Dead on my Feet

Baen Books by Wm. Mark Simmons

One Foot in the Grave

Dead on my Feet

Wm. Mark Simmons

DEAD ON MY FEET

A Baen Books Original

Baen Publishing Enterprises
P.O. Box 1403
Riverdale, NY 10471
www.baen.com

ISBN: 0-7434-3610-5

Cover art by Patrick Turner

First printing, June 2003

Library of Congress Cataloging-in-Publication Data

Simmons, Wm. Mark.
  Dead on my feet / Wm. Mark Simmons.
      p. cm.
"A Baen Books original."
  ISBN 0-7434-3610-5 (hardcover)
  1. Vampires—Fiction. I. Title.

  PS3569.I4774D43 2003
  813'.6—dc21

                                                    2003006195

Distributed by Simon & Schuster
1230 Avenue of the Americas
New York, NY 10020

Production by Windhaven Press, Auburn, NH
Printed in the United States of America

10   9   8   7   6   5   4   3   2   1

Battle not with monsters, lest ye become a monster,
and if you gaze into the Abyss,
the Abyss gazes also into you.

—Fredrich Wilhelm Nietzsche
Beyond Good And Evil

*Flectere si nequeo Superos,
Acheronta movebo.*

(If I cannot move Heaven,
I can raise Hell.)

—Virgil
The Aeneid

Author's Note: This is a work of fiction.
The twin cities of Monroe and West Monroe actually exist
on the banks of the beautiful Ouachita River, however
names, characters, places, and incidents
are either the product of the author's imagination
or are used fictitiously.
Any resemblance to actual business establishments,
events, specific locales, the U.S. government,
or persons living, dead, or undead, is entirely coincidental.

This one's for Dennis, friend & author.
While a number of people contributed time and advice,
he beat me mercilessly with a blue pencil through
conception and rewrites.
Any faults within are mine for advice ignored.

Chapter One

The beaded curtains clicked and rattled like finger bones as I brushed them aside. Hesitating on the threshold, I waited for my eyes to adjust to the dimness beyond. The first impulse is always to slip into the infrared band, but augmented perception of heat sources rarely comes in handy unless you're hunting prey. I was here hunting information.

Candles provided most of the illumination, although a lava lamp glimmered in one corner and the crystal ball at the center of the table seemed to shed a soft luminescence all its own. Tiny red eyes of burning incense glared through the dimness. Oriental rugs and tapestries vied with hand-woven god's-eyes for supremacy in the general decor. A couple of human skulls counterbalanced the effect of plaster saints and dangling rosary beads.

I stepped across the threshold. Technically, I didn't require an invitation, yet, but the appointment set by telephone would have served at any rate. I looked around, my eyes still working in the range of normal, human vision. Now that I was inside, the rest was less impressive: a step below a Jaycee's tour-the-haunted-mansion-and-your-donation-will-help-charity shtick.

"Nice," I said. "I'll bet the rubes just eat this stuff up."

"Atmosphere," said Mama Samm, "is very important in opening de gates of belief. Please," she indicated a chair, "sit down."

I sat. The chair was surprisingly comfortable. I sank down into its cushiony depths and discovered, belatedly, that it might be difficult to extricate myself in a hurry. Not that I should have to worry about busting out of a faux fortune-teller's parlor, but if I had learned one thing during the past year or so of my "after-life," it was the value of charting all potential escape routes when walking into unfamiliar territory.

And my on-the-job motto was: "Never relax."

"Relax," Mama Samm said.

She was immense. Her caftaned body seemed to fill a third of the room like a giant, glimmering white mushroom and her white turban floated above her dark features like a disembodied ghost.

"You have questions," she said. She wasn't asking.

I nodded. Opened my mouth.

"You are here on behalf of anot'er," she continued.

"Well—"

"A client. Someone wishes to know if I am legitimate. De real ting." She still wasn't asking.

"You've checked me out," I said, deciding to drop sixty percent of the bluff.

She nodded.

"And?"

She smiled. Her teeth were all white and even so that ruled out one ever-present concern. "You made your appointment under de name of Jon Harker. Your driver's license, social security card, in fact all of de right pieces of paper, plastic, and computer files say your name is Samuel Haim."

"Yes," I answered, interjecting just the right tone of "you've found me out."

"Even though 'Samhaim' is de ancient Celtic festival of de dead, its proper pronunciation is 'Sow-en.' So you see, Mister . . ." she paused, arching an eyebrow, " . . . Haim . . . it is not a very good pun for all de trouble dat you or someone else has gone to in leaving de proper paper trail."

I tried to say "I don't know what you're talking about" but my mouth wouldn't engage. Anyway, she was on a roll: "You come to Louziana six month ago—supposedly to open a blood bank here in Monroe. Ot'er people run it for you. You do not keep office hours and you have money.

"You live on de west bank of de Ouachita River. Big house, tree stories, lots of property, fenced and rigged with expensive security systems. You value your privacy. No record of any family. In fact, no record of any ting prior to your appearance here.

"You suffer from insomnia, rarely go out in de day, and have no personal physician. In fact, you have no life or healt' insurance. You do, however, have an interesting hobby: last mont' you opened a separate office wit' 'After Dark Investigations' stenciled on de door. Now you are here."

I shrugged. "Not much nightlife in Northeast Louisiana."

"So why come here? Nawlins has all de nightlife someone like you could want."

"New Orleans already has blood banks."

"Nawlins also has vampires," she said mildly.

I blinked. "Excuse me?"

"Owner of a blood bank, pale skin, an affectation for sunglasses, nocturnal lifestyle—some people might tink that you were a vampire, yourself."

I blinked again. "I have a medical condition that makes me allergic to sunlight. I'm highly susceptible to skin cancer."

"Of course. If you really were a vampire, you would hardly be able to roam about in de daylight. And you have been seen to roam about in de daylight on several occasions."

It didn't seem necessary to point out that this was one of them. "You have an interesting sense of humor," I said.

She dimpled without actually smiling. "Don' I? It is odd, however, dat with such a medical condition, you have not found a personal physician or done business with any pharmacy since you have moved here."

"You really have checked me out, haven't you?"

She smiled again. "I have clients, too, Mr. Haim. Your presence, here, has raised certain questions."

I felt a chill creeping up my spine. "I came here," I said, trying to keep my voice disarmingly pleasant, "thinking that I was going to be the one asking the questions."

Her smile grew more pronounced and she reached across the table. "You have a client who is wanting to know if I really am a true psychic with prescient abilities. Let me see if I can answer such questions with a personal reading of your own. Give me your hand."

Essentially I had three choices: refuse and still try to get the answers I was hired to get, get up and walk out now, or go along and risk that "Mama Samm" D'Arbonne was everything she was purported to be. The first course of action was unlikely and the second would mean that I might as well give up my newly chosen avocation and take up some less risky nocturnal pursuit.

Maybe needlepoint.

I put out my hand, the skeptic in me murmuring that a bona fide medium was about as likely as—what? An actual vampire? A real-life werewolf? Too late: Mama Samm clasped my right hand in her left. Engulfed, actually. The index finger of her right hand moved across my palm like a doodlebug on acid. "My, but you have de most interesting lifeline, Mr. Haim."

"I'll bet you say that to all the marks."

She shook her head and the white turban did a ghostly hootchy-cootchy. "No, *chère*, I not be funnin' wit you. According to dese lines, you already died."

"Really." My mouth loosened into a smile.

"Truly. More dan once, in fact."

"Is that so?"

She sighed. "You are about to tell me dat you have no idea as to what I am talking about. Dat you do not believe in fortune-telling."

My smile grew, showing teeth. "Maybe you really are psychic."

She closed her right hand over her left, trapping mine in-between. She squeezed. I felt a tingle, like a low-voltage electric shock, and Mama Samm's head snapped back. The turban wobbled but held.

She moaned and her eyes rolled back in her head. The electric tingle intensified, crawled up my arm.

"What are you doing?" I asked. Her only response was another moan as the tingle crawled across my shoulder and up into my head. I tried to pull my hand back but it was enclosed in a grip of velvet-sheathed iron.

The current slammed home in my brain, knocking me out of the room and down a dark corridor, a tunnel not unlike the one I had traversed when I had nearly died the year before. Memories fragmented and unfolded, waltzing across my eyelids like an acid-edged kaleidoscope.

The Barn . . .
   Vlad Drakul Bassarab . . .
     The transfusion . . .
      The crash . . .
       The morgue . . .

I cried out at the memory of two mangled bodies on the stainless-steel tables, and wrenched my hand free.

"My apologies, Mr. Cséjthe . . ."

It felt as though the temperature in the room had dropped a full ten degrees: She not only knew my real name, she had nailed the Hungarian pronunciation, "Chey-tay."

" . . . I did not know you were *oungan* for the *Gédé*." Her voice sounded strange, distant.

"What?"

"Tonight you will meet *Je Rouge*. It will hunt you for the *Ogou Bhathalah*. The shadow of *Ogou* is long here. . . ." Her eyes had rolled back in her head, showing a disturbing amount of white. "You must seek the grail, she will be the key. The Witch of Cachtice has helped them open the fifth seal."

"What?" I gripped her two hands with my left as the fine hairs suddenly lifted on my neck and arms. "Who did you say?"

"Unless it is closed," she continued, oblivious to my question, "the sun will turn black and the moon to blood." A shudder went through her. "Stars will fall like rain and the end will come before the Appointed Time!"

"You said the Witch of Cachtice!" I stammered. "Tell me what you mean!"

"Find the Grail before the *Ogou* sows the wind. Find *Marinette Bois-Chèche* and unmask the whore of Babylon before she puts her red dress on!" She moaned and her eyes fluttered.

I stared at her, waging an internal war over which was more upsetting: revisiting the deaths of my wife and daughter or a chance reference to a monstrous ancestor nearly four hundred years in her grave. "Save the gibberish for the gullible," I said, my voice harsh with the rawness of fresh memory.

Her eyes snapped open. Refocused. Her brow furrowed. "You are angry, Mr. Haim. What did I say?"

I snorted, feeling some control of the situation pass back to me. "Some fortune-teller; you want me to do your divination for you."

She stared at me for a long moment. Then: "Why don' you ask your wife to join us?"

Now I was angry. "My wife is dead."

"She must be tired of waiting in de car."

Like a flash fire, the anger was suddenly gone but a taste of ashes remained in my mouth. "I don't believe in ghosts."

"Or vampires? Or werewolves? Or legitimate psychics?" She smiled, white teeth erupting into a gleaming crescent in her dark face.

"Who are you?" I asked, rising shakily to my feet.

"Mama Samm D'Arbonne. Siddown, *chère*; I'm not gonna hurt you."

"What do you want?"

"De trut', Mr. Haim. De trut' is always important."

"And what do you do with the truth?"

"Depend on who it help and who it hurt. Keep it secret, mostly."

"Why?"

"We all have our reasons, *chère*. De Prince of Wallachia had his when he let you live—gave you a set of new identities and de money to lead a new existence down here in Louziana."

"And what are yours?"

"As I told you before, I have certain clients who are curious."

"Curious?"

"About you. Who you are. What you are. Why you've come here. What you intend to do."

"And now you can tell them, right?" I moved back so that my chair was added to the furniture between us.

"'Can tell' is not the same as 'will tell.' As I said, I keep secrets, mos'ly."

"Mostly?"

A cat jumped up on the cushioned arm of her chair unacknowledged as she nodded and repeated: "Mos'ly." The cat should have been a Chocolate-point Siamese except for one thing. . . .

"Your cat has two tails."

Mama Samm turned to consider the Siamese and it jumped into her arms. "Ah, my Taishi is usually too shy to enter dis room while a stranger is on the premises. You must have an unusual affinity for cats, Mr. Haim. It's not every day dat Shōtoku Taishi presents himself so boldly." She stroked its head as it regarded me with pale blue eyes that lent intensity to its cool appraisal.

"It's not every day that one sees a cat with two tails," I said, taking another, shaky step backward.

"An interesting mutation," Mama Samm agreed. "It is extremely rare. Did you know dat de ancient legends of Japan held dat deir vampires could assume de form of a cat? De one distinguishing difference between such unnatural felines and normal cats was de Japanese vampires always had two tails."

"No kidding," I said, fumbling for the doorknob behind me.

"Mr. Cséjthe. . . ." There was something in her voice, the way she said my name, that locked my legs on the threshold. " . . . Your name is hers. . . ."

It wasn't just a chill: an entire army was conducting close order drill on top of my grave.

" . . . But de Loa say that her blood . . . is not yours."

"Who?" I could hardly get the question out again. Maybe because I didn't want to ask it in the first place.

"You know who, Mr. Cséjthe. The legacy you bestow is life. Hers is death. Marinette Bois-Chèche will haunt your dreams until you unmask her. Before she devours you."

"That's not her real name," I said stubbornly. "And if we're talking about who I think we're talking about, she died in 1614."

"You do not know her real name, you only think you do. Do not forget that she is a liar. She has always been a liar. Her true power is in those she deceives. Do not give her your power, as well."

"Your accent is slipping," I said.

"The Loa say one more thing. . . ."

"Chatty folk, these luau."

"They say this is very important. They say you must save the child twice and bury the dead three times!"

What do you say to that?

There was nothing to say to that.

I forced my feet to carry me away from the fearful quality of her voice. I was careful not to slam the door. And I tried to exhibit dignity and decorum as I walked back to my car.

Mostly I tried to not break into a panic-stricken run.

The 1950 Mercury Club Coupé crouched in Mama Samm's rutted driveway like a prehistoric panther. The chopped roofline, narrow tinted windows, and minimal chrome chasing were swallowed up in the darker than black paint job that would render it practically invisible after sunset—a state I wanted to achieve soonest. Sliding behind the wheel, I counted to seven before turning the key in the ignition and pressing the starter button.

"So what did you think?" Jenny asked as the engine growled to life.

"You know what I think," I growled in turn as I backed the car up the long, hedged drive toward the main road. "You were right there inside my head through the whole visit."

She sighed but remained invisible, sitting in the passenger's seat. "Eventually, you're going to have to break down and admit that I am not just a virus-induced hallucination. Look . . ." The passenger window rolled itself down. "How could I do that if I'm not real?"

I leaned my head against the wheel and reminded myself that I was doing nothing more than conducting an internal conversation . . . externally. "Some of the by-products of my altered brain chemistry are certain telekinetic abilities," I announced to the empty seat. "If I can transport my body along the dreampaths, I can certainly fiddle with a car window without tweaking any of my conscious brain cells."

"Car," she said as I started to back onto the main road. As I hit the brakes, a gold Dodge Stratus popped into view from around the curve.

"Doesn't prove anything," I muttered as I got turned around and headed back toward town.

"Check the answering machine when we get home, Darling. You've got a couple of calls that sound promising. They were both long distance so I think your web page is starting to pay off."

"What do you mean 'promising'?"

"The first was an invitation to investigate a purported haunting in Tulsa, Oklahoma. The second was from Kansas City, Missouri. Something about a missing mummy."

"Missing mummy?"

"Uh huh. Couple named Satterfield. Said they had a mummy that was stolen out of their house. Since owning a dead body is not exactly legal, they couldn't exactly report the crime to the authorities."

"I see," I said. "And when did this unreported crime take place?"

"About six months ago. They said they had loaned an authentic copy of the Scroll of Thoth to an acquaintance the day before their mummy disappeared. Really, Chris; you need to do a much better job of cleaning up after yourself in the future!"

"Hey, I had no idea that the scroll would even work, much less have any long-distance peripheral side-effects."

"Ignorance is no excuse," she argued. "You still have an obligation to a former client to tidy up."

I cleared my throat. "Sounds like a pretty detailed answering machine message."

"I picked up during the call," she said. "I told them I was your secretary."

"You can't do that," I said.

"Why? Because I'm only a subconscious manifestation of your deteriorating psyche?"

"Something like that. How come you're still invisible? No one can see you but me."

"I didn't want to distract you while you're driving."

"Distract me?"

"I'm not wearing any underwear."

"How could I tell?"

"I'm not wearing anything else either."

I thought about that. "You're not real."

"You certainly didn't act that way last night."

I glanced at my watch at the next intersection and decided I had time for my evening run before heading back to the office. Glancing to the right, I noticed odd bits of anatomy starting to materialize in the passenger area.

"Darling, did you know that the French term for orgasm literally means 'the little death'?"

"You're not real, Jen."

"We should be home in another twenty minutes. Then you'll have another opportunity to prove your silly little theory."

I shook my head. "You're not real," I repeated. "And I have stuff to do."

"Stuff . . ." I heard her say.

"Can't miss my workout. Sun's going down and I've got to drop some tape off at the office and review my caseload. If I don't stick to my schedule, I'll start blowing off the exercise at every little opportunity."

"Just remember that you were the one who used the phrase 'little opportunity.' "

I switched on my turn signal and began humming "Strangers in the Night."

Chapter Two

The Witch of Cachtice remained on my mind as I jogged into the gloaming.

Gloaming. What a lovely word for that deepening purple twilight between the setting of the sun and the actual fall of night. My state of mind, however, was anything but lovely as skies downshifted from azure to indigo and the first stars of the evening faded into timorous glimmers.

Of all the mumbo-jumbo that the so-called fortune-teller had thrown at me, that one phrase continued to burn in my mind. What else had she called her? *Marinette Bois-Chèche?* I wasn't familiar with the reference but she had mentioned the "Loa" and that meant *Vodoun* or voodoo. I'd have to do a little research from that angle, maybe drive down to New Orleans this weekend.

Or, better yet, fly to Haiti, I decided, loping back up onto the sidewalk as a car approached. Aside from the assumption that the island source material would be purer, I knew there was a vampire enclave down in the Big Easy—reason enough to not make a return visit.

While Haiti had its own supernatural blood-drinkers—specifically the *mauvais airs* and the *mauvais nanm* of voodoo origin, and such West Indies imports as the *loogaroo* of Grenada, the *asema* of Surinam, and the *sukuyan* of Trinidad—I doubted that the island had any organized demesne system. The Crescent City enclave wasn't much on structure either but, sooner or later, every badass vampire wannabe decided to make the pilgrimage and few were said to return. Perversely, I was probably safer in the jungles of an alien nation than the back streets of an American tourist trap.

Mama Cséjthe didn't raise no dummy.

Unless you count my buying any part of Mama Samm's sideshow act.

The car passed by and I hopped off the sidewalk, sprinted across the street, and cut across a vacant lot. The streetlights were old and mostly out of order in this section of town, which was why I liked to run here. Even though I didn't huff and puff anymore, I detested being on display for the neighbors. The only thing I hated worse than jogging out in the open was running laps on a fixed track where the repetitive scenery is slightly less boring than watching the Golf Channel on cable.

A row of decrepit shotgun houses loomed ahead. Their coffinlike silhouettes provided an appropriate backdrop to my thoughts as I considered Mama Samm's veiled warnings and her troubling reference to *Marinette Bois-Chèche*.

The "Witch of Cachtice" made sense in only one context.

The ruins of a castle remain today in the Slovak Republic—Cachtice, Slovakia, to be precise. Once upon a time it lay within the borders of Hungary and was known by a different name. It was the ancestral home of Countess Erzsébet Báthory, who practiced the dark arts and came to believe that the blood of virgins would keep her eternally young and beautiful. During the opening years of the seventeenth century, she murdered over six hundred young women, practicing abominable tortures and draining their bodies of blood for her horrific beauty regimen.

Mama Samm's admonition to "unmask the whore of Babylon before she puts her red dress on" might have made sense four hundred years ago. But the infamous Blood Countess of Hungary died, walled up in her dark tower, in 1614. How could that have anything to do with me?

Other than the fact that the Báthory castle had two names.

Today it is known as Cachtice in the Slovak tongue.

In Erzsébet's time, the Hungarians called it Castle Cséjthe.

❖   ❖   ❖

Five blocks up and one over was the Community of Christ church.

I took a shortcut through a long alleyway, going from late evening to near midnight conditions in one swell foop. As the sidewalls of the alley blocked even the ambient light, my vision shifted over into the infrared spectrum without conscious thought. Perhaps it was a reflexive response to the sudden darkness. Or maybe the thrumming rhythms of the physical act of running triggered ancient predatory presets in my hindbrain. No matter, I went with it. I needed the practice and it made the scenery more interesting.

Imagine humidity as a color: blackish red. With swirls of dark purple like eddies of smoky black light. Mindful of the glimmering yellow splotches signifying the thermal decay processes of rotting garbage, I thought about dropping by to see if anyone was in this late in the evening. I dodged the small red-orange heat signatures of rats scurrying along the alley walls and recalled that the Book of Revelation in the New Testament said something about the "Whore of Babylon." If memory served, there was even something about a red dress or something. Maybe the pastor would be available for a quick Sunday school lesson.

Maybe we could have a nice friendly chat about eternal damnation and whether the blood of Christ could wash away the sins of those who must take bloody communion from human hosts.

The issues of sin and salvation were abruptly back-burnered: I was not alone.

Two human-shaped openings knelt in the crimson-flecked mists. The victim was a flickering yellow-orange, like a candle flame slowly guttering down. The executioner was a dark hole in the reddish curtain, its flesh too cool to register as a heat signature.

Too cool to be alive.

Wrong shortcut! I decided as it turned a dark, head-shaped emptiness up to stare at me. I whirled and ran the other way.

At the mouth of the alley where the warm darkness shied away from the icy wash of a corner street lamp, I stumbled against a garbage can. I dropped out of the infrared spectrum and shifted back to normal vision.

What are the odds? I wondered, shifting from a sprint to an all-out run. *Move to another city, another state, complete change*

*of identity, paper trail erased: a brand new friggin' life and I run
into one of them by accident!*

I kicked it up a notch so that I was doing twenty-five, maybe
thirty mph.

Once upon a time I had taken up jogging as a healthy pastime.
That was in another lifetime. In my present incarnation I ran more
to alleviate my boredom than to condition my transforming flesh.
Except now I was anything but bored and was literally running
for my life: two birds with one stone, as it were.

The sun had been down an hour but the temperature still
hovered in the mid nineties. The edges of my vision still regis-
tered in the infrared band and the pavement glowed brick red out
of the corners of my eyes.

How could I have been so stupid?

If hot summer nights had seemed a soothing balm for my
too-cool flesh, wouldn't it be all the more attractive to those whose
bodies had grown eternally cold? In thinking of my own comfort,
I had probably raised the odds of this encounter by a hundred-
fold. I glanced over my shoulder, expecting pursuit. Saw none.
Swung my attention back to the front and saw him come floating down, out of the night sky, like a lunatic Peter Pan.

Black chinos, black shirt and shoes, black duster: a very Goth
Peter Pan and overdressed for the season, to boot.

I braked, leaving gummy streaks of rubber sole on the hot
asphalt. Then I cut to the right, turning down a side street, and
picked up speed. Six blocks ahead and two streets over I could
see an on-ramp for the highway.

He elected to catch up to me on foot. I think it was intended
to spook me; his running just ahead of me, turned backward to
converse as if we were participants in a casual stroll—not running at breakneck speed down a darkened city street.

"My, but you're a fast one," he hissed with grinning, bloody lips.
"I like it when the rabbit tries to run a bit."

"Do you?" I puffed. Ten more minutes of this and I might break
out in a sweat—an increasingly rare experience in my "after" life.

Now that I had the occasional street lamp to manage the "visible" spectrum, I could make out a face—doughy, round features
overlaid with a ruddy glow, and overly prominent eyes. His sun-
burned appearance had nothing to do with the sun and his bulgy

eyeballs weren't tied to a thyroid condition. Rather, he'd overfed just moments before and so he was no longer motivated by hunger.

He was just tidying up; making sure there would be no witnesses.

"What is your name, little bunny?"

Not that he was in a big hurry, you understand. Like many predators, he liked to play with the prey.

"Bugs," I answered, trying not to "puff" too much.

"What . . . ?" My lack of terror was throwing him a little off-balance.

"Can you say 'Wascally wabbit'?" I asked.

And shoved him. Hard. He wasn't expecting it and his momentum carried him down in a tumble that sounded none too gentle for the parked car at the side of the road.

Now I ran as fast as my lungs would permit, inadequate draughts of air rasping in and out of my chest like a fiery crankshaft. I started up the on-ramp. If there had been more than one of him, I would've been dead already.

"Lit-tle bun-neeeee!"

And even with only one, it was just a matter of time.

He settled across my back and shoulders like a stack of cold, wet, woolen blankets, riding me like a grotesque jockey. He was surprisingly light, but far too strong for me to dislodge on my own.

"Little bun-nee," he whispered with a sniggering giggle, his wet lips close to my ear, closer to my neck. I threw myself down, twisting in midair and thrusting with my legs to ensure a long, sliding skid before I stopped.

It hurt!

It would have hurt a lot more if I hadn't put the vampire between the concrete and myself as I went down. I tumbled to my feet and limped the last dozen yards onto Interstate 20.

Traffic was light: a couple of semis and a dozen or so cars and pickup trucks. Playing dodge-em at 60 mph was better odds than what I had just left behind. As I ran, jumped, and spun across three lanes of traffic, I found it odd that no one swerved. I expected the sound of horns and the squeal of brakes but the drivers seemed oblivious to my presence. Reaching the concrete divider, I risked a glance back.

The creature stood at the entrance to the freeway, directing his attention to the oncoming traffic. He was obviously concentrating, using vampiric mind control to delete my image from the drivers' consciousness. For all intents and purposes, I was invisible for the moment! He turned his face to the right as I vaulted the divider, clouding the minds of motorists in the eastbound lanes, now.

I took my time as the traffic was heavier and he wasn't moving for the moment. As I reached the far side I risked another glance back and saw him launch himself into midair, off of the hood of a sedan that had slowed on the ramp. I climbed over the side of the elevated highway, dangling some three stories above the ground as he sailed across four lanes, headed directly for me. A large semi in the fifth lane intercepted him as I let go. There was a squall of surprise and rage heading eastbound with the truck while I prayed for only a broken arm or dislocated shoulder on the way down: either was survivable, while a broken leg or ankle would leave me helpless until he returned. The semi had only bought me some time—probably seconds rather than minutes.

Power cables broke my fall. Three lines of electrical burns across my back and buttocks, a flash, a pop, and I was thrown under the overpass. I rolled, trying to minimize the impact and discourage my singed clothing from bursting into flame. Came up on my feet. Took two steps. Fell down again.

The buzzing in my head diminished after a few moments and I regained some motor control in my left leg. I creaked to my feet and staggered into an ungainly sort of run, barely resisting the impulse to lisp: "Sanctuary . . . sanctuary . . ." in a bad Charles Laughton impression.

There were lights up ahead and I was staggering across a parking lot when the creature came floating back down some twenty yards ahead of me.

His clothes were torn, transforming the black-on-black Goth look to more of a punk statement. His face was bruised and one hand bloodied. The semi had made some impression, at least. So had I: "What *are* you?" he pondered, his googly eyes narrowing.

"I'm what goes bump in the night, Junior," I growled. I hunched forward, hands on skinned knees, and considered my next move as he contemplated his.

"You're too warm to be one of us," he mused, "but not warm enough to be human . . ."

"Sticks and stones."

"Killing you would be prudent but . . ."

"But?" He was stronger and faster and it was a miracle that I was still breathing, so I wasn't making plans past the next thirty seconds.

" . . . You may have your uses."

Uses? I was beyond fear, now, and edging into seriously pissed off. "What is it with you guys and the black-is-the-only-color-in-my-spectrum get-ups?" I snarled. "If it isn't black trench coats and eye-shadow, it's leather and chains."

"Black is the color of death," he intoned, saying it like some bad Vincent Price impression. He pulled a cellular phone from his pocket, activated it and punched in a number.

"Color of death, my ass," I hissed, still trying to re-inflate my lungs. "Color of brain-damaged losers who watch too much MTV and think a lack of fashion sense makes them look dangerous. Too bad Wal-Mart doesn't carry a Pretend-I'm-A-Badass line; that way you wouldn't have to accessorize at Dweebs-R-Us."

He cursed and shook the phone. Between our little tussle and his unexpected ride on the semi, it was apparently DOA.

"Hey," I said, bracing myself, "even Marilyn Manson moved on to color and spandex: get a clue."

As he attempted to return it to his pocket, he was off-balance for all of four seconds.

I hit him with my shoulder on the third. He went down and I went right over him. If I'd been wearing pants instead of jogging shorts he would have snagged me. Instead, long clawlike nails raked my leg and clutched my left Reebok. I left it in his grasp, sprinting across manicured grounds and rounding the corner of the next building. A door was open! I leapt for it and nearly collided with an elderly black couple who were just emerging. A twisting pirouette and I was safely inside!

He was right behind me standing on the steps, hands clenching and unclenching in impotent fury. I glanced over my shoulder and saw the large, wooden cross on the back wall of the entrance hall. Felt a smile start to bloom across my face: he couldn't enter a church. I turned back and saw that he was already gone. Just as well: I was too spent to gloat.

"Sir, are you a friend of the family?"

I turned again and found myself face-to-tie-clasp with one of the deacons. Or so I assumed. He was tall and elderly with pale, seamy features and a snowy pompadour such as only a mature, Southern gentleman can properly cultivate. He wore a plain, black suit and tie, sharply contrasted by a crisp white shirt and the man, himself, was nearly as monochromatic as his apparel.

"Beg pardon?" I asked, resisting the urge to grab my trembling knees, tuck my head down and gasp for air.

"Are you a friend of the family?" he asked once more.

"Um, sure," I said cautiously, hoping that, whatever family I was claiming association with, it would be large enough to allow me unobtrusive passage. . . .

"Would you care to sign the book, then, sir?"

It took me another moment to figure the trajectory from his gesture: an ornate guest book sat atop a podium near the doorway to the right.

"Um, sure." I took a couple of steps and recalled that one of my shoes was outside, near the edge of the parking lot. In fact, I was suddenly aware that, overall, my appearance and apparel were hardly appropriate for a church service.

Or a funeral.

A closer look at my surroundings revealed that I wasn't as safe as I first assumed. A church enjoys the automatic presumption of "holy ground" and, therefore, out of bounds to creatures of darkness. A funeral home, despite its religious symbols and services for families of the departed, is a debatable edifice on the sacred footage issue. The vampire had not followed me across the threshold, but then it couldn't follow me across any doorstep unless it received an invitation to enter.

While this might have been an impediment in the nervous North, we were down here in the sociable South: all that ole fang face needed to do was amble around to the back door, knock, and ask permission to come in. Sanctuary would give way to sanction.

The deacon cleared his throat behind me. I hurried to the guest book and grabbed the ballpoint pen that was glued to the bleached ostrich feather. Having spent the past six months living under an assumed name, I suddenly found myself unable to concoct another fake moniker: Caving in under the pressure, I signed my real name, figuring no one here was going to attach any significance to Christopher L. Cséjthe's signature.

Outside of taking a little detour through Weir, Kansas, a year or so back, it would prove to be one of the biggest mistakes of my life.

"We'll be closing in twenty minutes," the deacon intoned, nodding toward the doorway to the visitation rooms. "The funeral is tomorrow morning. Ten o'clock." He looked at me expectantly.

Expecting me to turn and bolt out the front door, most likely.

I glanced out at the darkness beyond the double entry doors: *not bloody likely!* My best bet was to find a hiding place and wait till an hour before sunrise. I turned and limped through the side doorway to the visitation rooms.

So much for low profile: I wasn't the only white person in attendance but the three or four of us were a distinct minority. A young black woman in her twenties was surrounded by a throng of young men who seemed to be competing for the opportunity to offer solace. Other faces turned and began to notice the banged-up white guy in the scorched tank top and running shorts. I kept moving, trying not to step on the flailing laces of my remaining shoe, and ducked into an adjoining room.

It was blessedly empty—if you didn't count the open casket at the far end. I limped over to a chair next to the coffin and started to retie my shoelace then decided to just chuck the whole footwear thing.

I sat down heavily and tried to let my lungs catch up to the rest of my body. As my respiration slowed, I thought about Mama Samm D'Arbonne's warning. What had she said? Something about *Je Rouge*—a rough translation suggested "the blush" but I'd heard the phrase used once before in a more compelling context. It was during a lecture on Haitian Vodoun. *Je Rouge* was the name given to cannibalistic, evil spirits by the *boku* or sorcerers who invoked them. The interpretation meant, quite literally, "Red Eyes."

Which certainly seemed to fit my fanged foe.

What else had she said? That it was hunting for the Goo-goo Battleaxe—or something like that. I should have paid more attention.

So now what?

Scoot out the back door or find a hiding place and wait until morning? The deacon would be closing up shop shortly and I needed to find a broom closet if I was going to stay. As I straightened up, I glanced down into the open casket. An elderly black man wearing a brown suit lay in repose. "You wouldn't happen to know where they keep the broom closets around here, would you?" I murmured.

Wrinkled eyelids twitched, slid upwards; yellowed eyes rolled in the corpse's sockets, focused on me.

"Uh!" I said. The question had been implicitly rhetorical.

A skinny arm shot up and dark, cold fingers closed on my wrist before I could react. "Bairrr," the old man croaked, "rrunnn . . ."

"Oh mama!" I said.

" 'Tect . . . of enge . . ."

"Say what?" I tried to pull back but the old corpse's grip was like refrigerated iron.

"Baarronnn . . ." The dead jaw creaked audibly as it tried to form the words.

"Hey!" said a voice from behind me.

"Pro-tect," the dead guy was saying.

"What are you doin'? Get away from there!"

I glanced over my shoulder. It was one of the consolers from next door. He was a lot bigger than me and looked more angry than anguished, now. "What the hell you doin', man?"

I turned, trying to show that I wasn't the one doing the doin'. Maybe he couldn't believe his eyes—I knew I couldn't.

"Moses! Elvin! Some cracker is messin' with Mr. Delacroix!"

Maybe it was one of those perspective-based optical illusions: the two guys who appeared in the doorway behind him looked big enough to push the first guy around in a stroller. The only way this could get any worse was if the vampire came back.

There was a blur of black and white at the edge of my vision and my luck for the evening was just about complete.

No one is here. Although the creature's lips did not move, his thoughts echoed through the room like a public address system on the edge of feedback. *Leave this room and close the door behind you.*

The three mourners shuffled backward like extras in an extremely corny zombie movie from the '40s.

Forget what you have seen. . . .

Or as Oz, the great and powerful, had once thundered: "Pay no attention to that man behind the curtain!"

The door closed and it was just the two of us. Or three, counting Mr. Delacroix. Who I suddenly realized had released my wrist. Trouble was, the vampire was now between me and the two exits from the room.

"Nice," I said. "A real 'Men In Black' sort of thing. How about I forget what I've seen, too? I'll go close the other door." I took a step.

Instantaneously, he was across the room, slamming into me like a freight train. I went down with the thing on top of me, Mr. Delacroix and his casket landing on top of us both.

Then, just as suddenly, he was off of me. I didn't waste time looking around to see why. I took off on all fours, plowing through a clutch of folding chairs on my way to the other exit.

I almost made it.

The vampire caught me three feet from the doorway and threw me into the wall. Or through it—it was only double Sheetrock with two-by-four bracing, after all. But I was in luck: I had found the broom closet.

A taloned hand reached in and clutched my leg.

Yanked.

I grabbed a mop on the way back out and slammed it across the newly made opening, halting my momentum. Momentarily. As I chinned myself into a sitting position, he yanked again and the mop handle snapped in two with a loud crack. As I exited the closet, feet-first, it seemed obvious who was going to mop the floor with whom. But as he climbed on top of me and bared his fangs, he got careless. He also got the jagged end of a broken mop handle planted in his chest. He screeched and fell backward. I scrambled up and headed once more for the second exit.

This time I made it. I ran down a connecting hallway and found myself in the chapel. Dodging between the pews, I had almost reached the podium at the front when I heard a familiar hiss behind me. To quote my realtor, "location is everything": I had evidently missed the monster's heart.

Rounding the podium, I cut to the left, behind an ornate screen of carved wood. As I reached for the door set in the far wall, the vampire crashed through the screen and into me. I crashed through the door and we both went tumbling down a flight of stairs into the basement.

The vamp was still stronger and faster than I was but, surprisingly, I was the first one back up on my feet. Maybe I just had more experience in taking punishment. I saw a door to my left and a heavier, reinforced door to my right: I gambled on the one to the right. I slammed it behind me and fumbled for the lock.

There was no lock.

I fumbled for the light switch.

There was a light switch.

I had just enough time to take in the general layout of the mortuary's workroom and vault the first embalming table as the vampire kicked the reinforced door off its hinges.

He stalked into the room and glared at me, now crouched between the steel table legs. No mocking smile, no "little bunny" now; he had finally figured out that, despite my appearance, I was more dangerous than a human. And the mop handle through his chest had pushed his need for fresh blood to a dangerous level. I wouldn't catch him off guard again.

Slowly, deliberately, he reached over and flipped off the light switch, plunging the room back into darkness.

Unlike the hot, humid air outside, the embalming room was kept cool by refrigeration units that were separate from the central air system serving the rest of the building. That kept the room temperature in the upper fifties for the customers who passed through for their final cosmetics. With the lights off, he could still see my heat signature in the infrared spectrum. Down in this air-conditioned bunker, I had the disadvantage: he wasn't warm enough to register as a heat source and the surrounding air wasn't warm enough to offer a contrasting backdrop.

Blind man's bluff and I was "it."

I rolled under the embalming table as he vaulted it in turn, his heels smacking down on the tiled floor where my head had been a second before. I upended the table, throwing some four hundred pounds of steel over and onto my undead assailant. I heard him toss it aside as I fell across a second table. The metal edge knocked half the wind out of me but, more discomfiting, this one was already occupied. Instinctively, I flung myself to the left and the vampire smashed against my former location, sending the dead body flying in one direction and the heavy structure careening in another.

A light glimmered at the far end of the room, a tiny wisp of blue-gold flame. I stumbled toward it—stumbled being the operative word as I caught my toe on some unknown part of a corpse's anatomy. As I went sprawling, I felt the intimate breeze of someone passing just overhead.

He caught up with me just before I reached the glimmering light. I was slammed against the wall—brick this time and not as forgiving. As I slid downward, the rough surface peeling my cheek like a cheese grater, I grasped a dim projection. A knoblike handle. It twisted in my hand and the tiny flicker of the pilot light erupted into multiple rings of flaming gas jets behind oven-tempered glass.

As an icy claw closed around my throat, I looked at my assailant's face in the flickering light. His lips were split and one eye was puffed shut. He grimaced and I was rewarded with the sight of one and a half fangs instead of two, now.

I tugged futilely at his wrist with my right hand while my left scrabbled behind me for leverage. I found another handle, pulled down. The door of the crematory oven creaked open and, with a puff of hot air, the flickering light intensified. His eyes widened, the puffy one showing a little iris, now: rings of red surrounding the pupils glowed with a crimson incandescence.

"*Red eyes,*" I croaked.

"*Je Rouge,*" intoned a dead voice from just behind the monster's head. A cold, dark hand appeared and pried the vampire's fingers from my throat. He whirled and another dark hand clasped his shoulder, tearing him away from me and into a stranger's embrace. Mr. Delacroix had come, it seemed, to cut in and demand his own dance with the devil.

I eased aside as the dead man forced the vampire toward the open oven. The monster struggled and snarled, slashing at the corpse's throat with his teeth. Dark flesh tore but no blood emerged, just the slow trickle of embalming fluid dripping down and tinting the edge of Delacroix's collar a pale green.

"*Baron...*" the dead man croaked. The vampire twisted and squirmed in his grasp. His face swiveled from the vampire's to mine. "*Baruhhhnnn.*"

"You talking to me? Are you talking to me?" Great: two dead

guys are dancing the tango and I'm doing Travis Bickle impressions.

"...Baarruuhhhnnn..."

"What!"

"...*A boon*..."

"Boon?"

"...*A bargain*..."

"Bargain?"

"...*Protect...my...daughter*..." He lifted the vampire off of the floor and threw him headfirst into the crematory oven. The creature screeched and spun, clambering out like a great, smoking spider. Delacroix pushed him back into the flames. "...*Avenge...me*..." He blocked the vampire's second attempt to escape and, shoving the undead thing back once more, climbed into the oven to hold him in the fire.

"*Promise...me...Baron!*" Delacroix bellowed as the vampire exploded in flames. A great jet of fire shot out from the oven's opening like a great blowtorch and I blistered my hands getting the steel-and-tempered-glass door to close over it.

"I promise," I whispered to the writhing knot of flames on the other side of the glass.

I heard the sound of footfalls on the stairs.

Time to leave.

Chapter Three

Once upon a time my barbarian ancestors roamed large portions of east central Europe—sort of like the bison's dominance of the North American prairie before the coming of the white man. My forebears probably would have liked that analogy. In fact, it worked on more than one level. But, rather than run down the list for an appalling side-by-side comparison between those lumbering smelly beasts and a herd of buffalo, just trust me: there are worse things to be compared to.

Like my great-to-the-something-power, great-grandmother for instance . . .

As if to punctuate my ancestral musings, the wind suddenly shifted as I limped toward home. An odor even worse than a hoard of unwashed Hun settled over the area as the local paper mill cranked up an olfactory distraction from the aches and pains wrought by my evening's dance with the dead.

If you've never experienced the airy fragrance of a paper mill when the smokestacks go on-line then I invite you to picture a cute little baby.

With an overfull bladder.

Now imagine the wettest, soggiest baby diaper it's ever been your misfortune to change—no baby putty, strictly "number one." But a lot of "number one." And in an old-fashioned cloth diaper, none of those sissy, disposable, paper-and-plastic jobs. Next, take that sopping, dribbling diaper and, without wringing or rinsing, deposit it into a large plastic bag. Seal the bag so that it's airtight. Place the bag outside in the hot sun for three or four hours. At the end of that time remove the diaper from the bag.

Finally, place the empty bag over your head.

That's a vague approximation of what it's like when the industrial venting process and the local wind patterns collaborate: this was turning into *such* a special night for me.

My driveway was a long winding tunnel through a half-mile of trees and shrubbery to my property. Actually, the half-mile of trees and shrubbery was my property too, but my philosophy is if you don't have to mow it, weed it, or water it, you can call it God's property and cross another set of worries off your maintenance list.

As I staggered closer to the roadside entrance, I found the way well lit by a column of flame.

Fires in the night. More reminders of my ancient relatives, the Hun. Now there was a group who knew how to keep the darkness at bay with the application of large quantities of combustibles. Of course the people they overran would say they brought a lot of the darkness with them. Jenny claimed that my "doesn't play well with others" attitude came from the sap that flowed through my family tree from the roots up. Hey, at least I didn't go around raping and looting and pillaging and burning down entire villages.

At least not yet, anyways.

I limped over and looked down the incline where the ground fell away from the road and slid into the tree line—which is what someone's automobile had tried to do. The Lexus had left the pavement and the steepness of the hillside had just carried it along until it met unmovable objects in the form of a five-pine cluster. The crumpled car must have ignited on impact and now the flames licked at the overhanging branches some thirty feet in the air.

In the distance I could hear approaching sirens: a good thing as a half-hour from now we would likely have a birthday effect spreading to the rest of the woods. Think mint cake with flaming candles for a five-hundred-year-old giant.

I thought about how much the Hun would have liked that. My own blood was too diluted by the intervening generations: *I hoped the fire would be out very soon*. Maybe somewhere back along the line I had an ancestor who was adopted. Preferably *after* great-times-something grandmamma.

She descended from one of the largest and most powerful clans, the Gutkeleds, who occupied territories that would eventually become Poland, Hungary, Slovakia, Romania, and a couple of quaint fiefdoms named Wallachia and Transylvania.

Cataloging my family registry kept my mind off the pain that jarred through my leg, back, and ribs as I hobbled along home. I turned and gimped back across the road and oriented on my property line.

Where was I? Oh yeah . . . by the thirteenth century the Gutkeleds had given up the nomadic, tribal lifestyle and become landowners. They also went for a name change, adopting the moniker of one of their "estates." The word Bátor meant "valiant"—had a nice ring to it—and, somewhere along the way, it became Báthory.

Maybe, I pondered, there was something in a name since the Báthorys grew in power and influence, producing a number of notable personages. There was Stephen Báthory, a loyal adherent of John I of Hungary. In 1529, he became *voivode* of *Transylvania*—more governor than warlord by that time. His youngest son, also named Stephan but with an "a," became king of Poland in 1575—which allowed his brother, Christopher, to succeed him as prince of Transylvania.

I turned off the main road and started up my long and winding drive as the first fire truck flickered around a curve in the distance.

Alas, in-breeding produced a flip side to all this royal success, surfacing when Christopher married Elizabeth, sister of Stephen Bocskay.

Sigismund Báthory, his son and successor, seemed of the opinion that sanity was somewhat overrated. That attitude may have actually helped his political ambitions. In 1594, he crushed the pro-Turkish faction of nobles and was recognized by the Holy Roman Emperor, Rudolf II, as a hereditary prince. Court intrigues proved a bit more challenging than kicking Turkish ass and taking names: Siggy abdicated in favor of the Hapsburg king of Hungary in 1597, then came back to assume power in 1598. He then abdicated again the following year in favor of his cousin, Andrew Cardinal Báthory, who died that same year so he had to be "coaxed" out of retirement a second time. With the help of Stephen Bocskay, he returned to power as a vassal of Sultan Muhammad III but abdicated (*finally*, this time) in 1602—once more in favor of Rudolf—and retired to Silesia. Maybe he wasn't crazy, just conflicted.

And maybe I wasn't tired to the point of hallucination: Maybe there was someone walking up the driveway, ahead of me.

The encompassing trees and encroaching shrubbery effectively blocked ninety percent of the moon and starlight. The flames from the wrecked car and the flashing red and blue lights from the emergency vehicles gave me just enough ambient illumination to see that the figure was man-sized. It didn't reveal whether it was man-shaped. But it appeared to be moving up the drive, away from me.

I thought about calling to him—not that I could be sure it was even a "him." I decided, instead, to close some of the distance while "he" was still unaware of my presence. I picked up my pace and, as I limped along, a detached portion of my mind continued to review the Báthory legacy.

Gabriel Báthory was a nephew of Andrew Cardinal Báthory, who became prince of Transylvania in 1608. His efforts to become the "Carpathian Caligula" eventually provoked a rebellion by the nobles. Since impeachment was a political concept whose time had not yet come, he was conveniently murdered. He did manage one notable accomplishment before the nobles served the ultimate recall petition: by marrying his niece Sophia to George Rákóczy II, he oversaw the union of these two noble families. Some say the Rákóczy line has never been the same.

Up ahead, my "quarry" seemed to be having as much difficulty walking as I was—perhaps he had lost his shoes, too. This was silly: stalking an unknown pedestrian in the dark. I decided to approach him but I was determined to do it carefully. In my experience, the Twilight Zone still lurks around certain corners. Too bad Rod Serling's dead and gone: more than once I would have benefited from his stentorian warning—*Look, there's the sign-post up ahead. . . .*

In Erzsébet's case, the warning signs were in place before she was even born. Her mama, Anna Báthory, married Gáspár Dragfy and gave him two sons: János and Gyorgy. History is closemouthed about the details but Gáspár died in 1545. Then Anna moved on to hubby number two: Antal Drugeth. He died shortly thereafter. In 1553, she married her cousin, Baron Gyorgy Báthory, then gave birth to four more children before the Baron croaked in 1570. Again, no details were forthcoming in my reading but, given Anna's run on husbands, I would be more inclined to hire a cook than let that woman anywhere near the kitchen.

Thinking of kitchens, mine was nearby and my stomach was starting to rumble in anticipation of some much-needed sustenance. I was also close enough to my target for him to know he was being stalked. He was either one cool customer or stone-cold deaf.

Which brings me to "stone cold" Erzsébet, better known in the West as "Elizabeth" Báthory. She was born August 7, 1560, into one of the oldest and wealthiest families in Transylvania, the second of the four siblings fathered by the baron. Although their dominance would decline by 1658, at the time of her birth she had a very distinguished pedigree with a cardinal, several princes, members of the judiciary, clergy, civil posts, a prime minister of Hungary and a couple of kings sharing her lineage. There was even a connection—one for sure, the second only hinted at—to my dark Sire, Vlad Drakul Bassarab.

Nearly a century earlier, in 1476, Dracula rode into Wallachia to regain his throne. Accompanying him was Prince Stephen Báthory, leading a contingent of his own forces. Both families had a dragon design on their family crests and a Dracula fief, Castle Fagaras, became a Báthory possession during Erzsébet's time.

That association is a fact of history.

The other, a hundred years later, was a matter of gossip and speculation.

My own connection to the Báthory line was unclear. My great-great-grandparents were from Romania. We bore the name Cséjthe but records between the seventeenth and nineteenth centuries had largely disappeared. The oral traditions regarding the Witch of Cachtice or the Blood Countess of Cséjthe are rife with tales of blood and torture and death and degradation—but notoriously mum on any other aspect of the subsequent generations. It was as if the family went into hiding.

My blood ties to Dracula were more recent and disturbingly clear. . . .

So what Mama Samm's disjointed ramblings meant beyond a red-eyed vampire with a cell phone remained to be seen. As did my walking companion. I reached out and tapped him on the shoulder as we came out of the tunnel of trees and onto the expanse of recently mowed grass.

He didn't start, didn't jump, and didn't even flinch. He had almost no reaction, at all. He took a couple of additional steps before stopping and then turned as the motion detectors turned on the security lights around the house.

"Can I help you?" I asked, trying to peer into the backlit silhouette where a face should be.

Maybe I had startled him: it took him a few extra moments to answer.

"A phone," he said slowly. "I need . . . to make a call . . ."

"Sure," I said, after a little hesitation of my own. "This is my house. Come on up." I moved to take the lead and he fell in behind me after another protracted pause.

Standing on the front porch, I fumbled for my key. After a minute of fumbling it became apparent that I had lost my key along with my shoe. Now what? Yell for an invisible, disembodied spirit to come down and unlock the door? Not with company standing behind me. *And damn but the paper mill was venting something particularly odious tonight!* What kind of chemical makes wood pulp smell like burned pork?

"Hold on," I said. "I've got to go around back to get in. I'll come through and let you in the front in a minute or two." Stepping off the porch I got a better, sidelong glance at my visitor. *Hospital,* I thought, hurrying around the side of the house, *got to get an ambulance for this guy ASAP!* The driver of the wrecked car looked like he was in worse shape than I was. It was a wonder he had managed to walk all the way up the hill. He was probably in shock.

I got to the back door, which was just as tightly locked as the front, and sat on the step.

I closed my eyes. Squeezed my breathing into a regulated cadence. Worked on regulating the rest of me.

Relax!

Be calm.

Focus. . . .

"Death is but the doorway to new life. . . ." I whispered.

We live today.

We shall live again.

In many forms shall we return. . . .

This time there was no dream state, no hallucinations, nor a sense of falling between dimensions.

I opened my eyes, expecting this attempt to have failed like most of the others. Instead I found myself sitting on the floor in the kitchen.

Naked.

That's the problem with translocation. In vampire lore they have Dracula and a dozen other long-toothed clones turning into mist and flowing through keyholes and under doors and such then reassembling, perfectly coiffed and without a wrinkle in their formal evening wear.

In real life—and don't you even get me started on the concept of "real" life—translocation doesn't involve mists or fogs, at all—unless the practitioner uses a little hypnotic suggestion on his or her audience. It's actually a psionic talent brought about by the vampiric mutations in brain chemistry. And it isn't a gift that most undead develop. It is restricted to the Domans of the underground communities who secretly break the *wampyr* taboo against mingling their blood with that of a lycanthrope—something that Lupé and I had ignorantly done on a couple of occasions.

Perhaps it was my not being "technically" undead that made successful translocations, even without my clothes, so unreliable.

That, or the lack of a discipline and frequency in my practice sessions. I scrambled to my feet and unlocked the back door.

Grabbing my puddle of clothing from the back porch, I hurriedly dressed and then grabbed the cordless phone on the way to the living room. The man on my doorstep flinched away from the light as I opened the front door. I caught a glimpse of a blistered cheek, a singed moustache and goatee, and a bloody eye socket before he stepped inside and pulled the wall switch back down.

"Why don't you come inside and rest?" I invited. *Before you collapse from shock.*

He took the phone and punched in a number. "Got to get back to my car," he said slowly, remaining just inside the doorway.

"At least let me get you some bandages, some ointment."

He raised the receiver to a bloody ear as I backed toward the first-floor bathroom. "Hello, Susan?" he said softly. "I'm going to be late . . . I just wanted to tell you that I love you. . . ."

It took me a couple of minutes to gather a handful of first-aid supplies. When I returned, the outside door stood open and the phone was on the floor buzzing a fresh dial tone.

I went to the doorway and peered out across the front yard. Between the outside security lights and the flickering illumination of the burning car and flashing lights from the main road, I could make out a lone figure shuffling back down the driveway between the trees. I looked down at the bandages and salves in my hands. The emergency vehicles down at the accident site would be better equipped to deal with any serious trauma. I closed the door, picked up the phone, and headed back to the bathroom.

The phone rang as I finished putting away the bandages. "Haim residence," I answered, leaving the first-floor bathroom and starting up the stairs.

"Hello?" The voice was feminine, hesitant. "Hello? Is Bradley there?" Undertones of fear and barely repressed panic were layered into her precise diction.

"Bradley?" I asked, trying to remember if I knew any Bradleys.

"Sinor," she elaborated. "He just called me. The number didn't come up on my caller-ID so I hit star-sixty-nine. Is he there?"

"Is this—" What name had my accident victim said? "—Susan?"

"Yes!" Overtones of relief crept into her voice. "Is he still there?"

"Um, no." I opened the front door and peered down the hill. "He left." It was as if the night had swallowed him whole.

"Is he all right? He sounded so strange!"

"Well . . . ?" How to phrase this so it didn't sound worse than it really was? "He had a little accident. . . ."

"Accident?" Relief took a powder: panic surfaced like a submarine with blown ballast tanks. "What kind of accident?"

I told her. Described the crash site, suggested that the car might be DOA but Bradley must be pretty okay if he could walk up the hill to my place and right back down again. Most healthy folk find the uphill trudge leaves them a little breathless. I assured her that Bradley would probably call her from the hospital. . . .

Which set off a new round of quavery questions in spite of my reassurances that any crash you could walk away from was not that serious.

She didn't seem inclined to wait by the phone so I gave her directions and threw in my address for good measure—though the fire and flashing lights would prove beacon enough once she got close. Since most ERs treat nonfatalities with the speed and promptness of a tax refund, she was probably right in deciding to not "cool her heels" at home.

She most likely had a cell phone anyway.

I hung up and the phone rang again. Unlisted number, line-filter against caller-IDs, and they still track me down. I glanced at my own caller-ID: the block was one-way so I could still see who was calling me even if they couldn't see who was calling them. It was the office.

"Haim Mortuary," I announced blithely, "you stab 'em, we slab 'em; you plug 'em, we plant 'em."

"Sam." It was my secretary. Her tone suggested I might want to be a little less blithe.

"I'm running a little late, Olive." In point of fact it was just a little before ten P.M. I glanced back to see if I—or my transitory visitor—had dripped any blood on the carpet.

"Sorry to bother you at home, Boss, but I figured you'd want the heads-up."

I groaned. "The Snow Queen?"

"My, my, a detective *and* a psychic!" I heard laughter in her warm, dulcet voice.

Walking into the hall bathroom, I turned on the lights, and considered my reflection in the mirror. It was just a little blurry tonight. "I—I've run into a few complications so I won't be in right away. Try to set up an appointment for Mrs. Cummings next week."

"I'll do my best, Chief, but—you know . . ."

I sighed. "I know."

"Are you okay? Want to take the night off?"

I considered my bruised face and throat. Even without an infusion of hemoglobin I was starting to look and feel better. Already the dark purples and reds were fading to pinks and pale greens. My cuts were closed. Were I still completely human it would have taken two to three days to heal to this point.

Of course, if I were completely undead, I would have totally recovered in minutes, if not seconds. "I'm fine," I answered. "I'll be in shortly. But don't tell her that."

"Do my best."

I opened the shower doors. "See you soon." I clicked off and reached over to turn the hot water faucet enough to start the showerhead dribbling on the floor of the tub. Then I wrenched the cold water handle as wide as it would go. A few minutes later I was properly thankful that a well-insulated house and twenty acres of property kept my neighbors from wondering about all the yelling.

It was closer to eleven-thirty by the time I squeezed the Merc past the fire trucks, drove down to the river, and parked next to the abandoned railroad spur.

In 1867, George Pullman, already renowned for redefining the concept of railroad luxury, rolled out the acme, the pinnacle, the Alpha and damn near Omega of the Pullman Palace Railway Cars. Called "The President" and essentially a hotel on iron wheels, it incorporated the finest accommodations imaginable for sleeping, dining, and passing many a long hour with all of the amenities of a penthouse suite. The sleeping compartments had been lined with cherry wood, and heavy, brocaded curtains afforded each window a measure of elegance to go with complete privacy. Over fifty feet long and ten feet wide, the interior was paneled and trimmed with teak, mahogany, and black walnut. Chandeliers hung from the ceiling and French plate mirrors adorned the walls. All of the upholstery was plush and the floors were softened with thick Brussels carpeting.

Once I'd finished the project, I couldn't say which was more expensive: acquiring a genuine Pullman and setting it up on an abandoned railway spur on the western bank of the Ouachita River or restoring this relic from a bygone age to all its former glory.

The forty thousand I spent on converting the toilets to chemical recyclers, the oil lamps and chandeliers to electrical, and getting the solar-powered heat exchanger to interface with the plumbing was a mere dribble in the bucket in comparison.

But I could afford it: Prince in Exile, Vlad Drakul Bassarab had treated me well. Between the suitcases of cash he had provided and the protected investments he had set up in my name, I could buy a whole train if I wanted to.

Never mind that it was essentially blood money for the lives of my wife and daughter.

I grabbed my equipment bag out of the back seat and walked to the end of the Pullman. Up the stairs, onto the platform and, sure enough, there it was on the glass window of the narrow door: "After Dark Investigations." Just as Mama Samm had "foreseen."

Too bad she hadn't been more forthcoming about *Je Rouge*.

"Go long!" I called, as I opened the door.

Olive looked up and kicked her rolling chair back from the desk as my camcorder went sailing across the room. One arm went up for a perfect, left-handed catch. Before I could launch into my crowd-goes-wild routine I became aware of another presence in the front office.

It was the Snow Queen.

"Miz Suanne is here, axing to see you," Olive added unnecessarily.

I cocked an eyebrow at her: the polite "darkie"-mixed-with-street patois was an affectation she reserved for the crackers who annoyed her. The Snow Queen was no cracker but she did tend to overdo the *noblesse oblige* bit for those of a darker skin hue or a lighter social status. I considered telling her that my secretary did the *New York Times* crossword puzzle in ink but I knew Olive would not appreciate my blowing her cover.

Suanne Cummings hadn't always been the Snow Queen. Once upon a time, I'm told, she had been a cheerleader and a model and a beauty pageant runner-up. She didn't acquire her royalty status until after she married Dr. Hyrum Cummings—eye, ear, nose, throat and just-about-anything-else specialist—and she, subsequently, became the top realtor in Northeast Louisiana.

She had everything a woman could want: money, success, social standing and, at the age of thirty-seven, she still possessed the body of a twenty-five-year-old. That her natural blond hair was now bleached an unnatural shade of white and that the extra layer of makeup was no longer sufficient to hide her frown lines, did little to distract from the overall package. Suanne was a babe, a power-babe, in fact, and the world as a rule stepped aside and held doors for her.

"Mr. Haim," she said, extending a hand dribbling jewelry.

"Mrs. Cummings," I countered. Her touch was nearly as cool as mine and I ran a quick check on her eyes. Nope: reputation notwithstanding, she was still human. "Your lawyer hired me and I really should be talking to him."

"But I'm paying the bills and retainer, and it *is* my husband." She kept her cool, elegant fingers twined about mine and nodded toward the door to my office area.

"I'm not really ready to make a report, yet."

"Then tell me what you do have."

"Nothing solid enough on which to build any kind of a case."

"Then tell me what you have done to date." The frown lines deepened, putting stress on her makeup base. "Or have you done anything to date, Mr. Haim?"

I turned to Olive. "Get me the most recent surveillance tape on the Cummings case."

She extricated a tape from the camcorder and placed it on the desk before opening a locked door set in the side of her credenza. She extracted several cassettes and checked the labels. "Go short," she retorted, selecting one, and flipped it to me underhanded.

I caught it underhanded and escorted Mrs. Cummings through the next door and into my office.

"Make yourself comfortable," I said as I popped the tape into an adapter, then the VCR and hit rewind. "I'll be back in a moment."

I stepped back into the reception area, closing the door behind me. "Olive, get me the number for Mama Samm D'Arbonne."

"The fortune-teller?"

I nodded. "In fact, give her a call, see if she'll see me tonight."

"Tonight?"

"If not tonight, set me up an appointment for in the morning."

"Rather late to be calling civilians, isn't it, Boss?"

"Maybe." I reached behind and ran my hand down my back: the electrical burns barely twinged now. "But I'm not so sure she's a civilian. And I think she's anticipating this call."

The cassette had reached the beginning of the tape when I returned to the inner office. I picked up the remote and fired off the two codes that activated the monitor and the VCR. "I don't think you're going to like this," I murmured.

"I don't expect to," she said.

But it wasn't what she expected.

The monitor displayed a stretch of green-black water, bracketed by cypresses and evergreens decked with bursts of gray-green Spanish moss and black-brown underbrush tented with cascading canopies of emerald-green kudzu. A silver-gray blob resolved itself into a canoe as the video camera was focused. "Black Bayou," I announced as the zoom kicked in and we were brought up to hailing distance of the canoe's two occupants: a bespectacled man in his early forties with thinning hair, and a pear-shaped woman with more gray than brown in her hair that might have been styled in a blunt-cut pageboy before the wind got hold of it.

"Hyrum Cummings and Delores Hastings," I announced unnecessarily. We watched for a few minutes as they drifted along, propelled by an occasional dip of a paddle in the still, brackish water. Hyrum and Delores wore expressions of quiet contentment, the occasional movement of lips indicating the briefest of verbal exchanges.

"This was taken two weeks ago, Saturday. They spent close to four hours on the bayou, together."

Suanne shook her head. "Hyrum played golf that Saturday. Hyrum goes to the country club every Saturday and plays eighteen holes of golf."

It was my turn to shake my head. "Your husband never plays golf more than once a month—and then it's no more than nine holes, never eighteen. He drops by the country club every Saturday, puts in an appearance so later on someone can say that they saw him there. But he leaves after twenty to thirty minutes."

"I find that hard to believe."

"Mrs. Cummings, how often does your husband clean his clubs?"

"Hyrum stopped cleaning his own clubs some time ago. There are people at the club who do it for him."

"Really." I produced a photocopied page of receipts. "According to the clubhouse records, your husband has had his golf clubs cleaned a total of three times this year. He gets more exercise hauling them to the car and back than he does from actually using them."

Her face darkened as she turned the logistics over in her mind. "All right, so he's cheating. I wouldn't have hired you if I hadn't had my suspicions."

"Depends on what you mean by 'cheating,'" I said.

"Oh, don't get Clintonesque with me," she snapped. "Let's cut to the chase; let's see some video that catches them in the act."

"The act." I nibbled a dry patch on my lower lip and considered the bookshelves on the far wall of my office.

"I can presume from your expression that you don't actually have any tape of them in bed together." She studied Delores' Rubenesque figure that wasn't exactly minimized by the flowery muumuu that she wore in the canoe. "I suppose I should be glad to be spared the sight of that woman naked. Gawd, it would be so . . . disgusting." She tapped a finger armored in gold against her perfect teeth. "But video of them going into or coming out of a motel would be just as good in court."

"They've never gone near a motel."

"So where do they do it? Her place?"

"They don't."

"Don't what?"

"Do it."

"They don't . . ." she paused, " . . . do *it*?"

I nodded.

"You're suggesting that they've never consummated the affair?"

"Define 'affair.' And, no, I am not suggesting, I am telling you that they haven't done 'the act' or anything closely resembling 'the act,' since I put your husband under surveillance seven weeks ago."

"Impossible!"

"Impossible for them to consummate, based on the evidence to date. My associates can account for your husband's and Ms. Hastings' whereabouts for every hour since you hired me and I have backtracked on all available records for six months previous to my hire. Other than the fact that they prefer to spend time together, there is just no credible evidence that Dr. Cummings and Ms. Hastings are lovers. At least in the conventional sense."

She shook her head. "I don't like it."

"I said you wouldn't." I stopped the tape and pressed rewind on the remote. "I have additional tapes of them at a concert, a monster truck rally, bicycling through Kiroli Park . . ."

"Where there's smoke, there's got to be fire."

I tapped the intercom on my desk as the cassette finished rewinding and ejected. "Olive, round up the Cummings' files and tapes with something to carry them in." I glanced up at one of the cut-glass mirrors set in the cabinet doors and noticed that my tie was askew. I had loosened it on the drive over and neglected to rebutton the collar before coming in. I also noticed that my reflection was a little vague—something that might be difficult to explain to the uninitiated.

I turned my back and moved to block my reflection as I struggled with the button. "Mrs. Cummings, aside from my files and a set of dossiers, I've got a dozen or so tapes, six hours each. I invite you to review all of them minute by minute and find even the suggestion of a kiss or improper body language."

"So what is your next step?" Suanne's head appeared just over my reflection's right shoulder: the woman was tall. The stiletto heels helped.

"I don't know that I have a next step in your case, Mrs. Cummings."

"But what about me?" Her arms appeared from my sides and reached up to adjust my necktie.

"You take the tapes and go over them with your lawyer."

"And?"

"Decide what you want to do next."

"If I understand you correctly, there isn't enough here to guar-antee a hefty divorce settlement." She pulled my tie snug. And then a little beyond.

"I gather evidence, Mrs. Cummings, I don't manufacture it."

"I'm not asking you to falsify evidence," she murmured, "just stay on the case until you can get something solid." Her hands continued to fuss with my tie even though it was as straight and snug as could be.

"That may never happen."

"And . . . ?"

"And I find that I am no longer interested in pursuing the case."

"I'll up your retainer and fee."

"I'm not interested."

"Isn't there *anything* I can do to change your interest?"

I started to turn around but thought the better of it when I noticed Suanne was disinclined to step back. I glanced at my office door: Olive, *help* . . .

"I'm not really keen on doing divorce cases, Mrs. Cummings . . ."

"Please call me Suanne."

Olive, help!

" . . . As you may know, I do this more as an avocation than an actual job . . ."

"Yes, I know. The stories are you're quite 'well off.'"

Help me, Olive!

" . . . Anyway, I find that I'm not really willing to take money from you to continue a surveillance that is unlikely to produce the results you're looking for."

"If you're not interested in taking my money," she said silkily, her mouth way too close to my ear, now, "then perhaps we could make some other arrangement for your remuneration . . ."

Dammit, Olive: get your ass in here RIGHT NOW!

The door opened and my secretary poked her head in. "I'm sorry, Boss, but did you call me?"

Suanne had stepped back but not before Olive had taken in the entire tableau. "Oh, it's that pesky tie again, huh, boss?" She marched over, took me by the arm, and spun me around to face her. As she fussed with the knot (that was just fine now), she launched into Mother Mode. "I swear! Why a man your age can't learn to tie his own ties . . . can walk out of his house without dressin' hisself proper?" Mindful of Mrs. Cumming's scrutiny, her speech patterns devolved as she warmed to the performance. "Mm-mmm, an' lookit dis collar! When is your woman gonna get herself back home, here? I gots a good mind to call Miss Lupé up right now an' tell her you is goin' to the dogs, for sure!" That with a sidelong glance at my client. "Tell her to git her shapely little butt out of Hollywood and git back here afore you pile up so much laundry it ain't never gettin' done in this lifetime!"

"Did you get Mrs. Cummings' materials together?"

"All done, boss. Everything but the billing." I had lucked out in hiring Olive Purdue. Especially when you consider the number of secretaries willing to work a night shift.

Cummings finally took her cue: "Why don't I come back at a more convenient time? I can run everything past my attorney and then we'll see what business remains for us to . . . consummate." She breezed past us and into the outer office.

Once she was outside and starting her BMW, Olive started to giggle. "I could've sworn I heard you yelling for help, Sam."

I loosened my tie. "I totally didn't see that coming."

"It's that old PD thing, Boss."

"What old 'PD thing'?"

"You know; in all the books it's where the sexy client wants to find out where the term 'Private Dick' came from." She guffawed— I mean there is no other term for the sound coming from her mouth.

"Yeah, well, I figure that she's pretty pissed at her husband and I'm the most immediate form of payback at hand for the moment."

"And there's that," she agreed. "Seriously, Sam; when is Miss Lupé coming home?" She returned my frown. "You say it's none of my business then you done answered both my questions."

"Both your questions?"

"You said she had an opportunity to do some stunt-work for a movie. But it's more than that, isn't it? Some sort of lover's quarrel."

"Some sort," I said reluctantly.

"Well, I know that it can't be another woman . . ."

Actually, if you considered the ghost of my dead wife to be another woman . . .

" . . . and I really don't want to know what it is about." She put her hand on my arm. "But what I do need to know is: is she coming back?"

"I don't know, Olive. I just don't know."

"Do you want her back?"

My head snapped up. "Hell, yes!"

"Then why don't you go after her?"

"I can't."

"Can't? Or *won't?*"

Both actually. I didn't know where she actually was and what name she was using. And, even if I did, going after her would put us both in serious danger.

"It's more complicated than that," I said finally. "Trust me, it's better if I wait for her to come home."

The telephone rang and Olive snagged it. "After Dark Investigations." She listened and started to frown. Covering the mouthpiece, she said, "No one's there."

"No one's there or someone's not talking?" She shrugged and I felt a prickle of apprehension spidercrawl up my spine. "Transfer it to my office," I said, heading back to my desk.

I grabbed the receiver on the second ring. "Samuel Haim . . ."

Jenny's voice crackled in my ear: "Darling, it's me."

I leaned back and pushed the connecting door shut. "I've told you to never call me at the office."

"Or you've told *you* to never call you at the office, if you believe your silly little theory about virus-induced hallucinations," she countered.

"I don't have time for this," I hissed. "What is it?"

"Someone's dropped by the house. I think he's looking for you."

"Who is it?"

Maybe the accident guy had wandered back up to use the phone again. . . .

"He isn't saying. He's dead, dear."

Then again, maybe he hadn't.

"Dead?" I struggled to keep my voice down. "He's a vampire?"

"No, honey; that would be an *undead* person. This gentleman is . . . well . . . dead. Has been for quite a long time, it would seem."

"He's a ghost? A spirit?"

"No, more like a rotting corpse. Walking dead. You know, like a zombie."

"A zombie?"

"That's what he looks like."

"What does he want?"

"How should I know? Do you want me to invite him in? I could put him on the phone and you could ask."

"No! No. I'll be right there." I hung up the phone. "Goodbye."

Oops. Get a grip, Cséjthe.

The clock showed a quarter past midnight as I came back out. "I think I'm going to take your earlier advice and call it a night, Olive. I'll be in tomorrow after my night class."

She was back to her desk, organizing a spill of paperwork. "I left a message on Miss Samm's answering machine. Want me to try again?"

"Not tonight. I'll just drop by tomorrow, unannounced. In fact, I think I prefer it that way." I dug my spare set of keys out of my pocket, trying not to drop them in the process. "Oh, and Olive . . ."

"Yes, Boss?"

"Three things. First, call the cop shop and see if any exsanguinated corpses have been turning up."

"Discreet or direct?" she asked.

"Hmm?"

"If the police *haven't* run across any bloodless corpses, they'll think we're mad for asking. If they *have,* well, they'll be wanting to know—"

"—what we know, how we know, and when we knew it," I finished, embarrassed for being so distracted that the obvious had escaped me.

"Especially since 'we' would be a very misleading term in this case."

"Sorry, Olive. Trust me; you don't want to know. But if you can run sources *and* be discreet, find out if there have been any unusual corpses in the morgue of late."

"Mmhmm. And if that's your first request, I'm not real keen on finding out about numbers two and three."

Yep, Olive Purdue was a gem and if I seemed to have caught a round of bad luck it was probably because I'd used up all my good luck in finding her. "Item number two: I'd like you to pull the obituary on a Mr. Delacroix for me before tomorrow night."

I don't know how she did it but my secretary managed to look both relieved and wary at the same time. "And the third?"

"Memo me in triplicate: No more divorce cases!"

Relief now battled surprise as she contemplated our accounts receivables. "But that's eighty percent of our case load."

"Better to kill time than have time kill me." I paused at the outer door and leaned my head against the frame.

She chuckled as she made shooing motions with her hands. "Maybe you're right. You look like you're dead on your feet."

I eased out the door. "More than you know, Olive." It closed behind me, the dim light from the pebbled glass barely adequate for my feet to find the platform stairs.

More than she knew.

I stepped down into the deeper darkness and set my face toward the heart of the night.

Chapter Four

It was one-ten in the a.m. when I turned the Merc off the road and started up the winding drive. The vinelike branches of a dozen weeping willow trees stroked the roof of my car like fleshless fingers; my tires swirled up a backwash of crushed pink mimosa blossoms made bloody by the glow of the taillights. I was bracing myself for—what?

My accident victim from earlier this evening wanting to call Triple-A? Mr. Delacroix, returned from his fiery tryst with my pop-eyed vampire?

I parked in front of the garage and walked across the vast, sloped lawn, expecting a troupe of reenactors from *The Night Of The Living Dead*. Instead I was treated to a diorama of Van Gough's *Starry Night*: not a soul, living or shambling dead, in sight.

I walked the boundaries of the "yard" twice, the motion sensors triggering the house "security" lights that, perversely, made me an easy target for hidden assailants while effectively destroying my night vision for the next fifteen minutes. And it took that long just to run primary and secondary checks of the immediate area.

If you're thinking that floodlights are a useless security feature for someone with infravision, let me tell you now that it doesn't mean diddley-squat when your intruders have the thermal equivalent of ice water in their veins. Still, being outside with the lights on *me* wasn't part of the original design concept.

I cut corners on doing the full perimeter sweep: proof that I had been wise to cut my military career short. *Though not as short as the men I'd helped court-martial back all those years ago.* Funny how you can face down a real monster in the here-and-now, yet find yourself more haunted by the ghosts of old memories.

I kicked an old pinecone into the woods and wondered whatever became of Birkmeister and his men. I had no real hope of finding out as their records had been sealed along with mine. One way or another, Uncle Samuel made us all disappear as a means of cleaning up the mess that had been made. I had gotten off easy.

But was it because I was innocent? My JAG lawyer had certainly made that case.

Or was it because my testimony had simplified matters for the military tribunals charged with laying the entire matter to rest?

I felt a flash of nearly forgotten anger—more proof that not everything that is buried, stays buried. I shook my head and turned to survey the slope leading back up to the house. Screw Lieutenant Lenny and the rest of the squad. That was then; this was now. I decided that I wasn't primed—mentally or practically—to do a wider sweep of the woods that bordered my property on two sides. And it just wasn't practical to step off the banks and into the waters of Gris Bayou in the back.

Still, there was plenty of lawn in-between. Not to mention pecan and oak and willow and mimosa and magnolia and dogwood trees—although they had lately begun to do battle with creeping vines of wisteria, clematis, trumpet, and honeysuckle. While I paid to have the grass cut regularly, the shrubbery had taken advantage of benign neglect. You could hide a whole marching band of corpses in my front yard—never mind the odd, ambulatory cadaver. Unkempt kaleidoscopic bursts of azaleas and lilacs and creeping phlox and fiery explosions of dwarf burning bush had mutated since Spring into unidentifiable, alien greenery that resembled kudzu on steroids. They had gone on to multiply like riots of bacterial blooms infecting a green petri dish. Some days I felt more like George of the Jungle than Milton the Monster.

I looked back at the silhouette of my stone-and-brick two-story house that was more fortress than home. *Three—Mama Samm had said "three stories."* Or *tree* to be precise. Did that mean she was less informed than she thought?

Or was she counting the subterranean level—the one with the safe room and the gun vaults that didn't show up on the official blueprints?

Stepping up onto the porch, I felt an unaccustomed grittiness under my left foot. I unlocked the door, rekeyed the alarm pad, and switched on the porch light. A mound of gritty white powder had been scuffed over and onto the doormat. Picking up a pinch, I rubbed it between my fingers and touched it to my tongue: salt.

Okay.

I studied the rest of the porch more carefully. Maybe I saw a couple of small stains on the concrete that hadn't been there previously. Or maybe not: Maybe it was residue from the accident guy who had dropped by earlier this evening. Hey, who studies their porch on a regular basis? I suppose someone, somewhere, is on intimate terms with their doorstep—but not because the ghost of his dead wife called him at the office to report an arrival of the departed.

I sighed and pushed the door open. My life would have been simpler if I had just gone ahead and died in the crash that killed my wife and daughter. Or if I'd become truly undead after my transfusion in Bassarab's barn. Being stuck somewhere between alive and undead made everything infinitely more complicated.

"Honey, I'm home!" I locked the door behind me and rekeyed the alarms. "What happened to our company?" I walked through the dining room and the den, half-expecting to find a stiff, relaxed and ensconced in my easy chair and making small talk with my now-you-see-her-now-you-don't wife.

Ex-wife.

Or, rather, deceased wife: ex-life.

I went through the entire house, basement and bathrooms included: no dead bodies, no ectoplasmic ex.

Olive Purdue didn't hear a voice on the other end of my phone call because there was no voice. My wife was more than a year dead and the dead don't come back and behave like refugees from a Thorne Smith story.

Yeah, tell that to my absent paramour.

Not that it would do any good. When Lupé stormed out of the house nearly two months before, she made it clear that I had to decide, once and for all, whether Jenny was just a psychic manifestation of the hemophagic virus mutating my brain cells—or the actual ghost of my dead wife. Either way, I was to resolve the situation so there would be no further *ménage-a-haunts*.

If I couldn't . . .

I gazed at Lupé's strong, dark features in a photo on the fireplace mantel. Her bronzed skin, dark eyes, and smoky black hair bespoke her Latin American ancestry more than her second-generation French Canadian heritage. Her features were strong and sensual in contrast to my dead wife's delicate porcelain beauty. There were no pictures of me. Cameras had a difficult time capturing my actual image now that I was becoming . . . what? The jury was still out on that issue. And since the my photos prior to the crash included Jenny or Kirsten, I had put them away months before meeting the woman who best understood my twilight existence.

If only she could understand my inability to let Jenny go in the more literal sense. If only I could. While I tended to agree with her theory that Jenny was only a manifestation of my inability to permanently "commit," I had yet to figure out how to exercise the marital clause of "'til death do us part."

Perhaps "exorcise" was more apt.

Sighing, I walked into the den and booted up the computer. While I waited for it to churn through the latest infestation of Microsoft Windows, I scanned my bookshelves for material on Elizabeth Báthory and voodoo, telling myself that the dead don't go AWOL from the local cemetery and ring doorbells at midnight.

And, of course, there's no such thing as vampires.

It took a little digging to run down "Marinette Bois-Chèche."

Vodoun or voodoo is not a set theology, per se. When African slaves were transported to the New World, they brought a range of belief systems as varied as the tribes and countries of their origins. As tribes were blended with other tribes, separated, then diluted by subsequent generations, these beliefs were mixed and muddled with the white man's religions—particularly Catholicism—producing a general form and structure identifiable as voodoo but by no means definitive across time and geography.

The supreme and most powerful voodoo "god" is Damballah-Wedo, whose symbol is the snake and is sometimes merged with the image of Saint Patrick because of his reputed influence over all serpents. I skimmed over a chapter on the symbology of snakes in myth and religion and noted that Ayido-Wedo was Damballah's "wife"—"the moon to his sun." Their children or "companions" are the Loa who manifest in over two hundred variants or avatars and are divided and shared among fifteen or so different sects.

Of course, the various source materials were mildly contradictory at best. And trying to quantify the Loa was nigh impossible. They weren't really gods or godlings, angels or demons. And "spirits" was such a generic, all-purpose term as to be virtually useless. The Loa were, well, just the Loa.

And, even then, they weren't always who you thought they were since they manifested different "aspects." As this happened rather frequently, each aspect or manifestation was identified through a variation on each one's name. Erzulie—or Ezili or *Maîtresse Erzulie*—for example, was the idealized figure of womanhood, the Loa of love and beauty. And, like most women, she expressed herself through a wide range of identities. There was *Erzulie-Séverine-Belle-Femme,* Erzulie as a beautiful woman; *Erzulie Taureau,* the aspect of Erzulie as the bull; *La Grande Erzulie,* the aspect of Erzulie as an elderly, grief-stricken woman; *La Sirène* or *La Sirènn,* the sea or serpent aspect of Erzulie; and *Tsilah Wédo,* the aspect representing wealth and beauty.

Like most characteristics of Vodoun there was a flip side. Erzulie could also manifest in facets of vengeance and ugliness. Some of these were *Erzulie Mapiangueh, Erzulie Toho, Erzulie Zandor,* and—most interestingly—*Marinette* Bois-Chèche. Unfortunately, there was little else chronicled beyond the names. Just a list of a few additional aspects—*Erzulie Boum'ba, Erzulie Dantor, Erzulie Dosbas, Erzulie Fréda, Erzulie Fréda Dahomin, Erzulie Gé Rouge* and *Erzulie Mapian.*

If this doesn't make a compelling argument for the simplicities of monotheism, I don't know what does—even the concept of a Three-in-One trinity seems terribly uncomplex by comparison.

And the confusion didn't end with these multiple personality disorders: there were sects or families of Loa who couldn't seem to make up their minds as to who belonged to which clan. And then there was the little matter of form and intent as applied through invocation and ritual. Most voodoo was practiced in the *Rada* or "right hand" forms—healing, blessing, purification, praise and thanksgiving. *Petro,* on the other hand is for cursing your enemies, raising the dead, invoking evil spirits, and basically turning Loa's bad boys loose to raise some Hell. The vast majority of Vodoun's adherents practiced Rada rites and had nothing to do with the Petro perversions—Hollywood notwithstanding. But it was another example of how the same Loa could be invoked for both good and evil.

The Gédé clan, for another example, was the Loa of the dead—but they were also potent healers and the protectors of children. Their colors were purple and black. Baron Samedi, the head of the Gédé family, was a powerful arbiter of justice between the living and the dead, and very popular for a cadaverlike spirit who hangs out in graveyards. But, then, he was a snappy dresser, wearing top hat and tails and, as everyone knows: "The clothes make the man."

Another clan, the Ogou, comprised the warrior Loa whose dominion was often symbolized by the sword, metalworking, fire, lightning, and the color red. Different "aspects" of the Ogou were said to manifest as *Ogou Baba,* a military general; *Ogou Badagris,* the phallic or fertility aspect; *Ogou Bhathalah,* the Loa of alchemy; *Ogou Fer* or *Ferraille,* Loa of the sword, iron and metals; *Ogou Shango,* the Loa of lightning; and *Ogou Tonnerre*—or Baron *Tonnerre,* the aspect of thunder.

I sat back in my chair and contemplated Mama Samm's cryptic warnings. She had said the Ogou cast a long shadow here. Meaning . . . what?

It took nearly another hour of digging to find a significant reference to Marinette Bois-Chèche, also listed as *Marinette Bras-Chêche, Marinette Congo,* and *Marinette Pied-Chêche.* There wasn't a whole lot of material on her—a single sentence, in fact, was all I could turn up.

"Powerful and violent principal female Loa of the Petro rite."

That didn't sound good as the Petro spirits were already considered to be "highly vengeful, bitter, and most dangerous" of all of the vodoun Loa.

So whom was Mama Samm trying to warn me against?

The Witch of Cachtice?

Elizabeth Báthory?

And what would happen when she finally "put her red dress on"?

Normally—a word that was becoming more and more infrequent in my vocabulary—I went to bed around sunrise and slept through the day. Tonight I decided to retire early. I wanted to get a running start on the Delacroix matter and I was just plain exhausted.

Jenny "reappeared" as I put the finishing touches on my makeshift first aid. The electrical burns had settled into a dull ache but my leg still throbbed as if the wound from the vampire's claws had occurred just minutes before. I had smeared antibiotic ointment into the red furrows and was taping an old but clean pillowcase around my calf when the medicine cabinet opened in the bathroom and a bottle of hydrogen peroxide floated out and down to the edge of the sink next to the toilet.

"Did you clean the wounds thoroughly?" she asked.

I let it bleed and then rinsed with alcohol.

"I'm not a mind-reader, darling; you have to answer out loud."

"Not if you're a figment of my imagination." I wrapped a few more strands of tape to add pressure as well as anchor the bandage. "Where have you been?"

"I don't know. One minute I was looking out the window at the dead person on the front porch. Then I was someplace far away and it seemed to take me a long time to get back."

"You're telling me you had some kind of blackout?"

The bottle drifted back up to a shelf in the open cabinet. "Why do you ask? If I am a figment of your virus-ravaged imagination then you already know."

"Yeah? Humor me."

The mirrored door swung shut and I fancied I could see her dim silhouette in its silvered depths. "Why, hunkered down in the stygian pit of your subconscious, of course," she said sarcastically, "awaiting my turn to torment you afresh—just like the rest of the fairytale creatures that have haunted your life this past year."

"The real Jen never used words like 'stygian.'"

"The afterlife has a way of expanding one's vocabulary. But you've got bigger problems than whether or not I'm real."

"Not according to Lupé."

I heard her sigh. "I know you blame me, Chris, but I think she has issues."

"Hell yes, she has issues!" I sputtered. "*You're* the issue!"

"If I'm not real, then how can I be the issue? Wouldn't that make *you* the issue?"

I grunted. "Me . . . you . . . *she* made it clear that she didn't want to come back until this particular issue was settled."

"I don't see what the big deal is, here. I thought I'd made it clear from the very beginning that I approve of her. I think she's very good for you."

I took a deep breath and let it out slowly. "It may be one of those woman things that we men are kind of clueless about but I think she doesn't appreciate being 'approved of.'"

"Well, that's too bad. What am I supposed to do? Disapprove? I've gotten a lot better about knocking before I come into the bedroom. Let's face another possibility: She just may not be the right woman for you."

"Not the right woman for me?" I jumped up and stalked back into the bedroom. "She's a werewolf, for God's sake!"

"And . . . ?"

"My God, Jen! I'm infected with one-half of the combinant virus that turns the living into the undead courtesy of a blood transfusion with Count Dracula—"

"Prince, not count," she corrected, "Vlad Drakul Bassarab."

"—I've shared blood with a lycanthrope and sampled Tanis leaf extract," I continued, ignoring the interruption. "I've got vampires and metamorphs from at least three major enclaves hunting me, a dead wife haunting me. Then there's this necrotic virus ticking away in my brain like a time bomb that, when it goes off, will blow my eccentric little coping mechanisms into a total disconnect from reality. What kind of normal woman is going to put up with that?"

"You'd be surprised what 'normal women' are capable of putting up with," she answered quietly. "But you've got a bigger problem, right now."

"What? The dead guy on my porch tonight?" I fell back on the bed. "I think you must have been mistaken. There was a car crash just down the road and the driver—who was pretty banged up—came by earlier to use the phone. It may have been him coming back. . . ."

"What? You don't think I know dead when I see it? No. And I'm talking about that vampire that seriously jacked you around tonight."

I crammed the extra pillow under my throbbing leg to elevate it. "*He's* dead. Case closed."

"Maybe the virus *is* starting to rot your brain. What if he was rogue?"

That stopped me. "What are you getting at?"

"As I see it—or as *you* do since *I* am only a figment of *your* imagination—there are three possibilities. One, there is an enclave in Northeast Louisiana . . ."

"Not bloody likely," I said. "I looked at all the maps back in Seattle. The only demesne in Louisiana is down in New Orleans. There are only eighteen in the entire country and there hasn't been a new enclave since the 1960s. There will probably never be another enclave—the other demesnes wouldn't permit it."

"So that leaves us with two possibilities, darling. Your vampire is either a rogue or an enforcer."

During last year's Seattle sojourn, Stefan Pagelovitch had acquainted me with the demesne system by which territory was divided and held by the various undead populations. These little "underground" fiefdoms were quite jealous of their own autonomy and, as a rule, only cooperated on the issue of rogues.

A newly minted vampire, left to its own devices, was a danger to the safety of every demesne. As a result, there were rules governing the existence of all who were reborn as creatures of the night. Broken down to basics, if you make another like yourself, you're responsible for "it." Teach it to exist subtly, hunt judiciously, and eliminate all evidence of feeding. It shouldn't leave telltale corpses lying about or visible bite-marks on the living. It should learn how the delicate art of mental domination can erase those awkward memories that might otherwise require a bloodier solution to the problem of witnesses.

And, most importantly, you bring it into the enclave where it must swear fealty to you and to the Doman, the ruler of the demesne who adjudicates all of the laws for that particular enclave. Any vampire attempting to exist apart from the watchful "protection" of its Sire's society was declared rogue and automatically assumed to be a risk to all demesnes.

"And it doesn't really matter," I said slowly, "whether this one was a rogue or a hunter."

If Robert Delacroix's dance partner was a rogue, I could expect a dozen or more vampire regulators to be hot on his trail. If he wasn't rogue, then it was likely that he was a rogue hunter hot on another newborn's trail and that there would be others around like him—the cell phone practically guaranteed it. Either way, it meant that my home territory was about to come under a lot of undead scrutiny.

And I had a bigger bounty on my head than any ordinary rogue.

"So, the question is," I continued aloud, "whether to hunker down and hope that I can stay off the radar as the Wild Hunt passes by or pull up stakes—"

"So to speak," Jen smirked.

"—and move again. The problem is, it's probably too late to make such arrangements without calling more attention to myself."

"Then you'd better hope Mama Samm is the only speed bump in your elaborate paper trail," my ghostly conscience warned. "Seriously, Chris; I feel a constant prickling in my ectoplasm these days. It's like there's something very old and very evil hovering just beyond the range of my senses. I felt it coming closer just before I . . . went away. Something is out there, something terrible! And its power is growing! This might be a good time to call Olive and tell her—oh I don't know—something like you're taking a couple of weeks off to go fishing."

I considered it as I walked into the closet and punched in the combination on my gun safe. "Blowing town might be just as attention-getting as actually moving," I decided finally, reaching in and withdrawing a box of ammo and a zippered pouch. "But I do think I'll give up jogging for a couple of weeks."

I closed the safe and walked back out and over to the bed.

"Now this looks like a bad idea," she said.

"I have a license to carry." I unzipped the pouch and removed the handgun. "This is a ten-millimeter auto Glock 20."

"Does that mean it's special?"

"The Glock 20 ranks with the most powerful automatic pistols ever made."

"Isn't Dirty Harry's gun bigger?" she asked with that gee-whiz, innocent tone that signaled standard baiting mode. "Or is that just Hollywood special effects?"

"If you add up the total foot-pounds of muzzle energy represented by the fifteen rounds in its high-capacity magazine, it's more like: 'Go ahead . . . make my week.' "

She giggled. "Was that supposed to be Jack Nicholson?

"Clint Eastwood."

"Don't quit your night job."

Laying out the cleaning kit, I proceeded to strip the handgun down and repeat the cleaning and oiling process I had just completed two weeks before after visiting the shooting range.

"I think this whole P.I. fantasy has gone to your head."

"If it had gone to my head I would be sporting a shoulder rig every evening as I chase after unfaithful husbands and follow up on insurance claims."

"Do you really think that will protect you from things that are already dead?"

I grinned as I reassembled the Glock and wiped it down. "Well, it won't protect me from your nagging but I don't mind. You nag me when you're worried about me." I laid the pistol on the nightstand and picked up a pair of magazines. "As for stopping dead things, I've got some special loads that I've been wanting to try for a while."

"Why is it that every guy thinks a gat in the hand means the world by the tail?"

"You watch too much Bogart."

"No, you watch too much Bogart," she said. "I'd like to watch the Lifetime channel but you've always got the satellite set to Turner Classic Movies. If we had cable, I could go watch in the other room."

I opened the box and began loading bullets into the fifteen-shot magazines. "These are 10 mil Glasers."

"Wad-cutters?"

"You didn't learn that from watching Lifetime." I held up the epoxy-jacketed projectile. "It's the equivalent of a standard 'Silver' Glaser—which isn't really. They call them that to differentiate them from 'Blue' Glasers."

"Who comes up with these names, anyway?"

"Originally? The inventor, Colonel Jack Cannon, named it for his friend Armin Glaser. I'm not sure why or whether Armin's still proud of his namesake. The idea was to produce a round that wouldn't endanger innocent bystanders from over-penetration. APs and FMJs have a tendency to pass through various substances— bad guys, walls, cars—"

"Honey, you're lapsing into SEALspeak and losing me."

I thought about arguing that she understood perfectly since she was really—*aw, hell with it.* "Armor Piercing and Full Metal Jacket ordnance are designed for military use as you really need that penetrating ability." Not to mention the fact that the Geneva Convention had decided they were more humane than mushrooming bullets and minié balls.

"Law enforcement, on the other hand, needed bullets that could be used in populated areas, hostage situations, and so on. If you shoot the bad guy, you don't want the bullet going through him and into the house across the street."

I paused as I considered the idea of the local cops using ammo that was outlawed by the Geneva Convention.

"JSPs and JHPs—sorry—Jacketed Soft Points and Hollow Points were designed to mushroom or flatten once they entered the target, expending their energy on impact so they wouldn't keep going."

"Sounds humane."

I knew that tone all too well. "Well, it is. For the innocent bystander."

"But for the person who's shot, it makes a little hole going in and a great big hole coming out."

I nodded. "Except, for my purposes, it's better if it doesn't come out. That's why I'm trying modified Glasers." I started back to loading the ammo magazines. "The rounds are filled with birdshot covered by a crimped polymer end cap. Upon impact, the projectile fragments, with the birdshot spreading like a miniature shotgun pattern. The frag-spread guarantees most major arteries and blood vessels in the vicinity will be penetrated, causing immediate unconsciousness from catastrophic blood-pressure drop and possible death from exsanguination within minutes.

"The 'Silver' Glaser uses slightly larger birdshot and has a couple of extra inches of penetration and stopping power over the 'Blue' version."

"Except," she interrupted, "*your* so-called 'Silver' version uses actual silver for the birdshot, anticipating major damage to undead flesh. Sort of like the Lone Ranger using a shotgun."

I looked around again; this open-mouthed response was getting to be a habit.

"Don't look so surprised, Chris. I'd have to have been pretty inattentive all these years not to know how your mind works by now."

Well, that made one of us.

The dream slammed through my head with all the ugly power of last year's memories of Bassarab's barn.

Four large, flaming braziers, one in each corner of the room, can't provide enough warmth or enough light to adequately illuminate the dark stone walls. *She likes it that way.* Even though she has many aboveground chambers as well as the courtyard to work with, she prefers the dark, underground warrens where she can practice in the eternal shadows beneath the keep.

The Dark Arts aren't so named on the basis of intent and final product alone.

The sounds of the great Carpathian forest echo in these man-made canyons of dressed stone and iron-girt doors: the constant moaning of the wind, the screech of the owl, the scream of the lynx, the growls, yips, and howlings of the wolves . . .

Only, there is no wind down here in the blocky bowels of Cachtice, no winged birds of prey, no four-legged animals—the beasts that inhabit this burrow, the hunters and the prey alike, walk upon their hind legs and make fading claims to being human.

Other sounds shatter the auditory illusion: the harsh slap of leather upon splitting skin, the subtle hiss of the heated irons, the skeletal shiver of chains and the perverse squeal of hinges.

And the soft pattering sounds of rain that falls, not from a cloud but from a spasmed clutch of flesh embraced by a metal cage of bars and blades and spikes.

The moaning fades as if the wind—or something—has nearly died.

She stands beneath the Devil's showerhead like Botticelli's *Venus*—if that master had painted his masterpiece during a scarlet period in counterpoint to Picasso's blue. Clad in nothing but crimson from head to toe, she opens her eyes, making two hollow openings in a curtain of red. She cups her hands above her groin and scrapes her belly in an upward motion that fills her palms until her insolent breasts are given a second undercoating.

Then she holds her unholy offering out to me, the thick, viscous (steaming!) blood dribbling between her fingers.

Share my bounty, she says, her teeth surprisingly white and shockingly long.

Share my power . . .

I jolt awake to the shrill bleating of the telephone and a disturbing hardness between my legs.

I rolled over and peered, bleary-eyed, at the telephone next to my bed: I had switched the ringer off but had forgotten the downstairs phone. The clock on my "night"stand proclaimed the time as 10:17 in the a.m. Picking up the phone was easier than getting up to close the bedroom door so I did.

"Mr. Haim?"

"Speaking." But just barely. My mouth was dry and my throat clotted.

"You're the private investigator with the office in the old railroad car?"

"Ummm." A migraine started to unfold between my temples like an origami sculpture made of pig iron. It pulsed in counterpoint to the throbbing in my leg.

"I want to hire you." A small portion of my mind not occupied in cataloguing my misery noted that the voice belonged to a woman.

"My office hours are eight P.M. to four A.M. I'm teaching a night class at the university and won't be in until after nine tonight. Come see me at ten."

"I work the night shift."

"So do I. How did you get my home number?" It was unlisted, of course.

"Mama Samm D'Arbonne gave it to me. She said you'd want to talk to me."

So all of a sudden the old fortune-teller was giving me referrals? I furrowed my brow. It hurt.

"Did she say why?" I tried to arrange a *ménage a trois* between my head, the telephone receiver, and the pillow.

"No sir . . ."

"Is it a divorce case?"

"No sir, it's—"

"If it's important enough to take off work for, you can tell me after nine tonight. At my office."

"Well—"

"Goodnight, Ms.—"

"Delacroix. Chalice Delacroix. Good morning, Mr. Haim."

I sat straight up in bed as the receiver clicked on her end and a bloody iron rose bloomed behind my left eye. My turn to dial star-sixty-nine.

"Ms. Delacroix? Sam Haim. I'll meet you at my office at twelve noon. . . ."

Imagine Vanessa Williams and Halle Berry as the ugly stepsisters: Chalice Delacroix was Cinderella.

Even half-blinded by the daylight and wearing polarized contact lenses behind EPF10 Ray-Bans, I could see why admirers at the funeral home had surrounded her last night. She was chocolate perfection in a black pants suit and crisp white blouse. All the more impressive as hardly anyone's clothes are still crisp by midday between July and October in Louisiana.

Most impressive of all: she held a doctorate in biology and worked in the genetics division at BioWeb Industries. Where her father was a janitor. Hmmm. . . .

"My father's funeral was supposed to take place today," she said. "We should have lowered his casket into the ground two hours ago." Her eyes glistened. They were moss green and liquid like deep woodland springs where only the surface seems still. "Now that there is no body to bury, there doesn't seem to be much point."

I steepled my fingers and leaned my elbows on the desk blotter. "The body is missing?"

She gave her head a little shake while she searched for the words or her voice. Maybe both. "My father's body was vandalized. Stolen from his casket and . . . and . . ." She looked down and tears dripped into her lap, some finding the handkerchief clutched in her hand, some not. "It was shoved into the crematorium oven in the basement and half incinerated before the fires were extinguished. The medical examiner recommended that we complete the cremation process once the police are finished with their investigation."

"So the police are investigating?"

"They're running the paperwork."

"You're anticipating racial bias?"

She gave her head another little shake. "Nothing so virulent, Mr. Haim. This is, after all, the New South." The irony in her inflection was nearly invisible. "But Robert"—she pronounced it "*Robaire*"—"Delacroix was an old and poor black man. He was already dead and there was no physical harm done to anyone else. Emotional harm doesn't count for much when the court dockets are filled with stabbings, gunshot wounds, and lost and found bodies. The police would be unlikely to do more than push paper for an old and poor white man."

"So you want me to look into it."

She nodded and I resisted the impulse to take her hands in mine. "Did your father have any enemies?"

She shook her head.

"Ms. Delacroix," I cleared my throat, "in order to do my job I have to know as much about your father as possible. That means poking around and asking personal questions—even embarrassing or insulting questions."

She nodded.

"For instance, did your father gamble? Did he owe anyone any money?"

"No. He was a custodian and he spent every spare dollar that he had to put me through medical school. Between the two of us, we still owe the government a good deal of money in student loans. Do you think the Feds might be upset that he defaulted by dying?"

Now I did take her hands in mine. "Ms. Delacroix, I am sorry for your loss." *You don't know how sorry.* "But there is a standard series of questions that come with an investigation like this..." *Who was I kidding? There was nothing standard about Robert Delacroix's assignation with a crematorium oven.* "... and I have to pursue every possible lead until I can reasonably prove a dead end. I promise to be discreet and remember that you and your father are the victims, here. But I wouldn't be giving you your money's worth if I didn't consider every possibility."

"Money," she said, withdrawing her hands from mine. "I don't have much but I was thinking that if you were to speak with the management of the funeral home—"

"I'm sure they'd be more interested in a settlement than a lawsuit."

She gave a little shake of her head. "I do not wish to extort money from them, Mr. Haim. I was simply thinking that it would be in *their* best interests to help bring this... vandal... to justice. That they might contribute to your expenses and we could fund your investigation jointly."

"I'll talk to them. I'm sure something can be worked out. Plus I'm giving you a fifty percent discount over and above what they contribute to the case."

She looked a little startled. "Why?"

"Because this *isn't* a divorce case. And one further stipulation: if I don't find out who did this, I won't charge you one red cent."

She gave me a look that asked the question I dared not answer honestly.

"Company policy," I lied. "I guarantee results."

The truth was her father had saved my life. Robert Delacroix had already gotten my promise to avenge his death and protect his daughter. The creature that precipitated his fiery dissolution had already perished and discorporated in the furnace in question. And the only person that witnesses could place at the scene of the crime was yours truly. The fact that I had been front row and center when Chalice's daddy ended up in the crematory oven didn't mean that I could just fake an inconclusive paper trail and blow off the investigation. I couldn't take money from the Delacroix family when the debt was mine here. And, whatever I might finally reveal to Ms. Delacroix, *I* needed to find out how many other red-eyed bloodsuckers with cell phones were hanging out in Northeast Louisiana.

And what forces were at work when corpses climbed out of their graves and coffins to battle vampires and do business with a man trapped in the twilight realm between the living and the dead.

Chapter Five

Robert Vernon Delacroix was a fifty-three-year-old black custodian who had gotten a bad case of the flu and an even worse case of congestive heart failure during one of his coughing fits.

That was the extent of the rather terse autopsy report that Olive had clipped to the file. It did not shine any light on Mr. D's potential motives for dancing with my pop-eyed vampire. The fact of the autopsy, itself—removal of vital organs, including the brain—made the old man's behavior even more unlikely as opposed to someone who was "merely dead."

Olive had also attached a printout of Mr. Delacroix's credit report and had typed in a variety of forms to gather additional information should I choose to do so: an MV198G requesting a copy of his driver's license, an MV15 for obtaining a copy of his license registration, a UCC-11 for listing such financial information as loans taken out by or liens against Mr. Delacroix, and a list of Internet websites for short-cuts to credit reports, tax assessments, and government databases. Each lead might not tell me much but put them together and I would find bits of information connecting to other bits of information that could tell me where to look next.

Normally, that is.

Unfortunately, this was no find-the-hidden-bank-account/trace-the-stolen-property/locate-the-missing-person kind of investigation;

it was more of a figure-out-why-the-dead-guy-saved-my-ass-and-what-protecting-his-daughter-was-all-about kind of case.

Complicating everything was the fact that there were vampires in town—emphasis on the plural.

A year and a whole lifetime ago I didn't believe in vampires. Or ghosts. Or a whole raft of night-creatures that had heretofore been relegated to fairytale stories and B-minus cinema. That was before a detour through Weir, Kansas resulted in an episode of "lost time" and the onset of a peculiar wasting disease that dulled my appetite and sharpened my sensitivity to sunlight. Although it seemed to be stealing my life, it also made me highly resistant to death. The automobile accident that killed my wife and daughter landed me on the morgue's autopsy table, where I woke up and proceeded to scare the bejezus out of the coroner and a hospital janitor.

Not to mention myself.

Maybe I didn't really die in the crash: my heart still beat, though with a vastly different rhythm, and I still required air—but having one foot in the grave and the other in the land of the living made these distinctions moot. If the necrotic virus from Dracula's transfusion didn't actually kill me someday, it still seemed destined to drive me mad. Half-believing that Jennifer's spirit remained behind to "haunt" me was just the earliest stage of its effect on my cerebral cortex. What would come later? Would I become another soulless vampire predator? Or would I become something more monstrous? More evil?

More like my ancient forebear?

Generations of inbreeding certainly set the stage for the madness to come at the close of the sixteenth century. Erzsébet Báthory's neurological problems manifested at an early age with seizures and blackouts when she was just four or five. A sadistic, bisexual aunt and a schizophrenic uncle provided perverse tutelage at an impressionable age. And then there was Lord Acton's axiom: spoiled, wealthy child of privilege raised by a series of governesses employed to cater to her every need—it would have been a miracle if her relationships hadn't been dysfunctional to some degree.

And what's easier to forget in this kinder, gentler world that we oh-so-civilized folk now inhabit is that she was very much a child of her time. Hungary was experiencing a turbulent period in its already tempestuous history. It had served as a battleground between the Turkish forces of the Ottoman Empire and the Hapsburg armies of Austria and there were continuous and mostly ineffectual efforts to send the Turks back home—or at least keep them at bay. War, battle, death, and retribution unfolded all around her on a regular basis. Life was harsh and the administration of justice—or, rather, rule—was even harsher.

As a young girl Erzsébet witnessed numerous punishments and executions, including numerous whippings, floggings, hangings, forced cannibalism, and burnings at the stake. Three peasant boys were accused of trying to rape her when she was eight years old. She had a front row seat when they were publicly castrated.

A fanatical Lutheran called Preacher Hebler was one of her childhood tutors. He tried impressing upon his young charge the importance of piety with vivid and heartfelt stories of the horrors of Hell and the tortures of the damned. As gruesome as the churchman's imaginative parables were they proved no match for the every day brutality that was up close and impersonal. In later years these stories may have actually provided inspiration for her own appalling "hobbies."

One night, while still in the formative years of her childhood, Erzsébet was taken from her bedchamber to witness a special execution. A gypsy had been accused of selling children to the Turks and his sentence was offered as public entertainment. Who knows what emotions filled her young breast as she watched? A horse was brought forward and pulled to the ground where its belly was sliced open. Did the dying beast scream more pitifully? Or the accused while he was stuffed, struggling and shrieking, amid the steaming entrails? Did she clutch at the arms of her velvet chair in dismay as the equine guts were closed and sewn shut? Or in excitement during the delayed and drawn out suffocation that followed such a gory entombment.

One might guess at her emotional bent by now but the intellectual lesson was unavoidable: if you were noble-born, commoners might be abused or disposed of with impunity and without fear of retribution. Could I depend upon my civilized upbringing, the lateness of my infection, to make me a more civilized monster? Or did the same dark blood that burned in her savage breast lie dormant in our shared genetic codes? Would that viral key eventually unlock my own murderous id and send it rampaging through the twisted convolution of sulci, gyri and fissures in my cerebellum to mirror her dark acts? How would I know until it was too late?

Maybe it already was.

The phone rang, interrupting my mental *detour-de-force*.

I picked up the receiver and announced: "After Dark Investigations."

"I would like to speak with Mr. Haim." The voice was familiar. As were the subvocal stressors.

"Speaking."

"Mr. Haim? This is Susan Sinor."

Ah. "Yes, Mrs. Sinor. How is your husband?"

A pause. "He's dead, Mr. Haim."

My turn to pause. "I'm terribly sorry, Mrs. Sinor. Is there anything I can do?"

"Yes." She drew a deep and ragged breath. "The police told me he died at the scene."

So much for my assurances that he would call from the hospital. "I didn't realize that his injuries were so serious."

"They were serious, Mr. Haim. He died in the crash."

"Excuse me?"

"The Medical Examiner thinks it might have been a heart attack. We will have to wait for the autopsy to be sure but he's sure that my husband was already dead when the impact threw him out of the car."

"I—I don't know what to say."

"Well, say *something*, Mr. Haim. Tell me how my dead husband got up and walked all the way up to your house, called me from your telephone, and then ended up back down at accident scene when the police arrived! Can you explain that?"

I couldn't, of course. Other than to suggest that the M.E. must be mistaken. It wasn't a satisfactory explanation but it was better than the alternative.

She was sobbing when I finally hung up and I cursed myself for picking up the office phone during the day. I had a secretary for that at night and an answering machine for during the day. Another good reason I shouldn't even be here (or anywhere) during the day.

The phone rang again. I sat and stared at it, rethinking my communications strategy: *e-mail*, I thought; *sever all relations with Ma Bell and only deal with people on-line.*

The answering machine picked up. "After Dark Investigations," it announced in Olive's chipper tones, "Samuel Haim, licensed private detective, and associates. Our office hours are eight P.M. to two A.M. You may call back or leave a message at the beep."

Please, I thought, *be anything but a divorce case.*

It was.

Not a divorce case, that is.

My secretary's voice continued to come over the machine's speaker but it was no longer a recording: "Sam, this is Olive. I've left a message on your machine at home but, just in case you miss it, I'm leaving one here at the office, as well. My sister is at the hospital and needs me to sit with her. I don't know how long we'll be there so—"

I picked up the receiver. "Olive? Sam here."

"What are you doing in so early, boss?"

What was I doing here? Oh, yeah . . . "Meeting with a client."

"Must be some client."

"Must be," I agreed. "Is everything all right?"

The barest of hesitations for my ebullient secretary spoke volumes. "It's my sister's boy. . . ."

"Jamal?" I had used Olive's nephew on several cases involving daytime surveillance, including the Snow Queen's "alienation of affliction."

"Is he all right?" I asked.

"It's the flu." She said it as if the boy had been diagnosed with cancer.

"They had to hospitalize him?"

"Maybe you haven't heard but there's a particularly virulent strain going around."

I remembered that Robert Delacroix's fatal coronary was occasioned by the flu. Of course, Jamal was young and healthy and whoever heard of a nineteen-year-old dying from the flu in these early years of the twenty-first century?

"Anyway, I wanted you to know that I may be late or even absent tonight. If that's all right with you."

It didn't matter whether it was all right with me or not. It was family and that mattered more than showing up to sit by a drowsy telephone for my little fly-by-night detective agency-cum-hobby. Olive was just being polite and I completed the formalities by saying "that's all right" and "take all the time that you need."

"Thanks, Sam. I'd better get going."

"Do you need anything? Is there anything I can do?"

Again there was that quarter-beat hesitation, imperceptible to anyone else.

"What?" I pounced. "Tell me, Olive." And knowing she was too proud to ask any favors, I *pushed*. Mental Domination is not a simple process in face-to-face encounters and I had only tried "pushing" over the telephone once before. It hadn't proved effectual in getting my cable installed any quicker.

"My car's in the shop," she finally admitted. "I need to call a cab."

"Cancel the cab," I said, "I'll drive you."

Despite Olive's protestations that it was a sunny day and I should stay inside, I picked her up forty-five minutes later.

She was fully signed on to my explanation about extreme susceptibility to skin cancer. It was certainly true that I had developed a few epidural carcinomas before I figured out that my stopover in Weir had effectively cancelled my membership at the tanning salon and necessitated a career move to the night shift. But what she didn't know was that cancer was only a secondary issue.

Sunlight made me sick. It sapped my strength, clouded my mind, and made me itchy and jittery, and downright nauseated. Wearing hats and long-sleeved shirts and wraparound shades and slathering on a ton of SPF100 sunblock served as talismans against the tumors.

But there was always that nagging apprehension that, one of these days—just like the undead whose blood I shared—I was going to spontaneously combust.

Olive didn't know anything about my preternatural biology but she kept apologizing as if she knew the gamble I took to chauffeur her across town. The Merc's heavily tinted windows made the trip bearable but I was on the verge of developing a nervous tic as we approached the hospital.

"Forget it," I said for the fifth time. Obviously five had not proved sufficient so I added: "I actually have business at Greenwood so it's no inconvenience at all." That seemed to help, but now I would have to park the car and go inside for a little while, wander around as if I actually did have someplace to be.

At least it beat tailing Hyrum Cummings to evening City Council meetings.

The closest available parking slot was a good two-block walk from the visitors' entrance but I smiled, crossed my fingers, and trusted my fate to Coppertone. Outside the car the solar radiation staggered me, the light bearing down with a palpable weight on my back and shoulders. I immediately slapped a straw fedora on my head—a Dobbs' Palmer with a moderate brim—but my scalp itched and tingled throughout the long walk to the hospital's entryway.

A double-set pair of sliding doors formed an airlock that kept the lobby cool and soothed my buzzing nerves and twitching skin. It didn't do anything for the fresh migraine simmering at the back of my brainpan like the embers of a banked fire. I took my sunglasses off before my eyes had time to recover and nearly ran into a potted plant and then a trashcan on the way to the elevators.

Olive—at least I assumed it was Olive—laid a hand on my arm. "Are you okay, Boss?"

I tried a grin and attempted to put reassurance in the middle of it. "Well, if I'm not, I'm certainly in the right place."

"Maybe you better let me drive you home."

"Seriously, Olive, how are you getting home?"

"My sister will drop me off."

"I can wait."

"I won't leave while she's here. If necessary, I'll be her excuse to go home before she's totally exhausted."

I reached out, located her shoulder, squeezed gently. "How bad is it?"

I think she shook her head. "It's killing black people."

"What?"

"Mr. Haim!" A new voice derailed the conversation before I could make sense of what I thought I had just heard.

"What do you mean—" I was saying when another dim blob

emerged from the haze. As my hand left Olive's shoulder, it was enveloped by another and shaken vigorously.

"Lou Rollins, Mr. Haim; I sent you a letter last week!"

"I'm afraid I don't—"

"BioWeb Industries," the voice continued, filling the emptiness of the corridor like an auditory tidal wave. "My people are very keen on joining your client list!"

"Client list," I repeated.

"Sam, I'd better get upstairs," Olive said, excusing herself.

Lou Rollins maintained a firm grip on my hand. He added another to my upper arm. "I'll check in on you before I leave," I called after her retreating form.

"Say, this is perfect!" Lou-from-BioWeb exclaimed. In fact, every sentence from Lou's lips had sounded exclamatory so far. "I'm on my way up to Pedes to work another handshake deal and this way I get to kill two birds with one stone!"

Two birds with one stone. I grew less fond of that old saw with every passing day.

"Let's walk this way . . ." He released my hand but steered me toward the elevators with an arm that hovered dangerously close to my shoulders. "Now, the area hospitals pay you how much per unit of blood?"

Ah. A light clicked on at the end of my tunnel vision. "Mr. Rollins—"

"Lou!"

"Lou," I amended; "that is privileged information between my blood bank and my clients. And the client-list is very short because I simply don't do enough volume to service all of the local hospitals. We're really more of a boutique as blood banks go."

"We can help you change that!"

The elevator doors slid shut behind me as I pondered that. My Glock was neatly holstered and zippered and locked in the glove compartment of my car while, for the briefest of moments, I considered the odds of being trapped in this metal box with a homicidal maniac.

"Oh, *Sam*—may I call you Sam? Your expression!"

I could now see that Lou Rollins had a face like my Uncle Harry: round and capped with a fringe of curly brown hair, large eyes with smile crinkles at the corners, and a wide mouth that perpetually alternated between laughing and grinning.

I never did care much for Uncle Harry.

"I'm talking about a combined fundraiser and blood drive!" he continued. "BioWeb is hosting a big bash at its conference center this weekend and I think you'll find it very profitable to come on board with us!"

"What does your company want with my blood bank?"

"Product, of course! Blood!" The doors slid open and I stepped out, not caring if this was the right floor or not. "We do research, Sam, and we've embarked upon some new trials that require more than double—nearly triple the volume of blood, plasma, and platelets that we utilized last year!"

"Well, Mr. Rollins—"

"Lou!"

"As scarce as my resources are, I would rather my 'product' go to the people who need it the most: the sick, the injured, the dying."

"I respect that, Sam, I really do! But let me tell you a little story . . ."

With some alacrity I suddenly realized that I wasn't so much affecting a retreat from Lou as he was herding me toward his destination.

"Once upon a time there was this town that was situated near a cliff that overlooked the sea. Now, from time to time—on a pretty regular basis—people would get too close to the edge of the cliff and fall off. The fall usually wasn't enough to kill them but it would bang them up pretty good! So the town council held a bunch a' meetings and came up with two plans."

"I think I've heard this," I said.

"The first involved getting a fancy ambulance and parking it at the bottom of the cliff. It would be outfitted with all the trimmings: life-saving gear, specially trained paramedics, the works! And a specially paved road that would get the ambulance up to the hospital in record time! That was Plan A!" Dramatic pause. "And do you know what Plan B was?"

"A wall," I answered.

"A wall!" he continued with no indication of having heard me. "A plain and simple wall to be built so as to keep people from getting too close to the edge at the top!"

"Prevention versus treatment," I observed. "With the town choosing the more expensive and painful back-end solution."

"So, with the estimates running to five-thousand dollars for the wall and five-hundred-thousand for the ambulance and stuff, which do you think the town council decided to fund?" He looked at me expectantly.

"Lou," I said, "I think you're telling me this story to try to make the point that an ounce of prevention is worth a pound of cure and that your research is going to save a lot of lives down the road. Of course, to make the analogy more truthful you'd have to add the stipulations that the ambulance could be in place tomorrow while the wall couldn't be built for another year or two."

"Yeah, the ambulance . . ." He looked at me curiously. "Say, have you heard this one before?"

"I used to belong to an HMO. Look, Mr. Rollins, I'll consider your request if you can send me some info on this research project of yours. Diverting already scarce resources for research is a gamble. A worthy gamble, but a gamble nonetheless. Before I roll the dice on an expectant mother hemorrhaging in the delivery room, I want a sense of the stakes for future lives."

"You think we're playing God, Sam?"

"One way or another, we're all playing God, Lou. Most of us just won't own up to it."

A thin wail pierced the conversation and I noticed that we had ambled into the maternity wing. The neonatal unit was to my left and I caught sight of a dozen tiny beds and four closed incubators beyond a large glass window. Five babies rested or squirmed in their hospital cradles while a sixth shrieked its pain or anger from the back of the room.

"Well, I'm sure I can get the company to send you some information," Lou was saying, "but I gotta warn you—it'll probably be pretty technical."

"That's okay," I said absently, "I've been reading a lot of medical research papers of late."

A nurse was carrying the screaming infant against her shoulder, walking back and forth, trying to soothe it into restfulness. *Not anger,* I decided, *the pitch and tone are pure misery. Acute discomfort, if not actual suffering.*

"Well, let me set you up with a tour of the BioWeb facilities,"

Lou was saying as he pressed some cardstock into my hands. "And here's a couple of free passes for our 'Death Sucks' blood drive and Halloween dance! Bring a friend. Hell, here's two more: bring *friends*!"

I nodded absently as if I had friends. Instead, I concentrated on the baby's wails, trying to clarify the pattern. Obvious—blatant even—once I figured it out but Rollins had distracted me, preventing me from seeing it sooner. Every time the nurse brought the child in close proximity to the window on the far side of the nursery, it cried all the harder. It might not be obvious to the untrained human ear or a nurse nearing the end of a thirty-six-hour rotation but Lupé says I have the ears of a wolf.

And she should know.

"Excuse me, Lou; did you say you had a meeting in Pediatrics?"

Startled and derailed, it took him a moment to shuffle through his mental scripts. "Actually, I've arranged a sit-down with the neonatal supervisor. . . ."

"Great! Can I get an introduction?"

"You want to sit in on the meeting?" Caught between company pitches, he hadn't regained his balance. Or maybe he didn't fancy any third parties at the next deal cutting.

"No. I just need a few minutes of whoever's in charge here's time."

"That would be me." The voice belonged to a short, round woman in pale blue scrubs, cap, and booties. "I imagine one of you is Mr. Rollins."

"That's me!" Outstretched hand and thousand-watt smile, Lou Rollins was back on track. "And you must be Anita!"

"Nurse Jensen," she said with a mild smile. "You'll forgive me if I don't shake your hand. I just scrubbed and I have to get back to my babies in a few minutes."

"Ma'am, what's the matter with the baby that's crying in there?" I asked politely. I learned early on that it never pays to be rude to those in authority.

She frowned at me anyway. "I'm a nurse, not a 'ma'am.' Are you family?"

"Maybe," I said. And gave her a mental *nudge*.

The frown lines deepened but she nodded and answered anyway. "We don't know, yet."

"What do you know?" I *pushed* a little harder.

"Baby Helen has an enlarged liver and spleen. She's anemic and her bilirubin is elevated." Her frown deepened. "Doctor suspects EB."

"EB?" I asked, trying to blend a "please tell me more" tone with a subvocal command to *never mind my stranger status and keep talking*.

"Epidermolysis bullosa. It's an inherited disorder that causes blisters to form on the skin at sites of trauma to the body."

"The child has trauma injuries?"

"She has blisters," Jensen snapped, eyes narrowing as she shifted her attention away from *the what* of my question and more toward *the why*. "Infants with EB are sometimes born with blisters."

"Sounds as if you need a genetics consult," I suggested, preparing to mentally cram that request down her throat if necessary. I was spared having to mind-wrestle Nurse Jensen into placing the call by the arrival of a familiar face.

"Mr. Haim?"

I turned and looked at my newest client. "Ms. Delacroix?"

"Dr. Chalice," Nurse Jensen said, "I was just explaining the infant's symptoms to this gentleman."

"Really?" Chalice Delacroix nodded briefly to Lou Rollins, who nodded back. "Why? Is he family?"

Jensen looked a little confused; her frown lines squirmed.

"In a manner of speaking," I answered. "I think this baby and I have something in common."

"Oh my," my client said with a good-natured smile. "I don't know how I can resist passing up such a wonderful set-up line, Mr. Haim." She turned and nodded at Lou. "Mr. Rollins. What brings you to neonatal?"

He smiled but leaned forward and lowered his voice to answer: "Umbilical cords."

I mentally grabbed my eyebrows before they could rise.

"What's that?" Nurse Jensen's frown deepened.

Rollins turned back to her and upped the wattage on his smile. "Is there someplace we can sit down and talk?"

"Let me just collect those blood samples and I'll be on my way," Delacroix said, placing an insulated carrier on the counter of the nurses' station. "Then you can palaver to your heart's content."

Jensen turned to the small refrigerator at the back of the station and stooped to open the door.

"What makes you think EB?" I asked Chalice.

"I don't think EB. Doctor thinks EB. I run the samples on the parents and child and screen for a variety of genetic disorders and see what pops up."

"I thought you worked the night shift."

"Ditto."

"An emergency came up," I answered.

"Ditto," she repeated with a smile. "Here's mine. Where's yours?"

"Downstairs." I was spared a longer answer by Nurse Jensen's return with four vials of blood.

"I should have an answer in forty-eight to seventy-two hours," Delacroix told her.

"Will you screen for Xeroderma pigmentosum?" I asked.

"What?" Jensen asked.

"Why?" Delacroix seconded.

I nodded toward the nursery. "The child shows signs of increasing distress every time she's carried close to the window." Another thought occurred and I turned to Jensen. "You said her bilirubin was elevated. Has she had photo-therapy?"

"I don't know," Jensen replied, "I just came on duty. Let me check."

As she went off in search of the chart I looked back at Rollins and Delacroix.

"Billy who?" Rollins asked with a half-smile.

"Bilirubin is a byproduct of red blood cell destruction," Delacroix explained before I could open my mouth. "Hemoglobin is broken down to heme and globin. Heme is then converted to bilirubin and carried to the liver by albumin in the bloodstream, where it's further processed and then excreted in the bile."

The expression on Rollins' face wavered between "huh?" and "so?"

"The problem," I said, continuing the explanation, "is that a newborn's liver isn't as efficient as an adult's—it's just started working for one thing. It takes a few days for an infant's system to gear up the entire process for breaking down red blood cells and eliminating the byproducts. Sometimes there's a brief period where the bilirubin builds up in their systems, causing their skin and the whites of their eyes to appear jaundiced."

I noticed that Chalice Delacroix eyed me with the same look that most zoo-goers gave the duck-billed platypus.

"Most of the time this is a temporary condition but there are occasions when the bilirubin levels can get dangerously high. If too much accumulates for too long, it can find its way into the central nervous system and cause brain damage."

"Kericterus," Chalice said, nodding.

"So I'm wondering if the hospital has tried photo-therapy."

"Photo-therapy," Rollins repeated. If he had been following me up to this point I'd clearly lost him now.

"It's the most common treatment for reducing bilirubin levels in infants," Chalice explained. "By positioning special fluorescent lights over a newborn, a chemical reaction can be stimulated that speeds up bilirubin breakdown in the bloodstream."

"So," Rollins pondered, "you think they ought to try it on the baby in there?"

"*No,*" I said a little too sharply. I softened my tone. "If this baby is photo-sensitive, it would be harmful—possibly fatal—if she's exposed to excessive light!"

"What makes you think the child is photo-sensitive?" Chalice wanted to know.

Nurse Jensen returned with the chart and spared me the necessity for elaboration. "Yes. She's had photo-therapy. In fact we have two blood samples on her, one taken before and the other after, to see if there's been any changes in the blood chemistry."

"We need to see the baby," I said.

"What?" Jensen shook her head. "No. I'm afraid that's out of the question."

Chalice glanced at me before giving the charge nurse her full attention. "I really think it might be a good idea, Nurse," she said.

Jensen's mouth was set in a tight line. "You have no jurisdiction here, Dr. Delacroix."

"Let us take a quick look," I said reasonably. *You won't regret it!* "You won't regret it."

"I—I shouldn't—"

"It's all right," I said. *Really!* "Please?"

"Perhaps . . ." Jensen was wavering. Rollins just stared at us, bug-eyed.

"Think of it as getting a second opinion." *Let us in!* I pushed, finally out of patience as the infant continued to squall in the next room.

Jensen opened the half door that permitted egress into the nurse's station and led us into the adjoining nursery. The nurse who had been carrying Baby Helen had placed her back in her isolette and was tending to another infant now. She looked up at our approach. "I couldn't get her to stop crying, Anita."

"It's all right," Jensen said. "We'll—I'll take over for now."

"I think her blisters are worse," the other nurse said as she made notations on another chart. "When is our consult coming?"

"I'm here," Chalice answered. "I've already logged the tests as high priority but I'll camp in the lab and try to push to the front of the line if I can."

While they were talking I reached into the isolette and retrieved Baby Helen. "Oh dear God!" I whispered as I drew her close to me. The child was covered with vesicles or bullae—quarter-sized blisters. I touched one and, as it gave under the light pressure of my finger, it oozed clear fluid. It could still be XP but I had another idea. "I need a Wood's lamp."

"Put that child down," Jensen said, reaching for Baby Helen.

"Get me a Wood's lamp *now*!" I barked, applying enough pressure to jumpstart my own headache.

Pain and confusion in her eyes, Jensen turned and hurried away.

Chalice eased her hands between mine. "May I?" she asked carefully. Just as carefully she eased the infant up and over just enough to get a good look at her back. "See the bullae here? The vesicles are smaller and more newly formed."

"The blisters on her front are probably from the bili-lights," I reasoned. "Her back would have picked up indirect sunlight while she was being carried close to the window."

Chalice nodded. "A difference in time and light intensity. Let's check the diaper."

I laid the baby down on the changing table. Jensen returned with a Wood's light as we unfastened the diaper and folded it down. Stains, as though someone had spilled a small amount of red wine, marked the inner layer. Also telling was the absence of blisters on the skin that had been shielded by the diapers.

"See this?" I said to the group as they gathered around closely.

"The reddish color in the urine? Someone douse the lights and plug in that lamp."

While Chalice plugged in the Wood's lamp and positioned it, Jensen turned off the room's lights and the other nurse lowered the shades over the observation windows to block the light from the hallways.

As the Wood's lamp flickered into an eerie purplish fluorescence the stained area of the diaper began to glow an unearthly pink.

"What you're seeing now," I continued, "are the abnormal proteins that have been excreted through Baby Helen's renal system."

"Porphyrins," said Chalice.

"Right. And I think the proper tests will confirm one of the porphyries—probably CEP."

"CEP?" Jensen's licorice frown was even scarier in the violet murk of the Wood's light.

I nodded. "Congenital erythropoietic porphyria."

"It's pretty rare," Chalice observed. "Even among the known porphyrias."

"Less than a couple of hundred known cases worldwide," I agreed. I looked over at the head nurse. "You're going to need a serious genetics consult. I can give you a list of experts in the field of porphyrias and photo-sensitive disorders such as XP if the hospital doesn't have ready access." I switched off the Wood's lamp, and the purple and pink luminescences faded. Now immersed in darkness, the room's only illumination came from a Christmas-y constellation of red and green LEDs on the natal monitors.

"They'll recommend more specific treatments but, starting right now, you've got to keep this infant away from direct light sources. No windows. No bili-lights. In fact, she will be safer around incandescent bulbs than fluorescent lamps as they emit less porphyrin-exciting wavelengths. But any light at all is a hazard. Keep her in the dark as much as possible until you've got a doctor on the case that knows CEP!"

"How serious is it?" Jensen asked as she picked up a blanket and began to drape Baby Helen's isolette.

"Very serious. Although a lot better now than once upon a time." I explained as best I could how the absence of the enzyme uroporphyrin in the body's cells created two serious problems. First there was the issue of heme, an essential ingredient of hemoglobin that victims of CEP couldn't manufacture. Transfusions and bone-marrow transplants could help, assuming the right genetic donors could be found, but that was a trickier business than one might assume. The second problem echoed the bilirubin issue: the uropor-phyrin enzyme deficiency prevented the breakdown of heme's toxic protein precursors—porphyrins. The buildup of toxic levels of these porphyrins in the bloodstream and urine produced a number of unpleasant side effects. The photosensitivity not only produced blisters on the epidural surfaces but also caused scarring and even patches of hair to sprout where it might not normally grow. Porphyrin deposits on teeth and bones produced a reddish dis-coloration and made them brittle. Even so, with proper treatment and careful avoidance of sunlight, most patients with CEP could now anticipate a life expectancy of forty to sixty years.

"Once upon a time they would have lived short, painful lives," I concluded. "Shorter, if the locals decided they were vampires."

The other nurse gasped as she turned on a small lamp at the far end of the room. "Vampires?"

"Receding gums giving the teeth an elongated appearance, already stained red from the porphyrin deposits . . . reddish urine . . . extreme pallor and a nocturnal lifestyle." I omitted the fact that garlic was also a no-no, due to the fact that it painfully stimulated heme production.

Jensen made a call as we left, demanding an immediate genet-ics consult and would someone please page the attending Pedes physician. Stat!

"You're extremely well-read on the porphyrias," Chalice said as we rode down on the elevator together, "for a private investiga-tor."

"I have a wide range of interests."

"You work the night shift, wear a hat, sunglasses, protective clothing . . ." her nostrils flared, " . . . sunscreen . . . pardon my nosiness, Mr. Haim, but do you have something like CEP?"

"No," I said as the doors slid open on the second floor. "Nothing like, at all."

Unfortunately.

I stepped out and walked away as the doors closed behind me.

Chapter Six

I found Olive and her sister camped out in the visitors' waiting area just down the hall.

"I just don't understand it," Claire said, staring dully at the floor. "He was as healthy as a horse yesterday. Wakes up this morning with a cough—just like Mr. Lloyd."

Olive slipped her arm around her sister's shoulders. "Jamal's had the flu before."

"Not this flu. This flu be killing people." Claire shook her head. "They won't even let family in to see him."

The first hint of distress crept into my secretary's voice. "They won't let you see him?" The receptors in the vomeronasal region of my nose caught a faint odor of Olive's stress pheromones behind the miasma of fear surrounding her sister like a clammy fog.

"They let me stand outside a special room and look at him through a window. They say they have to keep him in isolation."

"It's for your protection as much as your son's," said a new voice.

We all looked up at a man who had seemingly appeared out of nowhere. With broad shoulders and blond hair in a crew cut, he looked like someone had locked Drew Carey in a gym and taken away his glasses. His three-piece suit fit oddly, as if tailored for someone else. Or maybe it was that the man, himself, was proportioned just a bit strangely. "May I speak with you about your son's situation?"

Olive's eyes gave him the quick once-over. "Are you a doctor?"

"No ma'am—"

"Is this about the insurance?" Olive was clearly up for running interference for her sister.

"I'm here to offer some financial help, actually," the man said with a smile.

Olive's mouth bloomed into a reciprocating smile that suggested Mr. Three-piece-suit was just about the most welcome person in her world right now. I knew that look and felt vaguely sorry for this guy. Olive and her people had heard them all: promises of assistance, grants, loans, opportunities, future windfalls . . . promises that had evaporated, twisted into something else entirely, or had come with hidden daggers, snares, and pitfalls. Seeing the teeth in Olive's smile reminded me that there are still tribes in the world who regard the act of smiling as a sign of aggression.

"I'm John Jones," he said, offering his hand. "I'm with BioWeb."

My third BioWeb employee within the hour. I wondered what Mama Samm would say. She did not strike me as a rabid adherent of coincidence. Maybe John Jones wasn't his real name. Maybe he was one of the Red Lectroids ("It's not my planet, monkey-boy!") or maybe he was J'onn J'onzz, the Martian Manhunter. Maybe his middle name was Paul and he had not yet begun to fight. . . .

Maybe it was time to go home and lie down.

"You want to help with Jamal's hospital bill?" Olive asked, taking Jones' hand. It was suddenly obvious that she wasn't letting go until he answered the question to her satisfaction.

"Actually, yes. In fact, we'd like to cover all his expenses." His smile stayed in place and he didn't seem at all discomfited that Olive still held his hand in her grasp.

"Why?" Depend on Olive to cut to the chase. "You run some kind of charity program?"

"No ma'am. This is business. But good business for everyone, I think. May I sit?"

Olive nodded and released his hand. Jones sat and tucked his tie back down into his puckered vest.

"My company does medical research. We're in the business of developing medical techniques and finding cures to improve the human condition." He produced a couple of brochures from his briefcase and handed them to Olive and Claire. "This new strain of influenza that's going around—well, we're interested in finding a vaccine for it."

"You want Jamal for a guinea pig," Olive said bluntly.

"That's not the way I would put it."

"But I would," Olive continued pleasantly, smile still in place. "So, let's get down to it, Mr. Jones. You want to try some new experimental drug on my nephew?"

"No. No, nothing like that." Jones had a smooth delivery, I'll give him that: a little off-balance but barely rattled. "Before we can develop any kind of a vaccine, we need to understand the development of this particular strain. We want to be intimately involved in the case histories of as many people who have this flu as possible. The hospitals are only geared up to give their patients a relative degree of attention based on the severity of their individual conditions and just enough to make them well. We promise a level of involvement that will include around-the-clock monitoring and testing. Your nephew, ma'am—" he turned and nodded to Claire, "—your son, will have the best medical care available."

"Tell us more about this medical care," I said. "Specifics, I mean." I'd been listening closely but now I specifically focused on subvocal stressors, clues that he might be lying on any specific points.

As Jones explained it, the deal that BioWeb proposed was that they would have twenty-four-hour access to Jamal for observation and permission to take the full spectrum of samples—blood, urine, stool, even breath—on a regular basis. In addition, non-invasive scans and tests would be administered regularly. BioWeb personnel would administer no unusual treatments or drugs without mutual agreement between the family and the hospital. That was the clincher: Jamal would remain a patient of the hospital and under their medical care. BioWeb would pick up the full tab for the privilege of testing and monitoring access.

The deal seemed foolproof. Jamal would receive hundreds of thousands of dollars of additional medical care and it wouldn't cost the family a dime. Olive looked over at me and I nodded once, my assurance coming from my inability to pick up any false tones in Jones' pitch. But, as Claire signed the paperwork and I headed back to my car, I felt troubled by the old proverb: "If something seems too good to be true, it probably is."

As I headed for the outer doors I passed by the emergency entrance and a wave of dizziness hit me. Seconds later I recognized the scent that triggered it: I turned and watched as paramedics rushed a stretcher on wheels toward one of the trauma rooms. An arm flopped loose from the restraining straps and a dribble of dark blood suddenly became a bright red arterial spray, spattering a column and linoleum tiles with a gory spoor. The wave became a tsunami, pulling me under into a hot, dark tunnel. I turned and ran blindly for the doors.

The sun caught me unprepared.

It was like running into a white-hot furnace. My skin felt as though it was starting to sizzle as I groped for my sunglasses. I was blinded by the light (revved up like a deuce) and my car was out of sight.

As I fumbled my shades into place I had the distinct impression that my hair was beginning to smolder. I yanked my hat down to my ears, the straw crackling as it gave way. At least I hoped it was the straw doing the crackling.

It took another minute for my eyes to adjust to the excessive amount of solar radiation, only partially blocked by my heavily opaqued and polarized lenses. I oriented on my car and set off at a run as the first blister appeared on the back of my hand. I jammed my hands in my pockets and all but danced at the crosswalk as I waited for the traffic signal to change. As I reached my car I knew I was going to have a bad time of it.

It wasn't just the sunlight.

Think of the worst sunburn you've ever had and remember the sleepless night that followed. Multiply by ten. Bad enough. Not awful but more than a little unpleasant. And it wouldn't be the first time: while there were some tasks that just could not be delegated or postponed until after sundown, I rebelled against my nocturnal condition by signing on for more than my necessary share of daytime excursions. Like today.

But it wasn't just the sunlight.

The scent of human blood filled my olfactory epithelium, trickled across the gustatory cells at the back of my throat, and sent bright, hot golden threads of chemosensory hormones surging toward the limbic region of my chemically altered brain.

The Hunger was returning.

It was a good night to stay home.

An even better night to lock myself in and take a series of cold baths and showers until burning, buzzing, itching, crawling sensations receded.

Unfortunately I had a class to teach and, with a schedule of eight nights a month, a missed lecture was the equivalent of a week's worth of day classes.

I lay beneath the icy waters of a full-drawn bathtub, holding my breath for ten minutes, and then climbed out like a hairless, blue-skinned polar bear. A pot of water had come to a slow boil on the stove and I padded to the refrigerator, leaving pawlike puddles of water in my wake.

No pig's blood or mixed beef stock tonight. The Hunger had been triggered and those occasional stopgaps weren't sufficient now—especially after taking solar damage. Maybe with extensive rest and meditation . . .

But tonight I had obligations: I reached into the crisper bin and retrieved two plastic pouches labeled "Bayou Blood Bank."

I glanced at the clock: even with the water already a'boil, the microwave would be faster. But there are some things that microwaving ruins. After a half-dozen experiments I'd come to the conclusion that hemoglobin sat at the top of the list. I dropped the pouches into the roiling water and hurried upstairs to dress.

Once a teacher, always a teacher.

And the opportunity to teach again had seemed too good to pass up. As an adjunct professor at the university I would not be required to teach in the daytime and the paper trail was less complicated.

On the other hand, there was the matter of the dead body in my classroom.

The amphitheater in Stubbs Hall is one of those inverted ziggurats that's supposed to serve as a classroom and lecture hall. In reality it's a chair-lined concrete pit whose ambience seems more appropriate to cockfights and bear-baiting than *Intro to American*

Lit 101. Mr. DOA slumped in the middle seat on the third row so he sat right at eye-level where I couldn't miss him.

I looked around as I opened the class roster but none of my students had yet noticed the corpse in their midst. That was hardly surprising given their attention to detail in last week's pop quiz. And, to be fair, I'd probably had a good deal more experience with the "deceased but not quite departed" than the rest of them combined. The question was: what should I do?

I took roll.

And started the evening's lecture on "Themes on Death in American Literature." I almost smiled as I realized how ironic and apropos my preplanned lesson was, considering this new addition to my class. I wondered if he was auditing the course.

There are rules for dealing with the dead and I figured my best bet was to try rule number two, first: "Ignore them and maybe they'll go away."

Of course, rule number one ("Dead is dead") is such a joke that the rest of the rules are just as suspect.

"Maurice Blanchot writes that death is 'man's greatest hope,' " I began, "for it 'raises existence to being' and 'is within each one of us as our most human quality.' " I paused to let the idea sink in and see if anyone might question why I would quote Blanchot in a course on American lit. Not that any of them would know the slightest difference between Maurice Blanchot and Maurice Chevalier. They were probably thinking of Maurice the ex-astronaut on reruns of *Northern Exposure.*

"Literature, on the other hand," I continued, " 'manifests existence without being, existence which remains below existence, like an inexorable affirmation, without beginning or end—death as the impossibility of dying.' "

My gaze swept the lecture hall. They stared back at me, emulating rows of sightless corpses. The only eyes evoking any signs of thought processes were those of the dead guy.

"What does Blanchot mean by that?"

Thunderous silence met my inquiry.

"Anyone?"

No one moved: No one wanted to do anything that might draw attention to him- or herself.

"Bueller?" I called.

Nobody smiled.

I hunched my shoulders, settling down into the lectern as if anticipating a long wait. "Let's hold that thought. We'll return to it after we've discussed 'A Rose For Emily.' " I looked around the room: nearly fifty faces deeply buried in their books. It was probably the first time they'd opened their texts this week.

"This was William Faulkner's first short story to be published in a national magazine. Other than that, what makes this story memorable?"

I fancied I heard a cricket in the storeroom at the top and back of the lecture hall.

"What is Faulkner really writing about?"

I heard a creaking sound. Swear-to-God, the dead guy's jaw actually creaked! "Death . . ." he intoned.

"Well, *duh . . . !*" someone murmured. I heard muted giggling.

"Well, obviously," I agreed. "At least for those of you who actually read the story." I sighed and mentally threw in the towel. "Okay, take out a sheet of paper: we're going to have a pop quiz. A pop-*essay*-quiz!"

I endured the groans all around and despaired for this generation. By the time I had reached their age I had learned to volunteer answers for the professors' early questions: it took you off the firing line with a presumption of intelligence once the questions got harder. And it usually provided proof against the number-one weapon in the professors' arsenal of vengeance. This sorry lot would probably need another week before they figured out that a lack of response was always a prelude to another unscheduled, and potentially grade-point lowering, pop quiz.

I preferred the intellectual brutality of the essay test. Oral exams were for dentists and grad students surrounded by doctorates conducting their exit interviews. Other "written" formats, like multiple-guess or connect-the-dots, did little to rehabilitate the average "luck-is-my-copilot" slacker. If Pavlovian conditioning was going to work in a reasonable amount of time, I had to terrorize them into classroom participation. Oral avoidance, if you will: speak up and we won't get around to today's written essay. Maybe I could have them actually reading their assignments and involved in verbal participation by mid-semester.

In the meantime I told them to write a brief synopsis of the plot and then defined "synopsis" for those who looked hesitant. Then I asked for a succinct essay on what they thought the story was really about.

I thought about defining the word "succinct" as well but decided it was too demeaning.

To me.

The dead guy wasn't writing. And, despite his condition, he was the only one who wasn't buried in the text. He just sat there, staring at me. To say he stared strangely was a given under the circumstances. But I saw something in his death-slackened face, his clouded eyes, that indicated a strangeness of attitude. The majority of the dead I had dealt with so far had evinced attitudes of arrogance or rage or cold-blooded ruthlessness. Of course, the majority of the dead I had encountered hitherto now were vampires.

Student X appeared to be cut from another bolt of grave cloth: like Mr. Delacroix, this was one of the walking dead. Or sitting, anyways. And, like Mr. Delacroix, there was an attitude of respect in those cloudy, staring eyes. And *that* was the most unnerving aspect of this encounter.

So far.

I dismissed the class early: it was like—if you'll pardon the expression—beating a dead horse. I sent them home (or to the bars, most likely) with additional reading assignments—Robert Frost's "Home Burial," selected poems by Emily Dickinson, and excerpts from Walt Whitman's *Leaves of Grass*—and the clearly articulated threat that there would be more essay tests and pop quizzes if they came to class unprepared to discuss the material. I had nearly forgotten how much similarity there was between freshman entry-level courses and boot camp. The temptation to yell: "Awright, you maggots; drop and *read* me twenty!" was overwhelming.

I skimmed the first couple of essays as the last of my students shuffled out the door. From the look of things I wouldn't be spending hours grading this stack. When you haven't read the assignment you basically have two options. And while this class had suddenly acquired a dead guy, I didn't expect to find any psychics.

"Dr. Haim?"

I looked up. For a moment I thought the dead guy had brought a date. Then I realized she was one of my regular students. Third row, seat twelve: Theresa . . . something. Kellerman.

"Yes, Theresa?"

"Call me Terry."

"All right, Terry. What can I do for you?" Most of my students had departed now and, as soon as the rest were gone, I intended to have a serious sit-down with my terminal transfer student. I glanced up at his chair and was startled to see that he was gone, as well.

"I was wondering—"

"Excuse me a minute," I said.

There were only two ways out of the lecture hall: the main entrance just twenty feet to my right and the emergency exit at the top and back of the hall to the far left. I felt sure he hadn't passed by me on the way out. But the alarm should have gone off if the fire door had opened. I ran up the stepped aisle and examined the crash-bar on the door: wiring had been ripped out of the latching mechanism. I pushed it open and stepped out onto the fire escape.

All together maybe twenty students were in view, some headed for the library, others headed for their cars in the parking lot. I refocused into the infrared spectrum and quickly counted eighteen heat signatures. Dropping back into the normal visual parameters I did another tally: twenty-one. Three *cold* humans climbing into a—I started to laugh and nearly choked: a hearse!

Hello, Officer; I'd like to report some corpses—they've stolen a hearse and are out joy riding.

Sure, son, sure; 'tis a grave violation of the local curfew and we'll get right on it. . . .

I watched them pull out of the lot and drive leisurely down the street before I turned back to the fire door.

I see dead people. . . .

Where's Haley Joel Osment when you need him?

Theresa was waiting for me by the lectern when I returned.

She wasn't alone. The guy with her looked like a vampire wannabe. Come to think of it, both of them looked like cover models for an L.L. Goth catalog. Both wore long, black hair hanging past their shoulders in semi-permed waves, eye shadow and silver earrings. Both were dressed in black, though Theresa seemed intent on an understated look while darkboy's ensemble screamed "*The Crow* rules!"

I was trying to decide who had more piercings when darkboy gave Theresa a shove. She staggered into the podium and rocked it. "Oww! Rod, cut it out!"

"That's exactly what I'm gonna do, T, if you don't come along now," he said with a nasty smirk. "Haul out my shiny long-tooth and cut it right out of you. Won't that be a tasty little feast?"

"Quit it!" I heard an overlay of anger in her voice but, underneath, a multilayered stratum of fear.

Feeling a subtle rumbling in my upper chest as I walked down the stepped aisle, I said with pleasantness that I did not feel: "Yes, Rod, quit it."

He looked up at me, startled at my unanticipated presence. His eyebrows came down along with the corners of his lip-glossed mouth. "This is between me and my bitch," he said in a studied attempt to be menacing. He needed to study more.

My chest rumbled again and, with a start, I realized that I was repressing an actual growl. My impromptu soup-in-a-pouch had taken the Hunger down a notch but this little jerk was pushing my predatory buttons. I had to resolve this quickly and without violence or my control would start to slip.

He backed Theresa against the podium until it was close to tipping again. "C'mon, T! Unless you want maybe someone else to get hurt." He looked meaningfully at me as he reached out and grabbed her arm.

"Are you a student here?" I asked him as I continued down toward the front of the lecture hall.

"No, so you can't threaten me." He grinned, savoring the idea that he was smarter than some pansy-assed college prof.

"Can't I?" I stopped. "Rod?" I could walk down there, easily break both of his arms, and then turn him over to campus security. But I needed to keep a low profile for the next several weeks and any violence right now would kick the Hunger into high gear. "Look in my eyes, Rod," I said in still-pleasant tones. "Look at me and see if I can't threaten you."

It was relatively simple. I didn't try to get him to do anything, convince him to act against his will, or send a verbal communication. I simply bundled up all the dark and terrible thoughts, memories, and experiences of my past year and sent it, unedited, right at his forehead.

It wasn't a nudge, a push, or a shove; it was a mental shotgun blast. I peppered his cerebral cortex with batshot that turned into squirmy nightmare worms squiggling about and searching for access to his hindbrain. He dropped Theresa's arm and staggered, a dark stain emerging around his crotch like a Rorschach blot.

"So what do you think, Rod?" I asked as he stumbled away toward the door. "*Can* I threaten you?"

Rod's only reply was a muffled sob as he disappeared down the outer hall. I looked at Theresa-call-me-Terry. "Are you all right?"

She stared at me as if she'd caught a portion of the Sending.

"Are you a Dark Master?" she asked.

Chapter Seven

"So, like Miss Emily is really a symbol of the Old South and the events in the story are really about the changes that were taking place—abandoning the old ways and manners," Terry said. She raised the coffee cup to her lips, masking her face below bluer than blue eyes.

I nodded. "That interpretation works for most of the critics. It's certainly about the death of illusions."

"Oh yes!" she burbled. "Like someone who wears rose-colored glasses! I mean, there's the rose-colored curtains in the bedroom and the rose-shaded lamps on the dressing table . . ."

She took a sip of her coffee and I thought about how I wished I had a dozen students with her enthusiasm and curiosity. And noticed how the vein alongside her brow pulsed with each beat of her heart.

" . . . Which sort of parallels the 'rose' in the story's title. A rose for Emily is sort of what that dead man was. Like how we cut roses off and stick them in a vase or press one inside a book—to preserve them. Like she preserved him.

"And the decay," she continued after another swallow. "Though Faulkner really has Miss Emily's surroundings *fading* more than actually rotting. Kind of like a pressed rose would fade. And the way the old ways were fading and being replaced by the next generation." She took another sip. "But something I didn't catch until I read it a second time was that Miss Emily was actually slender and maybe even attractive while her father was still alive. It isn't until later that she takes on the appearance of a dead body that has spent too much time underwater. The way time and events are rearranged in the story sort of throws you off."

"Have you ever seen a floater?" I asked.

"Oh yes."

My eyebrows went looking for my hairline.

"On the Internet."

I smiled. It wasn't the same thing as real and close-up. When the smell hits you close range with only the acrid perfume of automatic weapons fire to cut the odor, you're momentarily grateful for the distraction of the enemy trying to kill you.

"So," she continued, "I'm thinking that when Homer dies—or maybe even before, when she decides to poison him—that's when Emily starts to turn corpselike herself. She becomes that pasty, bloated, coal-eyed thing. Am I right?"

I smiled. "Why don't you ask that during the next class? These are issues that beg more than one viewpoint and it might jumpstart some other people's thinking."

She contemplated her coffee cup and then considered my lack of one. "Aren't you going to have any java?" she asked. The question came out as if my answer might be loaded with import.

"I don't drink . . . coffee." I shook my head. "Are you a fan of Faulkner?"

She gave back a little shake of her head and chased it with a half shrug. "It's more of a Goth thing."

"A Goth thing?"

"I'm fascinated by the subject of death." She smiled.

"Fascinated?"

"Stimulated." Her smile grew. "Intellectually. Emotionally. Sexually." Her lips parted to unveil perfect white teeth. "Does that appall you?"

I felt a sigh coming on. "Do you really care if it does?"

"It depends," she said, looking down into her coffee cup. She picked up a spoon and stirred it even though she had ordered it without cream or sugar.

"On what?"

"Whether or not you're a Dark Master." She looked up. "Are you?"

I looked around the coffee shop. Only three or four students remained and the counterman would be locking up soon. "Suppose you tell me what a 'Dark Master' is?"

Her face took on a solemn mien. "Dark Masters," she intoned, "are those who have transcended this life and understand that there are other planes of existence. They are sent to us to teach us the hidden pathways in our flesh and how our spirits may be unfettered from the linear view of life to death. They know the secrets of being and not being. They are transcendent, yet secret. It is said that when the acolyte is ready, a Dark Master will appear."

I fought a smile through her explanation but nearly lost my hold on it with the last sentence. Another thought sobered me. "This Rod character, he fancies himself a Dark Master, does he?"

She nodded but smiled sadly. "I thought he was, at first. He taught me things. Like how to turn my cutting into a blood ecstasy ritual."

"Cutting?"

She turned her left wrist so that I could see the inside of her forearm. There, up near the inside of her elbow, I saw a series of raised red lines, like barely healed cat scratches. "I used to cut myself when I'd get depressed." She smiled—she did a little too much of that from my perspective—and said: "All the girls I hung out with would do it. Rod taught me that it can be so much *more* than a way of relieving stress."

"But Rod hasn't worked out," I prodded, hoping to sidestep any additional details of "blood ecstasy rituals."

"He's just a selfish manipulator. He wants sex and power. True Dark Masters don't force their acolytes, they come in response to the drawing of the ki."

"The 'ki'?"

She nodded. "You know what ki is?"

I nodded in turn. If she said: "I am the Gatekeeper, are you the Ki-master?" I was gonna lose it right then and there.

"And why," I asked, trying to anchor this sudden turn of the conversation into some seeming reality, "would you think that I'm one of these—um—Dark Lords?"

"Masters. Dark *Masters*." Her face grew solemn again. "You have the knowledge: I can see it in your eyes. You know things that others cannot even imagine or dream, save in the darkest depths of the soul's midnight." *Now* I missed the smiling. "You have power and its aura envelops you like a dark cloak."

"Golly!" I said.

Her eyes looked down but a hint of a smile returned. "I've embarrassed you."

"I think it's been a stressful night and that you need to go home and hit the books or the sheets," I said kindly. "I have business to which I have to attend."

She turned and looked out the window into the darkness.

"I don't think he's out there," I said, answering her unspoken question. Considering with what—and the force with which I'd mindsmacked him—it was likely ole Rod would want to be safely inside, behind locked doors and garlicked windows, before sundown from now on. I'd probably start feeling guilty about that.

Eventually.

"Will you give me a ride home?"

I knew it would be quicker to drive her than to spend another ten minutes trying to reassure her. And, as my eyes were drawn more and more to the half-healed cuts on her (creamy, soft) arm, it was best that I conclude our business as quickly as possible.

Walking across the parking lot I fancied I could see someone standing by my car.

"Have you ever tasted blood?"

I almost stumbled. "Excuse me?"

"It's part of the blood ritual," she said. "Rod taught me."

I looked around to see if anyone was within earshot.

"Rod says my blood has a very unusual taste," she continued conversationally, making no effort to lower her voice. "He says it's very sweet."

"Is it, now?"

"I dunno. Rod's tastes like nasty pennies. So maybe mine is sweet by comparison."

"You've tasted his blood?" I struggled to keep disapproval out of my voice: we academic types espouse multiculturalism over political incorrectness.

"Sure. It's—"

"Part of the blood ritual," I answered along with her. "Are you taking precautions?"

"AIDS? Yeah. And we always sterilize our blades."

I shook my head. Sepsis and HIV shouldn't be her only concerns. "I'll bet Rod's switchblade has been places you wouldn't like."

She had no immediate answer to that and I pulled out my car keys. Perhaps the Hunger's hormonal rush was messing with my perceptions: no one was there when we arrived. And, parked in a lavender pool of streetlight, it would be difficult to run and hide so quickly.

I checked the floor of the backseat before unlocking the doors.

"I want to learn from you," she said quietly as we headed down Desiard Street.

"Good. Do the homework and don't skip any classes."

"You know what I mean."

"I'm not sure that I do but it isn't important because, even if I was a Black Lord—"

"Dark Master."

"—I am an instructor at the university and you are a student. Anything extracurricular," I turned and looked at her, "*anything*— is out of the question."

"I don't want to go home."

"I know that feeling," I said. "Now, where do I turn?" She wouldn't give me her address, just directions as the next turn-off arrived.

"What if Rod comes over?"

"He won't."

"But what if he does?"

"Do you have a friend with whom you can stay?"

"Define friend."

I shook my head: in retrospect the coffee was a mistake. I knew that Rod wouldn't be bothering anyone for a while but she wouldn't be sure of that. "I have business to which I must attend, Theresa. Where do I turn next?" That sounded a little cold but dammit . . .

"Here," she said in a small voice. "Do I have to go now?"

I nodded. "'Now finale to the shore! Now, land and life, finale, and farewell!'"

"'Now Voyager depart,'" she muttered, "'much, much for thee is yet in store . . .'"

"You know your Whitman," I said.

She looked out the passenger window. "I know my *Death*," I heard her say.

I swung by my office and retrieved my messages. Or "message" as it turned out. Olive had called to beg off working tonight: her sister still needed her more that I did. The answering machine listed twenty-two messages but the rest were merely bursts of silence followed by disconnects.

I opted to shut down for the evening. *After Dark* was really more of a hobby than a business: I didn't anticipate any clients tonight and the Hunger was still sending a low-level buzz through my body. I needed to go home and lock myself in. Maybe go down into the basement and try a little primal scream therapy.

Instead, I drove around. What waited for me at home but a big, empty house and the resonance of my own approaching madness?

I had built a large house: why not, I had money to burn and more. Except big houses are very empty when you're the only one living there.

More room for the ghosts, said a voice inside my head.

Jen? That you? Anybody there?

Nobody.

I thought about driving by the blood bank: hello, I'd like to make another withdrawal. How much? How about enough to fill my bathtub? What was that old joke about the milk bath: "Pasteurized?" "No, just up to my knees will be fine. . . ."

Maybe if I lay down and submerged myself long enough, my skin would stop prickling and burning, my muscles would stop aching and this boiler factory inside my head would shut down for the night. Maybe the Hunger would be appeased and go back to sleep.

Maybe I could just drown myself.

Thinking of a tubful of blood brought me back to the increasingly obsessive topic of Erzsébet Báthory.

Other vampires and hemofreaks were content to taste their victim's blood. But not Erzsébet. Oh no.

According to popular legend a servant girl was brushing the countess' long black hair when she accidentally pulled a little too hard on a tangle. Erzsébet slapped her so hard that she split the girl's lip and splashed blood across her own hand. Licking the blood from her fingers, my forebear discovered that she not only enjoyed the taste but that her skin seemed younger and more attractive where the blood had landed—sort of a macabre cross between Vascular Intensive Skin Care and Oil of *Olé!*

It launched a grisly beauty regimen.

Unlike Lizzie Borden, who had to figure out how to wash off after giving her mother forty whacks (not to mention her old man's forty-one), Lizzie Báthory was always trying out new ways to fill tub and basin with the red stuff. And it couldn't be just any old blood; it had to be virgin's blood if it was to be effective in restoring her youthful looks.

You don't have to be a whiz at algebra to see the eventual problem. According to records kept in her own hand, over six hundred young women disappeared before her bloody reign was stopped.

As you might suspect, the numbers eventually did her in.

For years the nobles refused to take action against one of their own. Erzsébet's attitudes toward the peasantry were hardly confined to her own sick and twisted little mind—as I said before, life was cheap and the nobles traded regularly in its perverse coinage. But first she made the mistake of losing her husband.

Ferencz Nádasdy, the "Black Hero" of Hungary, was rarely home, spending the greater portion of their marriage on the battlefield striking terror into the hearts of the Turks. His status as a national champion protected her proclivities on the home front while he was alive. But the hazards of a soldier's life eventually caught up with him: he was stabbed to death in 1604 by an angry whore who claimed Ferencz had stiffed her after, well, "stiffing" her.

Greedy eyes began to consider the count's estates and potential scenarios wherein the family landholdings could be made forfeit.

Then the Widow Báthory made a political mistake that was her undoing.

Over a ten-year period Lizzie had not only exhausted her primary source of virgins, it was beginning to look like the original formula was losing its effectiveness at turning back the clock. Anna Darvula, who was rumored to have been a witch and Erzsébet's lover, had died by then and the work of procurement had been taken over by one Erzsi Majorova. Erzsi's take on the problem was that peasant blood was too base and coarse to have the proper qualities. Her advice was to switch to virgins of more noble birth.

It was really bad advice.

When some highborn girls disappeared, the aristocracy finally stepped in and said: "Up against the wall, red-to-the-neck mother!"

She and her servants were tried for "crimes against nobility," there being no such thing as "crimes against humanity" back then. All the servants, save one, were found guilty and executed in a most unpleasant manner.

Liz, being a noble herself, was above such vulgar things as capital punishment—not so different from today, I suppose—and was placed under house arrest. Lacking the technology for electronic ankle bracelets, they did the next best thing: They walled up the doors and windows of her private chambers and slid her food in through a slot where the door used to be. Since there's no mention in any of the accounts of openings large enough to allow the emptying of chamber pots, one might question the compassion of life imprisonment over the death penalty.

Anyway, maybe the historical take on the countess was wrong. Maybe she didn't start her bloody baths as an elixir of youth. Maybe she got an overdose of sunshine and it was the first-aid treatments that got her hooked.

If so, maybe I was closer to the precipice than I initially feared.

Not the same, the voice murmured inside my head. *That which you may take from the blood bank vault was given willingly.*

Maybe, I thought right back, but it was given willingly so that others might live. That the precious gift of life might continue to flow through the veins of those whose time should not come prematurely. Not sit in the belly of a man who had no place among the living or the dead.

What about your time? Did your life not end prematurely? What about fairness? What about justice?

Hey, if life wasn't fair, why should I expect anything different to come afterward?

You make your own justice.

Yeah, pervert the gift of life and steal it—keep it from reaching the twelve-year-old victim of a hit-and-run accident or the father of four children undergoing open-heart surgery; head it off before it reaches the hemophiliac who just might find the cure for cancer if she lives to spend another couple of years in her lab.

Yeah.

Sure.

Make justice out of that.

The other voice shut up for awhile and I drove past the blood bank.

I turned around before crossing the Ouachita River and headed for the eastern edges of Monroe.

I drove past churches, their lighted crosses and illuminated spires offering refuge against the spiritual darkness in this world and that which came from beyond. Was there succor there for me? Or was I already damned, like some unholy Buzz Lightyear, "to eternity and beyond?"

Away from the main part of town was a huge complex of buildings—fairly new buildings from the look of things. It looked like some freeze-frame from a Jerry Bruckheimer/Nipponese Sci-Fi flick where a lustful oil refinery runs amok and tries to mate with a nuclear power station. And it was all tricked out with barbed electrical fencing, security checkpoints, and the words "BioWeb Industries" trapped inside a huge block of clear Lucite. Even from the road you could see the letters change colors, shading from blue to purple to red and back again.

I eased on down the street without stopping, but I gave the place a good look-over from the front and pondered the little I knew to date.

BioWeb was involved in cutting-edge medical research and treatment options. Chalice Delacroix mentioned working in their R & D labs during our first interview and apparently was involved in the area of genetics from what I could put together so far. Call-me-Lou had been hot to discuss business with Nurse Jensen and the words "umbilical cords" had slipped from his trembling lips. I could think of only one likely reason: stem cell research.

My Hunger was momentarily forgotten as I swept back toward the highway. The security lights from the BioWeb complex glimmered in my rearview mirror like multiple beacons in the darkness.

Brighter and more promising of redemption than any glowing crucifix or floodlit steeple.

✧   ✧   ✧

They were waiting for me as I pulled into my driveway: three adults, one child. I wasn't sure of the genders until I was close enough to make out their clothing.

Even then I wasn't sure.

The boy was white. The adults—I wasn't really sure. What skin remained showed a mottled gray. Those facial features that still existed had become puffy and distorted past any kind of racial profiling.

One of the adults had misplaced his lower jaw.

I've known women who will never appear in public without wearing makeup. This woman (I think) seemed willing to come out for a visit without putting on her face.

I opened my mouth to ask what they wanted and caught my first whiff. I turned away and nearly spewed a liter of half-digested blood. *Tic-Tacs,* I thought, my mind tilting crazily—they were in the glove compartment. *Maybe I should offer them some.*

"We have come to beg your justice," a wheezy little voice said.

"W-what?" I clamped down on my gag reflex and turned my face back to the charnel-house smell.

"We seek justice, Your Excellency." The boy sounded like he had gargled with acid. His voice had a horrid, raspy timbre that grated on the ear like a bone saw.

I eased to my right, trying to put the security lights to my back before they came—*damn!* I was momentarily dazzled but at least I was a little closer to being "upwind."

"Why have you come to me?" I asked. A couple of days ago I might have freaked. After Robert Delacroix's dance with the damned I had progressed to the next level.

Whatever that was.

"Jussstisss," the faceless woman hissed.

Mr. Jaw-be-gone just nodded, his exposed trachea rattling as if he wanted to add something.

"Um," I said. "I'm a private investigator. I do divorce cases. Yep. That's my specialty. I don't do justice. Just divorce cases. Y'all aren't looking to do a custody battle, are ya? Because I don't—"

"You are The Baron," the boy wheezed.

"The Loa," whispered the third corpse. Not as old as the other two, I decided after a closer look. She was ("was" being the operative term) on the downward side of sixteen and now (and forevermore) an adolescent for eternity. Her skin looked like a dirty lace doily and she was missing both of her hands.

Hello, a nightlight kicked on in the back of my head. "Whoa. Hold on. Have you got the wrong guy!"

"Baron," they sighed.

"I'm *not* Baron Samedi."

"Help usss. Avenge ussss!" the faceless woman hissed.

The girl without her hands stepped forward and extended her right leg. I was stymied. If I couldn't put a stop to this, I might well be overrun with disgruntled dead people, all demanding some sort of revenantal recompense. And now I had a corpse threatening to do the hokey-pokey on my driveway.

I looked down and saw that someone had dumped a couple of handfuls of salt on the concrete. Okay. Certain ceremonies invoking the zombie dead required salt as a material component—that much I could remember from the "Raise Dem Bones" chapter of the Voodoo Practitioner's Handbook.

But I didn't know what it meant.

Was somebody raising the dead from the local cemetery and pointing them in my direction? Or were they self-motivated and finding their way to me here on their own?

While I considered the desirability of going on a sodium-free diet, the other two adults came over and took the girl by each arm to steady her. Her bare foot came down, toes curled and she began to scratch at the salt with her big toe.

Off in the distance I heard a cockcrow. I looked at my watch: *tempus fudge-it*—not quite one A.M. Someone must have goosed a rooster. I looked up to see my decaying delegation already in motion, heading off across my lawn and toward the woods.

"Hey!" I said. And then wondered what I was "heying" about. Did I really want them to come back and continue this conversation? Let rotting corpses lie—that's my motto. As they headed into the tree line I looked back down at the toe-scratches in the salt.

The crooked lines formed letters and those letters spelled a single word.

HOW

Dead people.
First they want justice.

Then they want vengeance.

And then they rudely walk away after starting a game of Twenty-Questions.

They made the Snow Queen seem the ideal client.

Someone came out of the woods, walking toward me. It was Mama Samm D'Arbonne. With a rooster under her arm.

"Siddown, *chère*," she said as she lumbered on up to the porch, "you look like you could take a load off."

I sat on the edge of the concrete slab. "I'm tired."

Mama Samm sat beside me. "You not sleepin' well, you?"

"I've had a few nightmares," I admitted.

"So it is foretold in de Bible."

"My nightmares are in the Bible?"

"And it shall come to pass in the last days, says God," she quoted, "that I will pour out of My Spirit on all flesh; your sons and your daughters shall prophesy, your young men shall see visions, your old men shall dream dreams. De book of Acts, second chapter, seventeen verse."

I sighed. "I don't know which implication is more upsetting. That I'm an old man or that these are the last days."

"Honey," she said, sounding very like my Great Aunt, "I don' tink you be ready for this, yet."

"Ready for what?" I asked, staring back at the woods. "Being Dear Abby for the dead?"

"More den dat, *chère*. You mus' be they champion. Bot' de living an' de dead." She patted my knee. "Remember dis one ting: dere is power in de blood."

"Yeah. And you know what the vampire motto is? More power to me."

She chuckled and adjusted her rooster. He crowed again. "You make a good start, tho. Already you find de grail. Keep her close, Hefe. De Whore of Babylon, she on her way."

I groaned. "As if I don't have enough woman problems."

"And dere is one who is lost between: maybe she save you, maybe she bury you—I don' see everyting."

"No joke."

She rose to her feet, the creaking of her massive knees making me wince in sympathetic pain. "De grail is de key."

"The ki?"

She nodded solemnly. "Maybe it so. Maybe you be him for true."

"Him? Him who?"

"Samedi, Lord of de Crossroads. For de Gédé clan. They all gone missing and here you be." She reached down and touched the side of my face. "Remember, de dead who come to you, dey do not seek a selfish vengeance. Dose who come to you, dey seek justice to protec' de living."

"And who am I to give that to them?"

She stepped back and stared down at me. After a long silence she nodded. "I see wings over you. De Darkness is coming for you but you will go down to de Valley—dey will lose you dere. . . ."

Like I wasn't already lost.

"And you will help to open de way back. Maybe dat more important than de gray men and all their plots. Take dis." She handed me a little red bag, tied shut with colored strings and tiny feathers and beads. "Keep it in your pocket. Ti-bon-ange."

And with a final nod of her head, she turned and lumbered back down my lawn and into the woods.

I sat for the longest time.

I see wings over you.

Yeah, batwings . . .

Mosquitoes flying reconnaissance in from the bayou circled my head in a whiney cloud, then broke formation and continued their search for sustenance out toward the road. Professional courtesy, I guess.

I gazed up at the whiteness of the moon and considered the mottled gray shadows that spotted its face like patches of corruption on a communion wafer. Grey men, I thought. Who are the grey men?

Maybe T.S. Eliot could enlighten me. There was a collection of his poetry on my nightstand. I picked myself up and brushed the salt from my rump and pants legs. Who says the dead are an "unsavory" lot?

Already you find de grail. Keep her close . . .

Something danced at the edge of my consciousness as I unlocked the door and rekeyed the security system. I meandered into the kitchen, pulled another blood bag from the refrigerator, and pressed the chilled plastic against my fevered brow. "Holy crap!" I whispered. "The grail—keep her close."

Wm. Mark Simmons

Chalice.

My headache turned savage and I stumbled toward the stairs and my bedroom. The night was still young but I wasn't as I grabbed the banister and started up. "Honey," I called, the old joke worn way past thin now, "I'm home!"

"I've been waiting for you," answered a familiar voice from the bedroom.

I pushed the door open, recognition starting to dawn even before I took in the all-too-solid white flesh, the shocking deep crimson tumble of hair, familiar lips distorted by unfamiliar fangs.

"Holy shit!" I said.

"Hello, Chris."

"Deirdre!"

Chapter Eight

When I first met Deirdre, nearly a year before, she was fully human.

She and her vampire lover Damien had befriended me when I was abducted and brought to the Seattle demesne. They were very much in love and troubled by Damien's inability to "bring her over." Forget the books and movies, making vampires is more like making babies than you might think—sometimes it happens on the first attempt, sometimes it never happens at all. When it comes to reproduction, there's no such thing as a sure thing.

They had exchanged all of the requisite bodily fluids and Damien had carefully taken her right up to the point where the virus should have caught hold—more than once, in fact. But it didn't happen. And, although she was willing to risk death—final and irrevocable—to truly be one with her vampire paramour, he wasn't willing to push the chance of losing her eternally.

Tragedy enough, but Fate had a crueler twist up its bony sleeve; it was the powerful and all but invulnerable Damien who preceded his mortal lover into the eternal darkness, staked by assassins from the New York demesne trying to get to me.

In an act that was equal parts compassion, grief, and madness, Deirdre had come to me as I lay helpless, recovering from what should have been mortal wounds. She comforted me, healed me.

First, with her body.

Then, with her blood.

And finally, while I slept in her soft embrace, she took the deadly dental appliance that Liz Bachman had given me and used it to take her own life.

When I escaped the Seattle demesne, Deirdre was a lifeless corpse on a drawer in the morgue.

Now, a year later, stretched out in my bed, she looked very lively.

And, except for a small corner of the rumpled top sheet covering practically nothing of consequence, she looked very naked.

"Hello, Deirdre," I said.

"Hello, Chris," she said with a slow smile. "Or should I call you 'Master'?" Her smile dimpled, revealing sly fangs.

It wasn't hard to figure out—even without Deirdre's fill-in-the-blanks account of her subsequent awakening. The virus, long dormant in her bloodstream, had been activated with her death. It took longer for her to rise—probably because Damien's gift had been diluted in the time that had passed since their last exchange. And by the time she had sundered her sarcophagus and emerged like a great and fearsome Luna moth, I was long gone down the road to Kansas and about to drop off the radar altogether.

"And now I've found you," she concluded happily.

"Why?" I asked.

"You are my Master."

I shook my head. That was a mistake: something seemed to tear loose behind my left eye and went rattling around inside my skull. "Ground Control to Major Tom . . ." I said, leaning heavily against the doorframe, " . . . or is that Major Nelson?" I felt my legs start to buckle. "Somebody send for Dr. Bellows . . ."

She was across the room with inhuman speed, catching me as the floor tilted toward my face. I felt myself lifted by slender but impossibly strong arms and carried into a roaring vortex of darkness.

Being dead was bad enough. The unrelieved blackness was worse. But being interred in a frost-free meat freezer was way past cruel and seriously starting to piss me off. I shuddered and gasped, fighting to orient my sludgy brain in the lightless void.

Something touched me.

Something cold.

But it was soft and not nearly as cold as I was.

"You fool!" said a voice.

=*How long have you gone without?*=

Without what? Adrift in the black infinity of this starless space there were eternities of emptiness: loss, loneliness, regret. And what had I not gone without of late?

=*You can't resist The Hunger with this!*=

Something was ripped from my numbed, nerveless fingers.

=*Here . . .*=

Pressure was applied to the back of my head.

My face pressed into yielding softness.

A trickle of warmth touched my lips.

=*Drink.*=

A thread of heat stung the tip of my tongue.

=*Drink! Swallow!*=

My throat convulsed but my mouth remained dry.

=*Suck! Have you forgotten what every infant knows from the womb? Pull at it!*=

A bare half-swallow and I felt a nudge of strength.

=*More! I have fed recently but you will need something warmer than that which already grows cool in my breast.*=

A bit of tepid warmth eased into my throat and the pain receded. I moved and felt the press of the mattress along my side. My hand glided to my face and found wetness. Found . . .

I opened my eyes. "Oh, God," I moaned softly.

Deirdre drew away. "I should hunt something for you before the sun comes up."

I tried to shake my head. Not good. "You mean some*one*," I whispered.

"You will suffer if I don't."

"I'm good at it . . . lots of practice . . ."

"The sun will be rising soon," she said.

"Stay. More blood downstairs—"

"Yes, I saw. It's cold."

"Boil water. Heat—"

"It's not fresh," she said like some fussy produce shopper. "But it will have to do until tonight," she finally decided.

I started to relax and slide back down that murky chute into the total dark.

"But first a little more to anchor you," she said, reaching down and reopening her self-inflicted wound. She pulled me to the freshet of gore once more. I was powerless to resist.

Finally I surrendered, feeling like a total boob.

Like they say: you are what you eat.

I awoke to the vague glimmer of sunlight behind the heavy bedroom drapes: the embroidered, dark green leaves glowed against the black fabric like a phosphorescent jungle. I looked at the bedside clock: five twenty-seven in the p.m. I looked at the rest of the rumpled bed: empty. A few drops of dried blood were the only tangible evidence of her presence last night.

So where had she gone?

I rolled to the edge of the bed and tried to sit up. Flashbulbs went off behind my eyes.

I made it on the third attempt and stared down at the carpet, about a mile or so below. "I can do this," I whispered. "There's nothing wrong with my legs, there's nothing wrong with my eyes; I'm just a little tired."

Never mind points for proper form, the will triumphed: five minutes later I crawled out of the bedroom and made my way down the hall on my hands and knees. The stairs were a bit of a challenge but I managed to go down feet first—and butt second. As Deirdre had wrestled me out of my clothes during the night, I picked up a wicked carpet burn by the time I reached the (ahem) bottom.

By the time I staggered into the kitchen I was wobbling erect, on my own two feet. *Think Weebles!* I kept telling myself. Weebles wobble, *but they don't fall down.*

I pulled on the refrigerator door. It resisted. I pulled harder. Reluctantly the magnetic and rubber seals gave way and I retrieved a couple of blood bags. I started back to the stove but the idea of going through the process of boiling the water and then cooling the contents back to an approximate ninety-nine degrees just wore me out thinking about it. Grabbing a paring knife out of the kitchen drawer, I ambled to the dining table and prepared the plastic tubing like an overlong silly straw.

The cold hemoglobin hit the back of my mouth like chilled Tabasco sauce. Halfway down my throat it started to burn then exploded in my stomach like cold fusion. My nerve endings started to tingle and strength returned to my arms and legs. The trembling in my extremities died down from a series of quivers and quakes to a mild vibration, then ceased altogether. My head began to settle and my mind started switching on the internal lights again.

I felt better. Not great, mind you, but almost human again.

Almost.

But probably never quite ever again.

I sat slumped against the table long after the pouch was empty whispering the old mantra: *I am not a monster, I am still a man; I am not a monster, I am still a man—*

I am not . . .

I felt even better after a long shower and some clean clothes. I stripped the sheets off the bed and dropped them down the laundry chute. Clean sheets from the linen closet and shortly thereafter I had a pristine bed to sleep in.

The question was how long would it stay that way?

Lupé, when (if) she came back, would not appreciate finding out that another woman had shared my bed in her absence. Never mind that we hadn't had sex, what Deirdre had done was more intimate than sex for a vampire.

And more complicated for me.

If Deirdre was calling me "Master" and sharing blood with me, it indicated that she considered me her "Sire."

But I hadn't "created" her.

It was Damien's blood, not mine, that had sown half of the combinant virae in her bloodstream, Damien's saliva that had injected the other half with his "love-bites." Had he still walked the earth when she resurrected, Damien would have been her Sire, her Master. Apparently she considered the fact that she had died in my bed, with her blood upon my lips, sufficient involvement in her *turning* to nominate me for the vacancy.

If true, I held the power of life and death over her. Or the power of "unlife" to be technically pure.

I could tell her when and where she could and could not hunt. Of course, she had apparently been hunting and feeding for the better part of a year without my input so dictating boundaries might prove a little difficult.

Especially since I wasn't fully undead. And could be considered peripherally responsible for Damien's death.

Now I faced two disturbing questions. One: how had she found me? If Deirdre had been able to hunt me down seven months later and a half continent away, who else might find me in time? And two: if I could not dissuade her from hunting human prey, how complicit would I become in the suffering and death of her victims? Could I stake her—essentially murder her—in the name of protecting humankind as the greater good?

I was just realizing that maybe that constituted "four" questions when the doorbell rang.

I pulled the drapes back and tried to check the driveway without standing in direct light. Whoever was on my doorstep was hidden under the first-story eaves and there was no vehicle in my driveway. There were, however, flashing blue lights strobing down at the end of my lawn by the woods. I glanced around the bedroom and then scanned the hall and the stairs as I hurried down to answer the door. Nothing suggested anything but a normal house with normal occupant(s) but I crossed my fingers, hoping that Deirdre wouldn't suddenly show up ahead of schedule.

I opened the front door and took in the tall skinny guy with long brown hair and a jutting, curly beard to match. The hair was topped by a small porkpie hat with a tiny feather peeking over the headband on the side. His sports jacket clashed with his pants and his tie seemed to be an attempt to catalog all the colors that didn't naturally occur in nature. A detective's shield was displayed on a leather flap that hung from the pocket of his jacket.

"Mr. Haim?"

For a moment I thought he was a ventriloquist, then realized the voice originated near my diaphragm. I looked down at a small Hispanic woman in a brown pants suit. She had a similar badge in her hand.

"Yes?" I said, standing back from the light but not so far as to indicate an unspoken invitation to enter.

"Detective Ruiz," she elaborated. "This is Detective Murray."

I nodded. "What can I do for you, Detectives?"

"We'd like to ask you a few questions if you have a moment." She smiled almost as an afterthought.

"Would you like to come in?" I asked reluctantly.

Ruiz looked back and up at Murray. Murray didn't look at anything in particular; he just maintained his own pleasant half-smile and waited.

"Well—" she prevaricated, "—I'm afraid we can't right now. We're waiting for the coroner's wagon and need to keep the area under surveillance until they arrive."

I glanced meaningfully at the tall, skinny guy with marked lack of fashion sense. I noticed he was wearing sneakers with mismatched socks.

"Murray is on loan from Vice," Ruiz said as if that explained everything.

"Ah," I said as though I completely understood.

"Would you be willing to take a walk down to your property-line with us, sir?"

I looked past her shoulder: the sun floated just a little ways above the tree line and threw a dim golden haze over the land. Maybe I could endure about ten minutes of it without protection.

"If you'll give me a moment," I said, "I need to apply some sunblock. I—"

Ruiz held up her hand. "I understand, Mr. Haim. We're aware of your sun sensitivity. Come down and join us when you're ready." She turned and started down the lawn. After a moment, the still-smiling Murray nodded to me and followed along behind.

I slathered on two coats of sunblock and selected another hat from my closet shelf, a buff-colored Stetson with a low crown. I popped in the polarized contact lenses but skipped the sunglasses for this outing.

As I walked back down the stairs, I heard something stirring up in the attic.

The coroner had arrived while I was primping. As I walked down the slope of my front yard I wondered about Ruiz's awareness regarding my sun sensitivity.

I wondered what else she knew.

And I wondered what had happened to the salt someone had spilled on my driveway last night: it was gone.

Two men wrestled a stretcher up from the midst of the trees with a black body bag strapped atop it. Ruiz motioned me over as it reached the back of the coroner's wagon. "I'd like you to have a look at this," she said, motioning me closer. She nodded to Murray, who unzipped the top of the bag.

I stared at a familiar face—if you could still call it that—while Ruiz and Murray stared at mine. It belonged to the young woman who had dropped by the night before—the one missing her hands and wrists. She appeared to be very dead. Even more so than last night.

"Well, Mr. Haim?" Ruiz asked after a long pause.

"Well," I said indignantly, "this was *not* a boating accident!"

"What?" Her eyes grew large.

Murray's smile expanded.

"And it wasn't any propeller, it wasn't any coral reef, and it wasn't Jack the Ripper!" I continued. "It was a shark!"

"All right," Ruiz said, jerking her head.

It sounded like Murray mumbled "Thank you, Mr. Hooper" as he closed the bag. We stepped back as the coroner's team wrestled the stretcher into the back of the van.

"No," I said.

"No, what?" Ruiz wanted to know.

"Depends on which question." I watched them close the doors on the van. They clanged like the gates on a steel sarcophagus. " 'No,' I didn't kill her or 'no,' I've never seen her before in my life."

"No one's accusing you of anything, Mr. Haim."

"And nobody's confessing here, either, Detective." I smiled at her, trying to approximate Murray's pleasant, laid-back demeanor. "I'm not personally offended that you just tried one of the oldest tricks in the book, Sergeant . . ."

"Lieutenant."

I knew that. But if she could trot out one of police-work's hoariest old clichés, so could I. " . . . but I can be offended that it *is* one of the oldest tricks in the book." I smiled a little more. "So, what other questions would you like to ask me?"

Her smile grew in turn. "Well, we thought it couldn't hurt to run some things past a fellow professional."

I looked for the note of sarcasm but the diminutive detective was making every effort to be friendly. Which really set off the alarms in the back of my head. I would have preferred sarcasm to insincere flattery.

Plus it meant I was still in the suspect column on her list.

"I need to get back inside," I said. "Will this take long?"

"No," she said pleasantly. No snarl, no "we can haul your sorry ass downtown and question you there..." Instead, she gestured back toward the house and said, "Let's get you back inside."

As we walked back up the lawn she asked the basics: Had I noticed any activity in the woods in the last few days? Or nights? Had I seen any strangers or unusual people in the neighborhood? Had any vehicles caught my attention in the past few days—maybe driving past slowly? Or come by more than once? What hours did I keep? Or, rather, when was I away for work or teaching and when was I home when I might observe any unusual comings and goings? Was I light sleeper?

And so on.

When she was done, I asked her about the body.

A couple of kids had found it in the woods this afternoon, she told me. The grave was shallow and they saw the toes of one foot protruding above the ground.

How long did they think she had been buried there?

Ruiz and Murray exchanged a look and I *pushed*.

"The victim has been tentatively identified as Kandi Fenoli," Ruiz said. "Believed to have been abducted while hitching. The cops in Winn Parish described ligature marks and so we're assuming strangulation. We think the perp removed her hands so she couldn't be traced via fingerprints. Makes no sense, though..."

"Winn Parish?" I asked.

"That's where the body was found," Ruiz said.

Murray finally spoke. "The first time."

"The *first* time?"

He nodded. "A little over a week ago."

"How did it get over here?"

"That's what we'd like to know," Ruiz said, looking me square in the eye. "The body disappeared from the morgue the night before the autopsy was scheduled. So tell me, Mr. Haim: do you honestly think it got up on its own and walked nearly a hundred miles cross-country to seek a shallow grave in those woods down there?"

I have a fundamental rule: never, *ever* lie to the police—you'll just end up making things worse.

I looked the feisty detective right back in the eye and unhesitatingly broke that rule with no compunction.

"No," I said.

Ten minutes after the Ruiz and Murray show departed, I was on the phone to Chalice Delacroix. When I told her that I wanted to visit her at BioWeb tonight she agreed without hesitation. I didn't even have to push. Maybe my luck was starting to turn.

Maybe not: as I hung up the receiver, I heard the door to the attic slide open and saw Deirdre come floating down like some heavenly creature from an ethereal plane—an ethereal plane whose inhabitants just happened to have pointy, sharp teeth and iridescent, red eyes.

Still, Deirdre's angel face and crimson hair made her scarlet eyes more haunting than horrifying. As in life, she was somewhere beyond beautiful, and her undead form was seemingly enhanced in ways I could not immediately fathom. The sweet, young woman I had met a year ago was somehow more—*compelling*—now that she had become an inhuman predator. I had to wonder: was it something in her?

Or in me?

"Sire," she said softly, "you are recovered." Her smile was almost better than sex.

You could find out so easily, said the voice (mine? hers?) inside my head.

"Deirdre, I'm not big on formalities. Let's just drop this 'Master' and 'Sire' business and call me Chris. Okay?"

Her smile expanded and she adjusted her big blue bathrobe where it threatened to do the same. "I'm not surprised that you're uncomfortable with 'Master' but you are my Sire."

While that could be debated on more than one technicality, I thought it best to let it lie for now. "Just call me Chris."

"Yes Chris," she said with amused obedience.

"Well . . . did you sleep well?"

She waggled her hand. "You have squirrels."

"I have squirrels?"

"And you have light leaks."

"Ah, the attic."

"And I am rather dusty. I need a shower."

I gave her a choice of bathrooms, upstairs or down, each outfitted with unused guest towels.

"Wash my back?" she asked, untying the sash of her robe.

"There's a loofah on a cord inside the shower stall."

Then she suggested a way to conserve water to which I pointed out that I had already had my shower. Clearly, this was going to be even more complicated than I had initially expected.

While she was in the shower, I went through the luggage I found stashed in one of the spare bedrooms: clothes, quite a bit of cash, fake IDs, otherwise nothing suspicious or very telling.

I moved the luggage so any settling of contents would seem natural and opened dresser drawers and the closet to prepare the room for occupancy. Deirdre appeared at the door as I was tidying up.

Taking in the change in sleeping arrangements, she said: "It's Lupé, isn't it?"

"Lupé?"

"You're monogamous, aren't you?"

I nodded.

"Monogamous, monotonous—it's not the natural state of our kind."

"Your kind," I corrected. "I have no 'kind.'"

She stared at me then looked around the room. "Where is she?"

"Away." I suspected California but there was no way of knowing for sure. She might have found stunt work for some movie being shot on location. "Working."

"When will she be back?"

I shrugged. "The fewer who know, the better."

"You don't trust me?" Her attention was back on me, now. Her eyes narrowed and she brushed blood-red tendrils of hair away from her face. "Or *you* don't know when, yourself?"

I shrugged again. "Her schedule changes from week to week."

"So you don't know *when*. Maybe it's more a matter of you don't know *if*."

I folded my arms. "If I am your Sire and Master, you should show me a little more respect. Especially in the matters of my personal life."

"It's my life, too," she said. The water from her hair seemed to have trickled down into her eyes: she blinked furiously.

"How did you find me?" I wanted to know but, even more, I thought it prudent to change the subject.

"It wasn't easy," she answered, unwrapping the towel.

My first impulse was to turn away or at least be gentleman enough to avert my eyes. But Deirdre had "thrown down" so to speak and looking away would be tantamount to a flinch on my part. I didn't want to lose points so I kept her in my field of vision as she searched for something to wear. It wasn't just social gamesmanship. We were both predators, now, and Deirdre was the more dangerous. While I had no desire to be her Master, any alternative could well be worse. And any sign of weakness could shift the ground under our feet in a heartbeat.

Besides, bitching and moaning about having to gaze upon unclothed perfection is hardly my style.

"Had we formed a true blood-bond, I probably would have found you months ago," she continued, selecting a simple green sheath dress. "There were days when I could hear the whisper of my mortal blood in my dreams, nights when I could hear it murmur in your veins. Had I tasted yours then, the whisper would have become a song. You've now taken my immortal essence into yourself. You were too weak last night, but once we have exchanged heart's blood, the bond will become a shout."

"And then you will be able to find me anywhere." Another reason I wasn't particularly keen on the process. "So what about you? With whom else do you share a blood-bond?" I noted as she wriggled into the dress that she wasn't wearing underwear. Come to think of it, I hadn't noticed *any* lingerie while rummaging through her luggage.

Her head reappeared and she gazed at me under half-lidded eyes. "Are you jealous, my Sire?"

"Just practical."

"Oh," a hint of disappointment in her voice, "oh, I see. You're worried that someone could use a blood-bond with me to find you."

I nodded. "Something like that."

"Well, they won't. There was pressure but I rejected every offer back in Seattle. I knew, once you were declared rogue, that I would follow you into exile." She slipped on a pair of green, snakeskin slingback heels that looked positively dangerous. "I think some of the others thought so, too. I told them I was mourning Damien, that I would enter no blood-bond for at least a year. I was very careful, when I slipped away, to leave no trail. There is no way that anyone could trace you through me: I spent two months just doubling back to see if I had picked up any tails. I did not seek you out until I was sure my back trail was clear. Trust me: you are absolutely safe."

The doorbell chimed.

I went downstairs, glad of the interruption and fearful that Detectives Ruiz and Murray had returned with a search warrant.

They hadn't.

Stefan Pagelovitch, vampire Doman of the Seattle demesne was standing on my front porch. "Hello, Christopher," he said pleasantly. He nodded, looking past my shoulder: "Deirdre . . ."

Beyond him, standing out in the yard, were another five undead foot soldiers from the Pacific Northwest.

Pagelovitch smiled, showing inch-long canines. "Aren't you going to invite me in?"

Chapter Nine

The Doman of Seattle wasn't imposing in appearance.

He stood about six feet tall with a slender build and had dark brown hair and features that were vaguely hawklike. You had to really stare at him when he wasn't looking back to get a sense of his true appearance. The older vampires were like that: it was the young ones who wanted to make an issue of their looks. By the time they figured out that calling attention to themselves was not the best strategy for longevity, it was generally too late: undead Darwinism.

Stefan Pagelovitch didn't exude a tenth of his actual menace—which made him all the more dangerous. So I wasn't happy about inviting him across my threshold. And I wouldn't even consider letting any of his enforcers inside. Even after he assured me that my red-eyed, cell phone-wielding vamp hadn't been one of them.

"So," I said, "what you're telling me is that there's another group of fanged enforcers in town."

Pagelovitch nodded. "New York has had a presence down here for some time. I'm surprised you hadn't noticed until now."

I shrugged. "We run in different social circles."

"I, of all people, should know better than to confuse you with your legend."

I unfolded my arms. "My what?"

"You shared blood with the legendary Dracula and then took him out."

"Well, we never actually dated—oh, I see." I looked over at Deirdre. "People been making up stories about me?"

She looked very small and despondent huddled on the couch. "It's well known that you killed Kadeth Bey and Lilith. And that you then destroyed Vlad Dracula. Is it surprising that the tale has grown with each telling?"

"Dracula is—" I stopped myself. Bassarab wanted the rest of the enclaves to believe he was dead and gone: we had set it up that way. I was already on the docket for a half-dozen vampire fatalities, what was one more?

Pagelovitch shook his head. "The Impaler, the four-thousand-year-old Necromancer who hounded him throughout the last five centuries, and the traitor who compromised the security of my entire enclave—any one of them might have made you a legend in death. Overcoming all three and then turning up alive—well—" he walked over to the drapes shielding the picture window, "—we all believe in the Boogie Man. You seem to have moved up the list to the number-two position."

He didn't say who topped the list at number one. He didn't have to.

"Is that why you let Deirdre leave? So you could follow her and find out whether I was a living legend or a musty myth?"

Deirdre's face tightened into a mask of misery.

"She didn't betray you," he said, pulling back the curtains to give us an unobscured view of the grounds. Or, more likely, to give his people an unobscured view of the interior of my living room.

"You mean not consciously," I said, unmoved by the stricken expression on Deirdre's face.

"We didn't follow her, if that's what you mean." He leaned back into the sofa and crossed his legs, putting a pair of Traversi alligator shoes on display. "I don't know how *she* found you." He hesitated and looked thoughtful. "Although I understand that Dr. Mooncloud was helping her with some sort of focused dream-trance-interpretation something. . . ." He shook his head. "No, my dear Christopher, it would appear that you have betrayed yourself."

"Okay. Mind telling me how?"

"You are familiar with the FBI's 'Carnivore' software?"

"You mean the computer setup that intercepts and reads mass volumes of email, scanning for key word combinations?"

Pagelovitch nodded. "We have something similar that we use to keep tabs on various government and law-enforcement communications. As you might imagine, we've added your name to the key words and phrases for which we maintain a constant alert."

"And my name is being bandied about by the local constabulary?"

He nodded again. "It turned up. It seems there was a—how would you say—ruckus—at a local funeral home. . . ."

I almost slapped my forehead. "Damn! I signed the guest book as Christopher L. Cséjthe!"

"It didn't take long to hack the City Hall computer databases to see who had appeared in town about the right time. From there it was a matter of narrowing the list of suspects." He smiled wolfishly and steepled his fingers. "This house was our first stop on the list."

"Lovely. Now what?"

The Doman sighed and placed his fingers against his lips. "Christopher, you place me in a very difficult position."

"What about my position?" I growled.

"Christopher, you are rogue. Not only that but Lupé and now Deirdre have followed you into exile. Under the law you all must either return to my demesne or be destroyed."

I moved my eyebrows up for maximum effect. "*Your* demesne? Under the law we are required to ally myself with *some* demesne. I don't recall the wording that gives you unequivocal rights to our persons."

"The law," he observed placidly, "requires me to destroy you if you are not allied with *some* demesne. So, if not us, then who?"

"We have a demesne," I said. "My Doman knows where I am, I have his approval, and we," I glanced back at Deirdre, "are under his protection."

"And your Doman's name is . . . ?"

"Christopher L. Cséjthe."

Pagelovitch didn't bat an eye. "Christopher," he said patiently after a long pause, "you know that is unacceptable. I need a real answer, a final answer."

I stared at him. "Only Regis Philbin gets a final answer."

He stared back. "Not if you're the weakest link."

I blinked. "How much time do I get to give you a final answer? Fifteen seconds?"

He smiled patiently; the teeth remained hidden. "You've been gone for better than half a year; how much time do you need?"

"More than fifteen seconds."

"What if I give you a day?"

"I need more than a day. How about a week?"

Pagelovitch shook his head. "I don't think you have a week."

"What does that mean?"

He sighed and rose to his feet. "It means if your signature led us to you, it will lead others to you, as well. Sooner rather than later." He put his cold hand on my shoulder. "Come back with me and help me rule the Northwest. You'll be a colleague, not a prisoner. If New York claims you, you'll be a prisoner—or worse."

"You think they'd actually kill me?"

He shook his head. "There are worse things than death, my friend. You know who rules there?"

It was hardly a guess by now: "Elizabeth Báthory."

It made sense, of course.

When Vlad Drakul Bassarab V had retired from the neck-stabbing politics of ruling the New York demesne, he found it necessary to disappear. The new Doman of the East Coast was very jealous of her then-and-future power-base. She put her own hounds of hell on the old *voivode's* trail, forcing him to go into hiding—in Kansas, of all places.

At the time he had told me of his need for anonymity and I had briefly wondered who could put the fear of death into history's number-one bloodsucker. Other distractions had prevented a follow-up question at the time but it certainly made sense now. Off the battlefield, the Countess Erzsébet Báthory-Nádasdy was actually scarier than Transylvania's crown prince, a regular Torquemada of the Damned.

Pagelovitch nodded. "Then you know how terrible the consequences can be should you fall within her bloody grasp."

I just looked at him working hard on a nonplussed expression—heavy emphasis on the non.

He sighed finally. "I will give you a day. Maybe two if all remains quiet. But I will need an answer by then. And do not presume upon my friendship." He took his leave then with a promise to return the following night.

I gave him a few minutes to quit my property and then peeked out the window. Not all of his minions had departed with him. I now had extra security. I wondered what their reaction would be if any additional plaintiffs turned up for this evening's session of night court.

Returning to my library in the den, I turned on my laptop.

"What will you do?" Deirdre asked from the doorway.

"I don't know," I said, browsing one of the bookshelves while the computer booted up. "I'm not ready to leave, yet. It's not just a matter of freedom and personal choice. I think—" Actually it was best if no one knew what I was thinking just then. "I need you to do some research while I'm gone."

"Where are you going?"

"To see a client."

"What kind of client?"

"The kind that may have answers that I can't get anywhere else. I'm not blowing town when a cure for my condition might lie right here, in my own proverbial back yard."

"Every night you remain here you run a risk."

I shrugged. "Every day, every night, is a risk for me as long as the virus continues to mutate in my body. In the meantime, I'd like you to look up everything you can find on Elizabeth Báthory. Do you know how to do online searches?"

"I'm undead, not brain-dead," she said archly.

"Good. I have some reference material on the shelves, here, but you'll have to do a little digging. Print out anything you can find on the Internet. She was Hungarian so remember to try alternate English spellings of her name."

"I am yours to command." Soft, a little breathy, like a half-hearted attempt at Marilyn Monroe.

"Good. Whatever I end up doing, you're going back to Seattle with Pagelovitch."

"Why?"

"Do the research. It will answer your question better than anything I could say." I went to the closet and brought out a black, hooded sweatshirt. "Now, one more thing. I want you to put this on, pull the hood over your hair, and run out the back door and into the woods."

"I'm your decoy?"

"Pagelovitch left two of his watchdogs behind. Just get them to chase you for about thirty seconds—that's all the time I'll need to get the car started and out onto the main road."

She stood there, looking thoughtful.

"You think they might hurt you?"

She shook her head as if she were shaking off a thought. "No. I know Stefan and I know his lapdogs: they will kill when it is necessary. But he is patient in most things and particularly long-suffering when it comes to you. They will not like the deception but they will not harm me as long as Stefan considers you to still be under his protection." She pulled the oversized sweatshirt on over her head. "I will do as you command—"

"Request."

"—and neuter the watchdogs. After which I will do the research for you."

"Actually, the research is more for you than for me," I said, thinking of Countess Báthory's proclivities toward the fairer sex. I hoped she would understand the warning.

Clutching my car keys so they wouldn't jingle, I took up a position next to the door where I could watch the front yard without being seen. A minute passed and then the back door opened and closed noisily. The watchdog vamp in the front went tearing around the side of the house and I eased the front door open and slipped out onto the porch. Running lightly down to the car, I slipped behind the wheel and pulled the driver's door to the almost-closed position.

I smiled as I inserted the ignition key: One of the advantages of driving an antique car was the absence of buzzers and alarms for doors, seatbelts, and ignitions. While I had spent a fair amount of money upgrading the engine, drive train, brakes, and wiper/reservoir system, I had kept the stealth configuration of the Fifties. I turned the key and closed the door simultaneously. As soon as the engine caught I popped the transmission into reverse and went careening down the long drive backwards instead of wasting precious seconds swinging around the concrete circle in front of the house.

At any moment I expected two very irritated vamps to run back around the house and come charging down the driveway faster than any human could run.

It didn't happen.

I spun the car out onto the cul-de-sac, slipped into drive and hesitated: still no pursuit. At least not from the house. Apparently Pagelovitch didn't think two watchdogs were enough: as I drove away, I picked up a tail at the end of the block.

I drove out to BioWeb with the black Suburban in my rearview mirror all the way. There seemed to be no point in trying to outrun or lose my undead babysitters as long as they weren't trying to stop me. A high-speed car chase, on the other hand, was just the thing to get additional unwanted attention.

I took my time, whistling "Me And My Shadow" as I crossed over the Ouachita River by way of the Endom Bridge.

I had some time before I was supposed to meet Chalice Delacroix so I gave my watchdogs the nickel tour. I drove around Monroe until it was patently obvious to even the outtatowners that ninety-six percent of just about everything was closed down by ten P.M. Even the mosquitoes packed it in around midnight— there just wasn't enough food out and about by that time to make it worth their while. In terms of the public nightlife, Monroe wasn't a swell place for the Big City vamps to visit. Since I lived here, I could almost feel sympathy oozing from the vehicle behind me as we motored down another darkened thoroughfare: pickings would be mighty slim for any night feeder.

Fate was with me on this particular night, however. The lights were still on at St. Mark's and I pulled up in front of the church with deviltry in mind. By the time my tail had pulled in behind me, I was out of my car and running up the steps with a forty-two ounce Citgo "Big Swallow" cup I had rescued from the cup-caddy on the passenger side. I heard doors slam behind me as I ducked inside and then nonchalantly walked into the narthex and scoped out the holy water font at the back of the chapel.

It was nearly empty.

Great: when do they fill these things, anyway?

"Can I help you, son?" A man approached from the candle-lit altar at the front of the chapel. He was middle-aged with a dusky, dark complexion that looked odd in the lowered lighting of the chancel.

At first I thought he was the priest but, as he limped down the steps and came down the center aisle, I saw that he was dressed like a workman. Faded jeans that raised doubts about their original color were peg-legged over weathered brown work boots with bits of green vegetation snarled in the climbing Xs of tan laces. The sleeves of his chambray shirt were rolled up to reveal forearms corded with lean muscle and camouflaged by indecipherable tattoos. A ring glinted on the third finger of his left hand. His brown hair was shot with threads of silver and his deep-set eyes seemed to glimmer like the votive candles behind him.

"Are you all right?" he asked.

Calm down, I told myself. Relax. "I—I was looking for the priest." Oops, wrong answer! All I wanted was a quick in-and-out, not a prolonged, excuse-making conversation with the resident padre.

"He doesn't seem to be around at the moment," the dusky man said with a sad smile. "You look like a man in search of an answer."

More like a man in search of liquid ammo. But I said: "Actually I was just passing by and I wanted to ask a question about something in the Bible."

The man stared at me as if he were reading the truth in my statement.

"The Book of Revelation says something about the 'Whore of Babylon' . . ."

He nodded. " 'And I saw a woman sit upon a scarlet colored beast, full of names of blasphemy, having seven heads and ten horns. And the woman was arrayed in purple and scarlet color, and decked with gold and precious stones and pearls, having a golden cup in her hand full of abominations and filthiness of her fornication; And upon her forehead was a name written, Mystery, Babylon the Great, the Mother of Harlots and Abominations of the earth. And I saw the woman drunken with the blood of the saints and with the blood of the martyrs of Jesus; and when I saw her, I wondered with great admiration.' "

There were unexpected goose bumps on my arms. "Who is she?"

That sad smile again. "Now that has been the subject of endless debates. Some Protestants will tell you that John the Revelator was writing about the corruption of the Church Catholic.

Others say it is America . . . a secret organization . . . a nation yet to rise to prominence . . . some now say it's one of the terrorist organizations. Take your pick or make up your own." He shrugged. "The Book of Revelation doesn't come with a Rosetta stone or Little Orphan Annie decoder ring. It's more like a Rorschach test for the rabidly religious."

"So," I said, "this Prostitute of Perdition isn't a real person or thing. She's really just a symbol, representing a group or organization."

"That's what the theologians believe."

"Theologians."

His smile was a little less sad. "You say that like a conservative fundamentalist."

My turn to smile. "Isn't that redundant?"

"Not at all. True fundamentalists are radical, back-to-the-basics kinds of folks. Conservatives are—well—conservative."

I chuckled. "While theologians are lawyers with Divinity degrees."

"And," he said, seeming to read my mind, "they tend to discount the supernatural."

"Meaning," I elaborated, "that they couldn't possibly buy into the interpretation of the Whore of Babylon as an actual person."

"If one could properly call a demon a person," he finished for me.

"So, laying theologians aside . . ."

"You lay the theologians, they're not my type."

I grinned. " . . . who would this Strumpet of Doom most likely be if she wasn't a metaphysical metaphor? Any likely candidates?"

He stared at me as if trying to decipher the intent behind my question. "There was an ancient demon—or demoness, actually— who fit the profile for the Revelator's visions. In ancient Sumer she was called Ereshkigal and the Greeks knew her as Hecate."

"What about the Babylonians?"

He shook his head—a twitch more than an actual gesture. "They wouldn't have recognized an actual demon if it had bitten them on the ass. Which happened rather frequently if you've studied what passed for their culture. No, the Whore of Babylon was best documented by the ancient Israelites. They knew her as Lilith."

The name shook me: I had killed a vampire named Lilith back in Kansas who had seemed as evil as any undead I had yet met.

"Does that name have any significance for you?"

I nodded. "Wasn't she Frasier's ex-wife?"

He grinned. "Now you sound like a theologian."

If I could I would have blushed.

"According to Jewish lore she was the first wife of Adam," he continued, "or the second. There are two different accounts of human creation in Genesis, one saying "Male and Female He created them." Some ancient scholars interpreted this passage to mean that the creation of man and woman was simultaneous, while the account of Adam and Eve is obviously sequential—the whole rib/transplant thing. While the identity of Adam's other wife is somewhat tenuous, Lilith is referenced later in the book of Isaiah in her identity as a Babylonian night demon.

"More detailed references to Lilith can be found in the Talmud, the apocryphal text *The Testament of Solomon*, and 'The Alphabet of Ben Sira,' which emerged from Persia or Arabia around the eleventh century. She is described as having long, dark hair and a seductive, earthy appearance while in human form. After she deserted Adam over what seems to be issues of inequality and male dominance, she went and dwelled in a cave where—according to different accounts—she seduced God, married Satan or the demon Samael or Asmodeus, the king of the demons, and became the mother of the world's demons. Modern feminists wrestle with the Lilith stories portraying a negative female archetype who is assertive, seductive, and ultimately destructive."

"Is there anything in these texts about her putting on a red dress?" I asked.

"I'm not a chapter-and-verse man." His eyes flickered like troubled candle flames. "My memory isn't what it should be. Earlier passages in the Book of Revelation say something about a woman with child running into the wilderness. Whether it is the same woman who appears later, wearing purple and scarlet, is another point for debate. Her scarlet attire may be symbolic for sin, acts of wantonness, or of bloodletting on a massive scale. I only know the Whore of Babylon makes her appearance with the unleashing of great plagues in the end times."

"The opening of the seals," I said.

He nodded. "Widespread death and destruction."

"Any of those plagues resemble the flu?"

There was a muffled crash behind the chancel and the man turned toward the back of the chapel. "What was that?" He started toward the altar. "Michael?"

"Don't go outside!" I said.

He glanced back at me but didn't ask the obvious question.

While Pagelovitch's watchdogs couldn't very well enter the church even with an invitation, this man would lose that protection if he stepped outside. While his back was turned, I hurriedly scooped a little *aqua sacra* into the Styrofoam container and moved back into the narthex. I was lamenting the scant inch or so I had been able to collect at the bottom when I spotted the drinking fountain. Hey, dilution issues might be moot: they didn't have to know I watered down the water. A moment later I was coming back out the front door.

To an empty entryway.

No one around.

I ran down to the Suburban.

Still no vampires.

I poured a bit of my now-brimming cup onto the door handle. Made sure it was nice and wet. Then rushed around to the passenger side. Still no vamps. I needed to draw them back to the front before the handyman left the safety of the sanctuary.

Plus, the bluff wouldn't work if they didn't catch me in the act.

So, what did I do now? Yell: *Olley olley oxen free-o? Come and get it?*

Come and get me?

I glanced in the Suburban's window and saw nothing: dark, tinted glass. I tried the handle: it opened.

Ah: the door alarm dinged; the ignition buzzer buzzed. It brought them running.

I had the door closed by the time they reappeared round front. I smiled and raised my glass in a friendly salute. Tipped it so a nice little stream of water spattered over both door handles on the passenger side.

That slowed their charge. "What's that? What are you doing?" the black woman in fangs and 'fro demanded as she moved to cut me off from my car.

"Your door handles were filthy so I rinsed them," I said, "real good!" I held the cup up and tipped it so she could see its clear contents. "You know holy water not only cleans, it blesses, too!" I jerked the cup so a little slopped over the side and went splat on the pavement at her feet.

She said an unholy word and jumped back. By this time the other vamp had arrived, a Gen X slacker complete with knit cap and three-day-old goatee. He immediately took in his partner's strong reluctance to get anywhere near me. "Yolanda, what's wrong?"

"This—" Yolanda said another unholy word "—has a (unholy adjective) cup of (unholy modifier) holy water! He's soaked the (unholy adverb) car doors with the (unholy noun)!"

"Well don't let him drive away! We won't be able to follow him until the handles dry off!"

I told her that it would be a real shame to "rain on her parade," and she had a few more unholy words and phrases for his suggestion and my innuendo. It wasn't hard to get back into my car, especially after I sat behind the wheel and poured some more water over the outside of the door.

"Take off your shirt!" she yelled at her partner. "Use it to wipe off the handles!"

This one was no dummy.

"My shirt? Why does it have to be my shirt?"

Her partner, on the other hand . . .

I turned the key as she started peeling out of her own shirt. I drove away as she wrestled her top off on the way back to the Suburban. I cruised on down to the next intersection and waited for the light to change. It turned green about the time that they discovered that I had auto-locked their doors.

Eventually they would decide to smash one of the windows. I patted my pocket: at that point they would discover that their car keys were no longer in the ignition.

Another example that *homo vampiris* was not necessarily the next step "up" the evolutionary ladder.

Just about the time that the glow from the BioWeb facilities became visible through the trees, I felt an overwhelming sense of *something* coming into the car.

I jerked the wheel as something grabbed me and the car skidded off the road in a spray of gravel.

"Oh, Chris!" It was Jennifer. And she was sobbing.

For a moment I thought my heart might break.

And then I remembered that my wife was nearly two years dead and I had promised myself no more psychic circle-jerks.

"Oh, Chris, it was horrible!" she/it/something wailed.

"What?" I asked, in spite of myself.

"Something—_Evil!_ It—it knocked me away—threw me back into that—that faraway dark place!"

"Where were you? At home?"

I felt ghostly stirrings against my neck and shoulder as if someone was there and nodding. "And when—when I finally found my way back again . . ."

"What? What is it?" The ectoplasmic tears trickling down the side of my neck shot my resolve all to hell.

"I—I—couldn't get back in! It was like—like there was some kind of barrier—a barrier of darkness surrounding it—keeping me out!" She pushed back from me and I could almost see a face in the dim glow of the dashboard lights. "There's something evil there, Darling! No! Evil with a capital 'E'! You can't go back there! It isn't safe!"

"We'll see," I said. "I need a little time to think about this." I glanced at the dashboard clock. "Right now I have an appointment."

"But—"

"Shush." I adjusted the rearview mirror and studied the hazy reflection of my own eyes. What was I doing? Trying to psych myself out of going to the one place where I might find answers for my condition?

I turned on the radio. Static. I turned the tuner until I hit music, a gospel quartet:

Would you be free from your passion and pride?
There's power in the blood, power in the blood.
Sin stains are lost in its life-giving flow;
There's wonderful power in the blood.

I reached for the knob again.

Oh, there is power, power, wonder-working pow—

Hiss, crackle, pop. Then an oldies rock station playing "Total Eclipse of the Heart":

Once upon a time there was light in my life;
Now there's only love in the dark—

I snapped the radio off and pulled back onto the gravel side road.

By the time we—er—*I*—pulled up to the main entrance gate, she—or—hell! The situation was a bit calmer.

So what was my subconscious manifestation trying to tell me? That, deep down, I perceived Deirdre as a real threat? What kind of a threat? Physical? Emotional? Spiritual? Or was I more spooked by Pagelovitch's arrival? Or maybe I was just freaking out over this Baron Samedi mix-up with the restless dead.

Whatever it was, my most immediate concern was what fearful secrets I might find in the maze of laboratories inside the BioWeb complex—or the labyrinthine maze of my own circulatory system.

An armed and uniformed guard came out of the guard shack with a clipboard. "Mr. Haim? I'll need to see some identification."

I handed over my driver's license and a moment later was directed to the visitors' parking lot.

"Where are you going?" my displaced psyche asked as I opened the door.

"I haven't seen a doctor since Taj Mooncloud and I thought I'd get a second opinion. Wait for me here, okay?"

"I—I don't think I could follow you in there if I wanted to. That—that horrible darkness—I think it is coming from here!"

I stopped and considered that.

Mama Samm had said something—several somethings, in fact, but still unclear somethings—about the coming of the Whore of Babylon. Her coming was supposed to be connected to the opening of seals, the unleashing of plagues, the beginning of the end. If I were a bloodthirsty demon, I might want to pick up some something supernatural and malevolent from the pits of Hell to unleash upon the world.

Something biblical. Or, at least, Cecil B. DeMillical.

It would certainly be apocalyptic.

But if I had learned anything during my life and subsequent postscript, it was that Evil rarely arrived with a packed suitcase. Evil preferred to make do with what was already at hand.

I looked up at the surreal light show flickering on the sandstone exterior of the main building. The glowing letters of the BioWeb sign pulsed from red to blue, red to blue.

To red.

To blue.

Some say the world will end in fire.

Some say in ice . . .

Who needed demons and paranormal pestilence when there were labs with anthrax and smallpox and Ebola and terrorists or careless researchers or untrustworthy governments? Yessir, who needed underlings from the underworld when there was so much to work with up here: Genghis, Attila, Adolph, Idi, Saddam—the list rendered the need for interplanar interference moot. We were our own demons, followed our own devils.

"Chris?"

"All the more reason to take a little look around." I said it with more confidence than I actually felt. Maybe the lights of the BioWeb complex weren't so much beacons of hope as candle flames that draw the moth to a fiery extinction.

As I closed the door behind me I heard the lock snap shut. I hoped I wouldn't need to get back in in a hurry.

I was met at the front entrance by another security guard, who let me in and then called upstairs for Chalice to come and fetch me. While we waited by the elevators I learned that his name was Reginald and that he worked the lobby/night shift, Sunday through Thursday. By the time the elevator arrived with my client, Reggie had a subset of unconscious commands to let me into the facilities whenever I dropped by—no questions asked and no conscious memories later.

Maybe next time I could arrange for my very own passkey.

"Tell me about BioWeb," I asked Chalice as we rode back up in the elevator.

"Where do I begin?" she asked with a pro forma smile. "BioWeb is a research consortium dedicated to extending longevity and improving the quality of life. Our primary foci are in genetics with viral offshoots but there are also divisions that work in the development of pharmaceuticals, bionics, nanotech, surgical advances—even mosquito modification."

"Mosquito modification?"

"We had an outbreak of West Nile encephalitis right here a few years back. The National Guard was called in. Crop dusters, mosquito abatement trucks, larvicide in the sewers and storm drains, even a hundred crews with hand-held foggers and back-pack sprayers working their way through the city, street by street, could hardly make a dent until the cold weather arrived. And since winter, down here, typically means temperatures in the forties, it was still a pitched battle for months.

"But as bad as that was here in our little ole parish, the problem's a lot worse in other parts of the world. Malaria, dengue, and yellow fever. Mosquitoes have dealt death to more people throughout history than any other creature. You may think of them as an annoyance but they've defeated entire armies—from the troops that attacked ancient Rome to the Europeans who sought to conquer Africa. In the Pacific during World War Two, General MacArthur estimated that two-thirds of his men had verifiable symptoms of malaria. During the nineteenth century, mosquitoes turned some American cities into ghost towns. Now, here in the twenty-first, we've got a new series of mosquito-borne epidemics: St. Louis Encephalitis, West Nile Virus, Eastern Equine Encephalitis, West-ern Equine, LaCrosse Encephalitis . . . still, it's the big three—malaria, dengue, and yellow fever that infect a half a billion people each year with a mortality rate of over one million annually."

"So BioWeb is working on an eradication program?"

"Yes, but not the way you think. We're working on bioengineer-ing mosquitoes on two fronts. Manipulating the genetic structure to alter their breeding pattern—that's an old project. But we're also looking at ways to change the host environment for the viruses and parasites they carry.

"The mosquito's body has evolved into a safe harbor for these pathogens, enabling them to be transferred from one host to another, using the mosquito as a traveling incubator. We think we can disrupt that benign relationship and more. We want to splice in the genetic codes that will produce antibodies, causing the mosquito to not only destroy the disease in its own body but might well someday inoculate everyone it bites from other diseases. Maybe even this flu strain that is going around!"

I rubbed my chin. "Could be a tough sell to the public. Remem-ber all the hysteria over genetically modified food? I can see the headlines now: *Lab wants to create Frankenskeeter!* You'd probably have more success selling a cloning agenda."

"We do have a cloning agenda."

"Really?"

"Nothing human," she qualified.

"Define human."

"BioWeb has an equally strong commitment to bioethics."

"Everyone has a strong commitment to bioethics," I said. "It's just a matter of whose biology and whose ethics."

Her smile was more genuine, now. "Yes, there is that."

"Stem cell research?"

"Of course."

"Of course?"

"BioWeb is working on the conversion and harvesting of stem cells from umbilical cords, placentas, bone marrow, fat cells, other alternative source materials. We don't do embryos."

"Some do."

"We don't." The smile wasn't as friendly, now, and that made me a little sad.

The elevator doors opened and we stepped out into a beige-walled, tan-carpeted hallway.

"So, what do you do?"

"Me?"

I nodded.

"We'll get to that . . ." she said enigmatically.

For the next forty-five minutes I was taken on a brisk tour of the main building. Although the night shift meant a skeleton staff, I was introduced to cell biologists, gene therapists, bioinformatics specialists, virologists, and analytical chemist biostaticians. Along the way I observed artificial breeding ponds for mosquito research in one of the "outbuildings" out back. I was whisked through labs and libraries, computer rooms and conference halls, tissue banks and petri farms, even mini-hospital wards with private rooms. One floor housed twenty patients of both genders and a broad range of ages; their only common trait was their African-American heritage. The other ward housed both genders of Caucasian patients but these were of a similar age group: all were on the north side of fifty.

"Whatever happened to desegregation?" I asked as we continued down the hall.

"In case you haven't heard, we have a flu strain going around that primarily targets black populations."

"I heard something of the sort but I didn't take it seriously."

"Of course not." *You're white.* She didn't say the words but they hung out there in plain view, anyway.

"I mean, it sounds like some sinister government plot. . . ."

She smiled ruefully and I felt the warmth of absolution. "It does, doesn't it? Yet the facts remain, it's cutting a swath through the south side of town while the north side remains largely untouched."

"Couldn't exposure profiles—"

"You're suggesting that it started in the black community and patterns of social interaction have confined its infection patterns?" She shook her head. "That's not borne out from past epidemics. Besides, there have been no white fatalities so far while the death rate among African Americans is more than double the average from previous strains of influenza."

"So you think there's some kind of genetic link—like sickle-cell anemia?"

She nodded. "We have teams working around the clock on issues like genetic triggers in viruses. Our beds are full here and we're contracting for additional space at several area hospitals."

"Are you working on this?"

"Not directly. I'm contributing in my time off but all African-American staff are being distanced from serious research involvement at this time."

"For health reasons," I concluded. "So, what the hell are you doing walking through the flu ward?"

"There's an experimental vaccine—we've all been given precautionary dosages. And I only walked down the hall, I didn't enter any of the rooms." Her voice was unsteady and she stopped and looked up at me. "I'm sure this is what killed my father, Mr. Haim. His autopsy was done before we really knew what to look for but I'd bet my career on it!"

"Would you bet your life on it?"

"Don't you see?" Her green eyes were large and nearly luminous with a sheen of moisture that leaked around the edges. "I have to help! I can't—" She turned abruptly and started walking again.

What could I say? What could I do to comfort her? Nothing, really, except change the subject.

"So," I said, "how about all those old white people?"

"They're mine," she said unevenly. "I'm supposed to be looking for the Fountain of Youth."

It wasn't hard to figure her bitterness and frustration. While she was helping a bunch of old honkies live longer, her own people— old, young, children—were dying one floor down.

The two things their research projects had in common, she explained back down in her lab, were genetics and viral triggers. That's what helped her maintain a sense of equilibrium when the urge to run downstairs and do anything—even empty bedpans— became overwhelming. "And any breakthrough in extending the human lifespan helps all people . . . my people . . . your people . . ."

Briefly I wondered who "my people" were these days. Dracula and Pagelovitch and Erzsébet Báthory? I repressed a shudder.

"At this stage of the project, they're having me focus on telomeres." She gave me a sideways look. "I suppose you know all about telomeres?"

I gave her The Look back. "You must be kidding."

"I didn't—"

"Telomeres," I continued, "are the end caps on the chromosomes that are involved in adding new DNA to the chromosome when a cell divides. Some scientists like to compare them to aglets."

"Aglets?"

"The little plastic or metal caps on the ends of shoelaces that keep them from unraveling. Telomeres are like that. The problem is, every time a cell divides, the telomeres shrink a little. Obviously, this means a finite number of cell divisions before the chromosomes turn into old shoelaces. Are you working on the oncology angle?"

Her mouth was open and she was giving me that same look she had tossed out the day before in the hospital nursery.

"Most tumor cells," I elaborated, "switch on a gene for telomerase, a protein that manufactures the telomeres. Cancer cells work hard at being immortal and they proliferate all out of control because their telomeres don't burn out at the same rate as a normal cell. I rather imagine the trick is to apply the telomerase enzyme without letting the cells go into some bio-frenetic rampage that is typical of the cancer process."

Her mouth was still open but no sound was coming out.

"Like I said, I've read a number of medical papers over the past year."

She finally found her voice. "I would love to see your book-shelves some time."

I smiled. "How about I show you something that will knock your socks off."

"Somehow I don't think there's anything you can tell me now that will surprise me more that you have these past two days," she answered in a sultry, flirty voice as she pulled up her office chair.

Of course she was dead wrong.

Chapter Ten

The needle slid into my flesh as though skin and muscle were pretty illusions, distractions from the truth of vein and artery. As my blood welled up in the VacuTex tube, I told her the story of a man who spent most of his life being a pretty ordinary guy. Grew up normal in Middle America, went to school, bungled his first year in college and dropped out to do a hitch in the Navy. Picked up some training in radio communications and a Ph.D. in the school of Man's Inhumanity To Man.

I didn't go into the details of a Mississippi manhunt that became a jurisdictional dispute with the Coast Guard and ended up with my being loaned to a special ops group run by the Feds—a bollixed operation that went terribly wrong and gave new meanings to the words "collateral damage." The subsequent courts-martial were something I had tried to forget—with the blessing of my dear old Uncle Samuel, who had warned everybody involved against telling old stories that should stay dead and buried. It was my first real lesson in how evil can taint even the innocent despite its best efforts to do the right thing and that telling the truth is rarely expedient. . . .

Instead I skipped ahead and over the return to collegiate life, the examined life and a masters degree in English Lit, the pretty coed who became a lovely wife, then mother, and cut straight to the chase of a family vacation gone just as wrong as that Naval assignment fifteen years before.

How a chance detour and the instincts of a good Samaritan at a house fire in Weir, Kansas, got me overpowered in a moldering barn, knocked on my back, and forced to give blood to a burned corpse that should have been dead but wasn't.

To this day it seems an equitable exchange to Prince (never "Count") Vladimir Drakul Bassarab V: the unholy transfusion that revived his undead flesh also gifted me with one-half of the combinant virus that transformed the dead into the undead. Since I wasn't dead and never received the other combinant half of the super virus that resided in the vampire's saliva, the results were unforeseen but immediately catastrophic: I blacked out afterward and drove into the path of an eighteen-wheeler.

The virus had already mutated my biochemistry, enabling me to cheat Death.

My wife and daughter had no such advantage.

Chalice filled three glass ampoules and withdrew the needle. The puncture resealed itself before she could cover it again with the cotton swab.

"Now what?" she asked, not quite meeting my eyes.

"Now you spend a little time running tests on those samples," I said. "After you're convinced that I'm telling you the truth, you decide the next step."

"The next step?"

"For treatment. I want to be cured. I want the effects reversed. I want to be human again."

"S-sure," she said, a little shakily. *Humor the psycho until you can safely call down to security.*

"Oh," I said, "and Chalice . . ."

"Yes?"

"Look at what's happening to my eyes."

She looked, of course.

And that's when I gave her the rest of her instructions.

I left Chalice in her lab, figuring I'd find my own way out. She was engrossed in running the first of many tests on my blood samples and hardly noticed my departure. I didn't know how much of that was my post-hypnotic conditioning and how much was her obsession with what she had just glimpsed under the microscope.

My greater concern was how circumspect she might be while running those tests. It was one thing to plant subconscious commands to keep my test results a secret. While she might be mentally blocked from telling anyone about my condition, I couldn't completely guard against my blood samples being inadvertently seen by others. I could only cross my fingers and trust in those opportunities being reduced by Chalice working the night shift.

And I had to take some chances if I was to take advantage of the BioWeb facilities in the time I had left.

As I retraced a portion of my tour on the way out, I ran into one of the security guards making his rounds. It was no big deal to leave him without any memory of having seen or spoken with me. I could have avoided running into him altogether by heading directly for the exit but there were several rooms I had missed on the original walk-through and, like Charlie Rich, I wanted to know what went on behind closed doors.

There were storage rooms and utility closets behind most of them but I hit pay dirt on the third floor. I opened a door designated Gen/GEN and walked into an Antarctic whiteout.

It took a few moments for my eyes to adjust to the white-on-white-on-white furnishings without risking retinal burns. Everything was white from the carpeting to the ceiling, with counters and cabinets and monitors and keyboards and banks of computer casements that were distinguished here and there by a black line, a colored LED, or a chromed edge.

"Looks like a Clean Room," I murmured, considering the shelves of paper booties, hair caps, and plastic gloves inside the doorway.

"No," said a voice, "by Clean Room standards this is actually a rather grubby room." A portly bald man emerged from behind a bank of monitors. "May I help you?" Imagine Santa Claus without the beard. Wearing a lab smock like Delores Hastings wore a muumuu.

"Samuel Haim," I said, shaking his gloved hand. "Oops, sorry."

"Not to worry, I've finished running tonight's samples." He stripped off the plastic gloves and deposited them in a slot in the wall. "Are you here for the story?"

Was I? This was too easy!

"I'm Spyder Landon."

"Spyder?" I asked. He didn't look like a "Spyder."

"Well, of course, you've got the basic PR packet and human resource materials. I guess you'll write me up as Walter Landon."

I nodded sagely—hoping to look as if I knew exactly what he was talking about.

"I'm afraid this is a little unexpected," he went on. "I mean, I've been asking for five years now when we're going to go public with the Genetics/Genealogical project, but I expected a little more warning."

"Well," I said, "you know how it is."

He nodded. "I wasn't expecting you until next month but I guess they want to get something out to coincide with the big bash."

I shrugged. "They don't tell me the whys and wherefores anymore than they do you."

He grinned. "I'll bet. You're new aren't you? How long have you been with the PR Department?"

"Uh—a week."

"I'll bet it took them six months to get your security clearances, though."

My turn to nod. "I'm having to run to get caught up."

"So that's why you're here on the graveyard watch: getting additional background. I figured Dr. Coane would be the only source quoted."

"Dr. Coane?"

"Well, Phillip is the project head, after all. And then there's the matter of security clearances for certain areas of information. Can't just go printing all of the dirty doings behind the scenes, can we?"

"Well," I said, "of course not. But they told me not to worry. They'll run my article through Security and censor anything that seems unseemly before sending it out." Then I told him to tell me about the project as if I didn't already have the background materials filed away in my cubicle downstairs.

"Why don't we start with a little demonstration," he suggested, handing me a set of gloves, booties, smock, and paper hat. "Put it all on: it's still a grubby room but we do use some Clean Room technologies to keep surface and airborne contaminants down."

I looked around the room trying not to fall over while I slipped the paper coverings over my shoes. "Very impressive."

"Impressive? Hah! This is just the tip of the iceberg. The

terminals and the sequencers are connected to other labs and a series of Crays in the basement. But this is where you see magic performed. Remember the Human Genome project a few years back?"

I nodded, adjusting the cap over my hair.

"BioWeb completed the sequencing seven years before the others. You didn't read about it because it was all hush-hush government business."

"Amazing," I murmured.

"Not really," he said dismissively. "We had a head start, better equipment, faster computers, and an unlimited budget. Let me show you something that's really amazing." Landon opened a cabinet and retrieved a foil strip. Opening the foil revealed a plastic swablike apparatus. "Do you mind working up a little spit?"

"You're going to run my DNA?"

"I'll do better than that, Mr. Haim: I'm going to run your family tree. Open wide."

I almost refused. Signing the mortuary's guest book had been a serious security blunder. Giving out DNA samples was better than sending the FBI my fingerprints. But I had come here to see what BioWeb had to offer in decrypting my unique condition. I wasn't going to get very far if I suddenly got shy about running tests. I opened wide and Landon took a saliva sample with some mouth scrapings.

"Now forget everything you've seen about gene sequencers," he said, crossing the room and selecting a series of buttons on one of the cabinets, "they are sooo last millennium." A panel slid up and he placed the swab in a tray and pressed another series of buttons. The tray retracted and the door slid shut.

"Over here, now." He led me to a series of monitors and activated two of them. "In a moment we'll have your genetic profile sequenced and catalogued." As he spoke, the first monitor began to fill with numbers and strings of code.

"Damn, that's impressive!" I said, meaning it this time.

"No, it's just fast. Faster than anything else the rest of the world has right now. What's impressive is what happens next."

The second monitor began to run a list of names and dates. There were locations mixed in and cross-referencing codes as well.

"What is it doing now?'

"Who has the most complete genealogical library in the world?" he counter questioned.

"That's easy," I said, "the Mormons."

He shook his head. "The government does. The Mormons don't realize it but their Salt Lake City data banks have been tapped for years and we have everything that they have and then some."

I stared at him. "You're stealing data from the Mormons?"

"No. A certain agency of the United States government steals data from the Mormons. And not just the Mormons, I might add. And then a member of that agency makes the data available to us. To which we add genetic information to as many listings as we can."

"You're telling me you're building a genetic database on American citizens?"

"No," he said. "We're building a database on the human race. Past and present, with an eye to the future. And we're not using the information to harm anyone. It's purely for research."

I almost said: "That's purely bullshit." If the government was involved in gathering genetic information on people it was bound to be misused, no matter the original motive. But I kept my mouth shut: I wasn't going to maintain a low profile by arguing with the BioWeb staff and I certainly wasn't going to change corporate policy on this visit. "I still don't see how it's possible," I said grudgingly. "Even if you could get a sample from everyone alive today, you couldn't do profiles on people who've already died."

"Why not? It's been publicly done on the corpses of recent murder victims and on remains as old as forty-thousand-year-old mummies."

"But the logistics—"

"Of exhuming every grave in every cemetery in the country?" He nodded. "Unlimited court orders and an army of backhoes wouldn't make The Project practical in anyone's lifetime. Fortunately, there are shortcuts."

"Shortcuts?"

"A little EPA Trojan horse legislation about thirty years ago. Required testing for cemetery groundwater contamination. Over the years we've refined the design but the original concept is pretty much the same: a mini core-sampling auger that drills down four to eight feet and collects samples at the appropriate depth." He grinned. "Oops! If anyone actually exhumes a coffin and discov-ers a hole, well, that's fairly rare and—hey—accidents do happen, you know. One man with one of our present rigs can sample ten bronze or steel caskets in an hour, upwards of thirty if they're the older wooden models.

"Here, let me show you one of the latest shipments." He got up and walked to the back of the room. He pressed a button and the rear wall slid open like something from an old Matt Helm movie.

Behind the sliding panel were stacked racks of finger-sized glass vials, maybe three or four hundred in all. "I'll have to run these babies through the sequencer and database before sending them down to the vault. Of course, we can only store about fifty thousand of these samplings on site. Every month they move several hundred lots from the vault to a gargantuan storage facility back east."

"You were sampling DNA before it was anywhere near decoded?" I asked.

He shrugged. "The Powers That Be knew it would just be a matter of time. They wanted to be ready when—" He stopped and gave me another look. "How much are you actually cleared for?"

"I'm *cleared*," I said. With a little, reassuring push. "I'm just playing Devil's Advocate for the purpose of story perspective. How complete is your database?"

"Depends. There are millions, if not billions, of samples yet to be collected. But the database is actually functional thanks to a pattern-sequencing system that analyzes DNA patterns in genea-logical cascades and can fill in the gaps with ninety-two-percent accuracy."

I waved my hands. "Wait a minute, wait a minute! Let me get this straight. You're saying that you've got software that takes the genetic profiles already in the database and—and uses those known patterns to figure out what's not been catalogued? I mean, it guesses what the missing samples should look like?"

He puffed up a little and an expression of annoyance flickered across his ruddy features. "I would hardly call data extrapolation 'guessing'! Most of the existing computer programs run statisti-cal models based on samplings from one region of each DNA sample—the mitochondrial DNA that is passed from the mother to subsequent generations, for example. Even the GEODIS program developed by Templeton only analyzes DNA from ten locations in each genetic sample for biological population studies.

"Our program, on the other hand, actually studies twenty-two different sites per sampling. We will continue to gather DNA samples to verify and complete the existing gaps, but the database can extrapolate variations in DNA patterns based on earlier and later configurations within a genealogical line. For example, your DNA has already been decoded and the computers are now running your sequences for matches with other related patterns in the database. In a few minutes we should be able to look at your family tree, going back at least twenty generations."

The computer beeped and the monitors froze their displays.

"Here we go. This is you. Your genetic map and the significant tags." He frowned as he studied the monitor. "Without running any of the details, I must say that your overall pattern looks a little unusual." He tapped a sequence of keys. "You might want to come back during the day and have Dr. Coane look over your tags in detail—that's not my area. But we can take a look at your Six-factor."

"Six-factor?"

"Yeah, genealogically speaking, everyone's just six generations away from being related to Kevin Bacon." He rewarded himself with a hearty laugh.

Then he stopped.

He stared at the screen and his eyes lit up. A huge smile bloomed across his face.

I looked and saw one of my deepest nightmares come true.

I slipped out of the Gen/GEN lab nearly a half-hour later. I might have finished up in ten minutes but I wanted to make sure my samples were thoroughly destroyed and my records were thoroughly purged from the database—not just deleted but scrubbed off the hard drives and any backup sectors on networked machines.

The fact that Spyder Langdon knew who my forebears were was a warning shot across my bow. That he found my lineage significant had tripped every alarm wire in my head and body. His reluctance to assist me in purging the lab of my samples and the computer files of any reference to my deoxyribonucleic acid structures—even under psychic duress—necessitated some serious "pushing." More like extreme psychic shoving and shaking and pummeling. When it came to forgetting that we had even met, I found it necessary to be "insistent."

Maybe a little too much so: I left him sitting at a blank monitor, an even blanker expression in his eyes, and a dribble of spittle linking his chin and the spacebar on the keyboard.

If I was lucky he would remember nothing of our meeting this night.

If he was lucky he might remember something of the past year.

I was now monster enough that I could bet more on myself than on him.

It took another hour to find the other room I was looking for.

I had sensed it shortly after entering the BioWeb complex. A preternatural heaviness pervaded the air trapped inside the building. It was something more than the stink of disinfectant and the vague vapors of distant reagents circulating through the whispering vents and air returns. It was like there was a little more darkness hiding around the edges of the track lighting and between the shimmer of fluorescent tubes. Now, away from the distraction of other people, the presence of Something Else became more palpable, the sense of oppression more tangible.

I tried to focus on sensing an increase or decrease in the area of effect as I moved through the building. It was as if the whole complex was lightly saturated with a mild toxin but removed from the source. I was about to give up when I discovered a second set of stairs leading toward the basement. I had checked the basement level early on. If you're going to hide something diabolical or store something unmentionable, basements are "high" on the list of dark, out-of-the-way places for nefarious nooks and crannies.

The BioWeb basement level, however, housed nothing but the physical plant for the complex: boilers, furnaces, heat exchangers, generators, transformers, and miles and miles of pipes and conduits. Two service elevators and a back stairwell accessed it.

Except I had just stumbled across a second set of stairs leading down from the ground floor and there had been only one set of stairs when I had walked through the basement about forty minutes before.

So where did this one go?

One way to find out. I started down the stairs.

I went down and down.

And down again.

Past the level of the basement and another turn and a flight down.

And a dead end.

The stairs ended in a cubicle-sized landing with no visible exits. Overhead a single red lightbulb glowed angrily, enmeshed in a steel cage. The far wall was also colored red, with an elaborate green pictogram at its center. The two-foot by one-foot image looked three-dimensional. I walked up to the design and grasped it with my hands. It was a metal sculpture, an ornate grillwork that stood away from the wall by an inch or so.

The design was familiar. I vaguely remembered seeing iron grillwork very similar to it somewhere down in the French Quarter during my last visit to New Orleans. I considered the pair of idealized swords that flanked the grid of rectangles criss-crossed into interlocking triangles with curlicues and lightning bolts and hammers and stylized flames.

I had seen this pattern more recently. . . .

In a book somewhere.

And the color red was linked to it somehow.

"Swords . . ." I murmured, " . . . lightning . . . hammers . . ." Hammers?

Hammers—metal—the forge.

"Vodoun," I whispered. "A symbol—no—a *vèvè* of the Loa." But which one? Something clicked in the back of my mind. "The Googoo Battleaxe," I chuckled, butchering the pronunciation again. I cleared my throat and said it correctly this time: "The Ogou clan. Ogou Bhathalah, the Loa of alchemy. Ogou Ferraille, the Loa of the sword, iron and metals. Ogou Shango and Ogou Tonnerre, the Loa of lightning and thunder."

As I spoke the name of the Loa, something clicked again, only this time it came from behind the wall. Voice activation and password recognition security: voodoo gone high-tech. I pushed against the metal grill and the wall swung back on silent hinges.

The darkness beyond wasn't complete. A series of candles flickered in recessed alcoves providing a dim pathway into the unknown. The sense of oppressiveness that had infused the air upstairs now made breathing seem difficult.

On more than one occasion I'd remarked that Mama Cséjthe didn't raise no dummy. But she wouldn't hesitate to say that her clever baby boy could still make some bonehead decisions from time to time. Example: I stepped forward into the near darkness.

The wall swung shut behind me.

Part of it made immediate sense, I reasoned, as I moved slowly between the parallel rows of flickering points of light. The Ogou clan of Vodoun spirits was supposed to manifest in matters of war and alchemy. If they were tied to BioWeb's viral and genetics research, then the alchemy connection was apparent.

But what about war?

Mama Samm had said something about the fifth seal and the end of the world. The Book of Revelation tied the opening of that seal to the unleashing of great plagues that would devastate the earth. But those Biblical end time plagues were associated with the appearance of the Whore of Babylon, not some Johnny-come-lately third-world religion like Vodoun.

Voodoo was a mangled meld of African tribal spirit worship overlaid on a distorted template of Catholicism. It utilized a doubling approach to its principal gods, matching each Loa with a Christian saint, bestowing a dual identity of sorts.

So, maybe the Whore of Babylon had an "altar" ego among the Loa.

Maybe the Whore of Babylon—or Lilith—was also Marinette Bois-Chèche.

And if "magick" was involved, it might explain the darkness that Jenny had described or the odd sensation that had made my skin crawl since walking through the front door.

I looked around. The candles lining the walls were red. Red was the primary color of the Ogou pantheon, so that fit. But the Ogou clan wasn't typically known for significant acts of evil. And their sacred spaces were, as a general rule, located out of doors. Not underground, deep beneath a high-tech biological research facility.

The "aspect" or manifestation of the evil Marinette, however, would alter everything, corrupting even the pure motives of scientific research.

Up ahead, the darkness was starting to fade in patches. Glimmering eyes grew in intensity, became more candle flames. The pathway opened up into a larger area. A voodoo temple space: the *hounfort*.

My eyes were adjusting to the dimmer light sources and I could make out more details, now. I was entering the *peristil* or dancing area for the Vodoun ceremonies. The floor was hardened dirt and, at its center, was a great pole extending from the floor to the ceiling: the *poteau mitan*. Beyond lay the *djevo* or altar room, glowing like a great, rectangular ruby against a larger dim backdrop.

I moved toward the altar, a large table draped with a black cloth and decked out with a profusion of objects. There were bottles covered with colored sequins and glass beads. And here was a small bottle, nearly a match for the finger-sized glass vials in the Gen/GEN lab, but marked as containing a Zombi-astral—a spirit from a corpse kept in a glass container like a hoodoo battery for certain spells.

For most people the word "zombie" conjures up the Hollywood image of a corpse shuffling about like a retarded sleepwalker. That or the stage persona of White Zombie front man, Rob Cummings. But while I had seen more than my share of the walking dead recently, they didn't actually fit the true voodoo zombie profile.

The walking "dead" documented as parts of Petro and Congo rites were actually living people, not reanimated stiffs. They were the result of a bokor or sorcerer lobotomizing the victim's personality and higher brain functions through hypnosis, autosuggestion, and a complex pharmacopoeia that included fish, frogs, and ferns.

The puffer fish (*Sphoeroides testudineus, S. spengleri*), the porcupine fish (*Diodon hystrix*), and the balloon fish (*D. holacanthus*) have all been cited as ingredients from a variety of sources, but the most likely culprit is the Fugu species whose skin, liver, intestines, and ovaries are overripe with a neurotoxin called tetrodotoxin. This particular neurotoxin is not only a hundred times more deadly than strychnine, but a single puffer has enough joy juice to wipe out a roomful of people. The Japanese consider Fugu sashimi an exquisite delicacy that, properly prepared, will cause one's lips to tingle, one's senses to soar, and produces a pleasant near-death experience for the adventurous gourmand. Improperly prepared, you are either unpleasantly dead in short order or paralyzed for life—however long and equally unpleasant that may be.

You might remember that this is a delicacy to the culture that also produced seppuku and the kamikaze. For those not sufficiently put off by the mortality rate of Fugu fans there's a little death dish called *chiri* that specially licensed chefs will prepare for those diners who would rather "play chicken" than eat it. But I digress.

Moving down the zombie recipe list, you can go from Fugu to Bufo: the toxic glands of the toad, *Bufo marinus*. Down in Colombia, the native Indians discovered that toasting these toads over a fire produced a yellow liquid that dripped from the carcass: curare. Once they figured out that arrows and darts dipped in frog fondue were fatal no matter where the victim was hit, precision marksmanship went right out the window. In small amounts, the Bufo toxin would prevent oxygen from entering the bloodstream and cause massive heart failure. In smaller amounts, it could paralyze without killing but the horrific hallucinations that it produced would make you wish for death anyway.

Then there were plants like Albizzia and *Datura stramonium*, known in Haiti as the zombie's cucumber and in North America as jimsonweed. Producing a topically active neurotransmitter-blocking drug, the plant could induce disorientation, hallucinations, amnesia, coma, convulsions, and death. It had a long history of "curing" marital infidelity in Africa. "Permanently" in most cases.

The bokor had their own recipes for mixing such biotoxins along with ground spiders, powdered human bone, colored clays, lemons, and various leaves and branches of other plants such as Jamaican dumb cane (*Dieffenbachia seguine*) that paralyzed the mouth, throat, and vocal cords.

But I continue to digress.

The only truly "dead" zombies in Vodoun were the zombi astrals, being the spirit—or "ti-bon-ange"—of a dead person caught and kept in a bottle for medicinal or healing purposes. Think of it as something akin to a psychic battery. Since the soul is eternal, it keeps going and going and going. . . .

I wondered what spell this little bottled soul was running.

Around it upon the altar were small statues and porcelain dolls encompassed about with lengths of chain and cages of wire. Colorfully framed photos and drawings were propped up against machetes and knives and axe heads. Kongo packets, shredded palm leaves, and small mirrors were scattered here and there. A series of defaced medallions bound a clutch of kewpie dolls that had bead-headed pins stuck into their arms, legs, eyes, ears, torsos—each seeming to have its own, distinct pattern of torment. Bowls containing offerings—salt, cayenne peppers, Tabasco sauce, rum, palm oil and palm wine, cigars, roasted yams, and green plantains—formed a border around the table's edges. One bowl held blood, a deep maroon shading toward black as it coagulated. An ancient glass retort bubbled over an invisible flame while a dozen black candles and another half-dozen red candles provided eighteen dancing tears of shimmering light, casting fantastic shadows upon the red satin drapes that covered the back and side walls of the *djevo*.

At the center of the altar, wrapped in a whorl of scarlet silk, was a realistic drawing of a nude woman performing an obscene act with a crucifix—my money was on it being a representation of the vile Marinette Bois-Chèche. Her face was turned away so that her features were obscured. And the crimson cloth it nested in was a dress.

Perhaps *The* Dress.

The one that the Whore of Babylon would put on when the sun turned black, the moon turned to blood, and the stars began to fall like rain.

But that wasn't what caused my knees to go all rubbery and hungry motes of darkness to gather at the edges of my vision. Two photographs were displayed across from each other, the left one elevated to be ascendant, and the one on the right positioned upside-down and in descendant mode. A photo of a gray man wearing a gray suit held no special significance other than the fact that someone had drawn a military helmet over his head and medals on his chest with a ballpoint pen. On the other side was an inverted wedding photo that had been torn in half, lengthways, and then scotch-taped back together.

A very familiar wedding picture.

The same ballpoint pen used on the other photograph had blacked out Jenny's eyes and mouth and drawn fangs that protruded cartoon like from my lips. An "X" was deeply marked into the center of my chest.

A blackness rose up inside me and I leaned against the table, the stink of shriveled blood rising toward my face like foul incense.

What was I supposed to do? I was just one man!

Something had stirred the dead to leave their graves and seek me out by night. Something was mounting a psychic attack that affected my perceptions in the form of the ghost of my dead wife. Vodoun magicks were being invoked in the name of the Loa who ruled the realms of alchemy, the forge, and the military. The government—or some "aspect" of the government—was making a list and checking it twice. No doubts in my mind whether it was naughty or nice.

End of the world prophecies and an ancient demoness who was the mother of monsters.

In retrospect, the fact that vampire enforcers were in town and Erzsébet Báthory was involved seemed a minor annoyance: we were already at Defcon Four.

Except . . .

Oh, God.

If Marinette Bois-Chèche could be a manifestation of the Whore of Babylon . . .

Then why not my great, great-times-great grandmother, Erzsébet-the-Hun?

How could I thwart the schemes of an ancient vampire who commanded the undead might of the entire East Coast and God knew what biotoxic witches brews in this high-tech chamber of horrors? Even Dracula had gone to ground for fear of her power. And I knew Pagelovitch wouldn't risk the lives—or unlives—of his enclave over some fortune-teller's half-baked prediction or my questionable, fevered dreams.

It was *way* past time to leave town.

But where could I go if Erzsébet Bois-Chèche ended up destroying the world?

I thought about demolishing the altar, but they would only put up another one. And know that someone had penetrated security. I pushed away from the table and turned to leave.

Then turned back.

Screw the element of surprise—it was an illusion of security that I no longer had! I grabbed all three pictures and tucked them into my shirt pocket. As I did, I felt the little gris-gris packet that Mama Samm had given me. *Ti-bon-ange.* I reached for a candle but hesitated as sounds reached my ears from the candlelit hallway. I dove beneath the altar.

Moments later two men and three women entered the *peristil*, leading a goat. Crouching under the table, I could see the goat better than I could see the people. The women wore loose sack dresses and were barefoot and barelegged. The men wore loose shirts and pants with the legs cut off at mid calf. They were barefoot as well.

Imports, I guessed; not locals. While Vodoun doesn't hang out a shingle or erect well-lit signs like most churches, they tend to be known within certain circles in their neighborhood. I had checked into those circles during my past half-year of residency and hadn't heard a thing about this sort of going on. Báthory probably recruited them in New Orleans. Or maybe even Haiti. This was no Entertain-the-Tourists shtick so E.B. probably spared no expense in acquiring the Real Deal rather than apprentice wannabes.

The goat was tethered to the great post while one of the men squatted at the outer edge of the dance floor and began beating a drum. I was no expert but I had done enough research to recognize that someone was setting up to raise a *Baka*, a possessive spirit. Not a ritual for the squeamish or faint of heart under the best of circumstances.

All things considered, these were not the best of circumstances.

The women began to dance, bare feet shuffling along the packed earthen floor. They would be the *mambos* or *hounsis*. The men— they would be *hougans*—began to chant.

The language wasn't a French variant like some of the invocations I had run across in my research. It was more likely some African dialect like Yoruban, so I couldn't even take a wild guess here.

I changed my mind, watching the *hougan* as he poured a pattern of cornmeal and salt onto the dance floor, a rust-stained machete at his side. This one was more likely a sorcerer—a *bokor* or *caplata*. This was more than *Rada* or even *Petro* worship. With Marinette Bois-Chèche invoked and what appeared to be the pending sacrifice of a black goat we were seriously into the realm of "Left-handed Voodoo," probably a variant of the *Bizango* or even the *Cochon Gris*. Although the Ogou pantheon weighted heavily toward the realms of power and military might, it would not evoke such a dark and loathsome aspect unless black magic and sorcery were invoked at its core.

Lucky me: I had a front-row seat for the next session of Let's Open The Gates Of Darkness And See What Comes Out.

As the chanting grew louder and more insistent, the room suddenly grew cold and a gust of wind came out of nowhere, causing the candle flames to gutter like terrified spirits.

Maybe it was nothing more than the air conditioner cutting on . . .

A greater core of darkness began to unfold in the twilight at the room's center.

Who was I kidding? The only way this was going to get any worse was to add vampires to the mix. As the *bokor* approached the goat with a machete and a bowl, the wind intensified, extinguishing the candles as neatly as if someone had flipped a light switch.

My aborted vision shifted over into the infrared spectrum and I orientated on the red-and-yellow blob that represented the goat's body heat.

That was it.

I looked around the rest of the room and only saw darkness. With a greater stain of darkness growing toward the goat like a hungry thing. There were no heat signatures for the *bokor*, the *hougan* or the *mambos*. Belatedly I realized that someone *had* added vampires to the mix: voodoo for the undead!

Give me that old time religion . . .

Once the goat was dead and started to cool, my reduced-heat signature would become more noticeable in the darkness. And even if I remained hidden throughout this morbid and messy mass, there was still a time factor: if I was trapped down here for too much longer, I wouldn't have enough time to get back home before sunrise.

I didn't fancy spending another twelve-plus hours on the premises.

The chanting was extremely loud and strident now so it covered the sounds of the new arrivals. Gradually I became aware of a new voice, chanting in counterpoint.

Whereas the Vodoun invocation was in an unknown tongue, the new voice was uttering pronouncements in a very different language. I couldn't distinguish more than a word or three: it was Greek to me—in the most literal sense.

Another light source entered the room. Or two, actually. One was shaped like the outline of a man, shimmering like a chromatic rainbow in an oil slick, the black silhouette of a person at its center. The other was a giant sculpture of pale blue radiance, like a glow-in-the-dark plaster statue of a saint. Only this statue was larger than a man and appeared to duck its head as it entered the room.

The original chanting died away.

The goat bleated.

Someone took a flash picture and the room was rocked with a blast of light and heat that flung me against the back wall of the *djevo* and treated me to a planetarium show behind my fluttering eyelids.

I awoke to the smell of smoke.

I couldn't have been out for more than a minute or two, but the red drapes surrounding the altar were already shading to orange and yellow as tendrils of flame nibbled at their edges. I crawled out from under the table and saw in the growing glow of the flames that I was alone.

The goat was gone, rope and all. Five mounds of ash, one of them partially flattened by a toppled drum, marked the former positions of the Vodoun congregants. The elements adorning the altar had been swept to the floor and scattered, the kewpie dolls unfettered and unpinned.

So much for keeping the security breach hush-hush.

I patted my shirt pocket as I staggered down the corridor. I still had the pictures. Maybe destroying the altar wasn't such a bad idea after all. As I memory-wiped Reginald on the way out, I gave some consideration to reexamining my spiritual life. Maybe it was time to get religion.

Before religion got me.

Chapter Eleven

My wife was just as obedient in death as she had been in life: when I returned to the car she wasn't there.

Something else was: the odor settled over me as soon as I closed the door and buckled on my shoulder harness. It smelled of wet leaves and musty attics—a far cry from the rotted perfume of my three previous supplicants. I looked in the rearview mirror but the backseat appeared to be empty.

A wispy voice spoke behind me: "You're him, ain'tcha? That Baron fella?"

I swallowed. It didn't help. "Actually, I'm not."

A pair of ancient eyes appeared at the top of my seat in the mirror: he was behind me, crouching on the floor. "Sure you are. That old juju woman says you are. And you got the Shine. I kin see it myself." A pair of eyes and a nose was all I could see without turning around. A saggy, billed woolen cap of faded blue covered the top of his head.

A soldier's cap.

A Union soldier's cap.

Circa middle 1800s.

"She says you got some neezia or sumpin."

I sighed. "What can I do for you, son?"

"The captain sends his regards and wants to know what you intend to do about the incursion of the enemy."

I was tired and my skin was starting to itch and burn again. I closed my eyes and pinched the bridge of my nose. "Which ones?"

"Why—all of 'em, I guess. Them long-tooths, the carpetbaggers, the gray men."

"Carpetbaggers?" I turned around—or tried but found myself hampered by the shoulder harness. "You don't talk like a Yankee soldier, boy."

"Guess I ain't no Yankee soldier no more." His voice was soft and sad, a whispery, ghostlike sound less real than the pale flesh crouching behind me. "We're all not what we were anymore."

"You-all being . . . who?"

"Twenty-third Infantry down out of Iowa and a bunch of Johnny Rebs from Colonel Harrison's Fortieth Louisiana Cavalry. We mixed it up here in the winter of—" he paused as if searching through tattered memories, "—'63. Cut each other up pretty good. Then somebody up and shot that nigra woman. Probably an accident. Nobody knows which side and it don't matter. She cursed both sides afore she died and pinned our souls here in the swamp where we fell."

"Here?" I asked, looking over the BioWeb complex of buildings.

"They drained the swamps 'bout near fifty year ago. Found some of us then and moved those remains to the local cemeteries and museum. Dug some more of us up about five year back when they built this abomination. Dug up some dragon bones, too."

"Dragon bones?"

"Captain calls it a fossil. Says it died milyuns a' years ago so its bones have turned to rock. They never tol' nobody, they just put it back alongst with those of us they found. Why would they do thet? Deny a soldier his release and final ticket home?"

I shook my head. "There are laws that would have guaranteed your final interment and rest, soldier. But the people who built this place are a lawless band. They only use the laws that will serve their purposes and ignore the rest. It was more important to them to finish construction on schedule than to honor the dead."

I saw him nod in the rearview mirror. "So other'n that little bit of excitement, the rest of us been lyin' under the silt and clay just talkin' amongst ourselves these past hundert-and-fifty-some year, figurin' out what's what and what's not.

"And lissenin' to the plans of the gray men," he added with some heat. "It ain't right!"

"The Confederates?"

"Naw, we all the same now: dead men, soldiers, patriots. This is as much my land as theirs now and we all salute the same flag. Hell, we been together so long we even talk the same. The captain wore the gray but I take my orders from him now as he's the ranking officer on post. He's the one what sent me as I'm the most presentable so far."

"But you said 'the gray men.'"

"The enemy. They still breathe but they souls is all dead and gray inside. They the enemy. They allied themselves with the long-tooths and now they plot the deaths of millions. The gray men would destroy everything we've shed our blood for."

"The Civil War?"

"All of 'em! Revolutionary, 1812, 'Tween the States, WW One and Two . . ."

I unfastened my shoulder harness. "Tell me about the gray men. What are their plans?"

There was a distant ululation. "Cock's crow: I caint stay. Come back tamorrow night and we'll meet agin."

"I don't know that I'll be able—"

"There'll be a cotillion. Come out the west side and walk down to the pond. The captain will meet with you there."

The door opened and the dome light revealed a human caricature that was half flesh, half denuded bone, wrapped in rags. It flopped out and slammed the door shut behind it. As it galloped across the parking lot, flapping like laundry on a line in a high wind, I could only make out thin sticks where fleshed-out arms and legs should be.

No one was home when I returned: no ghostly wife, no Deirdre, no vampire watchdogs. If the dead had come looking for me, they had long since left as the sky was starting to lighten in the east. Maybe they didn't care for the weather. Even though the sky was relatively clear, a cold front had moved in during the night dropping the temperature fifteen to twenty degrees.

I reset the alarm system, then turned it off so Deirdre wouldn't trigger it when she returned. Then I wandered back into my study before retiring for the morning.

The bookshelves had been sampled, the texts and tomes still grouped by subject but slightly out of the order I normally kept them in. Over on the desk, a yellow legal pad was skewed between the computer and a couple of unshelved books. I picked it up and considered Deirdre's neat notations as I wandered back into the kitchen and opened the refrigerator.

There should have been three or four blood packs left over from the box I had brought home last month. I usually needed a single bag every week to ten days to stop my stomach from cannibalizing itself. In a pinch, I could go without—for how long? The last time I had quit, cold turkey, I had managed to last two and a half weeks while going through the most agonizing versions of the Two-Stage process I had ever experienced.

Stage One: you're afraid you're going to die.

Stage Two: you're afraid you're *not* going to die.

While I had serious reservations about getting the crimson monkey off my back I was determined to keep my need in check. Except for periods of stress or injury, I'd been able to limit my intake of hemoglobin on a consistent basis.

Until now.

Still, there should have been enough O-positive in the fridge to see me through a couple of weeks in the best of times, a couple of days during the worst.

But there was nothing. And I wasn't sure I could last until sundown.

I picked up a shrink-wrapped Styrofoam tray of raw hamburger and popped the plastic at the corner. Tilted and sipped the watery run-off. Eewwww.

Disgusting.

I parted the curtains and peered out the kitchen window. I could see the bayou in the ambient, predawn light, its black waters restive against the gray bank of grass at the end of my backyard. I calculated the time it would take to drive to the blood bank, use my passkey to boost another carton, and return home. I could do it without risking my life but the morning sun would likely negate any good a fresh pack of blood might provide.

Suck it up, Cséjthe, I told myself. *You can last another day.*

Under normal circumstances, I reminded myself, starting up the stairs. But even adjusting for spending the past year and a half in the Outer Limits, there was nothing "normal" about the past few days of my unlife.

Take the cast of characters that had joined my one-man traveling show of late.

Miguel de Cervantes wrote: "Tell me what company thou keepst, and I'll tell thee what thou art." I wondered what Mike would make of my ongoing associations with vampires, corpses, and a ghost.

Well, "maybe" on the ghost.

Maybe I could scratch ghost/wife off my dramatis personae.

Maybe along with werewolf/girlfriend.

Samuel Johnson advised that a man "should keep his friendships in constant repair" and wrote that "true happiness consists not in the multitude of friends, but in their worth and choice."

Obviously, I needed a lot of work on both counts.

Like the guy in that Barry Manilow song, I was "standing at the end of a long, lonely road" and was "waiting for some new friends to come . . ."

It suddenly occurred to me that if I was identifying with Manilow songs it was long past time to pull the plug.

I kicked my shoes off and flopped on the bed. The names on Deirdre's legal pad reminded me that I could be surrounded by far worse than I had right now.

Erzsébet Báthory had acquired a jolly group of sadists and psychopaths in her unholy hobbies. With friends like hers, the dead and the undead didn't seem like such a great social burden.

After the influence of some of her bent and twisted relatives at an early age, there was her old nurse, Iloona Joo—referred to as "Helena Jo" in some texts. She seemed to be involved in Erzsébet's practice of the dark arts and her sadistic inclinations early on.

Dorthea Szentes, an old maid who claimed to be a practicing witch, instructed her in the disciplines of black magic. While Dorthea—affectionately called "Dorka"—didn't start out teaching torture as a technique of witchcraft, she eventually became an enthusiastic participant.

Erzsébet had enjoyed a succession of lovers from a young age, and marriage to Count Ferencz Nádasdy, the "Black Hero of Hungary," did not hamper her sexual appetites for variety as he spent a great deal of time away from home on military campaigns.

Two of her paramours are worthy of note. The first was an unnamed stranger, described by contemporary accounts as being slim, pale, and possessing sharp teeth. The villagers took him for a vampire. Both Erzsébet and her mysterious lover disappeared for some time. She eventually reappeared. He did not.

Thus gossip—and probably nothing more than that—linked the Dracula and Báthory clans again, albeit briefly.

Her other notorious liaison was with her maid, Anna Darvula, reputed to be "one of the most active sadists in Erzsébet's entourage." A stroke eventually left Darvula blind and severely incapacitated, so she had to pass the torch (as it were) to the other perverts in Castle Cséjthe. This list included the dwarf majordomo, Johannes Ujvary, also called Thorko and referred to as Ficzko (which means "lad" in Hungarian) in Erzsébet's journals, a drunken peasant woman named Kardoska who helped obtain girls for the countess' sadistic pleasures, and Katarina Beneczky, about whom little is known other than the fact that she was the only one found "innocent" in the subsequent trials and released.

Erzsi Majorova almost escaped punishment, as well. She came into the story after Anna Darvula was forced into retirement and was said to be responsible for Erzsébet's eventual downfall by pushing the "noble blood is more potent than peasant blood" theory. She wasn't around for the first trial but they eventually caught up with her and she was beheaded after a second trial.

Thorko was beheaded, too. Extra precautions were taken: the sword used in the beheading was "blessed," the blood was drained from his body, and then his body was burned along with the bodies of his cohorts.

Iloona Joo and Dorthea Szentes were given even harsher treatment. Both were sentenced to having all the fingers on their hands—which had "dipped in the blood of Christians"—torn out, one by one, by the public executioner with a pair of red-hot pincers. After that was accomplished, their bodies were to be thrown alive on the fire.

Mercifully (if that word should even be applied here) the old nurse fainted after only four fingers were extracted. She was thrown unconscious into the fire. Likewise Dorthea Szentes, all fingers intact, who had fainted in the presence of Iloona Joo's torture. Justice gone soft, I suppose.

Anna Darvula died well before the trial so her punishment was doubtless taken to a higher court.

One hoped, anyway.

The concepts of justice, good, and even God were starting to dim in my mind like fading memories of playing in the sun. Was it because the virus was starting to color my thinking? Or was I finally more cognizant of the greater darkness that surrounds us all?

There are dreams that come with all the clarity of being a dream but that does not make them less terrible.

I walk into the castle's courtyard and believe the dream itself to be as monochrome as the old photographs in the trunks in my grandfather's attic. The walls and outbuildings, the keep, and especially the great, brooding tower are all constructed of black stone, quarried from the Carpathian mountains that encroach on the land like dark dreams made manifest. The sky is nearly as black; dark, swollen clouds block the weak winter sun and are dense with the wanton power of a gathering storm.

The architecture is harsh and brutal; the icy winds that blast down the mountain passes, even more so. Only the gentle slopes of drifting snow add any touch of softness to the iron-edged tableau.

The naked girl stumbles, falling to her hands and knees, sinking up to her elbows and haunches in the frigid bank of whiteness. Her skin, as white as the snow she wallows through, is marked by purple splotches of bruise, mauve stripes of whip marks and cuttings, brick-red punctures that weep scarlet tears: the first hint of color in the black and white and gray landscape. She struggles to her feet and I see her clearly now: young and yet old before her time, her malnourished and abused body could be fifteen or nineteen.

It will never be twenty.

The dwarf cracks a short whip behind her, driving her forward and across the courtyard. Toward the great, black iron cauldron.

An hour ago the fire beneath it had burned brightly, the water within bubbled merrily. Now the fire is banked, only a wisp of smoke suggests its previous existence; the water inside is already slushy with ice.

Two women move to the cauldron and dip buckets into its stew of water and ice. Like the dwarf, they are well wrapped against the piercing cold.

Their prey can only shield herself with blistered hands.

The women step forward and fling the contents of their pails as the girl tries to change direction. The water breaks over her like a wave, plastering her dark hair against her shockingly pale skin, sluicing her wounds so that they weep pink, washing away the last vestiges of warmth from her goose-dimpled flesh. She slips and falls upon her back, disappearing in the deep snow. She does not get up and the women turn back to the cauldron.

"This unnecessary cruelty will be your undoing, Betya," says a familiar voice.

I turn my face up to a window in the great tower. Even though they are hundreds of feet away, I can hear them over the howl of the winter wind as if I stand in the chamber, beside them.

"You are a fine one to lecture me, Old Dragon. Your atrocities were the excesses of legend a hundred years ago and time has done nothing to redeem your reputation."

"My so-called 'atrocities' were acts of war. Against superior forces. If I had not struck terror in the hearts of my enemies, Wallachia would have been overrun."

She dismisses his argument with a shrug. "Did any of it really matter? The Turks are everywhere, now. I barely see my husband because he is always off fighting the Ottomans. *On the battlefield,*" she adds archly. "I seem to recall certain events that were closer to home. Ambassadors at court and the use of nails, the poor locked up in burning buildings, forced cannibalism—"

"One's enemies are not confined to the battlefields, Betya."

"I know. Oft they can be found in the bedroom," she says with a red smile.

Down below, the two women raise the naked girl to her feet. A third woman joins them and helps the dwarf douse the pale, limp form with more buckets of water.

"In *your* bedroom, my dear, everyone is the enemy."

"Not so, dearest Vladimir. Unlike you, I do not fear those I take to my bed. I love them."

"To death," he agrees. "But they fear and hate you so that makes you the enemy. It makes your own bed a battleground."

"Oh please! You seduce your lovers with mind control and pretend they come to you of their own free will. You are such a poseur!"

"I do not torture them, Betya. I do not make new enemies when there is no need. As *voivode,* I served a higher cause than my own vanity. What do such cruelties serve here?"

The women release the girl and she now stands unsupported, her white flesh touched with a translucent blue sheen. The water has formed a transparent cast over her features, the mouth frozen open in a silent scream, the eyes dark and empty like piss holes in the snow, the wounds like jeweled adornments of rubies and tourmaline. An ice sculpture of torment frozen in time.

"I serve The Darkness inside me, my prince. I must feed it or it will surely devour me. As it would devour all of my bloodline. We are bound to its dark service."

"You serve the witch, Betya. She will betray you. She will betray you all."

The countess laughs. "Does she frighten you, my lord? You of all people?"

"You should kill her," he growls, "before she can make her power over you complete!"

I turn away and stumble into the extended arms of another young woman, her face a mask of frozen blood, her embrace the iron bands of winter. Cold limbs leech the warmth from my sides and I fall against the ice shelf of her bosom. I try to push away but my hands can't find purchase on the downhill slopes of shoulder and hip. I twist away and am drenched with another bucketful of icy water . . .

. . . icy sweat. I pulled at a cold arm and disentangled myself from her flaccid embrace.

Deirdre stirred and murmured something, lost in her own crimson dreams. I slid from my bed and pulled a sheet over to cover her snowy nakedness. Then staggered down the hall to the guest bedroom, shedding the clothes I had fallen asleep in earlier that morning.

I crawled into the empty bed.

Stopped and then got back up.

Went to the door.

Locked it.

Staggered back to the alien sheets.

And slid into a hazed and confused slumber where I crawled through a dreamscape of parched desert sands and over dunes of ground glass.

At some point the dream changed and I had become Quasimodo, perched precariously on the castle ramparts.

A mob storms the walls with scaling ladders while a semi-organized phalanx shoulders a great log and uses it as a battering ram.

"Sanctuary!" I shout down at them, "sanctuary!" I can barely hear myself over the noise. The bells peal in the bell tower above me while the pounding against the great gate below grows louder and louder.

"Leave me alone!" I cry. "Go away!"

But they won't go away. I will have to kill them to make them stop coming after me.

And, God help me, that is no longer a guarantee.

I opened my eyes to see Deirdre bending over me.

The doorbell continued to chime and the pounding on the front door reverberated throughout the whole house.

"Someone's at the door," she said.

I groaned. "Thank you, Lucas Buck."

"What?" She was still naked.

"Never mind." I sat up and felt something slosh inside my brainpan.

"Why are you in my room?" she asked.

"Why were you in mine?"

"Send whoever is downstairs away and I will show you," she answered lasciviously.

"Oh God . . ." I groaned my way off the edge of the bed and up and onto my feet. I stumbled back into my pants and fumbled into my shirt on the way down the stairs. Heedless of the afternoon sun, I yanked the front door open.

She was putting her full—if not particularly considerable—weight into her pounding. When the door gave way, so did she. I ended up on the floor with the diminutive woman sprawled across my lap.

"Detective Ruiz," I observed. "I see you favor the Lady Shaft line of faux leather trench coats. To what do I owe this . . . pleasure?"

She scrambled back onto her feet. Behind her, out on my doorstep, Detective Murray smiled affably. I thought about lending him one of my hats: the little Tyrolean number he was sporting today was especially hideous.

"The 'long arm of the law' is meant to be a figure of speech, Captain," I continued, starting the process of finding my own way back up. Murray extended a long arm of his own and grasped my hand. I was standing in no time.

"I'm still a lieutenant, Mr. Haim."

"Please, let's not stand on formalities, Detective. Just call me 'skel.' "

"You took a long time to answer the door, Haim," she said finally.

"This is the middle of the night for me, ma'am."

"We were making enough noise to wake the dead." Her eyes lit up when she saw that that phrase slide under my skin.

"Why don't you just mace me and get it over with?" I asked with a scowl.

Murray cleared his throat. "Dorcas . . ."

I looked at Ruiz. "Dorcas?"

"We wanted to ask you a few more questions," she said hurriedly.

"Always happy to assist the police," I said, "but your tone suggests I may want to consult a lawyer."

"All we really want to do is have your permission to look around your property," Murray continued in a rare burst of verbosity.

"The grounds or inside my house?" I asked.

"Does it matter?" Ruiz wanted to know.

"A dead body was found in the woods adjacent to my front yard. The murderer may have left evidence in the vicinity and there's always the possibility that some of it ended up over the property line. I'd certainly look around if I were you."

"Then you—"

My face hardened. "But the only reason to look around the inside of my house is if I'm considered to be a suspect." I gestured out the door. "Be my guest, tromp around my yard, crawl through my bushes, go around back and wade in the bayou. But you'll need a warrant if you want to come into my house."

"Something inside you don't want us to see?"

I stared down at her. "I have company right now. You're interrupting." I cocked an eyebrow.

She glared back up at me. "A *lady* friend?"

"Ever hear of 'don't ask, don't tell'?"

Murray started humming the theme from *The Flintstones*.

"Depends," Ruiz said, "on whether your 'company' is alive or dead."

I struggled to keep my expression neutral.

"Oh shit," said Murray. He was looking down into the flower bed beside my porch.

We all looked.

Between the impatiens and the creeping phlox was a ridge of white toadstools.

Then I saw that they weren't five little toadstools in a row: They were toes.

Curtis "Pops" Berry didn't look like a lawyer. Unless you were thinking of a lawyer from the 1800s who was taking a week off to go camping. His graying hair looked as though he'd missed his barber's appointment two months in a row and his beard hadn't seen a pair of scissors in two years. As usual, he was wearing a tee shirt, blue jeans and work boots. The tee shirt was emblazoned with the message: "Jesus Is Coming!" in bold red lettering. Beneath this platitude, in smaller, gold typeface was the addendum: "And boy is He pissed!"

He hadn't felt it necessary to don his denim ("working") blazer, he explained, since I was being released without bail, without even an arraignment. Apparently my whereabouts were fully checked out and accounted for during the period of time that Kandi Fenoli had once again disappeared from the morgue. My alibi appeared airtight.

It took Pops a little longer to get my hat and sunglasses out of lockup than it did to spring Yours Truly. He handed them to me before escorting me out into the late-afternoon daylight.

Outside the sky was heavily overcast and it looked about three hours later than it really was. I kept the hat and sunglasses on: clouds don't mean diddley when it comes to UV radiation.

"They did a quick search of your house," Pops said as he

shepherded me across the street and fished for the remote in his pocket.

"They what?"

"Detective Ruiz is citing 'probable cause.' Says you alluded to a potential accomplice in the house. I say it's pretty damn weak even if there had been another party present and you may have grounds for a lawsuit." He found the remote and a purple Lexus chirped a row away from us. Pops liked comfortable things—clothes or cars, cost wasn't the determining factor.

"Did they trash the place?"

"Nope. Checked it out, myself, on the way over. They just looked around enough to ascertain that no one else was inside. The real damage would seem to be to Detective Ruiz's ego: she says you deliberately set her up."

"I don't think I've seen the last of Dorcas."

We opened the doors and slid in, buckling up.

"Now that we're out of earshot I want to ask you the same question they did, and remind you that anything you say will fall under the umbrella of lawyer-client privilege." He started the engine and navigated us back out into traffic as a few random drops began to kamikaze against the windshield.

I sighed. "I know: do I have any enemies? Any enemies who would replant a corpse right next to my front door?"

"Son, I've seen a lot of weird shit during my life—especially the last five years—and I don't think anything would totally surprise me anymore." He looked at me sidewise. "You may be keeping a couple of surprises from me and that's okay—I have a sense about most people and I won't abide a crooked client. You may have a couple of kinks in your closet but I don't read you for anything crooked. But I can't help you unless I know what kind of trouble you're really in.

"Speaking of which, you want to stop by the emergency room on the way home? You look like hell on roller skates!"

We stopped by the blood bank instead. My "medical condition" is just vague enough to most people for them to accept that I self-medicate and require occasional infusions of whole blood. Being owner of the blood bank and having all kinds of official-looking paperwork was sufficient to have me in and back out the door in five minutes. I wouldn't have to come back after closing with my passkey.

"Looks like you have a welcoming committee," Pops observed as we motored up my driveway.

Theresa-call-me-Terry was sitting on my front step.

"Two dead bodies were found on your property," she said as I tried to keep her from noticing the blood labeling on the box I was sliding into the refrigerator.

"Just one, actually," I said, trying to figure out how soon I could get her into a cab so I could tear through a packet of blood. "They found the same one twice." I filled a pan with water and set it on the stove to heat up.

"*Really?*" she said, eyes opening wide.

Oops—not thinking clearly at all!

"It's complicated," I said. "Look, Theresa—"

"Call me 'T.'"

"—I've had a really rough day and I'm not feeling too well—"

"Is that why you brought home that blood from the blood bank?"

"—and I need to go to bed. Please go home."

She stared at me, daring me for an explanation.

I stared back, gearing up to erase her memory of the last ten minutes. The trick was to be precise enough so that she didn't end up wondering how she suddenly ended up here in the first place.

The telephone rang. The answering machine picked and went into its "leave a message" spiel.

"After this call, I'm calling you a cab."

Terry-call-me-T cocked her head to the side and studied me as if I had spoken in tongues.

"Sam?" Chalice's voice. Interesting: we were on a first-name basis, now. "I'm still at the lab. I'm sorry I haven't called sooner but I've stayed over and run every test I can think of on your blood and—and—I don't know what to say!"

I looked at my uninvited guest, whose attention had shifted to the answering machine: Uh-oh.

I dodged toward the telephone as Chalice said: "I never would have believed your story about vampires and werewolves if I hadn't been responsible for the results, myself. Your blood—"

I snatched up the receiver. "Chalice, I'm here."

"Sam! This is incredible!"

Unfortunately, answering the phone did not immediately dis-connect the answering machine: both of our voices were now amplified through the little speaker, producing squealy feedback.

"We've got to bring other researchers in on this!"

"No!" I said, looking back at Terry-call-me-T. "And I can't talk right now."

"But the genetic mutations in your hemoglobin, your DNA—you may be the key to all of our research projects! The more people we bring in on this—"

"*Absolutely not!*" I pushed, straining sub-vocals to impress my point. "You *cannot tell* anyone else!"

"I won't," she said, the pout evident in her voice. "But running samples through the analyzers and sequencers is a guarantee that someone is going to notice sooner or later."

Shit! "I cannot stress this enough, Chalice: no one else must find out! It could well mean my life!"

"What about my life? If you bit me would my blood—"

"I can't talk right now!" I slammed the receiver down and leaned over the machine with my back to my precocious eavesdropper.

"How about if you bit me?" she said after a moment.

"Nobody's biting anybody here." I turned around. "And you are going home."

"Am I?"

"Yes. Look into my eyes."

She looked. "Oh, I see. You're going to hypnotize me—use mind control. Like you did with Rod." She positively beamed. "Was I right about you or what?"

"It doesn't matter," I said. "Because you won't remember any of this. In a moment you'll be *leaving*. You *won't remember* any-thing about coming here. You *won't remember* anything you heard or saw. You *won't* ever have *the urge* to come back and visit my house." I hesitated. "And you *will go* to the Registrar's office tomorrow and *drop my class*."

She turned away from me and walked back into the kitchen. I heard the clack of the stove burner as she turned it off and then the sound of a drawer opening. She returned with a paring knife.

"You know what?" she said with a bright and chipper tone,

"you're the one who's getting sleepy. You can hardly keep your eyes open. You don't need that warmed-over stale plasma. You want the real deal, fresh and hot from the heart." She drew the blade across her forearm, and rivulets of red welled up in its wake. She extended the arm (the flow, *the feast!*) toward me as an offering.

I took a step, staggering. "No," I said. "Let me get you . . . some . . . bandages," I whispered. The world faded around me, Terry receded. The arm was all that was left. The ribbon of life, precious life—flowing, cresting, surging!

"Hello," said a voice from the stairway. "Are we having company?"

I forced my eyes away from the blood (the blood, yes, the blood) and looked over at Deirdre who was drifting down to the first floor. She yawned, putting three-quarter-inch fangs on display. "Planning on starting without me?"

Terry's eyes had grown large. "Coool!" she said.

Chapter Twelve

"I'm not hungry!" Deirdre pouted as I dragged her up the stairs and into the guest bedroom.

"Fine," I said. "But you're still coming. I need a date."

"You don't need a date. You just don't trust me to stay here with her!"

"This is one of those social/charity/fundraiser thingies," I continued, ignoring her, "and you need to dress nice."

"*You* need to lie down and rest," she retorted. "After all that you've been through, *you* should be lying on the couch with those two blood packs in your arm instead of hers. Better yet, you should have taken her up on her offer! You need fresh blood and she's done everything short of forcing it down your throat."

"I'm going to run through the shower and change. Be ready when I get back."

I stalked into my bedroom but left the door open—like I really had any chance of monitoring the stairs while I was back in the master bathroom. If Deirdre snuck downstairs while I was in the shower, well . . .

I should have just stayed out of it. Theresa was safer when she just had Rod to shove her around. Damn! I hadn't planned on attending BioWeb's Halloween social do but Theresa needed to lie down for a couple of hours while her blood loss was replenished and I didn't trust Deirdre—or myself, for that matter—to stay here while she was so enamored of the idea of being somebody's entrée.

I started the hot water and then felt my jawline so see if I needed a shave, yet. It had been a week or so since I had last applied the razor and I imagined that I was just about due: My screwy metabolism hadn't put my follicles into a total state of stasis but it now took me about five days to get a five o'clock shadow. I was thinking about growing a beard: When your reflection in the mirror starts playing hide-and-seek, shaving is a bitch.

On the other hand, beards have to be trimmed and a pair of scissors might well prove more challenging than a razor.

I hurriedly lathered up and raised the tri-part blade. Closing my eyes, I tried to invoke a Zen-like state: *my face and the razor are one, my face and the razor—*

The razor disappeared from my fingers. "Here, let me help you with that." I opened my eyes as Deirdre turned me away from the sink and tilted my chin up.

"I don't understand you," she said as she scraped lather and stubble from the sides of my face. I started to open my mouth but she pushed up on my chin. "No, don't talk. You don't have the juice to spare if I nick you."

I stared up at the ceiling while she worked her way down to my throat. "She's the perfect donor," Deirdre continued. "And she's way beyond willing. You wouldn't need any kind of mental domination with this one. Your mouth on her arm, on her throat— just the thought of it and her nipples are ready to tear through her bra." She rinsed the razor in the sink and checked for any missed patches of skin. "You can rinse."

I looked down at her. "Go get ready," I growled.

She left and I stripped down and jumped into the shower.

I promised myself I'd be in and out in less than five minutes but the hot water felt so good against my too-cool skin that I braced hands against the tiles, bowed my head, and let the warmth work its way into my tepid flesh. I nearly jumped as cooler hands came to rest on my shoulder blades.

"The heat is pleasant, isn't it?" Deirdre said.

"What are you doing?"

"The same as you: getting ready. If you're in such a hurry and don't want to share, I can use the downstairs bathroom—the one just around the corner from your excitable groupie."

"No!" More reasonably: "I'll be done in a minute."

"I'll wash your back."

"Deirdre . . ."

"And you can wash mine—it'll save time." She started soaping my shoulders.

I had visions of Lupé arriving home unannounced to find a disheveled co-ed on my couch and a redhead lathering me up in the shower. The heat from the water seemed to be penetrating too well: I felt a pleasant burning sensation in my solar plexus begin to radiate out toward my extremities.

"If you don't think that she can spare it, why don't you drink from me? I topped off last night."

"What?" My skin was starting to tingle and a pleasant knot was starting to tighten in my groin.

"Vampire blood, second generation," she elaborated. "More potent than a homogenized human."

I wrenched the shower handles so that the water turned suddenly cold. The pleasant knot unraveled. "Vampire blood? Deirdre, what happened to Pagelovitch's watchdogs last night?"

"I took them out."

"Took them out? You were just supposed to distract them!"

"They got a little rough. It got out of hand."

"Out of hand? Pagelovitch is going to be pissed!"

"He's already pissed. But he's not going to do anything to you unless he runs out of options. I'm a different matter, but he knows the rules and understands that it is my place to protect you. He won't punish me for acting within the law."

"The law," I repeated as I grabbed the shampoo and smeared a dab into my hair.

"Your ideas of honor and propriety are going to get you killed. And me along with you."

I was incredulous. "You feed off of two of Pagelovitch's enforcers—kill them—and tell me that my refusal to use violence is going to cause trouble?" The shampoo stung my eyes. I rinsed and groped for the washcloth. Encountered something I shouldn't have.

"That's nice . . ." she said, and sighed. "Look, it's a wolf-eat-wolf world. I don't just disagree with your refusal to fight your way to the top of the food chain, I'm at a total loss to understand how you can turn down the gifts that are freely—even fervently—offered."

I got my eyes cleared and started soaping my other necessities. "How about this," I tried. "A masochist and a sadist are shipwrecked on a desert isle. The masochist gets down on his knees in front of the sadist and says: 'hit me, beat me, slap me, kick me, abuse me, *hurt* me!' " I turned and looked at Deirdre, who lifted sudsy mammaries in my direction.

"Bite me," she invited.

"And the sadist just looks at him, then crosses his arms," I continued, crossing my arms, "and says: '*No.*' "

Deirdre studied my face for a long minute and relinquished her grip. "I don't get it."

"You see, the masochist wanted—"

She waved her hand. "I *get* the joke. I *don't* get the analogy." Her mouth hardened. "Other than the fact that you're both a sadist and a masochist. Do my back." She turned around.

"I think you're puzzled because Theresa seems to be offering me what I need and appears to do so of her own free will. *You* want to invoke the consenting adults clause but I'm afraid that just doesn't wash." I washed my way down to the small of her back.

"Why not? She's of age. And if it does no one any harm—"

"Who says it does no harm?"

"Yes, *who* says?" She whirled around so that my hands were suddenly soaping her belly. "*You?* Who are *you* to say?"

I handed her the soap. "Who is *she* to say?"

"It's her life."

"No man is an island," I said, stepping out of the shower and snagging a towel off of the rack.

"Donne? You're bringing John Donne into the argument?" She followed me out, dripping water. There was no extra towel.

"Look, the concept of the 'victimless crime' is an engaging myth," I said, heading for the linen closet, "but it just isn't true that 'what goes on behind closed doors' never comes out from behind closed doors."

"I should have seen this coming: you're a 'rules' person." She said it in the same tone that some people reserve for pederasts and IRS agents.

"Even if we want to break the rules of our society, those rules still define us."

She followed me down the hall. "Is it always so wrong to defy what defines us?"

I tossed her a clean towel. "Is it so unthinkable that human society must have standards of conduct for the common good?"

She caught the towel but made no move to use it. Not even to cover herself. "Maybe the 'common' good isn't the 'best' good. Who gets to decide those standards?"

"Hey, I know it gets dicey the moment we try to establish a central moral authority," I agreed, walking back into my bedroom. "But is the alternative any safer?" I closed the door.

I dried and dressed hurriedly, went back to the bathroom and brushed my teeth, then scurried down the stairs.

The couch was empty.

I looked around the living room: no Theresa.

Sounds behind me.

I turned and saw Theresa mopping the dining room floor. "I'm afraid the paper towels didn't get it all," she said.

"What are you doing up?" I asked.

She turned those large eyes upon me like deep blue searchlights. "I'm still upsetting you. I don't mean to upset you. I don't want to be a bother. . . ." Her eyes were luminous. "I want to serve you."

"Theresa . . ."

"Call me 'T.' "

I went to her, took the mop from her hands, and led her back to the couch. "Where are the blood packets?"

"I put them back in the refrigerator to keep for you. Your thrall said you need more blood—"

"My what?"

"Thrall. That beautiful redheaded creature. Will I transform so beautifully when I become your thrall?"

"*Deirdre!*" I bellowed.

The beautiful redheaded creature came stumbling out of the guest bedroom and hopped to the head of the stairs. "Yes, O Dark Lord and Master?" Her little black cocktail dress was askew; a black high-heeled shoe dangled from one hand.

"Never mind."

She looked down at us, perched precariously on one foot and tugged an errant spaghetti strap into place. "What is it?"

I sighed and stared at the carpeting between my feet. "Please tell Theresa—"

"T," she whispered.

"—that you are not my . . . 'thrall.'"

Deirdre's mouth twisted into a lopsided grin. It looked as if she was trying very hard to not laugh at one of us. I wondered which.

"Oh . . . no . . ." she said. "I am not his 'thrall,' T."

"*Thank* you," I said.

"I am his *blood slave*," she finished lasciviously.

"*Deirdre!*"

"I serve and pleasure him in untold ways!"

"Dammit, Deirdre!"

"Honey, you just lie down and rest for now and let's see how things work out when we get back." Deirdre turned and bent down to slip on her other shoe. It looked to me as though she was deliberately presenting her backside and suggesting via body language that I kiss it.

T lay back down with a sigh as my "blood slave" walked back to her room with an exaggerated wiggle. I consulted my watch as I fetched our tickets from the counter between the kitchen and the dining room. "We're gonna be late!" I yelled toward the upstairs as I walked back toward the couch.

"Theres—T," I said. "She—Deirdre—was just joking with—"

She gazed up at me with those haunted sapphire eyes.

"—you can't—T—oh hell, *look into my eyes.*"

She did.

It didn't do any good.

Maybe I was the one having trouble concentrating.

Or maybe she had a psychic immunity to mental domination—Rod notwithstanding. By the time Deirdre came down the stairs I had given up on getting Theresa to do anything via mind control.

Maybe after we got back from the party, I could get her drunk enough to shove into the backseat of a cab.

Or maybe I could just quietly leave town and start all over again somewhere else.

"Ready?" Deirdre asked, opening the front door.

"Don't invite anyone in while we're gone," I said over my shoulder as I followed my "thrall" outside.

"I think your problem," Deirdre said quietly as I fumbled for my keys, "is that you're still struggling to define your place in *human* society. What does human society have to do with either of us?"

I sighed as I locked the front door. "Well, *one* of us is still trying to hold onto his humanity."

"One of us," she agreed. "Though it seems a poor excuse to be so judgmental."

"You say that as if *I* am and *you're* not," I argued as we stepped off the front porch. "What makes you think you're making any less of a 'judgment'? And," I added, "did you check to see if the coast was clear?"

"I did," she said. "And *you're* the one who turns every pleasurable opportunity into a prissy exploration of the 'just say no' ethic."

I stopped and grinned at her. "Prissy exploration of the 'just say no' ethic?" I shook my head at the thought and then looked around at the sloping yard and the car parked a few yards away in the circle drive. "I'm surprised the Doman didn't set new sentries around the perimeter."

"He did." Deirdre continued to promenade toward the car, her long, pointy heels necessitating a slower, strolling gait. What was lost in speed was compensated for by the esthetics.

"He did what?" I asked, trying to shake off the distraction of the "piston effect" in her locomotion.

"Set more sentries," she said casually, stopping to lean over and adjust one of her shoes.

"What? Where? I thought you checked!"

"I did. And they're out here." She pulled the shoe off and then reached down to adjust the other. "Look, that girl offered you fresh blood when you needed it the most. When taking it was not only logical—and let's not forget pleasurable for you—but would have given her pleasure, as well. What could possibly be wrong with that?"

"It would be like having sex with a nymphomaniac." I looked around. No vampires were in sight. Ditto on the zombie front.

She put a hand on my shoulder for stability as she fiddled

with the other spiked heel. "Obviously, I'm not getting the point, here."

"Okay, it would be like inviting a kleptomaniac over to your house and leaving things out and readily available while you were conveniently absent." It wasn't a very good analogy but my mind was more on the Glock in the glove compartment of my car. "It would be exploiting someone's sickness, someone's vulnerability, for selfish reasons. Theresa is young and inexperienced and impressionable, and she's been involved with someone who has exploited and manipulated her for his own, selfish ends. I'm *not* going to be another reinforcement for her self-mutilation fantasies."

The vampire that had been hiding behind my car came vaulting over the hood like a psychotic jack-in-the-box sans container. Before I could react, Deirdre spun with superhuman speed and swung both shoes with deadly accuracy. The three-inch stiletto heels nailed him in the throat and chest. She went down under the impact of his body but he was already crumbling to dust as she hit the ground.

I ran over to help her up.

"And what about me?" she asked as I reached down and took her hand.

"I'm your Sire," I reminded her as I pulled her to her feet, "your so-called Master. If I would not validate Terry's self-destructive behavior, I certainly wouldn't permit—"

"That's *not* what I mean," she snapped, slipping her shoes back on. "I'm not young and impressionable. Do you think it symptomatic of some sort of mental or emotional aberration when I offer myself to you?" she added.

Careful, Cséjthe . . .

I glanced up and noticed the second vampire, crouching on the edge of the roof, just ten feet away. "Would you be terribly offended," I asked, trying to signal Deirdre by rolling my eyes, "if I were to say that I don't feel desire for you?"

The vamp launched herself but we dodged easily as she came down between us. Deirdre even had time to fumble with her purse as this one was turning her attention on me. I backpedaled, trying not to trip as I leaned away from her taloned grasp.

"I'd be offended that you'd *lie* to me," Deirdre answered with some heat. She snapped her purse strap over the vamp's head and jerked the gold chain across our assailant's throat. "You've transformed enough to know how easily I can read your physical responses. . . ." She twisted the chain-strap and pulled her arms in separate directions, tightening the golden loop. " . . . Your pupils and blood vessels dilate, your pulse quickens, your breathing deepens, your flesh betrays you through the pores of your skin, the autonomic reflexes of specific muscle groups!"

The vamp was tearing at the fine links, trying to dislodge the chain-strap from her windpipe but the muscles in Deirdre's arms flexed and the golden garrote continued to sink into that undead throat.

"You *do* desire me!" she insisted. "But you refuse me just the same!" A final yank and the chain closed its deadly circle: the vamp's head popped right off. "At least be *honest* about it," she finished, brushing more ash from her dress.

I grabbed her arm and pulled her toward the car. "Let's go! Before Pagelovitch sends any more our way!"

"They weren't Seattle's hounds," she said, recovering her shoes. "Our watchdogs are still watching."

"Then whose were they?" I slid behind the wheel and reached over to unlock the glove compartment.

"Hey, you're the gumshoe," she said, slipping into the passenger seat. "I'm just a leg breaker."

I slapped the zippered pouch onto the leather upholstery between us and started the engine. "Any more out there?"

"What do I look like? Miss Cleo? Drive, O Dark Master!"

I growled at her but slammed the gearshift and spun the car around the circle and headed down the drive at highway speed. Another fanged intruder erupted from the darkness and launched himself across my hood. He landed with his face pressed to the windshield, his hands clawing for purchase in our open side windows. I hit the retrofitted wiper controls and twin streams of fluid spurted up and onto the glass and ghast.

"I think you've thrown a rod," Deirdre said as smoke began to billow up in front of us.

"Naw, Rod's probably cowering under his bed right now; I don't know this guy's name." I hit the brakes and the vampire slid back down the hood and fell off the front of the car. A moment later he popped back up, the white planes of his skull glistening in the headlights where his face once was. Deirdre's foot stomped down on top of mine, pressing the gas pedal to the floor. A bump and a thump and we were moving again. The smoke had disappeared with our "hood ornament" but I gave the windshield a few more squirts and turned on the wipers.

Deirdre looked back at the smoking vamp on the concrete and then turned and studied the windshield wipers. "Holy water in the fluid reservoir?"

I nodded. "Keep it in mind the next time we fill up at a full-service station. And by all that's holy, don't get any on you."

Chapter Thirteen

"I've been waiting for you to invoke Lupé," she said after we had driven some distance in silence.

"Are we still having this conversation?"

"Where is she? Is she even coming back?" Deirdre stared ahead as though she were searching the darkness. "I think not. Maybe it's your inability to surrender to your own passions that drove her away."

"You don't know what you're talking about," I said quietly.

"Then please explain it to me! You can't use Lupé as an excuse—she understands the Rules of the Pack and the Coven. She would understand that you are my Sire and that you have obligations—"

"It would still hurt her."

"But she would accept it."

I silently counted off thirty-seven white divider stripes before she spoke again.

"And that's if she comes back." Deirdre cleared her throat. "And if she doesn't—"

"You're right, I'm using Lupé as an excuse. It would hurt *me*."

"I guess that really isn't a surprise." She tapped her fingers against the window glass. "Though I expected you to draw out some argument based on the power differential in our relationship—that, as my Master, such a coupling would exploit me. Or corrupt your sense of honor."

I didn't answer; I was too busy checking the rearview mirror.

"But I think it's more fundamental than that for you."

"We're being followed," I said, pressing down on the accelerator. "Unzip the pouch. Use the second magazine, it's loaded with ball ammo."

"*Ball* ammo?"

"Jacketed. I don't want to waste silver on a vehicle."

She picked up the pouch and opened it. "So is it simply a religious hang-up for you? Do you still fantasize that there is a God? That He would disapprove?"

She removed the Glock and checked the magazine while I strangled a bitter laugh. "Things have been done to me," I said, "that are changing me into an inhuman killing machine. Do you think I wring my hands and worry that God is concerned with my bedroom conduct when I'm starting to see human beings as slabs of meat? A smorgasbord of tasty treats who merely exist to give me momentary pleasure?"

The headlights in the rearview mirror drew quickly closer: our tail was accelerating.

"Then it's not a religious thing?"

"Depends on your definition of religion. Are you buckled up?"

She nodded but then loosened her belt strap, presumably to allow her to move and aim, if necessary. The human Deirdre I had met in Seattle would have been clueless if handed a firearm a year ago. Damien's murder had motivated her with a vengeance: she'd told me that she practically lived on Pagelovitch's shooting range after her "rebirth."

"Can you tell if it's a black Suburban?"

"Not yet," she answered. "And what do you mean by 'definition of religion'?"

I hunched over the wheel, trying to ease the tension in my back while gauging possible exit points—paved or otherwise. "Seems like everywhere you turn, there are laws. The laws of the Coven. The laws of the Demesne. The laws of the state of Louisiana. Me? I believe in the laws of physics."

She snorted. "Physics is your religion?"

"Why not?" I gestured toward the distant glow of the BioWeb complex. "Up there is one of its temples, where the pure laws of science are worshipped by acolytes in lab coats, meditating before the CRTs, invoking the rituals of mathematics and measurements. There are commandments and codicils from the subatomic level all the way up to the macrobiotic sphere. Laws of the seen and the unseen. Laws of the quantifiable and the unknown—sometimes silent and secret, but no less real while they await discovery."

" 'All kingdoms have a law given: and there are many king-doms,' " Deirdre murmured, " 'for there is no space in which there is no kingdom; and there is no kingdom in which there is no space . . .' "

I nodded, easing back into my seat and stretching my arms against the steering wheel. "Poetic, but as apt a description of quantum mechanics as one is likely to squeeze into a single sentence."

"The *Doctrine and Covenants* by Joe Smith, 1832." She smiled at my expression. "What? You'd forgotten that I read, too? That Damien and I met in a library? Do you think you're the only one who has searched the various theologies for a loophole? An escape clause? A chance to recover our souls, our humanity, before the long darkness closes over us?" Her smile faded. "Well, let me save you a little homework: we inhabit a different kingdom, now. A very different kingdom and we are ruled by a very different law."

"You use the words 'laws' and 'rules' interchangeably—like they're the same thing," I said. "I think of rules as something people think up to keep other people in line: the *rules* of the Pack, of the Coven, of the Demesne. If I'm rebellious and clever enough, I can break those rules and get away with it." I shook my head. "Laws, on the other hand, are immutable facts of existence. Doesn't matter whether you agree with the law of gravity or not: one way or another, it *will* be obeyed."

"Chevy Nova," Deirdre interjected. "Green."

"Not a black Suburban," I mused. "Still could be Pagelovitch's crew."

"So. You're differentiating between the 'rules' of behavior and the 'laws' of existence?"

"Or the 'rules' of religion as opposed to the laws of God."

"So you do believe in God?"

I hesitated. "I believe in the universe. And I believe its nature is evidenced by how it is governed by law."

"Can you be any more obscure?"

"Obtuse," I said. "I think the word you're looking for is obtuse. And hold on tight!"

"The word I'm looking for is 'hold on tight'?"

I wrenched the wheel while my feet danced over the floor pedals: our car spun one-hundred-eighty degrees and I floored the gas pedal immediately.

"Take sustenance . . ." I began.

"This whole conversation started because you wouldn't take it when it was offered," she said as the screaming tires found traction and we leapt toward our pursuers.

"Our choices on the menu may vary, our appetites may wax or wane," I continued, "but the one immutable law of food is that, without it, we *die*."

The driver of the Chevy Nova decided I was sufficiently serious— or unstable—and steered his vehicle into a ditch, effectively ending our game of chicken with twenty yards to spare.

"We may vary in caloric intake," I added as we passed our would-be tailgaters, "volume consumed, tastes preferred, but we will waste away and die without some form of physical fuel for our physical bodies."

She nodded. "Okay, bologna or blood—I'll buy that humans and vampires must obey a fundamental law of biology." She looked back through the rear window. "I think they're stuck."

I nodded. "Even though they don't want to be, I'll bet. That's the problem of factual conditions versus wishful thinking. Which underscores my point, here. As a theology, the tenets of physics are consistent; the laws of thermodynamics and gravity hold us all accountable before the bar."

She laid the Glock on the bench seat between us. "Physics is one thing but behavioral needs are quite another. As individuals, raised in different cultures and environments, we have different needs." She pulled down the passenger sun visor.

"Do we?" I turned down a dirt road that would bring us back around to BioWeb by a more circuitous route. "Are your so-called 'behavioral needs' really necessities or just issues of preference? Food is food and our inability to live without it is not the same thing as whether you prefer meatloaf to crepes suzette."

"Actually, I prefer Meatloaf to Mozart." She opened her handbag, peered inside, then reached up and switched on the Merc's dome light.

"Music or food, you make my point about preference. Desire is not the same thing as true need."

She looked up and then out the side window at the darkness that paced us with every passing fence post. "How do you measure either?"

"Desire?" I considered briefly. "I think we each define our own. But our needs truly define us."

"You're playing at words."

"Am I? Desire unfulfilled may make us strong. It may make us weak. But if we perish from its lack then it was not a preference but truly a need."

"How can you know the difference before it is too late?"

I shrugged. "Most people don't know the difference between love and lust."

"Oooo, listen to you! And I thought I was the jaded soul."

"Assuming you still have one," I observed dryly.

"Testy." She went back to rummaging through her purse.

"Yeah? Well, the subject of the soul is . . . subjective. And I think I've lost my perspective this past year."

"Or maybe gained it for the first time," she suggested. "Your problem is you're trying to measure and define the unseeable."

"For now we see through a glass darkly . . ." I murmured. "If the invisible actually exists, then it is quantifiable. Physics shows us that anything can be measured if it acts or is acted upon— even the unseeable aspects of existence. Gravity, electricity—"

"I've seen electricity." She pulled out a lipstick case and opened it. "And gravity isn't hard to miss." She flipped down her visor and studied her lack of reflection in Lupé's clipped-on vanity mirror. "Damn! I keep forgetting!"

I suppressed a grin. "You don't see yourself in the mirror—how do you know that you exist?" I elaborated: "You've seen the *effects* of electricity, you haven't actually seen the flow of electrons being passed from one atomic orbit to the next."

She evidently saw something else: She grabbed the Glock and, as she tilted the visor back toward the ceiling, I saw the flash of headlights in the looking glass.

"Chevy Nova?"

She nodded. "Looks as if they weren't that stuck, after all."

In retrospect the dirt road was a mistake: the dust trail had led them right to my rear bumper. Which they accelerated and bumped as Deirdre rolled down the passenger window. "I was wrong!" she called over the increasing noise from the wind and the two engines.

"About what?"

"About our date turning out to be a boring waste of a good evening!"

The car behind us dropped back and then accelerated to smack into our rear bumper again.

"You really know how to show a girl a good time!"

"Glad you're enjoying it!" I started to weave back and forth across the road: two tire tracks connected by packed earth and a handful of gravel didn't give me much leeway for evasive maneuvers. "Maybe you'd like to explain the rear end damage to my insurance agent!"

"Stop weaving, I can't get a shot!"

"It's a car, for Crissake! It's only five feet away! How hard can it be?"

Her head and one shoulder were out the window, now, and her hair streamed backwards, cloaking her face as she aimed the gun at our bumper car assailants. Nothing happened. The Nova banged into us again. Then a fourth time.

Deirdre pulled her head and arm back into the car.

"What's the problem?" I asked. "Gun jammed?"

"What's the problem?" She rolled the window back up and glared at me. "How about your chopped roofline makes the passenger window too narrow for me to fit through! I'm right-handed! I can't hit squat shooting left-handed from a moving car weaving all over a dirt road at high speed!" She turned around and knelt on the seat, bracing the gun in her right hand on the cushioned back support.

"What are you doing?"

"Aiming for their headlights."

"Through my rear window? Forget it!"

"You got a better idea?"

"I'm pretty sure," I said tightly, "the glass in this car is irreplaceable."

"And we're not?"

The Nova thudded into the rear bumper with enough force to jolt me against the steering wheel. Deirdre tumbled back against the dashboard.

"What about your rear end?" she asked, trying to extract her rear end from the foot well. "Isn't that irreplaceable?"

"Sheet metal is easier to rework than vintage auto glass," I sniffed.

She bared her teeth at me. "You need a moon roof."

I nodded. "Thought about it once. Too bad I didn't—*hey!*"

Deirdre fired off four shots into the night sky. Or rather, through the ceiling of my car, into the night sky. While I was still reeling from the noise and the smell of gunpowder she punched her fist through the roof and used her preternatural strength to peel back the metal and fabric like the lid of an old sardine can. "Don't get your panties in a wad," she groused. "I'll pay to have the job finished properly at the body shop of your choice—if we survive." She stood up and pushed her head and shoulders through the top of the car. The Glock barked twice more and the headlights in my rearview were suddenly dark.

The sound of our pursuer's engine receded as Deirdre squirmed back down into the car. She pulled the flap of metal back into a semblance of closure and ripped away the dangling swatch of ceiling fabric before she refastened her seat belt. "Now, where were we?" she asked as she laid the handgun back down and began to paw through her purse, again.

"Well. Um. You were saying that I needed a moon roof—"

"No." She produced a hairbrush and waved it at me. "Before. About seeing the unseen."

"Ah." I considered as she began working the tangles out of her auburn tresses. "I was just pointing out that we measure a myriad of unseen forces—physical, biological, emotional—all by way of their effects."

"And how do we do that?"

I looked in the rearview mirror but could see nothing. Now I needed a process for measuring the unseen. "We can, um, do that because we recognize a pattern of adherence to law. Consistency. Objects fall in obedience to the law of gravity. Not only fall, but must obey the same laws of velocity regardless of weight."

"Heavier-than-air craft fly in defiance of that law," she countered, working on a stubborn snarl behind her head. Her breasts rose in response as though seeking to demonstrate the Bernoulli principle in my defense.

"Gravity does not cease to exist, it remains immutable," I argued. The dirt road swung sharply to the right up ahead. "But airplanes and jets and even birds and bats and bugs rise in obedience to other immutable laws, laws of lift and velocity and aerodynamics. The courtroom of the airfoil administers 'higher' laws—if you'll pardon the pun."

"I'll pardon the pun if you'll make your point." Her voice shaded toward irritation. "And why is the rear window suddenly red?"

I glanced in the rearview mirror. The glass of the rear windscreen was aglow with blossoms of crimson, each bloom encompassing a bright red dot. The blooms moved like flowers stirred by a gentle breeze. As they migrated over to the passenger side of the window I reached over and shoved Deirdre's head down. "Designators!" I said.

"Desi-what?" Her head popped back up.

"Laser-sights!" I shoved her head back down.

"Laser—?" There was the sound of a small thunderclap and a round hole suddenly appeared in the windshield on Deirdre's side, radiating a nimbus of fine cracks.

"What was *that*?"

"Ah shit!" I said, glancing back and noting a matching hole—about the diameter of a pencil, ringed with a spider's web of cracks—in the rear window. The trade-in value of my car was definitely plummeting. "Nine millimeter."

"What?"

"A .22 short or a .45 ACP travel just under the speed of sound," I explained. "We probably wouldn't have heard it over the noise of the engine. A nine mil approaches mach one-point-five: that sound you just heard was a miniature sonic boom."

"They're shooting at us?" she asked with more than a touch of indignation.

"Actually," I said, wrenching the wheel into the turn, "they seem to be shooting at you."

"Why me?"

"Well, you did start it."

"You're the one who gave me the gun. Told me which ammo to use."

"Don't get upset."

"Don't get *upset*? They're shooting at *me*! How come they're not shooting at *you*?"

"Would you rather they shot at me?"

"No. I just want to know why."

"We could stop and ask them," I said reasonably.

She unbuckled her shoulder-harness. "Maybe I'll just shoot you myself," she said, falling across my lap and slapping the knob on the dash that controlled the headlights. Suddenly we were barreling along at sixty miles an hour in the dark.

"Hey!" I said, tapping the brakes. "What's the idea?"

"They have no headlights," she said, seemingly addressing my leg, "and we can see better in the dark than they can. As long as our lights are on, we make the better target and give them something to follow."

I felt the tires leave the hard-packed dirt ruts and tapped the brakes again as we slipped onto the grass. "Keep your foot off the brake," she demanded of my inner thigh.

"I can't see the bloody road!"

"Well, they can see our brake lights so just coast until your night vision kicks in!"

"I'm still half human, Deirdre; my infravision only registers major temperature differentials, not dirt roads after sundown!"

Her head popped back up and she grasped the wheel. "I'll steer. You just keep your foot off that brake until I tell you."

I glanced in the rearview mirror; once or twice a red dot swept across the back of the car but didn't stop or linger. Our pursuers were falling even farther behind.

"I don't like it," she muttered.

"You don't like it? They put holes in my windscreens! Never mind the cost, I don't know if I can get replacements for a 1950 Mercury Club Coupé!"

"I'm not talking about that. I'm talking about your whole 'physics as morality' premise."

I shook my head. "You really aren't going to let this go, are you?"

She smiled and I glimpsed the ghost of a fang in a faint

reflection of starlight. "You haven't finished explaining how the physics of the universe abrogates human desire."

I sighed. "If there is a connection between physical law and human need, it's simply this: in every kingdom, seen and unseen, the principles are the same. You don't get something for nothing, everything affects something, and every action has a consequence."

"My daddy used to say there's a price tag on everything and there's no such thing as a free lunch," she said, snuggling against me and steering around something sizeable in the darkness. "The universe bites."

"Why?" I asked. "It only means that everything has value. Consequences can be good as well as bad. Price tags can show you where the bargains are shelved and the treasures are buried. What you choose produces an effect, a result. On you. On someone else. On a place, a thing, or a pattern of existence."

"Now you're going to segue into the morality of physics," she said dryly.

"It's not about being right," I said. "When it comes to the laws of physics, it's only a matter of what *is*. Right or wrong have nothing to do with it. The law of gravity doesn't care if you're a good person or a bad person. Saint or sinner, you walk off the edge of a five-hundred-foot cliff and the law of gravity is going to slap a summons on your ass, court's in session, and sentencing phase is coming up in ten seconds."

"Turn off ahead," she announced. "Take your foot off the gas but don't touch the brake unless I say so."

I peered through the darkness ahead of us and glimpsed a gray ribbon bleeding out of the purple blackness. "Asphalt?"

"Very good! You just may be less human than you think."

Now there was a comforting thought.

Deirdre spun the wheel and, as we left the dirt ruts behind and bumped onto smooth blacktop, I goosed the accelerator. Dim light from distant pole lamps beside barns and fuel pumps illumed the road turning the ribbon of gray to dirty silver. I could almost make out the oil stains and crushed moths now.

"What about miracles?" she asked as I took the steering wheel back into my grasp. She stayed, snuggled against me.

I shrugged. "Show me one that negates a physical law without serving a higher one, like Bernoulli's principle, and we'll talk.

Otherwise, statistics suggest the saints tend to die younger and uglier than the wicked of this world."

"So, invoke the laws of physics and God has no place in the universe?"

"*Quid pro quo* or *ipso facto*?" I countered. Another pair of headlights popped up in my rearview mirror. "That the universe runs like a complex and self-perpetuating machine hardly precludes an intelligence behind the design. The self-winding watch winds itself—but someone designed it, crafted the parts, and assembled it before sending it off to its own self-contained existence." The headlights were too far back to be sure, but I was betting it wasn't the Chevy Nova. I turned our headlights back on. Driving with them off would just call more attention to us now.

"So you *do* believe in God," she said. The note of challenge in her voice was more wistful than accusatory.

"I did. Once upon a time. Now the idea only seems to make me angry."

She laid a cool hand on my thigh. "Nietzsche said 'we are all apes of a cold god.'"

I hunched my shoulders. "Which is worse: an empty universe where life is but a short distraction from the long nothingness that comes before and after? Or a Supreme Intelligence that is indifferent and unresponsive to suffering and injustice? Don't ask me that question: I'm already damned so, for me, it doesn't really matter."

She squeezed my leg. "So what does matter?"

"People. Loyalty. Truth. Love."

"Love," she repeated.

"The real deal. Not the pantomimes of hormones, hungers, and egos. By the way, it was Marx, not Nietzsche."

"Not Nietzsche?"

"Marx," I affirmed, "Karl not Groucho."

"I get them mixed up all the time—Karl and Groucho."

I nodded. "I have the same problem with the Lennon boys. Which one wrote 'Give Peace A Chance,' Vladimir or John?"

She picked up the handgun again. "Those headlights are still getting closer."

"I'm not going that fast."

"Then go faster. And finish your point."

"Which point?"

"Your definition of morality in an amoral universe."

"I don't think I'm talking about morality, really," I said, pressing down on the accelerator. "I'm just talking about what works and what doesn't according to the laws of the universe."

"Faster."

"Driving or talking?"

"Both."

The headlights in the rearview mirror dropped back and held for the moment. "We know that the universe is a series of physical kingdoms, each interactive and structured to be ruled under a set of laws. Some of these kingdoms are invisible. Some, as yet, unmeasureable. The fact that we cannot yet quantify or measure them makes them no less real than the atom was before it was quantified by John Dalton."

"Of the infamous Dalton Gang?"

"So why not kingdoms both natural and supernatural?" I asked, refusing to be baited. "Physical and metaphysical? Is there spiritual existence beyond the electro-chemical processes of the human brain? Perhaps we are merely waiting for another Madame Curie to open new windows into those yet unseen and unquantified realities?"

"The kingdoms of the soul," she murmured.

"Why not? We are physical beings and, as such, are subject to the laws of physics. Walk off a cliff, plunge to our deaths. Place our hand in the flame, our flesh is burned and we feel pain. Why wouldn't there be laws and consequences of a spiritual nature?" I noticed the headlights in the mirror were slowly closing the distance between us. "Where's the spare magazine?"

"Must have fallen on the floor." Deirdre leaned down and groped under the seat. "So," she pondered, "the laws of physics in commandment form might be: 'Thou shalt not walk off of five-hundred-foot cliffs.' And: 'Blessed is he who does not place his hand into the flame.'" She came back up with the spare magazine of silver-treated Glasers, which she tucked into her cleavage for safekeeping and ready access.

"Works for me." I tilted the rearview mirror to try to get a better look at the vehicle behind us.

She snorted. "Eventually, of course, religions would arise to teach us that God hates people who walk off of cliffs and delights in chastising those who wickedly play with fire."

I grinned. It felt like a death rictus so I lost it immediately. "But a loving and compassionate God would have nothing to do with that. He might say, 'I love you and don't want you to come to harm so I give you these commandments as warnings. It's not judgment or punishment. This is the way that the universe works and it is the laws of gravity and thermodynamics that must be obeyed. If you attempt to defy an immutable law, there's gonna be some hurtin' goin' on.'"

"So you're suggesting the vengeful and wrathful God of the Old Testament is a bad rap," Deirdre said, twisting back around for a better look at the car behind us. "Warn against the consequences of head-butting immutable law and the messenger gets the blame."

I nodded. "Especially if the laws invoke the commandments of the heart."

"It still sounds very Calvinistic to me."

"What would you prefer, something very Calvin and Hobbsistic?" I sighed. "*Some* people will always look for loopholes whether it's theology, biology, or relativity. 'Why doesn't God make the universe harmless,' they'll carp. 'Make fire cold, negate the pull of gravity?' They wouldn't have to figure out how to cook their food or warm their homes as they go flying off the surface of the planet, flung into the void by the law of centrifugal force. They'd lobby to have every law negated or rescinded until the universe was devoid of structure, without form and void—entropy and nihilism because somebody always chafes when they notice boundaries."

"The problem with all that," she said, raising her voice as she pulled down on the metal flap that used to be part of the car's roof, "is the interpretation of the unseen and immeasurable *has* to be arbitrary. No one's quantified the rules—excuse me, *laws*— of the spiritual kingdoms in measurable, even provable form. In the meantime you get people who nail other people *to* crosses or *wear* them around their necks as they burn witches and launch crusades!"

"You're right."

"I am?"

"And wrong," I added as the metal flap gave way with a distressed groan. The wind poured down into the car, swirling

Deirdre's hair into a twisting, flamelike dance and forcing us to raise our voices again. "The fiction of the fools and the foul doesn't make what's True any less true."

She tossed the flap into the backseat.

"They just obscure the path to discovering what really works and what doesn't," I elaborated. "The fact that I'm pissed at the universe doesn't change its actual nature. If there is no God—or if there is and He doesn't bloody care—it ultimately makes no difference whether I rebel or suck up or divert myself with ritual and poetry: the laws of the universe, seen and unseen, *will* have their way. So, for me, my own brand of religion is all about figuring out which rules are the real laws. And which are merely the diversions and obfuscations of misled or purposely evil people."

"Interesting," she said. "But we're still left stumbling around in the dark. Who can measure love? Is fear merely a biochemical reaction? Where does desire come from? Why do two men respond to the same oppression with such different thoughts and emotions?"

I shrugged. "The fact that I *do not* know doesn't equate that I *can not* know. The laws governing our unseen selves are consistent: without companionship we are lonely, without hope we come to despair, without love we wither. The degree and the timetable may vary from person to person, but we are so alike in our *needs*—even if we are unalike in our expression of those needs and the forms we desire to put upon them."

Deirdre unfastened her seat belt and turned, thrusting her head and shoulders through the open roof to look back.

"What are you doing?"

"Objects in mirror are closer than they actually appear," she announced over the rush of night air. She ducked back in and refastened her seat belt. "Black Suburban. Are we done?"

I noticed that she did not put the Glock back down.

"Just one more point," I said, "since you wanted to pursue this topic. If I kiss your lips, you would take it as a sign of affection. If I were to kiss you and then betray you, you would feel the betrayal that much deeper—either because the kiss was false, or the kiss was true but I betrayed you anyway. Our bodies, our nerve endings, our pleasure centers—what we *do* with them defines our relationships and our intent."

The Suburban made its move. It accelerated until it swerved

around to pull alongside, matching my speed. The tinted glass windows remained closed, keeping its occupants anonymous.

"When I lie with Lupé," I continued, refusing to gawk, "when we make love and our bodies are joined, we are one. One flesh. It is our covenant. It is our pledge that though we are often individuals, yet we have a union between us that makes us more than the sum of our separate selves. That physical joining helps define our oneness in our unseen and unmeasureable aspects. We say to one another in the most primordial and fundamental language: I am One with you. Together, we are complete. And that act is more than the cement of our oneness, it is transformative: it becomes more than a symbol, it becomes The Truth." I tightened my grip on the steering wheel. "As long as neither of us betrays that Truth."

The dark window parallel to mine lowered and I could see Stefan Pagelovitch's face limned by the pale glimmer of the dashboard lights.

I lowered my window. "Your timing is lousy: Deirdre and I are talking about sex."

)*A mistake, my dear Christopher,*(came his telepathic response.)*You should be discussing death; you are on your way to embrace it.*(

Jeez, and here I thought we'd just spent the last twenty minutes running away from it, I sent back.

"What?" he called aloud.

"So what's your advice?" I yelled back.

"Come back with me to Seattle! Tonight!"

"Other than that?"

"Other than that I cannot help you!"

"I am weakened by every recruit to my banner. Is not a man better than a town?"

"What?"

"Emerson. Ralph Waldo, not Lake and Palmer." I raised my window and accelerated. The Suburban dropped back and fell in behind us.

Deirdre just looked at me.

"If I were to lie down with you and join my flesh to yours," I continued, "I would be saying to you that *we* are one. I am one with Deirdre, and she with me. *We* are complete together. And if it wasn't a lie between us, it would diminish my bond with Lupé because our oneness would no longer be unique. It would be the start of a lie between her and me. *The* Lie." The entrance to the BioWeb facilities was coming up on our right and I decelerated and turned in. "If it was a 'lie' between *us* then my relationship with Lupé is still diminished but *you* and I have also lied to one another."

"I don't—"

"I can't truly be One with her," I said, cutting her off, "if I'm not exclusive." The guard at the gate came out and checked the invitations that I held out my window. He looked at the bullet holes in the fore and aft windscreens and the makeshift moon roof. I was preparing to use the old Jedi mind trick when he waved us on through.

"Love," I said, maneuvering around a phalanx of expensive automobiles with real sunroofs and unventilated windshields, "requires an act of trust. True love is that greatest act of faith. When we lie to one another in the pantomime of love, we do violence to our secret selves and damage one another."

I parked so that we were near the entrance but facing the road in case we had to leave in a hurry. "And when we have lied, or been lied to, often enough—our capacity for love, to give or receive, is harmed beyond words."

"So, if you were to lie with me," she said with a forced dimple, "you would have to *lie* with me."

"By Jove," I murmured, "I think she's got it."

"I think we should have stopped when you said you didn't desire me."

I tried to match her smile but felt the weight of my words pulling at the corners of my mouth. "Ah," I said as we opened our doors, "but that would have been 'to *lie* with you,' as well."

Chapter Fourteen

The walk from the parking lot to BioWeb's main entrance was too short to solve the mystery of the Chevy Nova encounter.

While our pursuit had been decidedly unfriendly and our pursuers certainly willing to do violence to my passenger, their seeming reluctance to shoot the driver took on the appearance of solicitousness for my well-being.

Assuming they even knew who was driving.

Pagelovitch was intrigued by our account—what little he was able to glean from our telepathic musings, that is. I didn't, however, sense that he was about to go running back to confront our backside besiegers. More likely, he hoped our little outing would convince me to hop in the back of his Suburban and make the return trip to Seattle. There I would be untroubled by the necessities of survival and could enjoy the peace and prosperity than came with being the prize specimen in his preternatural petting zoo.

Which moved him to the top of the list of likely sponsors for our troublesome troupe of tailgaters.

And, as I held the door for Deirdre, who had done a remarkable job with her tiny hairbrush for a second time, I didn't have sufficient time to think about my previous visit to BioWeb's Black Fortress, or even a chance to focus on whether or not tonight's air was charged with a similarly dark presence.

There was, however, just enough time to snatch the spare ammo magazine out of Deirdre's marvelous décolletage and slip it into my pocket as we stepped into the entrance hall where another "guard" waited.

The guardian of the gates wore a black sheath dress that did nothing to enhance her lack of a figure. She was a tall, thin stick of a woman, in her late forties but eerily reminiscent of grade school hall monitors. "Mr. Haim, you're late!" she scolded as she checked our tickets.

I forced a smile. "Considering the theme, being the 'late' Mr. Haim seems somehow appropriate, don't you think?"

Her frown, slightly exaggerated by the tip of an ivory fang, indicated she didn't. I did a double take, saw it was fake. A portfolio and a set of plastic teeth encased in shrink-wrap were thrust into my grasp. A second set was proffered to Deirdre.

"I don't need the teeth," she said.

"You brought your own?"

My companion nodded, pulling back her crimson lips to display her "natural" incisors.

"Marvelous," the hostess enthused. "Some people really know how to get into the spirit of things!" She directed us toward the double doors, then froze in mid-gesture. Frown lines appeared around her Egyptian-mascaraed eyes as she took in my gray slacks and blazer over a maroon shirt. "You're not wearing black. Didn't anyone tell you that this is a *theme* event?"

I shrugged. "I forgot." Warbled eight bars of Bob Hope's signature tune using the words: "Fangs for the memories..."

Deirdre saved the day—or "night" to be more precise. Not only properly fanged, but attired in the universally appropriate "little black dress," her whiter shade of pale complexion provided a stark backdrop to the rosy luster of the strand of pearls at her throat. She reached into her little black cocktail purse and produced a small wooden box inlaid with mother-of-pearl and ivory scrolling. "Here, Darling," she said, placing it into my hands, "didn't I tell you it was on top of your dresser?"

I opened the box and considered the razor-sharp fangs resting upon the velvet-sheathed interior. During last year's sojourn in Seattle, Liz Bachman had found a dentist who made unusual dental appliances for the special effects studios out in Hollywood. Using a dental mold of my actual teeth, taken in the name of research, she had commissioned a pair of "vampire fangs" that would fit over my actual teeth. They looked real, were actually "functional," and—most surprisingly—stayed in place without the need for any kind of oral fixative.

Back when she was still human, Deirdre had offered herself to me while I wore the teeth and had proven them every bit as effective as the homegrown kind.

Then, while I slept beside her, she had taken the appliance from my mouth and used it to open her wrists in a manner that left no question of her final intent.

"How did you find this?" I whispered.

"Aren't you glad that I did?" was her idea of an answer. "You certainly don't want to be wearing those plastic, one-size-fits-all choppers for the rest of the evening."

I grimaced and slid my faux fangs into place as the hostess opened the door into the community room. Whenever I wore my enhanced dentatia I tended to sound a bit like Humphrey Bogart doing Elvis Presley doing meth. I wasn't looking forward to any long conversations.

"Gude eevning," the vampire up on the stage purred in a so-so Bela Lugosi accent. He tapped the microphone. "Is dis thing on?"

I looked around the large room. The conference wing of the BioWeb complex was overrun with vampires in full evening dress, only a few of which were pausing to pay any attention to the spokesman up front. I was tired and depleted and the adrenaline rush of the past hour was bottoming out, but I had a brief pick-me-up of the ole "fight or flight" juice before internalizing the fact that the fangs were all plastic. At least they all seemed to be plastic. Perhaps tonight's background sensation of wrongness could be chalked up to fatigue and the jittery backlash of my hunger.

Not to mention the weirdness of using a vampire theme to elicit donations of both the red and the green stuff.

The Red Cross had established an annual blood drive and theme event called "MASH Bash" where the attendees dressed in uniforms and surgical scrubs like the characters in the old television show. It had been a resounding success in rounding up blood donors for years. BioWeb was trying for a more Halloweeny theme, kicking

off their first annual blood drive utilizing the image of the ultimate blood donee.

Pop culture: ya gotta love it.

Nevertheless, it creeped me out. I had to force myself to relax,
calculating an hour of obligatory schmoozing, a discrete check-
in upstairs with Chalice on my blood work, and then we could
go home and figure out what to do about Theresa-call-me-Terry-
call-me-T.

As the lights dimmed and a descending screen caught images
from a hidden projector, I worked the perimeter of the room,
making a conscious effort to effect a social promenade while
checking the layout, guests, and exits.

Everyone was dressed in black, the men in tuxedos, and the
women in tailored dresses with hemlines and necklines of various heights and depths. Here and there were various flashes of
color: jewelry and cummerbunds, but I was apparently the only
one out of step with the overall color scheme. So much for the
low-profile strategy.

As the spokesman made a painful attempt to be entertaining,
he reeled off statistics about BioWeb's recent successes in pharmaceuticals, genetics research, and even nanotech development.
Tuning him out, we passed by a food bar with rows of steaming
dishes wafting odors of sauces and spices . . . and . . .

I sniffed and nearly sneezed.

Deirdre cursed.

Garlic!

"Great!" I muttered as we hurried past the potent smorgasbord,
"Buffet the vampire slayer!"

"Ooo-ooh!" cooed a feminine voice just off my left shoulder.
"Mr. Haim? It *is* you, is it not, Mr. Haim?"

I turned and half-recognized a matronly woman from the society
pages of the *News-Star*. I couldn't put a name with the face that
showed up there three out of four weeks but she had pegged me
from somewhere.

"Amanda Benton, Mr. Haim, of the Tallulah Bentons! *Not* the
Moss Point Bentons, of course!"

I nodded numbly. "Of course."

"You have been getting social invitations for six months now
and yet I never see you! I am sooo glad you could see your way

clear to join us this evening! Although I am just *sure* you couldn't stay away when the issue is blood itself!"

I think I goggled a bit. "Excuse me?"

"What with you owning that new blood bank and all I knew it was just a matter of time before BioWeb hooked you up with a fundraiser! And the brilliance of combining the October Ball with a blood drive is genius! Sheer genius! *À bon vin point d'enseigne!* It has that certain *je ne sais quoi*! Don't you agree?"

"*Çe n'est pas croyable,*" I said. "*Ca me donne le frisson.*"

She gave me a blank look.

"*Ça sent le poisson ici,*" I tried.

When it seemed that I was finally done she swatted me playfully. "*Oh*, Mr. Haim—may I call you Samuel? I did not know that you spoke French!"

"I do not know that you do, either. And call me Sam."

"Money, community service, and an active wit! Why Samuel, you need to start accepting more invitations! You'll be the *life* of the parties!"

"That would be an interesting change," Deirdre murmured on my right.

"Samuel," the matronly lady laid a white-gloved hand upon my arm, "I simply must introduce you around!"

"Must you?"

She stared at me, a fleeting look of blankness stumbling across her features. Then she started laughing—a strange juxtaposition of whooping and chuckling. "Oh, come with me you droll boy!"

Deirdre released my other arm before I was caught in a tug-o-war contest. "Looks like I'm not invited," she said.

"Stay out of trouble," was all I had time for before the crowd closed between us.

The introductions coupled with the obligatory chitchat were pretty much one and the same—the names and faces blurred in memory after a few moments. That is, until I was introduced to a portly gentleman dressed like Charles Addams' idea of a farmer.

"And this is William Robert Montrose his great grandfather was one of Monroe's original founders." Mrs. Benton said it all in a rush as if punctuation had no place in separating a man's name from his ancestry. It had been much that way with her other introductions this evening.

Montrose was as color-coordinated as the rest of the guests but, while they sported ebony and claret-trimmed evening dresses or tuxedos with crimson-lined capes, he was decked out in black satin overalls, a ruffled red silk shirt with white wing-collar and cuffs, and a lacy black cravat.

"Billy-Bob," Mrs. Benton continued, "I'd like you to meet Mr. Samuel Haim. Mr. Haim moved here six months ago and opened that new blood bank near the river."

Montrose scowled down at my would-be social guide and interpreter. "Amanda, how many times have I told y'all not to call me that? It's not dignified." He turned to me, flashed a toothy grin complete with vampire fangs and extended his hand. "Pleased to meet you, Mr. Haim. Especially since you seem to be the only other person here who isn't dressed like a Bela Lugosi or Morticia clone."

We shook hands. "My pleasure, Mr. Montrose." I noticed that his grip was smooth and cold.

He laughed and I noticed something else. Montrose's incisors were almost an inch long and the real thing. "Call me Bubba."

Amanda looked as if she was trying to figure out why an old acquaintance couldn't call him "Billy-Bob" but a complete stranger was allowed more casual status.

I was trying to figure the new terrain: so far I had one vampire try to kill me, another try to bed me, a third bring along reinforcements to make me go home, and now I had one asking me to call him Bubba....

I *hate* high-society socials.

"Ooh," Mrs. Benton fluttered, "there's Victor Cascio—"

"Amanda darlin'," Bubba's arm cordoned me off like a crime scene, "I have business to discuss with Mr. Haim." He smiled and I felt a vague disturbance in the air. "Run along and I'll play host for awhile."

She smiled uncertainly then turned and, after a moment's orientation, trotted off toward a knot of upper-crust matrons like a Sioux warrior bent on counting coup.

"Thank you," I said.

He grinned. "Amanda could suck the life out of a person faster than a real live vampire."

I looked at him sidewise. "Isn't that an oxymoron? Real 'live' vampire?"

"Perhaps. But the world is filled with oxymorons."

"Certainly morons."

"I will concede that point quite readily, Mr. Haim."

"Please, call me Sam."

"With pleasure. Once we become good friends, perhaps you will let me call you Chris."

I looked at him sharply. "What?"

"Don't look so surprised, son. You're not such a bad detective for a Yankee who's been down here less'n a year. But we Southern boys figured out how to use and breed bloodhounds before the North even took notice that there was a South."

"Bloodhounds, eh? Are we talking about a certain fortune-tel—?"

He held up his hand. "Hold on there, son. I won't hold with casting aspersions on a lady. Especially the one you were about to name. It wouldn't be right and, furthermore, it wouldn't be *safe*. And if you haven't figured out that much, yet, maybe you should close down that detective hobby of yours and try your hand at gardening." His smile softened any presumed judgment in his words.

"You're her client."

He grinned. "One of 'em. And, more important, I count her as one of my friends. A good friend. A fella needs good friends when he's encompassed by the bands of death."

"Bands of death," I repeated. "Are we talking about heavy metal concerts?"

His grin faded. "Look around you. Not all of the plastic fangs are plastic." He caught my arm. "*Subtly* . . . let's not gawk like a chicken in a fox house."

Fatigue had dulled my senses—all six of them. Now that it was called to my attention, I saw what would have still been sneaky had I arrived on full alert. Here and there among the fake vampires were representatives of the Real Deal. Little details began to stand out: their erect carriage and attitude of aloofness—as if no one else was in the room but them. Their pallor was not the artifice of powder or paint but their true, sunless nature. And, with careful observation I could see that most of them seemed aware of one another: nods and gestures and fleeting eye contact. They were a group with a group's purpose.

"I didn't realize that there was a demesne in this area."

"There ain't, son. These boys are outtatowners. Northeast Teeth with a temporary assignment in our fair city."

So Erzsébet Báthory was importing undead from both ends of the compass. "What are they here for?"

"Well now, that's where I'm hoping you're a better detective than everybody says you are. I'd like for you to find out for us. . . ."

Count Bubba had pretty much concluded our conversation with directions to his "manse" and the invitation to drop by soonest for a more in-depth palaver about BioWeb's vampire connection. The little I learned from our brief conversation was considerable compared to my intelligence from the past six months of living here in the twin cities.

Although the BioWeb facilities were nearly five years old, the vamps on staff hadn't shown up until about eighteen months ago: a couple at first, then a couple more. Until recently, the numbers seemed to stabilize in the eight-to-ten range. That had changed a couple of days ago when those numbers had suddenly doubled.

I made a note to ask Pagelovitch how many fanged enforcers he had brought with him from Seattle.

Aside from the fact that these imports hailed from the East Coast, all but confirming Erzsébet's hand in all of this, Montrose claimed that there was no organized coven—much less actual enclave—here in north Louisiana.

He did, however, admit that he and I weren't the only rogues inhabiting the area.

I wanted to ask more questions but Billy-Bob was adamant about not drawing attention to us. Especially while we were surrounded by so many deadly undeadlies. I barely refrained from pointing out that this was advice coming from a man wearing black satin overalls.

"Keep that in mind as you work your inside sources," he said, nodding toward the "vampire" that was coming our way.

It was Chalice and she must have run Deirdre's little black dress through BioWeb's cloning labs. Her hair was piled up on top of her head, giving a clear view of her neck and the twin puncture wounds that dripped blood down to her bare shoulder. Unnatural teeth flashed behind full, red lips and jewels of blood glistened at the corners of her mouth.

I reached for her and grasped her arms as she arrived. "What happened? Are you all—" I got a closer look at her bite marks. "—right—that's not real blood," I finished lamely. "Lipstick?"

She shook her head and I could see that the teeth were Halloween plastic. "Nail polish. Lipstick just doesn't catch the light right for that freshly bled shimmer."

"I didn't expect to meet you down here," I said. "I guess the staff is expected to show support, though."

She nodded. "I didn't want to wait. I haven't slept since I started running tests on your blood samples." She kept her voice low and in the "confidential" range, but I was mindful of ears that could hear better than most dogs.

"Chalice, I'd like you to meet—" I turned but Montrose was gone, already blending into the tree-line of the crowd. "Never mind." I looked more closely and saw the haze of fatigue clouding her emerald eyes. "Hey, you've got to get some rest."

"Don't worry about me. I can sleep later."

"You should sleep now." I considered making it a command.

"There's so much to do!"

"And that's the other point. If you're tired, you're more likely to make mistakes. And that could set me—us—back more than those extra hours of sleep."

"But—"

Not here! I sent. *Not now!* "We should discuss this elsewhere."

Chalice swayed a bit—perhaps from fatigue, or my sending may have been a tad forceful due to my own discomfort with our surroundings.

"Outside," she said. "We could meet out back, down by the runoff pond."

I glanced around. Amanda Benton looked as if she might be working her way back in our direction. "I'll go now," I said. "Wait ten minutes and then try to slip out without attracting any attention."

She nodded and I bolted, weaving my way through the loose accumulation of bodies so as to avoid any conversational nibbles from the wrong parties.

I slipped out one of the back doors and waited for my eyes to adjust to the dark. It didn't take long because it wasn't really dark. The grounds were well lit in front and to either side of the main building. Enough ambient light spilled over behind the building to illume the area to predawn levels.

A service path led down to the ornamental pond back toward the electrified fence.

As I strolled closer, I could tell that the pond had more than ornamental purposes: a chemical smell rose from its misty, oil-slicked surface and a pattern of turbulence betrayed some stirring mechanism hidden in its black depths.

No crickets sang, no bullfrogs harrumphed; the only sound was the hum of electricity from the fence capacitors, chanting a mindless mantra of death for foolish trespassers.

I looked around. I was as alone in the bleached darkness as I had been inside my own heart since Lupé's departure.

A moment later I wasn't.

Alone, that is.

Faster than you could say "abra-cadaver" there was a corpse standing in front of me. "Baron . . ." said a quiet, fluttery voice. A familiar voice. "It's me."

"Of course it is," I said. "Who else could you be?"

"Introduce yourself, soldier," said another voice from the deeper darkness behind him. It had a clotted quality—like water trickling over clods of ancient earth fouling an old drainpipe.

"Oh. Oh! Sorry, sir!" He almost saluted, then fumbled his cap off his head. "I'm PFC Willie Blankenship, Twenty-third—" What I could see of his twisted face twisted some more. Along with the cap in his bony hands. "Sorry. Cap'n is always remindin' me that we're all Louzianans now. Been dead here longer than alive all them other places put together."

Something "cleared its throat" beyond his desiccated shoulder.

"Oh, and may I present Captain Jelly Worthington."

"Commanding officer of the First Monroe Irregulars," finished the not-quite-human voice. "You will forgive me, suh, if I do not advance into the light. I am not yet presentable to living eyes."

If he considered the remains of Private First Class Blankenship to be mostly presentable maybe I didn't want to see what was standing back in the shadows. Being sort of a Yankee carpetbagger, myself, I was unsure of the proper social protocols—I nodded my head and said: "I'm honored, Captain."

"Not as much as we are, suh. We've been a waitin' for you to come for near on a century and a half."

"Hum," I said, trying to think on my feet and be ready to run with them, too. "I don't think I am who you think I am. . . ."

"It doesn't matter to us if you're an actual baron or not, suh. Bessie Crow says you're the one who's going to deal with the gray men and give us our discharge papers."

"Uh, discharge papers?"

"Our bones may be bound to the soil in which we lie but our spirits have ties to other homes and kith and family—even if they are our great-great-grandchildren. We've stood picket for a hundred and fifty years. We're overdue for relief. And we like not the company of the dragon that slumbers beneath us."

"How—how can I help?" I asked, wondering if the word "slumber" was being used in the figurative sense.

"A more likely question is how can *we* help? Your flesh is solid, your bones intact. You can pass for human under most circumstances. We have not adequate form, yet."

"Uh, adequate form?" I asked. "Yet?"

"The gray men pump their runoff into a dry aquifer. From there this witch's brew seeps into the earth and laces our remains with poisons that would kill us twice over were it not for the old witch woman's enchantments. Instead, the chemicals bind to our sinews and swell the dried husks that remain. The old witch has promised that we will have our hands and feet in time. She says the time to muster is soon."

"She say anything specific about what *I'm* supposed to do?"

"You are to break the alliance of the gray men with a woman called Marie Bochay."

"*Marinette Bois-Chèche*?" I should have been happy that some of these loose ends were starting to line up into some sort of pattern. What I felt now had nothing to do with relief.

"Someone's coming," said PFC Blankenship. He stepped back into the darkness with his captain.

I turned and looked back toward the building. A figure was coming toward me, haloed by the spill of lights from behind. Its features were lost in the dark silhouette created by the backlighting.

I shifted my vision into the infrared spectrum and . . . no one was there. *Bubba Billy-Bob?*

I shifted back to the human-visible range and reacquired the silhouette at half the distance now: it was rushing me.

I leapt aside as it closed but it grabbed my jacket and we whirled about as though we were partners in some mad Cossack dance routine. I threw the creature off with a little help from centrifugal force, but it recovered quickly and advanced with its arms held wide, growling like some B-movie monster from the fifties.

"Look," I said, backing up and trying to maneuver so that I could regain the advantage of light and shadow. "I just came outside for a breath of fresh air. I'm sorry if I wandered into a security zone by accident. I'll just go back—"

"Cséjthe?" the silhouette growled.

"Geshundheit," I said.

What I really wanted to say was: *Shit!*

"The countess will be pleased," it rumbled. And lunged.

Where was Deirdre when I needed her? I dodged again.

It caught me again. This time I couldn't shake free.

We went down. I rolled. It refused to relinquish its hold. Maybe I could roll us both into the pond. Maybe that might be enough distraction to break its grip. Then what? The backstroke?

We stopped without ever reaching the pond. One moment we were rolling, the next we weren't. Although I ended up on top, the vampire still held me close in a three-handed grip. Something was wrong with that tally but before I could think through a recount, one of the hands released my arm and grabbed my assailant's biceps. Another joined it. And another. Suddenly there were more hands than I could keep track of. The vampire reluctantly released me as a half-dozen or more hands pried his arms back and pinned them to the ground.

The hands came in an assortment of sizes and degrees of decay. The only things they had in common were that they were attached to arms that were thrusting up out of the earth and they were all dedicated to restraining my attacker. Who began to howl and struggle all the harder as his clothing and flesh began to smoke where the dead appendages held him.

. . . this witch's brew . . . laces our remains with poisons that would kill us twice over . . .

Apparently undead flesh wasn't proof against BioWeb's toxic waste. I scrambled to my feet and stepped back. PFC Blankenship was suddenly at my side. "Captain's compliments, suh. He was thinkin' you might want to borrow his sword under the circumstances." He handed me a cavalry saber in its curved brass sheath.

The vampire continued to squirm and bellow as I drew the sword and considered its tarnished and rusted blade in the pale wash of amber light.

"Under the circumstances," Blankenship kibitzed, "it's the humane thing to do."

Actually, it was the smart thing to do: every screech and holler risked undead reinforcements. I raised the ancient blade above my head. "The humane thing to do," I echoed. "But is it the *human* thing?"

"Do whatever it takes to stay alive," the dead soldier whispered.

"Then it is our humanness that damns us," I said. And brought the blade down. The caterwauling stopped immediately as the head went tumbling away from the body. A moment later the vampire's remains crumbled to ash. The only evidence of our struggle was the churned earth where, even now, the cadaverous hands were withdrawing into its sour depths.

And my rumpled clothing, bearing grass stains and dirt smears and a scorch mark where the fabric was briefly grasped by poisonous phalanges.

"More company," another unseen voice called from the darkness at my back. I looked back up the path at another silhouette walking toward me. I shifted perspective: no heat signature. Shi—

"Mr. Haim?" The voice belonged to William Robert Montrose aka Count Bubba.

I relaxed but PFC Blankenship snapped to attention beside me. "Holy cow, Sarge! What are you doing here?"

Master Sergeant William Robert Montrose excused himself from the revenantal reunion he was sharing with his fellow Civil War vets—some of whom he'd helped plant here. I had assumed Billy-Bob—excuse me, Bubba—was a born and bred son of the South. I mean, what's in a name?

It turned out that he was originally from Des Moines, marched down here with the other blue bellies of the Twenty-third Infantry, and got forcibly assimilated a month after the war ended. According to his abbreviated explanation he had come through some twenty-odd battles without a scratch only to get bit by "some undead Yankee sonuvabitch carpetbagger" while on garrison duty.

I'd say he'd assimilated real good over the past one-hundred-and-forty-odd years.

Amazingly neither he nor his former comrades and foes had any inkling that either had lingered post-mortem for so long and in such close proximity. Just goes to show what a small world the afterlife can be.

"She's not coming," he said, a look of concern hardening his face.

"Who? Chalice? Deirdre?"

"Neither one's my guess." He caught my arm as I turned back toward the main building. "I'm out here for a reason: finding you was just a bonus."

"And the reason is . . . ?"

"Not to be in there, right now," he said. "Why don't you hang around here and, when the boys and me are done palavering, we'll take a walk over to the mosquito breeding ponds and see if we can figure out what the gray men are really up to?"

There was a disquieting look in his eyes—beyond the usual disquiet I generally feel when looking into the eyes of an undead creature.

"I have someone I'm supposed to meet."

"Sonny boy," he laid a cold hand on my shoulder, "this here's a fancy dress ball and that ain't nothing more than a dandified dance. One of the realities of any dance is that you don't always go home with the one that brung ya."

"What are you afraid of?"

He looked up at the building. "The Hunger," he said unevenly.

"Me, too," I said quietly. "But I can't hide from it."

"Not what I'm talking about," Montrose said. "Not my hunger, not your hunger. It's a Hunger beyond us. An Appetite . . ."

"Yeah? Well, ring my bell and call me Pavlov." I started back up the hill.

He caught my arm again after a dozen paces. "If you must go, go slowly. Go carefully. Stay close to an exit. And get away as soon as you can." He turned back to the shadows where his sesquicentennial comrades were waiting.

I stomped back up the hill muttering a string of curses. Divorce cases weren't so bad. Come to think of it, spouse stalking was a little bit like being cinematographer for *America's Funniest Home Videos*. I was going to memo Olive as soon as I got back in, tonight: from now on After Dark Investigations was going to handle nothing but divorce cases!

No more walking corpses!

No more End of the World conspiracies!

And absolutely nothing requiring attendance at social gatherings with dress codes!

The rear exit was one of those self-locking affairs, forcing me to hike all the way around to the front of the building to get back in.

Chapter Fifteen

The first thing I noticed was that there were fewer cars in the parking lot than when we had arrived. It was too early for the evening's entertainment to wind down and I knew of no other social events likely to siphon off the crowd tonight.

Three more cars drove off while I stood and looked over the lot. At least there had been one new arrival in the past hour: a green Chevy Nova was parked four spaces over from my car.

I affected a casual amble, moving across the lined asphalt in a roundabout route to see if anyone was loitering in the vicinity.

Nope.

As I drew near, I noticed that my car sagged a bit: the right rear tire was flat. So much for a quick getaway.

Upon closer examination the problem was clear: a slitted puncture in the sidewall of the tire. Stiletto? No . . . the slit was three times the width of a stiletto blade. More like the signature of an Army combat knife. One end of the cut was even abraded as if caught by the back saw-edge of such a blade.

I looked across at the Nova and then back at my poor, abused coupe. Talk about adding major insult to injury . . .

Whatever happened to the good old days when vampires rarely traveled by coach and spent most of their time lurking around castle corridors?

I opened my trunk, hauled out the jack and the spare. Took off my jacket and proceeded to set a new world's record for a tire change outside of a raceway pit crew. Put my jacket back on and grinned: now the element of surprise had shifted.

I looked back over at the Nova. There was room to shift it some more.

I put my ruined tire and my jack back in my trunk and looked around. Wondered a bit about security cameras. Remembered that my image worked about as well on videotape as it did on mirrors.

I hefted my tire iron and walked to the far side of the Nova. Doing my best Minnesota Fats impression, I poked a hole in its rear tire. Now we were even.

Except I was ahead of the game now.

But not enough ahead, I decided, curling my fingers under the lip of the Nova's trunk. I pulled and lifted using a little of the preternatural strength that my tainted blood had granted as a benevolent side effect. The catch popped with a groan of stressed metal. If I couldn't bend it back to close tight, they might still believe it was the sudden dive into the ditch that left it sprung.

Or they might not once they found out that I had popped their spare, as well.

The spare was not readily accessible. Under the amber wash of the parking lot lights I could make out tarpaulin bundles that lay across the flooring and wheel well. I pulled one of the edges back. Looked. Started opening the other bundles.

The handguns were on top: a couple of 9mm SIG Sauer P226 pistols, a .357 Magnum S&W revolver, and an HK 23 SOCOM .45 caliber handgun with suppressor and laser aiming module.

Four rifles were underneath: a Carbine automatic M-4 A1 5.56mm, a Chicom Type 56 (think AK-47), and two 7.62mm M-14 automatic rifles. Next to them were a couple of 12-gauge Mossberg shotguns, pump action with folding stocks.

This was bad with a capital B.

What made it infinitely worse (with a capital W) were the bundles on each side.

On the left I saw an N91 left-handed 7.62mm bolt-action sniper rifle. Next to it, a Barrett M99 .50 BMG bolt-action, magazine-fed sniper rifle. The sewing machines lay on the right-hand side of the trunk: an MK43 7.62mm machine gun and two submachine guns, MP-5 series, 9mm.

I didn't open the ammo boxes: I was afraid I'd find grenades.

I rewrapped everything and closed the trunk lid, pushing the lip back in so it would catch on the frame and hold shut for the time being.

I tossed the tire iron in the back seat of my car and pulled out my cell phone. I only used it for emergencies as it gave me headaches. I had already learned to step back while operating a microwave oven. It was fortunate that I had the number for the Monroe cop shop stored in memory: my hands were shaking so badly I would have had trouble punching in 911.

"Monroe Police Department," answered a voice. "How may we help you?"

"Uh, I'd like to report a probable crime."

"What sort of a crime? And may I have your name, please?"

"Name? I thought I could report a crime anonymously."

"Well, yes, but—Haim? Is that you?"

"What?"

"This is Detective Murray, Mr. Haim."

"Detective Murray?"

"Yes. I'm just covering the phones while the desk sergeant is using the can."

"I didn't know you worked the late shift."

"Well, truth be told we were just getting ready to come back out and see you." His voice held the easygoing tone of a man suggesting a pleasant social visit. Sometimes Murray's affable smile and pleasant tone suggested that he might be more dangerous than Ruiz for all her vinegar-and-piss attitude.

"We?"

"Lieutenant Ruiz is here."

I felt my heart sink: could this night get any more complicated?

"Seems your corpse has turned up missing again," he continued all too pleasantly.

"*My* corpse?"

"Yeah, Kandi Fenoli. Remember her? She's showed up at your place twice, now. The lieutenant thinks third time's a charm."

There was a brief mumble and fumble then Ruiz's voice blared in my ear: "Haim? I don't know how you're getting her body out of the morgue but I'll have a warrant tonight if I have to wake up every judge in Ouachita Parish! I'll commandeer a backhoe! I'll dig up every inch—"

While Ruiz bellowed my sinking heart found its Peter Pan "happy thought" and began to soar.

"No need to go all L.A.P.D., Detective," I said when I could finally squeeze in a word edgewise. "You know you've got nothing on me except a vague circumstantial and you've got nowhere else to look. You keep shaking my tree, hoping something will fall out."

She sputtered but I kept on talking.

"Well, to show you there's no hard feelings, I'm going to help you break the case. I think I know where the body is."

"*What?*"

I almost said "nice *Gladys Kravitz impression*" but why throw fuel on the fire at that point. "I think it's locked in the trunk of a green Chevy Nova in the guest parking lot in front of BioWeb Industries."

"What's it doing there? How did you get this information?"

"Well, I saw this Chevy Nova parked in the woods near my place this evening and remembered that I had seen it in the neighborhood on the other occasions when that corpse turned up on my property."

"Are you certain about this?"

"I walked over to see what was going on and found the car empty and the trunk open."

"What about the body?"

"Didn't actually see a body."

"Then why—"

"Though there was this tarp that might have been wrapped around a body."

"That's hardly—"

"I almost looked inside but there were all these guns."

"Guns?"

"Illegal stuff. Auto and semi-automatic weapons. Sniper kits. If these bubbas are going hunting, they sure as hell ain't looking for Bambi."

"You're telling me you saw contraband firearms in the trunk of this car?"

"And I think I saw a shovel," I said, "and maybe a bag of quicklime. I decided I'd better get out of there fast. Then I saw the same car right here."

"Parked in front of BioWeb?" Her voice had lost its bluster and taken on that vague distracted tone that meant she was writing everything down. I would have to choose my words carefully.

"You might want to bring a SWAT team, Lieutenant; these guys are loaded for bear."

"You're sure you saw automatic weapons? You know what to look for?"

"I did some time in the military. This was special ops stuff. Better get down here before they drive away," I admonished. And gave her the license number just to be on the safe side. "Gotta go."

"Wait!"

I disconnected and turned the phone off. I had intended to report an illegal weapons cache, hoping the police would come out and muck up the works for whoever was shadowing me in the Nova. Getting Ruiz had been sheer serendipity. There'd be hell to pay when Kandi Fenoli didn't turn up and Ruiz went looking for tire tracks in my woods, but the immediate fireworks would likely get both the police and the vamps in the Nova off my back for tonight.

If it *was* vamps in the Nova.

I was making more than one assumption, here. I hadn't actually seen how many occupants there were in the car when I had braced it on the trip in. I was assuming undead because that's where my current problems seemed to lie.

But the past has a funny way of blindsiding you when you least expect it, I thought, remembering the left-handed setup on the N91 sniper rig.

Let the police handle it, I decided. I was strictly limited to divorce cases from here on out. I almost felt a wave of contentment, having juxtaposed two problems into a single solution—that old "two birds with one stone" thing again. I almost whistled as I pulled the Glock out of my own car and fished a spare shoulder-rig out of my trunk.

Maybe my luck had turned, but I'd lived and died long enough to know the importance of making safety your first priority. I jacked the silver loads into the Glock, holstered it, and pulled my jacket across the forward thrust of the butt as I walked back toward the front entrance.

I had been gone only—what? Thirty, forty minutes?

During that time there had been a "sea change" in the main ballroom. The crowd had diminished by a good third or more, but it seemed more a result than a causal factor. It felt as though the air had been pumped out of the room and replaced with some thicker, viscous gas. The lights seemed dimmer, the music more harsh and edged. Last night's air of unease was a feeble precursor to tonight's atmosphere of dread.

The murmur of conversation had doubled in volume even as the numbers of conversants had dropped. Here and there, high-pitched laughs verging on hysteria spiked above the noise like an auditory flare requesting rescue.

" . . . Mosquitoes!" an old man was saying. "All that spraying and larvicide just a couple of years back and they're saying the numbers are twice what they were during the encephalitis epidemic!"

"But no viruses so far," Dr. Stoli responded.

Stoli taught American History at the university and reminded everyone but his students of a jovial Russian bear. "No West Nile, no Equine or St. Louis." He wasn't Russian, and Stoli wasn't actually his name. Lithuanian by birth, "Stoli" was an approximation of the first two syllables of his first name. "Mosquitoes are tiny down here. Up in Michigan they are huge. Bite through blue jean denim. Carry off babies!" He made a large gesture that threatened to slosh his drink in a ten-foot arc.

"Been to Michigan," the old man argued. "Ours may be small but they've got way more attitude. Travel in larger packs. Some carry switchblades. . . ."

As I passed beyond their orbit and set course for the crowd's epicenter, I saw a maelstrom of bodies rotating slowly at the center of the room, circling some eye of social power at its center. I thought about Poe's *The Masque of the Red Death* as I moved deeper into the melee and started trolling for Chalice and Deirdre.

"Sure, a lot of their work is theoretical," my banker opined, off to my left, "but there's government money involved and that most likely means biological counteragent development in the back rooms. If there's another terrorist incident you'll see BioWeb stock go through the roof!"

Mrs. Stein, old and rich and thrice widowed cocked a silvery eyebrow. "You're so sure the government would only be interested in *counteragents*?"

Sweat sheened the faces of those false vampires I passed as I nodded pleasantly to nothing in particular to maintain some social camouflage. The real vamps seemed to have thinned out but the two I passed within a ten-minute interval were clearly affected, as well. They stood still, eyes closed and nostrils flared open, oblivious to the press of the throng around them.

"For God sake," a young, thin man was ardently protesting, "you people think every instance of misfortune is some external conspiracy to oppress you and keep you down! It's the flu, for God sake!"

An elderly black man stood stiffly, staring back at him, through him, beyond him, as if contemplating some ancient fork in the road that led to different and alien landscapes.

I stopped a little ways beyond them.

Closed my eyes.

Sniffed.

A kaleidoscope of scents thundered through my head: the sweat and musk of a hundred bodies overlaid by a multitude of perfumes, colognes, and aftershaves, all lubricated with various soaps and powders, deodorants and antiperspirants. Makeup: foundation and lipstick and gloss and polish and spray with tobacco chasers tucked away in pockets, pouches, and cases. The food bar, the alcohol with three-dozen different blends spilling atomized distillations across my olfactory nerves.

And something else. Something sweet and sharp and exciting and familiar but—

It came to me.

The lunar cycle was not the only tidal force at play this night. Other cycles had converged for some of the female attendees. The sweetest perfume yet.

Yet . . .

Something more.

Something greater than the possible cyclic alignment of every woman on the premises . . .

I turned my head, searching.

The perfume wafted from the center of the social storm.

I turned and began a slow approach trajectory designed to bring me there in a great, arcing curve.

"All I know is the Social Security trust fund was in enough trouble before Bush instituted that irresponsible tax cut. The subsequent war footing has done so much damage to the economy and the surplus that my own kids are never going to see one dime of their retirement, never mind my grandkids . . ."

I had initially worried about making a spectacle of myself upon reentering the party. My clothes were rumpled, my knees stained, elbow scorched—if the vampires didn't take notice, I figured the social mavens would.

But no one did.

It was as if they were distracted by their own conversations, trying desperately not to look around. Some appeared to be listening to music that no one else could hear. Darkness seemed to be gathering in the corners of the room like shadowy dust bunnies.

Why do we do this? I wondered. Dress up and surround ourselves with the trappings of evil and pain and death?

Is it ancient mummery, designed to appease the elder gods with ritual obeisance? Or the modern trend of mocking that which we fear? Over the years I had rolled my eyes with every fundamentalist letter to the editorial page bemoaning the pagan observance of Halloween. Prissy, self-righteous, ultraconservative Christians with their panties in a wad over children in costumes going door-to-door to extort candy on October thirty-first. *Satan worship,* they railed. And the rest of us wondered who was really giving the devil his due: children embracing a yearly opportunity to dress up and collect free goodies or pinch-faced adults who feared such activities would lead them down the path of sin and degradation?

We honor that which we fear.

And in fearing something, we grant it power over us.

But perhaps we are wise to leave our bonfires dark on All Hallows E'en. If we light no fires we leave the shadows trapped in the greater darkness. When we burn, we call them to the edge of our guttering light.

Where they wait their opportunities . . .

I was closing in on the center of the room now and found Chalice first. A tall, thin, bald man stood beside her and had one arm twined with hers while the other hand gripped her wrist in what could be a simple gesture of affection or an artful pose to prevent her leaving. The bald guy was in animated conversation with a woman wearing a man's black tuxedo. "Government entitlements are like a lifeboat," he was saying. "Try to load too many people on board and it sinks: everybody drowns!" The woman wore her tux much better than he wore his. I wasn't sure about her but my client definitely looked as though she needed rescuing.

"Ah, there you are!" I said, working my way toward my last hope for humanity. "What about that dance you promised me?"

Chalice jerked her head toward the sound of my voice but the relief in her eyes was veiled by caution.

I got more enthusiasm from Chrome-dome the Cadaverous. "Ms. Delacroix, could this be our mystery man?"

She shook her head as I shook his hand. "Name's Haim," I said as I pumped his fishlike hand, allowing Chalice the opportunity to disengage. "Samuel Haim, private eye."

"Pleased to meet you, Mr. Haim," he answered. His voice had a nasal quality that would have rendered it unpleasant even without the rest of him showing up to put you off your feed. "Would you be our mystery donor?"

"I solve mysteries," I answered in my most chipper tones, "I don't donate them. Ms. Delacroix has hired me to look into a family matter for her."

"Oh *really*? What sort of case is it?" he asked.

"A sort of a private case," I answered with a smile. "Which makes it serendipitous as I am a *private* investigator."

His smile held but his eyes had a bit of a blank look pass across them. "Ah! Well! Perhaps we might avail ourselves of your services . . ."

"Getting divorced?"

"What? No. What I mean is we have a bit of a mystery here in our own laboratories."

"Ah," I said, nodding as if I were contemplating the Great Mysteries, myself: "research."

"Well, yes, of course," Baldy dissembled. He peered at me closely.

It was like being examined by a suspicious vulture. With halitosis. "But the mystery that we are currently discussing has to do with some blood samples."

"Oh," I said, "now *that* I can probably help you with."

"You can?" He smiled. Yep, a vulture.

"Most assuredly. For example, it's standard practice to collect at least two five-milliliter tubes of blood in purple-top tubes with EDTA as an anticoagulant for DNA analysis. For drug or alcohol testing one collects blood samples in gray-top tubes with sodium fluoride. I always identify each tube with the date, time, subject's name, location, my name, case number, and evidence number." Baldy was trying to get a word in but I wasn't about to let him. "But procedure doesn't end there," I continued with scarcely a breath. "You have to refrigerate, being careful to not freeze your blood samples. And when you have to ship or transport them, you pack the liquid blood tubes individually in Styrofoam or cylindrical tube containers with absorbent material surrounding the tubes, layered with cold packs, not dry ice." I paused and when he opened his mouth to speak, I added: "It's important to label the outer container with phrases like 'Keep in a cool dry place,' 'Refrigerate upon arrival,' and 'Biohazard.'"

"That's not what we're talking about!" the dome sputtered when I finally ran down.

"It's not?" I replied, all innocence.

"Dr. Krakovski is the Head of our Viral Mutagens Division," Chalice explained. My dumb and annoying act seemed to be serving some purpose: Krakovski was off-balance and Chalice looked a little steadier than she had upon my arrival.

"We're dealing with unknown blood samples," the "Head" clarified.

"Oh!" I said, "why didn't you say so up front instead of letting me go on and on about something so irrelevant as collecting *known* blood samples?"

"Well—" he began.

"Now collecting unknown blood samples—that's a real challenge!" I was off and gauging my rhythms and pauses to Krakovski's vain attempts to get this conversation back on track. "For instance, you got two kinds of blood when you're collecting it from a person— living or dead. For your liquid blood, you use a clean cotton cloth or swab—but you gotta leave a portion of it unstained as a control. Then you air-dry the cloth or swab and pack it in clean paper or an envelope with sealed corners. You don't use plastic containers— this is one of the mistakes you commonly see on TV."

The woman in the tux started backing away.

"Now dried blood is pretty much the same, believe it or not. You still use a clean cotton cloth or swab only you moisten it with distilled water. And, of course—" He chimed in with me on: "—you gotta leave a portion of it unstained as a control."

"Right," I said.

"Then you air dry the cloth or swab and pack it in clean paper or an envelope with sealed corners," he continued sourly.

"You don't use plastic containers," I reminded.

"It's one of the mistakes you commonly see on TV," he concluded. "Are we done?"

"Don't you want to know how to collect blood samples from various kinds of materials or surfaces?"

"Not really."

"Or in snow or water?"

He shook his head.

"Well," I said, "there are some variations, mostly in storing and transporting. But you've got the bulk of it with the cotton cloth or swab technique." I joined Krakovski in looking around. "Where did Ms. Delacroix go?"

"You're the private eye," he said with ill-conceived contempt, "why don't you go detect or something." He turned away and stalked off in a huff. I stared after him: I hadn't actually seen someone leave "in a huff" since I was back on the playground in grade school recess.

A hand fell on my shoulder. I turned and looked into undead eyes.

Bluffing was out of the question. It was obvious from first glance that this guy knew who I was and had sought me out deliberately. Worse, I've seen scary-looking vampires but this guy would super-size your goose bumps even if he was still human. Built like a muscular bowling ball, he was all heft and weight and hardness— nothing soft about this Bloody Harry.

"So," I said with the most pleasant smile I could barely muster, "every vampire I know was bit on the neck when they were turned. Since you haven't got one, how does that work, exactly?"

He linked his arm through mine. It was like being handcuffed to a steel I-beam. "She wants to meet you," he growled.

There was never even the slightest question of whom he was talking about.

"Growling? You're a hyper-mesomorph with fangs and, on top of all that, you're growling? I think someone is overcompensating."

He tugged and there was also no question of whether I would come along or balk: I staggered and the floor began polishing the soles of my shoes.

"Tell me the truth . . ." I whispered, " . . . you've got a little one, don't you?"

As he dragged me toward the center of the maelstrom of flesh and fear, I glanced down to see if I'd wet my pants yet.

So far, so dry.

The night, however, was still young.

A woman stood at the center of the room, her back turned toward me.

I knew even before she turned in profile that I was in the presence of the Blood Countess, the Witch of Cachtice. The fact that she bore little resemblance to the blurry images provided by surviving woodcuts was of no importance. Her aura of power and menace marked her more surely than any forensic technology of the twenty-first century.

Deirdre and Chalice stood beside her, one on each side, but I couldn't focus on them because *her* presence demanded my attention. She wore a black leather dress that blended well with her long, black hair and blacker eyes. It had a vulgar cut that seemed well matched to the woman wearing it. Individually, her features suggested that she should be beautiful. The combined effect had been spoiled, somehow, as if her beauty was skin deep and something unspeakable lurked just beneath her epidermis.

The neckline of her dress plunged and narrowed to the nexus of her cleavage then parted again, angling out to form an hourglass-shaped cutout baring her pale midriff. As if the "black widow" motif was too obscure, there were additional spiderweb cutouts on either side, artfully designed to show a great deal of flesh as she stood and even more when she moved.

I tried not to stare but failed miserably. It wasn't sexy; it was a crude attempt at sensuality that came close to failing as even a caricature. She turned as I approached and gave me one of those stagy "come hither" looks that just about completed the whole tacky tableau.

I arrived, "dragged" hither more than anything else.

Her eyes looked me up and down and then invited me to reciprocate.

I reciprocated. Smiled. "Wow," I said, "did Madonna have a garage sale?"

The bowling ball's hand tightened painfully on my biceps. "You will show respect to your betters!" he hissed.

"Sure, sure," I agreed quickly, my knees starting the transformation from solids to liquids. "Just trot 'em out here—"

"Sandor, be nice." Her voice was low and husky and triggered an involuntary shiver down my spine. I like it when a woman has a little more testosterone than estrogen jazzing her hormonal balance. But I'm still insecure enough to prefer that my T-levels be higher than hers—I'd met pre-op transsexuals who were more feminine than Sandor's lady boss.

I looked over at Deirdre. She only had eyes for the lady in leather. Ditto Chalice. Beside me Sandor the bowling ball was practically a-quiver like some great mastiff whose mistress has promised him a yummy doggie-treat if he will obediently sit until she tells him to move.

Which meant that, until then, I wouldn't be moving either.

"Mr. Cséjthe, I have been looking forward to meeting you for such a long time," the lady in leather said, extending her arm. "Allow me to introduce myself. I am Elizabeth Cachtice."

Sandor extended my arm for me. "That's not your real name," I said sullenly. A startled expression passed across her features so quickly that I almost missed it.

"Really? What makes you say that?"

"You're Erzsébet Báthory. Ouch."

Sandor had involuntarily tightened his grip but the Witch of Cachtice was more prepared. Her eyebrows rose politely and she said: "What an amusing idea. But please, call me Liz."

"How about I call you 'next week'?" I growled. I'd been taking lessons from Sandor.

"What?" Nice lift of the eyebrows again. "Oh. I see." She smiled. "Your reputation precedes you, Chris."

I smiled back. "As does yours, Bitch."

Sandor squeezed and it felt as if my radius and ulna were rubbing together. I forced my smile up a notch but couldn't do anything about the beads of perspiration that were erupting across my forehead.

"Mr. Cséjthe, I would love to continue our little conversation after I finish some business here. So, please stay for awhile," she said, her voice echoing in my ears, in my head. <*We have much to discuss and I want to give you my full attention.*>

And—that simply—I suddenly had no desire to leave. Sandor released my arm and I stood there, even more trapped that I had been a minute before.

Spiderwoman turned her attention back to a gray-haired gentleman in a gray suit who appeared to be in his late fifties. The fact that he wasn't wearing a tuxedo or fangs should have made him a standout in this crowd, but his nondescript appearance had the opposite effect: he seemed to fade into the background as if gray was the ultimate color scheme in camouflage and protective coloration. "You were saying, General?" she said.

I looked again: this was the man in the first photograph I had snagged from subterranean altar. I suddenly remembered that the Ogou pantheon manifested its military aspect in the form of one Ogou Baba.

As the gray-haired, gray-suited and—I looked more closely—gray-eyed gentleman looked around, his face hardened into an expression of displeasure. "I hardly think it appropriate to continue this discussion out here, in the open, and certainly not in front of outsiders."

"Dr. Delacroix works for me—"

"She's not cleared!" he snapped, cutting her off.

"She *works for me*," Báthory repeated, putting some heat and force behind the words. The "general" winced as if in pain. "It is now necessary to provide her with the essential clearances and briefings for her to continue her work."

I looked at Chalice. Her eyes had grown hazy with confusion and the anesthetization of mental domination.

Deirdre's eyes were different. I couldn't seem to get a reading on her.

"Mr. Cséjthe is about to become a major contributor to the Greyware Project," Báthory continued. "In a manner of speaking, General, he's about to become your very best friend. Yours and your friends on the council back in Virginia and Montana."

Walk away, Cséjthe, I told myself. *Move.*

I couldn't.

"I thought you started final testing three weeks ago," the general snapped.

"Of the virus? Oh yes. And aside from a little fine-tuning, I think we've cleared all of the major hurdles." Her smile twisted into a smirk. "But we've still got a ways to go on perfecting the vaccine. Mr. Cséjthe's hemoglobin may prove more effective in stabilizing the telomerase than pure vampire blood. And, unless the council is composed of superpatriots, I think you'll be waiting for the antidote before authorizing the broad-spectrum release."

The general looked thoughtful and I looked around for the exits. I had been able to resist Dracula's mental domination: Why couldn't I leave now?

"What about Phase Two?" he asked.

The brunette turned abruptly and spoke to Chalice. "Go upstairs to Lab Four. Wait for me there. Do not leave."

Chalice turned silently and headed toward the main hallway.

I tried to follow her.

I couldn't get my legs to move.

"We've begun testing on Operation Blackout," Báthory said as Chalice disappeared. "In fact we're mixing some of our clinical trials."

"Why?" the general asked. "Won't that just confuse the results?"

As much as I wanted to hear where this conversation was going, I knew that the longer I stood there, the slimmer my chances became of exiting of my own volition. Straining against the mental command to stay, I felt the straps of my shoulder rig begin to chafe my ribs. An idea began to glimmer.

"Not for us," Báthory answered. "The piggybacks are activated by two different triggers. For the Greyware virus, it's the length of the telomeres. For the Blackout piggyback, it's the racial subsets of DNA. That still requires a bit of fine-tuning, but since we're not even trying to develop any counteragents for the second solution, it's taken less time to get to the trials phase."

Gently, slowly, carefully, I raised my right arm, as if to adjust the front of my suit. Moved my hand toward the opening above the button at my waist.

"But you're right in that releasing both piggybacks will lead to some confusion. It should slow any effectual diagnosis and response on the part of the public health sector and the CDC." My fingers were just inside my jacket lapel and inches from butt of the Glock as she added: "I shall become very cross with you Mr. Cséjthe, if your hand gets any closer to that gun."

Cross? I'd show her frick'n cross! I grabbed the Glock and pulled.

"You *bastard!*"

I flinched as a gunshot boomed and waited for the shock of the bullet tearing through my armpit to reach my brain.

I heard a second gunshot about the time I realized my fingers were nowhere near the trigger and the voice wasn't Báthory's. Heads turned; mine with them.

The Snow Queen commanded the entryway to the main hall through which Chalice had passed just moments before. The beaded black sheath dress that Suanne Cummings wore wasn't cut for a proper shooter's stance—which was probably why she had failed to hit anything of consequence, yet.

The room erupted in screams—some of them feminine—and half the occupants threw themselves to the floor while the remainder rushed about in a variety of directions. Most of them ended up on the floor, as well, tripping over the already prone or colliding with other rushees.

"You *bastard!*" Suanne repeated. And Hyrum Cummings broke from the pack as his cover went down and ran in search of other shelter.

"Where is she?" Suanne shrieked. The hem of her dress gave way with a ripping sound as she spread her feet and the seams on both sides unzipped to her thighs. The nickel-plated, snub-nosed .38 came up in a two-handed grip and tracked her husband as he ran . . .

. . . toward us!

The temptation to lay down suppressing fire passed through my mind without tapping the brakes. I released my grip on my own gun and made a quick sending: *DROP THE GUN! DROP THE GUN!*

Suanne didn't quite drop her weapon but she did fumble with it. Another shot boomed like doomsday thunder and a bullet tore a bloody chunk out of my left biceps while Dr. Cummings was still twenty feet away. The countess and the general hit the floor simultaneously. I was suddenly free of Erzsébet Báthory's compulsion. I ran toward Suanne, hemorrhaging like an Internet start-up.

Chapter Sixteen

I slapped the gun out of Suanne's hands as I ran past her and then out into the main corridor. Taking the stairs meant that I would bleed that much faster, but the elevators would be way too slow. I pushed the door to the stairwell open and then clapped my good hand across my shattered upper arm.

So much for my renewed enthusiasm for divorce cases. Maybe the Monroe P.D. had an opening for a meter maid.

I was outside Lab Four in less than a minute, but even with the advantage of inhuman speed I wasn't moving fast enough. By now, Báthory and her goons would be up and moving and I was leaving a trail of gore that Mr. Magoo could follow.

I slammed the door open and ran to Chalice. "Come on! We're getting out of here!"

The hazed expression in her green eyes had faded but the anxiety that replaced it was scant improvement. Her gaze slid from my face to a focal point over my drooping shoulder.

"Howdy, Sparks," said a familiar voice. "Long time . . ."

" . . . no see," chimed in a second unwelcome greeting.

I turned slowly. Shock and pain had dulled my reactions but I deliberately kept my movements slow and careful, knowing that any sudden move would likely be my last.

Two men wearing ill-fitting tuxedos lounged against the wall, on either side of the doorway I had just pushed through. The one on the left towered over me. In the fifteen years that had passed since I had last seen him, the muscles of his body had been overlaid with a smooth coating of fat. He still looked as if he was strong enough to tip a Hummer over, though. I saw him do it once. I didn't doubt that he could still do it if sufficiently pissed. "Mouser," I said, "see you've gone for the Jesse Ventura 'do."

Joel Mouse rubbed his gleaming bald head and grinned. "Ya think?"

"A feather boa would complete the look if you wanted to go retro," I offered.

The short, barking laugh of the short, funny-looking man with gray teeth augmented Mouser's answering scowl.

"Fafhrd," I said. "I should have known you'd still be hanging with the Mouser after all these years." Fafhrd wasn't his real name and he most likely still couldn't spell the nickname that had been hung on him all those years ago. Just as well: Fritz Leiber would be turning over in his grave.

Shoot, he'd probably spin like a turbine.

Fafhrd stopped laughing. "Yeah. We even did time together after you spilled your guts to the brass."

"Spilling guts . . ." I scowled. "You're a fine one to talk about spilling guts . . ."

"Looks like someone started yours ahead of schedule," Mouser observed.

"Oh my god!" Chalice grabbed my arm to get a better look. *That* felt real good. "Sorry," she said, seeing the expression on my face. "Can you get that jacket off?"

"Just cut the sleeve off," I said through clenched teeth. The odds were bad enough at two to one. For all that I knew, the rest of the squad might be around the corner. Remembering the left-handed setup on the sniper rifle I could just about bet the bank on at least one more.

I closed my eyes and started focusing: *You will obey me, you will obey me . . .*

"I will obey you," Chalice said.

"That's nice," Fafhrd said. "*She* will obey you, but don't count on us being your happy little mind-slaves."

The Mouser nodded. "We got that hypnotherapy fix. You blood-suckers can't mess with our minds now."

That was interesting. Not only were they aware that vampires actually existed, they knew something about my condition, as well. The question was, who was acting C.O. for these Rambo rejects and what was his relationship with BioWeb?

The military connection was a given. But was it legitimate or paramilitary? There was the guy downstairs with the obvious moniker "General" and the not-so-obvious gray business suit. Which meant nothing as he could be legitimate and visiting covertly. Or he could be representing any one of the dozen or so private militias that had long fancied themselves a more legitimate alternative to our duly elected government.

Legitimate or not, the presence of these two soldiers of misfortune, along with Erzsébet Báthory's involvement, suggested really nasty business afoot. Bioweapons are ugly enough. Using them on segments of your own population takes the ugliness to a whole new level. Ike had warned us against the military-industrial complex. I wondered if he had ever, in his darkest dreams, imagined the world that was to come.

"Like you have enough mind to mess with in the first place," I retorted, slipping my hand inside my jacket as if to assist in its removal.

"Uh-uh, Sparky!" Fafhrd slide-cocked the 9mm that had suddenly appeared in his hand. "I ain't supposed to smoke you but I can blow your legs out from under you before you can clear your shoulder-rig."

I just shook my head. Anyone else would already have a round in the firing chamber: thumb the safety off and you've got a head start on the other guy. Not Fafhrd. He still preferred the retardo drama of slide-cocking his nine. Someday that pose would be his undoing.

"Want me to get his gun, Faf?" Mouser asked.

But not, apparently, this day.

"Think you can do it without blocking my shot, big guy?"

He smirked, trying for a knowing smile. "Hey, we're The Elite!"

"The Elite?" I said, and swore. "You bozos aren't anything more than SEAL wannabes. More Special Ed than Special Forces."

"You talk like you weren't one of us," Mouser growled.

"He wasn't one of us," Fafhrd snarled. "That's why he turned on us."

"A court of inquiry asked questions," I said. "I swore an oath to answer truthfully."

"What about loyalty? What about trust?"

I glared at the huge bald man. "What about dead civilians?"

Mouser shrugged. "There are always casualties in war."

"This wasn't war. It was a classic hostage situation and you guys hot-dogged it with no regard to SOP."

"Okay, so there was some collateral damage," Fafhrd agreed. "It was regrettable. We can agree on that. But what was done was done and, afterward, there was no taking it back. What purpose was served ratting us out to a bunch of Monday-morning quarter-backs?"

"You mean telling the truth under oath to my superior offic-ers?" I asked as Chalice took a scalpel from a dissection kit at the edge of the table. She began cutting away my blood-soaked sleeve. "Seems to me to me I'm answerable to them, not to you. Answer-able to them and the civilians we were charged to protect and rescue."

"Your first responsibility," Mouser said, circling to my left, "is to the man backing you up in a firefight. You've got to be able to trust every man in your squad with your life or one of you doesn't belong there. Too bad we found out about you after the fact."

"Don't lecture me about trust, Mouse. We were trusted to fol-low orders and we broke that trust." I winced as Chalice pulled my shirtsleeve away from the wound and fresh blood began oozing from my torn flesh. "If there was any betrayal, it was when you abandoned protocol and started your cowboy shit. I answered the questions I was asked truthfully and honestly. It's bullshit to think that company honor required that I lie for you."

"High-handed talk, Sparks," the little man retorted. "If you're so righteous, tell us why we're still working for the government while you're on their Most Wanted list?"

"I'm on the government's Most Wanted list?" It had been awhile since I had been inside a post office, much less checked the mug shot posters.

Of course, the real question was "which" government were we really talking about?

"Too bad it ain't 'dead or alive,'" Mouser added, reaching for the front of my jacket.

"You know, the sad thing is," I told him, "all these years I thought you were a cowboy; I never figured you for a Nazi."

Mouser's hand jerked to a stop. "Huh?"

"A Nazi, Mouse. In your case, more like a Schutzstaffel."

"What are you talkin' about?"

"I'm talkin' SS Stormtrooper, Herr Rat! I'm talkin' about genocide and gas chambers!"

Instead of grabbing my gun he shoved me back against the counter. "Why're you trash talkin' me like this?"

Faf laughed. "The Mouser is just a foot soldier, Sparks. He don't know policy, he just follows orders."

"But you're a smart guy, aren't ya, Faf? You know what I'm talking about, don't you?"

He shrugged. "I hear things. I can add two and two."

"Only we're not talking addition, here, Bucko. We're talking subtraction and in the millions."

"What are you talkin' about?" Mouse demanded to know.

"I'm talkin' about your mama, Herr Rat. How old is she?"

He shoved me again, jump-starting a lawnmower of pain in my arm. "Shut up about my mama, man!"

I focused past the renewed agony and said, "The people you work for are going to kill her, Mouser. The general is using these facilities to manufacture a virus that's designed to kill the elderly."

"Naw, man; you got it wrong," Fafhrd drawled. "The general is going to solve the race problem, old and young. Got nothin' to do with the Mouser's mama, she bein' white. She is white, isn't she, Mouse?"

Mouse suggested that Fafhrd look no further for sexual intimacy than his own genitalia.

"It's both, bozo." I pointed a trembling finger at the little man with the gray teeth. "Your general is collaborating with vampires to produce and disseminate viruses tailored to kill blacks as well as the elderly of any race or ethnicity." I heard Chalice gasp behind me as I turned back to the big bald guy. "Which means your mama, Mouse!"

The Mouser turned to his partner. "Is this true, Faf?"

Fafhrd answer was cryptic. "Urk!" he said.

Or something to that effect as the lab door flew open and smacked the little man back into the wall.

"What the f—"

Mouser never finished his query: I had spun on the balls of my feet and grabbed his throat with my good hand, my fingertips digging into the flesh over his carotid arteries.

"Nobody move!" I yelled. "Drop your guns or JoJo's Adam's apple winds up across the room.

"Suits me fine," said a familiar voice.

Fafhrd contributed another "urk" to the conversation.

I turned and saw William Robert Montrose standing in the doorway. He was holding the door with one arm so that it continued to pin Fafhrd against the wall. Although the old vampire didn't seem to be exerting himself in any way, cracks were appearing in the plaster, radiating out from behind the door.

"Hurry up and feed!" he said. "We've got to get out of here."

"Feed?" I echoed. I was suddenly aware of Mouser's dead weight and the strain on my good arm from holding the unconscious man by the throat.

A brown hand closed on my wrist and helped brace my arm. "What's this about a virus designed to kill blacks?" Chalice hissed.

"I'm a little short on the details," I answered, "but a pattern is starting to emerge."

"What do you mean?"

Between the dreams, the countess' historical MO, a fortune-teller's vague prophecies, BioWeb's sinister projects, and that conversation downstairs between Bloody Báthory and General Goebbels Goering, it was just too difficult to explain.

Especially under the current time constraints.

"Later," I promised. I saw movement behind Count Bubba. A kid squeezed past Montrose and into the room.

He was probably sixteen—or had been when he died. But he looked younger, smaller because of the suit that he wore. Or, rather, it wore him. Electric blue, it was strictly forties era and very zoot. The pants were crotched low with reet pleats and bluff cuffs. Above, he wore a racket jacket with a drapeshape and wide lapels. His keychain, in the hepcat lingo, was "long with links." On his head was a wide-brimmed dicer with a hatband that matched his Windsor-knotted choker. On his feet were two-tone barkers and—I was guessing under the saggy baggy striders—argyles held up by old-style garters. This was my first look at an actual, honest-to-God, zoot suit outside of old photos, and the whole package was totally killer-diller.

"Wowsers!" I said. "Beat me, Daddy, eight to the bar!"

"This him?" the kid asked incredulously. "This the one they're all bumping their gums about?" He turned to Montrose. "What's the wire on this Joe? He's still breathing!"

As if that was some kind of social blunder.

He turned back and peered at me, squinting his eyes. "He still has a heartbeat!"

"Which is mostly the point, I suppose," Count Bubba replied.

Fafhrd made another urky sound. The Mouser was unconscious and silent.

"You gonna eat that or play with it some more?" the kid asked.

I dropped Commando Cruddie and glared at Montrose. "You didn't tell me you were babysitting tonight."

"Hey!"

"We don't have time for this," Montrose said. "J.D. meet Chris Cséjthe. Cséjthe, J.D."

"Charmed," I said.

"More'n I can say about you."

"Now," my undead doorman continued, "take a few swallows of blood before you fall over...."

"I'm fine."

"Casper the Friendly Ghost has more color than you," he retorted. "And neither of us is keen on the idea of carrying you. What's the matter? Squeamish?"

I nodded. "I knew this guy a dozen years back. I wouldn't have let him handle my food then. What makes you think I would consider making him my food, now?"

The kid shook his head. "Besides being finicky about the torpedoes here, I think half-and-half's problem is he ain't got any teeth."

"I've got teeth!" I said, baring mine.

"Not the pointy kind."

He was right. Somehow in the grand melee and my subsequent flight, I had lost my prosthetic fangs.

Chalice had been standing there silently, holding the bloody scalpel by her side while we dithered. "Oh, for heavens sake!" she said now, stepping forward. She brought the blade up and touched it to the inside of her left forearm. "The BioWeb staff is required to take monthly blood tests and I can assure you that I am quite clean." She drew the edge of the blade lightly across her skin and the red line in its wake quickly became a ribbon, then a spreading film. She raised her arm toward me and said, "Come on, Sam. Or Chris. Or whoever you are. We're wasting time and I'd hate to waste any of this on the carpeting." She tilted her head. "What's the matter, don't care for the brown sugar?"

My head was spinning—though whether from blood lost or blood being offered, I could not say. Instead, I said: "What's the ideal woman?"

J.D. cocked an eyebrow.

"I'm a scientist, white boy," she shot back. "I'm curious. And, as long as you don't get greedy, I can spare a little. Besides, you told me, yourself, you haven't got the saliva factor to infect me."

I was in no condition to argue. I took her arm in my hands and bowed my head, bringing my mouth down to the cut. It was a terribly intimate act, and made all the more uncomfortable by the need to hurry and perform it in front of strangers. Chalice, herself, was nearly as much a stranger. All that was forgotten, however, as the first sip of blood entered my mouth.

It was more than drink, more than food.

It was the best sex I could remember and better than that.

It was speed and steroids mixed with honey and jalapenos.

It was molten sunshine seeking out the cold, dark regions of my innermost self.

All the way down to the cellular level I could feel a myriad of switches being flipped, the engines of life being revved.

A swallow and I could tell that my bleeding had stopped.

With a second swallow my head began to clear.

A third and I could feel tissue in my upper arm begin to re-knit. Not a lot but the healing process was already beginning.

A fourth and fifth were all I dared. I needed more for the process to quicken, for my strength and stamina to return to superhuman levels.

But I could not take the risks—the risk of delaying our escape any longer, of bleeding Chalice any further.

And the risk of losing my humanity, of feeding until she was utterly drained.

I raised my head and turned away as I licked my bloody lips. "Thank you," I said, my voice uneven from the twin shocks of my wound and my quickened hunger. "We'd better go now."

As we turned toward the door, Chalice balked. "I can't," she said.

Montrose and the kid looked puzzled.

"Báthory ordered her to come here and wait for her," I explained. "She's having trouble countermanding the geas."

"If she was still tranced," said the kid. "But get a slant on her peepers: she looks like she's wide awake now."

"Báthory must be reinforcing the command telepathically even as we speak," I said. "I've seen this sort of thing before."

"Then all the more reason to leave her behind," Montrose said. "If Báthory has a psychic link with her, she's not only a homing beacon but an open communications link, as well. She could listen in on everything we say; through her eyes, see everything we do."

I shook my head. "I won't leave her behind for that monster."

The kid pulled out a pocket watch, popped the cover, and consulted the antique face. "Time to take it on the heel and toe. Past time. Would-a been easier while the joint was still jumping. Bet it's a quiet riot downstairs, now." He produced an old "police special." At least it was special to the cops back in the nineteen forties. "Good thing you brought your own Roscoe; we may have to squirt metal on the run-out."

I looked back at Montrose. "*Where* did you find this guy?"

"Don't let the lingo throw you," Montrose said, reaching behind the door. "He's a solid back-up when he's straight."

"When he's straight?"

Montrose retrieved Fafhrd's nine and opened the door enough to let him slide to the floor. "Let's continue this discussion in the stairwell."

"I'm not leaving her!" My previous experience with Dracula's mental control taught me the futility of trying to countermand an older vampire's geas. There was, however, a chance that I could use my own fledgling powers of domination to put her to sleep and then carry her while she was unconscious.

If everyone would shut up long enough for me to concentrate.

"Ah, look," said the kid, shoving the ancient .38 back inside his baggy jacket, "I got an idea." He walked up to Chalice and stuck out his hand like an insurance salesman at a costume party. "Slip me some skin, babe, I'm J.D. and I'm your ticket outta here!"

As she tentatively extended her own hand, in turn, the kid looked up at the ceiling and exclaimed: "Holy crap! What's that?"

I imagine we all looked up: I certainly did. There was nothing to *see* on the ceiling but we got an earful: the loud *smack* of a fist against flesh. An unconscious Chalice was sagging into the kid's arms when I looked back.

Montrose caught my arm as I took a step toward them. "You wanted to bring her along. It's the only way."

"I'll carry her," I said.

"With that busted arm?" The kid hoisted Chalice over his shoulder. There was plenty of room: his jacket looked as if it used ironing boards for shoulder pads. "I got your frail. C'mon gate, let's perambulate!"

I wasn't happy about the arrangement but I didn't have a better plan. And it was long past time to go. We exited the lab and hurried down the hall. Choosing an elevator was like playing Russian roulette—with most of the chambers loaded, as a single security guard could cover all the elevators on each floor. The stairs were a slightly better bet—but not by much. Since the back stairs were the logical escape route, we took the front.

Montrose stopped us just above the second-floor landing. "Vamp below," he announced. "First floor."

I reached for the silver-loaded Glock in my shoulder holster.

"Nice heater," the kid observed. "Got a pillowcase to fit it?"

"What?"

"He means a silencer," Count Bubba answered. "Fire that thing off in here and everyone in the building is going to hear it. Time to detour." He reached for the door permitting egress to the second floor. It was a fire door and wouldn't open.

The kid shifted Chalice's center of gravity and kicked the door off its hinges.

"Oh," I said, "that was nice and quiet."

"Button yer yap," the kid said, shifting Chalice to a better position. "There's a bull down the hall wearing tin and packing iron."

"Let me guess: a security guard."

He looked at me as if I were slow. "That's what I just said."

Count Bubba stepped over the broken door. *"They're getting away!"* he said. *"Down the back stairwell! Hurry!"* The mental reverberation was making my temples buzz. I stepped through the doorway in time to see the guard turn and start hurrying in the opposite direction.

"Nice," I said. "I would've needed more time to convince him."

"You'll get better at it," Montrose said, "if you live long enough."

"And your odds would be better if we ditched the skirt," the kid added.

"If I ditch anybody, it'll be a certain hepbat," I growled, "who needs his film noir projected where the moon don't shine."

He slid Chalice from his shoulder. "Wanna try me, Tepid? Come on, then," he nodded at my dangling arm, "put up your duke."

"Settle down, Beavis."

"Hisst!" said Montrose. "The first-floor vamp is on his way up!"

The kid bent and moved Chalice away from the doorway. Both he and Count Bubba plastered themselves against the wall on either side of the door. All that was missing was some bait. What luck: I was available!

I started backing down the hall in the direction of the departed security guard, keeping an eye on the opening to the stairwell. As I moved, my shoulder bumped a projection from the wall: a fire alarm. I pulled it just as Báthory's fanged goon appeared in the doorway.

The blaring of the alarm klaxon might be sufficient to cover the noise of gunshots now. I hauled the Glock back out but my companions were quicker. The kid stuck out a leg, tripping the vamp, and Montrose produced a sharpened wooden stake from a pocket in his overalls. Sixteen bars of "Dust in the Wind" and we were back in the stairwell, headed for the ground floor.

Pandemonium had ceased but it was still a disorganized circus. Cops were everywhere, gathering evidence, taking statements, and guiding a handcuffed Suann Cummings into the back of a squad car. Across the parking lot I spied detectives Ruiz and Murray standing between my car and the Nova, which was lopsidedly hiked up on a bumper jack with the rear tire missing. They were questioning a man in dark clothing and a watch cap.

"I'm going to have to bum a ride," I said. "My car's staked out."

"My truck's just down the hill," Montrose answered. "I suggest we split up and J.D. will take Ms. Delacroix with him until we can meet up safely."

I looked over at the kid. "No offense, Junior, but I'm not keen on leaving a living, breathing human in the custody of a vampire."

"Hey, man, for a smoke chick she's a real eye-grabber and I might have been tempted when I was alive. But I heard the dish: her blood's too reet for my tastes."

"So, you're saying . . . what?"

Montrose interpreted. "J.D. has himself a nasty little habit. He prefers to mainline junkies. If they aren't high, he isn't hungry."

"Your steroid buddies back there were more to my taste," the kid added. "Too bad we didn't have more time."

"Well, it looks like there's more where they came from," I said. The man wearing the watch cap had turned his head and I got a better look at his face. It was Lenny. *Lieutenant Birkmeister to you, Ensign Cséjthe!*

The urge to whistle "That Old Gang of Mine" came and went quickly. "Louie" Lenny spotted us—more specifically, spotted me—and, for a long moment, it seemed that the jig was up.

One would think that carrying an unconscious woman toward the parking lot should elicit some response from the swarm of cops that were all around us. But, between the three of us, we seemed to be doing an adequate job of the old vampiric ability to "cloud men's minds." I doubted this little mental misdirection would be sufficient, however, once Birkmeister alerted Ruiz and Murray.

But he didn't.

A long, searching look and he turned back to answer more questions from my detective twosome. The Chevy's trunk was open but I couldn't see if damning evidence still lay within. If it did, no one seemed particularly concerned with cataloging the contents.

"Okay, what's the plan?" Montrose asked as we reached his pickup.

"Plan?" I hadn't thought that far ahead.

"So far, we're safe," Montrose said. "You're not. Nobody's made us, yet."

"Lieutenant Lenny just saw you with me."

"If he's human, it's too dark and we're too far away for a real description." He turned to the kid. "Get her out of here, J.D. Take her back to my place. That's where we'll reassemble."

The kid nodded once in agreement. Then he looked at me and grinned. "Now who's babysitting?"

I couldn't think of a suitable comeback even after he had dodged off into the darkness with Chalice Delacroix firmly balanced across his excessively padded shoulders. Instead I was thinking of Deirdre, still inside Erzsébet Báthory's BioWeb fortress, surrounded by rings of armed and fanged security forces.

I had never felt so helpless.

"Cséjthe. Cséjthe!" Montrose waved his hand in my face. "Any reason to go back to your place?"

"My place?" I thought about Deirdre

"That's the first place she'll look once she knows you're gone. If you need to grab something, it's now or never."

I thought about Terry-call-me-T whom I'd left on my couch like a complementary mint. I thought about Countess Báthory's tastes for young female flesh. For Deirdre's sake, I prayed that those tastes were confined to living rather than undead flesh.

I nearly pulled the door of the pickup off as I wrenched it open. "Let's *go!*"

Chapter Seventeen

Montrose's face took on a satanic cast in the red-orange wash from the dashboard lights.

"Okay," he said, "give. I'm doing this because Mama Samm asked me to. Reason enough, I suppose. But I might feel a sight better about risking my neck—not to mention a hundred and forty-some years of quiet, undiscovered residency—if you were to shed a bit more light on just what is really going on."

"What's going on?"

He shrugged. "You know. Genetics research, mosquito breeding labs, paramilitary freelancers, undead security, zombies. . . . I get the feeling that something just isn't quite normal, and I can't quite put my finger on it."

"Hardy har," I said.

"My military compadrés seem to be all lathered up about little gray men. Should I be adding flying saucers to my list?"

"I don't believe the diminutive was invoked. There is military involved—although I suspect they're either backroom or illegit. I think that's what they mean by the gray men. Nothing extraterrestrial." I sighed. "I hope."

"Glad to hear that. It's been a century and a half but I remember a couple of boys in our company had soldier's hearts."

"Soldier's hearts?"

"That's what we called it back then. Something would break inside. Disconnect. We'd say, 'he has a soldier's heart.' During World War I it was called shellshock. World War II: battle fatigue. I'm not sure about Korea—I slept a lot during the fifties. Boredom, I suppose. Then it was delayed stress syndrome after Vietnam."

"Soldier's heart," I said softly. "I like that."

"Nothing to like about it," he said grimly. "Especially when death doesn't bring release. You die and find that you're still lost, still crouched down in the cold and the dark. My boys need to go home, Mr. Cséjthe. Can you help us?"

Was there a Good Samaritan law for the deceased? My initial impression—once I learned that vampires actually existed—was that they were soulless killing machines, bereft of any semblance of humanity. Perhaps that was more a matter of "nurture" than "nature." Cut off from the world of the living, forced to live as both hunter and hunted, their alliances would predictably turn from the living to the dead. But the depths of Pagelovitch's concern for those he ruled in Seattle and now Montrose's allegiance to his former comrades continued to surprise me. "I wish I could," I said. "Honest to God—if there is one. But I can't even help myself."

"I thought you were Baron Samedi."

"You and half the dead in this parish."

"What do they want?"

"Justice."

"For what?"

I stared into the darkness beyond the windshield. "I don't know. There's a teenage runaway—" I hiccupped a short, bitter laugh. "That is so . . . un-funny. Kandi Fenoli. She was raped, sodomized, and murdered. Her killer cut her hands off so her fingerprints couldn't identify her. He either didn't have the time or the smarts to consider her dental records . . .

"After her death she escaped from two different parish morgues and walked a hundred miles to ask me a question."

"What was the question?"

I shook my head. "I don't know. We keep getting interrupted. Then there's Chalice's daddy."

"Chalice's daddy?"

"Never mind. Long story. Bottom line: I was supposed to protect his daughter and avenge his death."

"I take it his death is connected to the gray men?"

I nodded. "I'm starting to think so, yes."

"Suspicious circumstances?"

I thought about Delacroix's last words as he dragged that vampire into the crematory oven. "I think he was telling me that he was murdered."

"Murdered? As in after the fact?"

"The coroner's report stated he succumbed to a heart attack with complications induced by severe influenza."

"Interesting murder weapon."

I nodded again. "Murder by flu. Yes."

"So, who pulled the trigger? And why?"

"I think BioWeb is manufacturing the weapons. I don't know about the why, yet. Erzsébet Báthory is involved and there is some kind of military connection, but I don't know if they're legit, rogue black ops, or militia."

Bubba's brow furrowed like the cotton fields east of town. "Distinctions?"

"If it's private, paramilitary involvement then we've got home-grown terrorists taking the game to a whole new level. It will make the anthrax scare pale by comparison."

"There's heavy metal music involved?"

I gave him The Look.

He shrugged. "Sorry. I used to think I was an invulnerable badass but between you, Mama Samm, and that Romanian bitch back there, I'm starting to think about getting religion. Too bad I'm already damned."

"We may all be beyond damned. If some rogue black ops division is financing this it gets scarier. There've always been backroom operations that the government either forgets or decides it doesn't want to know about. When dirty work needs to be done, it's best to not to have too much knowledge or responsibility for the really nasty elements of your own counterterrorist resources."

"Sounds like you know something about that."

I stared out the passenger window as if there was something worth seeing. "I had my own encounters with Uncle Sam's heart of darkness. You pushed one of them into a wall back there."

"But it's even worse if the military connection is legitimate, isn't it?" he asked.

"God help us if our government is officially involved. Perhaps the gun nuts and the militia separatists are right, after all."

"Okay, we're still working out the 'who.' Any more progress on the 'why'?"

"BioWeb appears to be two separate entities," I said. "The front organization is involved in pure biomedical research. Employees like Chalice Delacroix are unaware that their work is being utilized for bioweapon development behind the scenes. Chalice told me that she's working on the genetic triggers to the aging process. A little while ago I was listening to a conversation between Báthory and some guy she called 'General' where they discussed a 'Greyware Project' and another called 'Operation Blackout.' Recently there's been a local strain of the flu killing a disproportionate number of blacks in the community."

"What about old people?"

"First thing I looked for. As usual, there's always a higher mortality rate among the elderly with every new strain of influenza. But nothing disproportionate to the death curves for previous years."

"Maybe it isn't perfected yet."

I shook my head. "Báthory spoke of work on an antidote. I think the virus has been engineered but the cure isn't ready, yet. They're not ready to let the chimera out of the lab until they can be sure of their own immunity. I think they've engaged in open-air testing of the second virus because they're not concerned about a vaccine."

The truck suddenly fishtailed onto the shoulder as Montrose stood on the brakes and swore. "They're targeting the black population and aren't worried about a cure because the people doing this don't think they need one?"

Like I said, you never knew what attachments the undead might form with the community around them.

"Which could be the first glimmer of good news we can pull out of this morass," I said, nodding.

The expression on Montrose's face shifted from passive horror to a willingness to make a little active horror on his own. "What the *hell* are you saying, boy?"

"The people behind this need a vaccine to protect themselves against a virus tailored to be fatal to the elderly. If they're not worried about protecting themselves from a mutant strain that targets blacks then they're not likely to be legitimate military. Even covert ops has been racially diverse for a long time."

"So we're back to private militia backing with an all-white membership?" The hostility in his face and voice ramped back down to bitter anger.

"Yeah," I said, "the KKK wearing kamouflage."

"Mosquito delivery?" he was asking as we turned in at my driveway.

"Why not?" I said, peering up at the dark, swaying forms of mimosas and willows beyond the headlights. "They've been working on genetic manipulation of—*shit!*"

Bubba was baffled. "Genetically modified excrement?"

I pointed at the swaying shrubbery that wasn't shrubbery after all. "We've got company."

Montrose took in the congregation of corpses assembled in my front yard. "*You've* got company, son; *I'm* just the taxi service." He pulled up and attempted to turn in to the circle drive. It was slow going as the corpses in his way were a little slow in granting right-of-way.

"Oh, man," I groaned, "I do *not* need this right now!"

"Got that right!" He tapped the horn at one particularly slow stiff. "You've got five minutes to get in, grab, and get back out! I'm out of here in ten, with or without you—Mama Samm be damned."

I opened the door and sent a fresh roll of saw-toothed agony through my arm as I tried to exit without unbuckling my shoulder harness first. Hitting the ground on the second attempt, I pushed my way up to the porch and turned around to address the crowd. "What do you people want?" I yelled.

They swayed like a grove of saplings in the wind and in a mass voice that fluttered like a breeze they whispered: "*Jusssticcce...*"

Oh God.

I didn't have time for this.

And all the time in the world wouldn't make any difference.

If there really was a Baron Samedi, I was going to hunt him down someday and seriously kick his ass.

"Go home," I said wearily. "I can't help you."

"Jusssticcce . . ." they sighed.

It wasn't fair. You stumbled and fought and bled your way though life with only the hope of rest and heaven and reward once you were done with it all. Why were the dead coming back?

And why were they coming to me?

It just wasn't fair!

To any of us.

"Jusssticcce . . ." they repeated.

I put my hands on my hips and bellowed back: "There is no Justice!" My voice cracked on the last syllable and I felt as if something were breaking down deep inside, as well. "No Justice in this life! And, from the look of things, no Justice in the life beyond!"

"Baaarrronnn . . ." they murmured.

"I am *not* your baron!" I yelled. "I can *not* help you. *No* one can help you! Go *back* to your graves and your tombs! Go back into the silence and the darkness! *Sleep!* Find your peace in oblivion! There's nothing I can do—"

"You're wrong," whispered a feathery voice near my waist. I looked down and found one of my previous, deceased visitors: the dead boy who was now much closer to resembling a puffy, white mushroom than he had during his last visit. Behind him were the mortal remains (and not so much of them now) of his companions: the faceless woman, Mr. Jaw-be-gone, and Kandi Fenoli, the Houdini of the parish homicide division.

"What?"

"You make justice where you can, when you can." The kid nodded at the chinless corpse: "Chuck?"

Mr. Jaw-be-gone stepped up onto the porch, carrying a sack, and the other cadavers moved back, clearing an open patch of concrete. He stooped and spilled the contents of that sack onto the cement, making a white, crystalline mound that glowed with a faint blue luminescence in the moonlight.

Salt.

"You make justice through one soul at a time," the boy said.

As Chinless Chuck stepped back, the faceless woman spoke, sounding like an ancient steam pipe: "Barrronnnn . . . you mussst level the pile . . . ssssspppread the ssssalttt . . ."

A moment ago I had been defiant. Anger formed in hopelessness, forged in helplessness, was already fading. I knelt obediently and leveled the mound into a smooth plain of white powder.

"Kandi?" the boy called.

I moved back as the handless girl stepped forward.

Again, as before, she dipped her toe into the salt and began to draw lines, making grooved letters in the grainy page of my porch. The first three letters were the same as before: an H, an O, and a W. Then three more followed in quick and sure succession as if she had practiced for this moment: an A, an R, and a D. Then a second line began and I could see that she wasn't asking a question but, rather, revealing a name. The pale cast of moonlight and the shadowy forms around me made it difficult to read but then the porch light came on and the letters clarified in their shallow trenches.

HOWARD
IGER
black chevy van
2109 Boudreaux
Sikes, La
basement

The toe stopped.

Kandi Fenoli stepped back.

I looked up at her shadowed face. "Is this the one?" I asked, my heart a cold lump of lead in my frozen chest. My own soldier's heart. "He did this to you, didn't he?"

She nodded. Once.

If there is a God, I thought, He must be an absentee landlord.

The front door opened. Terry-call-me-T peeked out. "Sam?"

I stood up and turned to my wide-eyed houseguest. As I did I saw a familiar red firefly dance across the doorframe and disappear into my shadow.

A giant fist slammed into my back, knocking me across the threshold and slamming me into Terry with the force of a battering ram. We both smacked into the vestibule wall and she went down beneath me.

I didn't think her eyes could get any bigger but I was wrong. Her mouth opened but no sound came out. I tried to lift myself off of her, but my arms had lost their strength and my legs their feeling. I had to roll to the side, flopping onto my back, and push myself up on shaky elbows.

The world lost its momentum.

Time slowed.

Moments became a succession of freeze-frames.

Even as deep shock probed my brain with muzzy fingers, my body was ramping up into preternatural battle-mode. Unfortunately, my legs had gone on weekend furlough.

I heard the door open on Montrose's truck and his head appeared above the cab. "What happened?" he called, his voice distorted into a bassy drawl.

Beyond his shoulder, something flashed in the branches of one of the trees. Wide-eyed, I stared in disbelief as a small rocket whooshed toward the pickup in slo-mo.

My heightened reflexes gave me just enough time to yell: "LAW!"

Master Sergeant William Robert Montrose, who had last seen action in 1865, couldn't know what a Light Antitank Weapon was. And even if he had, he could not have cleared the truck in time. The front yard turned the color of his red-orange dashboard lights and a gust of hot wind threw me down the hall.

It took me a moment to shake off the disorientation from my double battering. As I oriented myself I discovered that I had a small hole in my back and a larger one in my front. Judging from the alignment, I probably didn't have a liver any more. Curiously, there was no pain, just numbed discomfort and hazy exhaustion. I turned back toward Terry and saw that she had been flung onto her side, where it seemed as if a large carnivore had taken a bite. Her shirt was in rags, oozing raw, bloody hamburger and nubs of white bone where her pelvis and ribcage had been shattered. She blinked once. Twice. Stretched her arm toward me. Opened her mouth. No words came, only a freshet of blood. Her eyes stayed open but her body suddenly relaxed and her gaze went past me, focused on eternity.

Shadows appeared on the roiling, flickering play of yellow, red, and orange lights on the curtains and hallway walls. They moved like parodies of human beings, their distorted forms shrinking as their sources drew closer to the door and windows, backlit by Bubba's burning truck. I flopped over and began dragging myself deeper into the house.

Footsteps sounded behind me and the odor of cooked and spoiled meat heralded the presence of my ghastly supplicants.

"Baron," said the small, familiar voice of the dead boy. "Let us help you."

Outside, someone began yelling. The deep tones of concern suddenly pitched into a higher register of terror. Abruptly, the shrieking was cut off.

"We will protect you, Baron."

"You can't protect me," I gasped. "Others will be coming."

"What would you have us do?"

"Get me to the phone while I can still talk."

Spongy fingers grasped my arms. My wounded biceps had barely knitted, and I groaned as I was lifted and carried to the chair by the phone. Swollen hands, withered fingers assisted me in unknotting my tie and slipping off my ruined jacket. Folding the torn and stained material into a bulky pad, I pressed it against the exit wound in my abdomen as skeletal phalanges secured it with my necktie, re-knotted about my waist.

"There should be some blood in the fridge," I gasped. "Bring it to me, please." I didn't know what good it would do: I had already lost more than twice that amount through my sniper's wound and I was still leaking. I picked up the receiver and, after three tries, managed to dial 9-1-1 correctly.

"Nine-one-one," a voice answered, "please state the nature of your emergency."

"I'd like to report a murder." *My own?*

"Your name and the number you're calling from, sir?" It was standard procedure, even though my call was being recorded and the Caller ID was expected to log my telephone number. In a moment they'd realize that I had filtered the ID trace on my phone.

"I'm going to give you the identity of the man who murdered a young woman named Kandi Fenoli. Her body was found in Winn Parish a week or so ago."

"Have you contacted the authorities in Winn Parish, sir?"

"Listen closely!" I heard a click over the line and guessed that they had already started a trace. "Her murderer's name is Howard Iger. He lives at 2109 Boudreaux in Sikes, Louisiana. He drives a black Chevy van. Tell the cops to get a search warrant and check his basement. Got that?"

"How do you—"

Of course an anonymous phone tip wasn't going to convince a judge to fork over a search warrant but, now that the local constabulary had a name and an address, it would probably be just a matter of time and a little legwork. I slammed the receiver down and grabbed the half-empty blood bags that were offered. There wasn't nearly enough and I spilled some of that trying to get it to my mouth with shaky hands. It was cold and greasy-tasting and my stomach cramped as it went down. I couldn't be sure that it was doing any good at all.

"Baron . . ."

I looked up at the dead boy and found I was having trouble focusing my eyes. "I'm just a man, son. Only a man."

"You are more than a man, Your Excellency. You are the Adjudicator for the Dead. Kandi says she can rest now . . . that four others can rest now. And that many more will be saved because of what you have done."

"I made an anonymous phone call."

"We have no voice in the realm of the living. You are our voice. Speaker for the Dead."

"Great. Vampire enclaves from both coasts are after me and now Orson Scott Card is going to sue my ass. Can it get any worse?"

My question was answered by multiple burps of automatic weapons fire. The living room windows shattered and a couple of corpses a few feet away went down, cut in two. Normally that would just be a colorful exaggeration but some of these guys had been dead so long that a decent kick would scatter them to the winds. I looked down and realized sadly that there was no way I was ever getting all of them out of my carpet.

A grenade came sailing through the broken window. A half-dozen corpses piled on like it was a loose fumble at the New Orleans Superdome. A muffled *crump* and I was picking other people's scalps out of my own.

"That was a rhetorical question, dammit!" I hauled out my Glock and tried to stand. "That's all I can stands, I can't stands no more!" A couple of spastic attempts and it was painfully evident that I couldn't stand anymore.

"Please, Baron!" The kid put a half-cooked hand on the gun's barrel. "You cannot help us if you become one of us." His clothes were smoking and a large, twisted shard of metal jutted from his back.

Other arms encircled me, helped me up as the dead boy pulled the Glock from my trembling fingers. "I have a safe room in the basement," I mumbled. "Help me down the stairs and I can lock myself in."

But they steered me past the door to the basement and into the kitchen. Small arms fire rattled from the front of the house and the *crump* of another grenade echoed as they opened the back door. Something—maybe someone—was down on the ground with a knot of ruined corpses huddled atop, struggling as if to contain an extremely powerful man reduced to mindless hysteria. I lost a shoe and still could not feel the ground against my toes as my feet dragged nervelessly between my dead supporters' strides. Down the hill we went and then down into the dark waters of Gris Bayou. I felt the cold bite of the water from a distance as it reached my knees.

Then I was hoisted up and over into a pirogue. The sound of gunfire was closer but I couldn't see anything lying facedown in the tiny boat.

"Go with God," murmured a hoarse, new voice.

"There is no God," I whispered into the weathered planking as I felt a shove and the skipping rhythm of wavelets striking the prow as it moved out into the main channel of the bayou.

My forward momentum was spent in a matter of moments. Now I was a sitting duck. Without wind or oars, there is no actual current in a bayou unless you count inches-per-hour as actual movement. In a few minutes, Lieutenant Birkmeister's boys and Countess Báthory's hounds were going to reach the backyard. Then the only real question would be: bullets, grenades, or swim out here and haul me back in?

Using the last vestiges of my strength, I raised myself up enough to hook my right arm over the gunwale. I scooped at the water with my hand and was gratified that the pirogue's shallow draft actually allowed me some leeway. Unfortunately, one-sided paddling was also bringing me about, turning me back toward the shore. If I paddled long and hard enough I could probably execute several watery doughnuts before BioWeb's troops arrived to play Sink The Bismarck.

My head was beginning to spin again. As I brought my hand out of the water, a head bobbed to the surface.

A very pretty head.

Attached to lovely white shoulders.

The dark waters hid the rest.

Her eyes were sad and haunted. And just as green as her long hair that flowed down the sides of her elfin face.

"Hello," I said. "Do you know the aguane?"

She smiled sadly and a white arm came up out of the water and grasped the rope that dangled from the pirogue's bow.

A sudden squelching sound accompanied a row of geysers that stitched the water nearby.

"Go away, Honey; you're gonna get hurt if you hang around here. Shoo. Scat."

She ducked back under the water and I couldn't hold my head up any longer. I lay back down, my face resting in damp bilge that hadn't been there moments before. Either the boat was leaking or I was bleeding out even faster now.

Either way, it didn't make much difference.

I closed my eyes and sank into watery darkness.

Chapter Eighteen

The roaring beats against my ears, my skin, shivering and shaking my body, filling my head until I fear it must burst!

If I concentrate on the flames, I can almost forget the crowd, can almost believe the roaring comes from the great fire, alone . . .

That I am alone . . .

The faceless one comes, his head enclosed in a lopsided cone of dark leather. I try to see the color of his eyes but the eyeholes reveal nothing but deeper shadows. I look down and see the iron pincers in his massive hands, its curved and sharpened ends glowing a dull, cherry red like the baleful eyes of deep-dwelling demons from Hell.

I force my gaze away—away from the executioner and the judges. Away from the accusers and witnesses. Away from the coming horror . . .

A horror like that which I wielded when I took my turn beneath the castle as de facto judge, witness, and executioner . . . tormenting Her unwilling guests while She looked on, seemingly apart yet more the participant than we who wielded the whips, the pincers, the irons, and the blades at Her will.

At Her pleasure.

The others will hold their tongues despite this final, excruciating injustice. Erzsi has escaped their net, so far, but I think she will not live long. She is doomed as we all are for having come under the Witch's spell.

255

Our dark Mistress maintains Her hold over us still, though Her bloody reign of terror has all come unraveled and we have been bound with the chains with which we once played. She formed our answers as the questions were asked and the heated irons were applied like lovers' kisses, subtle, intimate, then ardent . . .

Even the countess, shackled not with chains but with stone and mortar, high in her dark tower—but I cannot dwell upon this last, great injustice.

She will not let me, still.

The secret will die behind our blackened lips.

The secret will only be told by the blood, the blood that has no voice of its own.

I turn back to the fire and stare into its shimmering depths. The fire is all. The flames fill my field of vision as they fill the town square. The screaming starts and the world begins to burn.

The fire is all.

Some say the world will end in fire.

Others, ice.

Perhaps there was a third alternative: water. Not too cold, not too warm. But dark. And something akin to desolate nothingness.

My return to consciousness was like a reversal of my descent into its watery depths. I was a bubble trapped under layers of dark silt and mud. Slowly, drowsily, I slipped the confines of my premature burial and began to rise, ascending through the heavier strata of cold, dim waters and moving toward the light and warmth that lay just beyond the surface, high above.

As I ascended, the murky, muffled sounds resolved into voices—clarified—until I could finally distinguish words and phrases. Then sentences.

Although the water was warmer and clearer, now, I still had a ways to go. My eyes would not yet obey my desire to open.

But I could listen now.

So I lay quietly and listened to my first sermon on the other side of the grave.

"You have heard it said that God is an *angry* God, a *vengeful* God! That He *delights* in punishing the *wicked* and destroying the *evildoer!*"

It was a strong voice, a powerful voice. But it became soft and gentle a heartbeat later.

"I know that you say in your hearts: 'I *am* wicked! I *am* an evildoer!' And you believe that you are *damned* because fearful men, ignorant men, men with *no* love in their own hearts, have told you so!"

Near the surface now, I cracked my eyelids a bare sliver and squinted against the harsh whiteness that seared my eyes.

"These same men, out of the darkness in their own minds, the fear in their own hearts, would presume to enslave you—to shackle you to their own fears, their own darkness! In *you,* they see the reflection of *their* own evil, *their* own sin and corruption, and they have made you into spiritual scapegoats—the sin-eaters for *their* twisted purposes!"

My eyelids twitched and I began to bear a bit more brightness, now.

Again the voice thundered, "I say to you, do not fear the judgment of men! That is what has enslaved you! Enslaved your fathers! And your fathers' fathers, going all the way back to the ancient times! It is not by men that you will be ultimately judged, but by God! It is God's judgment that matters and not the fearful imaginings of ignorant men. And some of *you* should understand this all too well because some of you were once fearful and ignorant men. And women."

I lay on my back. Above me flared a panorama of white. Flickering white.

"Now, *now* that you should know better, you are *still* held hostage to the fear and ignorance of those who cannot see beyond the grave!"

I saw seams in the whiteness ... stitches ...

"Do you truly believe that you are beyond redemption? Consider the words of Paul, an Apostle of Jesus, called Messiah by the Christian sects: 'There is *no one* righteous, not even one; there is *no one* who understands, *no one* who seeks God. *All* have turned away, they have together become worthless; there is *no one* who does good, *not even one.* Their throats are open graves; their tongues practice deceit ...' "

Shadows of limbs and moss-draped branches danced, faded, and reappeared across the whiteness with the shifting patterns of light.

" 'The poison of vipers is on their lips. Their mouths are full of cursing and bitterness. Their feet are swift to shed blood; ruin and misery mark their ways, and the way of peace they do not know.'"

The voice paused dramatically, then continued: "Paul goes on to say that 'all have sinned and fall short of the glory of God.'"

I turned my head and saw that my canopied ceiling descended to the floor in swooping drapes and folds. I was inside a tent.

"Have you done evil?" the voice asked. "Well, let me tell you that you are in good company!"

I wasn't sure about my afterlife theology. I might hear sermons in Hell . . . but would I see tents?

"This book that I hold in my hands contains a veritable roll call of evildoers! This Paul, the Apostle of Jesus, whom I just quoted a moment ago, went around arresting and executing Christians with a viciousness that made him hated and feared throughout his country. He held his friend's coat and watched in utter indifference while the man was put to death. And, when he finally repented of the evil that he had done, he had to change his name and assume a new identity, so utterly fearful was his reputation in the land!"

I looked down and examined my blanket-wrapped body. It lay upon a canvas and wood-frame cot. As far as I could tell, I still had a physical body and it ached like hell. Again, the theological rules regarding corporeal existence were unclear. Was I still alive?

"Remember the story of Moses? Moses was a murderer! Before his exile into the wilderness and his destiny on Mount Sinai, he killed an Egyptian with his bare hands! Not by accident, not in self-defense, but in a murderous rage—a rage not unlike that crimson tide of fury that has swept many of us to violent acts in our own circumstances!

"Solomon was an adulterer. His daddy, King David, was always getting into trouble on that front and even ordered his best friend on a suicide mission so he could possess the man's wife without complications! How's that for cold?"

As a matter of fact, *I* was cold. The blankets kept some of the chill at bay, but I didn't generate enough body heat for the blankets to trap it effectively.

"The prophet Jonah defied God. Jonah! Sent on a mission by his God, he effectively said: 'The Hell with this!' He defied God and abandoned his mission! Ran away from his responsibilities! *Not* because he was afraid for his life, *not* because it was too difficult! He ran away because he was afraid the people he was supposed to preach to . . . might be converted!

"He didn't want them to be saved! *He wanted them to suffer!* He wanted them to be damned to eternal hellfire! Now *what* kind of evil is that?"

I worked on unwrapping the blankets. Whoever had tucked me in had done a bang-up job of it. I felt like a moth seeking premature release from its cocoon.

"Peter. The Apostle Peter. What a *disappointment!*"

While the "Sermon in Hell" scenario seemed less and less likely with every spasm toward wakefulness, it seemed pretty clear that I hadn't fallen into the hands of the 700 Club, either. Nope, not the sort of material one would expect from Graham, Falwell, Robertson, or Swaggert. And definitely not in the province of those TV evangelists with the gold furniture and the lady who looked like the love child of Dolly Parton and Tammy Faye Baker.

"Peter who is all noise and thunder when it comes to proclaiming Jesus as the Messiah," the voice continued, "suddenly loses his spine and denies that he even knows this man! Not once, not twice, but three, count 'em, three different times! How's *that* for eternal damnation? Denying the Son of God!"

I managed to work an arm free and then lay quietly, waiting for the room—er, tent—to stop spinning.

"*Except the New Testament doesn't say anything about Peter being damned!*"

I—and, presumably, some unseen audience—endured another dramatic pause. The tent seemed to spin a little less. "So what is the message here?" the voice continued quietly. "It's a very powerful one."

I noticed a familiar quality to the voice when it spoke softly— I had heard it somewhere before. I couldn't quite put my finger on it but, in my present condition, I was just as unlikely to come up with my own telephone number.

"The message is simply this: the great men and women in the Bible, by and large, were guilty of great wrongs! They sinned on both sides of the aisle: the sins of 'commission'; *and* the sins of 'omission.' But—in spite of their failings, their fears, their acts of disobedience or destruction, even their acts of evil—God *used* them! In fact, God *blessed* them!

"Oh, there were struggles and consequences, to be sure. But the scripture says 'Nothing can separate us from the love of God!' "

I worked my other arm free and was gratified to see that, while the tent's interior continued to revolve slowly, the revolutions didn't increase in speed.

"Do you believe that you are damned for all eternity? Do you really believe that you are beyond the forgiveness of Eternity?"

A large shadow darkened on the wall of the tent, shrank and darkened as someone approached.

"The Bible says that there is only one sin that is unforgivable! Only one sin that is unpardonable! It is *not* murder! It is *not* denying the Son of God! These sins, though not inconsiderable in their consequences, are not beyond the possibility of redemption." The voice dropped in volume and then continued softly: "No, the only sin that the Bible claims as being beyond God's mercy is—"

Lost as someone swept the tent flap aside, the stiff canvas making the sound of a colossus striding about in gigantic corduroy pants. Three women entered, the last pulling the flap closed behind her.

"Ah. You're awake I see," said the first, an older woman with a scattering of long, dark hair amid the predominant gray. She could have been in her late fifties or early sixties—assuming she was human. Actually, she did *look* human, and more than a little Amerind, but I had long since learned to not go with my first impressions.

The woman just behind her left shoulder appeared younger, taller, and plumpish. She wore glasses and had a kerchief bound over her long, dark hair. The woman standing just beyond the first woman's right shoulder was smaller, roundish, with dark hair and skin tones evidencing Hispanic origins. All were dressed similarly in blue jeans, tee shirts, and sneakers. If they were the Three Fates they were remarkably casual dressers.

"How are you feeling?" Fate Number Two asked pleasantly.

"Like Hell?" I croaked.

"Well," said Fate Number One, "you'll feel better in a bit. We'll do a session, with your permission, and Father Pat will be collecting communion shortly."

I wanted to ask: "A session?" Then: "Father Pat?" And before I could even get my mouth open: "Communion?" Instead I bypassed all three and asked: "Where am I?"

They all looked at each other and Fate Number One asked, "Where are we, girls? I'm afraid I haven't been paying attention lately and lost track."

Fates Two and Three exchanged expressions of bemused befuddlement and shrugged.

"The swamps," said Two.

"There aren't exactly any streets, addresses, or postal drops out here," added Three.

"We move about on a regular basis," concluded One.

I sighed. "So, I guess I'm still alive."

The oldest one chuckled and her eyes crinkled up into a dozen smiling creases but her words chilled me: "Not necessarily . . . your aura is all wrong."

"My what?"

"And your chakras are all running backwards," chimed in Number Three.

"Angela!" Number One scolded.

"Well, they are."

"Reading someone's aura from across the room is one thing," One continued, "but we don't do scans until we have permission."

"But I didn't scan him—not really. I can see it from here! Can't you, Lynne?"

Number Two cocked her head and looked me up and down. Or, more accurately, from one end to the other as I was lying down. "Nooo," she said slowly with a slight shake of her head, "I need closer proximity to his energy field in order to visualize the patterns of flow . . . but his aura . . ."

"It is unusual, isn't it, girls?" One remarked.

"I've never seen anything like it!" Angela breathed.

"Except for the time," added Lynne, "that Brother Mike—"

"Ladies!" One sternly admonished, "we are being rude." She turned her attention back to me. "Forgive us our nattering. We would like to help you but first we must ask your permission."

"My permission?" I croaked.

"To do a scan," Angela elaborated.

"And adjust your energy fields," Lynne added.

"If we can," Number One amended.

"Marilyn!?" the other two gasped, as if she had suggested something unthinkable.

"Well, look at him," Marilyn said matter-of-factly. "He actually has three distinct auras. I'm betting that his chakras don't total the requisite number either. Tell me, friend; are you alive, dead, or undead?"

I shook my head, causing the tent walls to take a quarter-turn about me: "I honestly don't know."

She nodded, thoughtfully. "Well, you've got holes in your auras that I could drive a truck through. With your permission, we'll attempt to close those gaps and rebalance your ki."

"Anything to make the room stop spinning."

Marilyn nodded and the three ladies took their positions at my head, my feet, and my side. Hands were extended, turned palms down, and then floated over my body a few inches away from actual contact. Aside from a series of "hmmm"s, a sigh, and a couple of "now that's interesting," the tent was quiet for a time.

"Angela is right," One—er—Marilyn said after a prolonged silence. "I count fourteen definable chakras—doublings actually—and three, hmmm, I don't know—para-chakras? And more than half of them are running backwards!"

"Is that bad?" I asked, starting to raise my head. The tent started to shift to the right so I lay back and closed my eyes.

"Not necessarily," answered Marilyn's voice. "If you were completely human, your energy flows would be completely out of whack—you'd be one very sick puppy."

"Voilà," I said, making a weak gesture with my hand.

"But you're not human," she continued. "Aside from the evidence in your multiple auras and chakras, you simply would not have lived three minutes after being gut shot the way you were—never mind surviving these past two days."

"Two days?" I murmured.

"And not just survived," she continued, "but begun to heal. Wiggle your toes."

I complied as best I could, though my feet felt numb and far away.

"See? Already your severed spinal cord has begun to knit."

I pushed past that surprise to ask about my liver.

"I'd stay away from hard liquor for another week or two but you could probably crack a bottle of wine tomorrow."

I doubted that I would be up for much of anything by

tomorrow but I learned a long time ago to not argue with one's nurses.

Unless, of course, the topic was bedpans.

"So, to answer your question . . . we don't know."

"Um," I said, "you don't know what?"

"Whether half your chakras running backward is a good thing or a bad thing," Lynne answered, her eyebrows performing a series of merry pliés.

"Normally we would work on reversing the vortexes that are turning counterclockwise," Angela explained.

"But normal is not the operative word here," I croaked.

"And because it isn't," Marilyn elaborated, "we might end up undoing some aspects of your—ah—rather unique metabolism."

"Hey," I said, "if it puts me back on a normal diet, I'm all for it."

"Well, there is that. But I'm more concerned that we might switch off whatever energy pattern that's slammed shut Death's Door and is currently keeping it triple-bolted, padlocked, and barred. You're on the mend—but becoming human at this stage of the process could still be fatal."

I thought about that.

I thought about the fact that I had cheated death more than once.

That living on borrowed time always involved heavy interest penalties down the road.

That living as a monster was only defensible when you'd tried every other alternative.

And maybe not even then.

"I'll take that chance," I said finally. "Take your best shot: make me normal."

"What about Father Pat?" Angela asked.

"We probably should ask him, first," Lynne agreed.

"Mr. Cséjthe has made his choice," Marilyn answered. "It is *his* life. We must respect his wishes."

The others nodded and, once again, all extended their hands, palms down.

"How come everybody seems to know my real name?" I murmured.

"Lynne, take his feet and ground him."

I wasn't sure what she was doing down there but the numbness in my lower extremities began to work its way toward my head.

"Father Pat?" I mumbled. "Any chance he's available to grant absolution?"

"Are you Catholic?" I couldn't tell who was speaking now as tendrils of Novocain had started to tickle the underside of my brain.

"Nooo . . ." The Novocain had already established a beachhead in my lips and tongue. "Jus like ta keep my basssesss coverrredd."

"Well, neither is Father Pat. But I'm sure he—"

Whatever else was said, I was beyond hearing it.

Everywhere I look I see a crucifix.

Preacher Hebler would approve. Not only have my personal chambers been stripped of every luxury of the flesh, the walls and doors have been adorned with a hundred and more crosses—the Christian symbols of torment and death. The priests and magistrate tell me that they will serve as a constant reminder of the God whose laws I have violated in every way imaginable. That they are there to turn each waking minute to reflection and penitence. That although there can be no hope of forgiveness in this world or the next, perhaps some good may be achieved by surrounding me with the sigils of the only willing sacrifice of blood, the only holy use for which the elixir of life is sanctioned.

But that is mere sanctimonious posturing: I know why my walls have sprouted a veritable forest of Christ-trees. The so-called Holy Father of the Romans has blessed each and they hope that these sacred objects will reinforce the earthen strength of timber and stone to hold me in this place. The peasants pray that I will be bound here beyond my sorcerous powers to squeeze through the slitted windows and fly upon the midnight vapors to seek more prey.

They need not fear.

Not myself, at least.

Even should timber crack and stone crumble, I am held here by a dark power more terrible than they can yet understand. They believe that they are safe now that I am "bound." But it is not their strength alone that prevailed against us. And it will not serve them against Cachtice's Power.

I shall make the motions and the mumblings of atonement. Who knows, perhaps I am not so damned as they think. Are the children worthy of the same degree of guilt as the adult who parents them?

I shall repent of my dark artistries ... but, before I do, I shall make this one last spell.

A conjuring of the blood.

I shall bind the truth in my own blood that it may speak for me yet.

I shall send that binding through the blood, blood unto blood.

Someday, the issue of my blood shall reclaim my name. I do not believe it shall be through my children, Pál, Anna, Ursula, or Katelin. The Witch's reach is long and my grandchildren—Ferenc, Anna, Maria, Erzso, and Janos—may not exceed Her awful grasp.

In exchange for my silence, She promised to not touch my family unto the forth generation. She has even named them though they are as yet many years unborn: Ferenc, Nicholas, Pál, Antal, Michael, Tamas, Elisabeth Christine, Anna Teresia, Maria Magdolna, Orsolya, Juliana, Klara, Ilona, Zsigmond, Kata, Gregory, and the two Lazlos.

My issue beyond that may be hidden even from Her as the fate of my own, illegitimate daughter is hidden from me.

Strange that I should remember her now, as I have not thought of her since I wed Ferenc. So many years ago! She was taken from my fourteen-year-old breast, the issue of a summer dalliance with a beautiful peasant boy. A year later I was the mistress of Cachtice and wife to the Black Hero of Hungary. Though legitimately born and of noble pedigree, our children may not be so pure as that nameless, lost daughter of my childhood. Perhaps the witch does not ken her existence and it shall be her anonymous legacy that delivers my message.

I cannot see what my dark Mistress sees. But I make this spell and bind the truth through my blood to be passed from one generation unto the next.

Until those bindings shall be loosed for Truth's sake ...

I ascended into consciousness more abruptly this time, not as a bubble but as a drowning swimmer, choking on the flood of water ...

... of blood that filled my throat and flowed over my lips, dribbling down my chin.

"Careful," said a voice, "you're giving him too much. Give him a chance to swallow."

I turned my face away, sputtered, and spat the thick, viscous liquid out while a bit more dribbled down my cheek and jaw. I coughed and felt my heart leap within my chest.

I reached up to wipe my face and found my arm moved with a strength I had forgotten I could possess.

"How are you feeling, Mr. Cséjthe?" asked the familiar voice.

I opened my eyes and looked at the strange, discomforting visage that was somehow familiar.

"I know you from somewhere . . ." I whispered.

He nodded. "St. Mark's, the other night. You were looking for a whore." He laughed at what must have been the expression on my face. "The Whore of Babylon," he elaborated. "Or maybe you were looking for Elizabeth Báthory."

"Who are you?"

He smiled a death's-head grin and I finally realized what wasn't quite right about his complexion from our first meeting. The light, here, was different than the chapel at St. Mark's but his pallor remained ashen, a luminescent gray.

"Call me Father Pat; everyone else does."

"Maybe I should call you the 'late' Father Pat." Among other things I was discovering that my near-death experiences weren't improving my manners.

He chuckled, seemingly unoffended, and nodded. "We have much in common, Chris. We have both been tourists in that undiscover'd country—"

"—from whose bourne no traveler returns? Well, the border seems to have been left open for some time now and nobody's checking passports."

The bowl was pushed toward my face and I looked up. "Jeepers creepers: Lurch in a fright wig!"

While the giant leaning over me actually did bear a passing resemblance to Ted Cassidy (not Carel Struyken or John DeSantis), his face was as preternaturally pale as the shaggy white hair that framed it. The features were strong, as if a sculptor had intended to create an eagle or a hawk in white onyx and then changed his mind and tried for a rough approximation of a human being. The massive brow kept the eyes in shadow, the nose jutted and curved like an insolent beak, and the mouth was a slitted cleft in impassive stone.

Father Pat cleared his throat. "This is Brother Michael."

Massive white hands clutched the golden bowl with its bloody repast. They offered the bowl again.

"Um, not really thirsty, big guy. Maybe you should pop that back in the fridge."

"Please," said Father Pat. "You need it. And you shouldn't waste the gift of life: it will go bad soon."

"Won't we all. Where did it come from?"

"It is a love offering from the congregation."

"The congregation? It's human blood?" I don't know why I was surprised; by all rights I should never be surprised by anything ever again.

"Some of my congregants are human, yes. And it was given freely and specifically for you."

"I—I can't accept this," I said, staring down into its crimson depths. Saliva started to flood my mouth.

"You would refuse more than the gift of life, freely given," he said, his voice beyond serious and suddenly edging into—what? *Ponderously prescient?* "You would be handicapping your role in the battle that is to come."

"Battle?"

He nodded and his eyes seemed focused on something outside the frame of time and space. "The forces of Darkness are preparing to roll across the lands of the living. Unless she is stopped, the Whore of Babylon will put on her red dress, drenched in the blood of the innocent, and open the Fifth Seal. The end time plagues will be loosed upon the earth and will hasten the Day of Final Judgment for all of Mankind."

An electric shiver worked its way down my spine but I suppressed it with a medicinal dose of annoyance and said: "Why is my drinking some blood so all-fired important in the grand scheme of the Apocalypse?"

Father Pat appeared to consider for a moment and then said, "There was another man who questioned the necessity of certain sacrifices. He said: 'If possible, let this cup pass from—'"

"*Whoa!* Whoa, whoa *whoa!*" I pushed the covers back and swung my legs over the side of the cot. "I may *not* be a believer anymore—

maybe more of a secular unhumanist—but you're seriously edging into blasphemy, here!" A hand grenade of pain went off in my middle and I sagged back against my pillow.

"I am not anybody's Great Undead Hope," I said, a little more carefully. "I am not a leader, a Loa, a messiah, or a general! I am just a guy trying to make sense out of a universe that keeps changing the rules."

"We all are," Father Pat said agreeably. "But fate and circumstance call us to greatness out of need, not because we're ready and willing to answer the call."

"Yeah? Well: ring, ring . . . what's that? . . . nobody answering? Guess we'd better keep working our way through the phone book."

"Perhaps if you understood—" he began.

"Let me tell you what I *understand* . . ." The stress of the past few days, the repressed grief for the lives lost, my most recent trip to the edge of death and back were combining to fuel a desperate rage. "When I was a kid in Sunday school they told me I had to pay for my sins. Okay, that seems fair. What doesn't seem fair is when I keep getting the bill for somebody else's crap! Well, check returned, insufficient funds: I am closing out all my accounts! You want someone to do battle with the Powers of Darkness? Go recruit the WWF! Hell, I can't even wear spandex without getting a rash!"

A scream split the momentary silence as I drew breath. A second later the tent flap was pulled aside and a face that was half-human, half-wolf appeared in the opening. "Father Pat!" it growled. "Come quickly! It's happening again!"

Pat jumped up. "Michael, bring the Roman Ritual and the holy water! Hurry!" He ducked through the flaps and was gone in a human heartbeat.

The giant hunchback stooped over me and gently, but firmly, pressed the bowl into my hands. His face was like carved stone, not quite human yet gently reassuring in its stony calmness and resolve. He turned and shuffled like someone unaccustomed to walking, bowing deeply for his humped shoulders to clear the tent's human-sized opening. Then he was gone, as well.

Chapter Nineteen

I slept badly and awoke often. It was, however, a slight improvement over the alternative of not ever waking again.

During my fevered tossings and turnings I heard snatches of conversations ranging from the conditions of my chakras to the theological imperatives of free will. During the rarer times I was sufficiently conscious and cognizant, I was also ravenous: I essentially chugged the contents of three different bowls. Slept and drank again. Twice more.

I also picked up bits and pieces of my host's story during his visits and my occasional moments of lucidity.

He called himself Pat but that wasn't his real name. He apparently couldn't remember his real name any more than he could remember his former life. The specifics of his existence went back a couple of years and dead-ended in the Holy Land, where he had begun a new life and a new calling.

And, in a fit of rare humor, chosen a new name.

It wasn't short for Patrick.

It was shorthand, he said, to remind himself that there were no "pat" answers. And that, since waking up in a shallow grave in the Sinai wilderness, he had to physically pat himself, from time to time, for the reassurance that his existence was more than the flickering dream of a brain guttering out in its final, electro-chemical shutdown.

And then there was the matter of the giant hunchback, Brother Michael.

It was too good a synchronicity to pass up, he said: Pat and Mike. It seemed the perfect frosting on the cake of their peculiar partnership. Why not?

Brother Michael had found him wandering in the desert. It was the albino giant who kept him alive (if that was the operative word) and somehow got him to America. His memory was nearly as patchy of that first year out of the ground as it was devoid of all the years before. It was, he mused, like most lives in that we have no memory of a pre-birth existence and are hazy regarding our infancy and early childhood.

The only clues he had to go on were the remnants of semi-military garb that he had worn like a tattered shroud.

That and the violence of his original passing.

"Murder?" I asked.

He smiled that odd, thoughtful, slightly off-kilter smile that had caught my attention during our brief encounter near the holy water font. His resurrected body, he explained, not only bore the evidence of man-made death but suggested a prolonged period of torture, as well. Perhaps, he considered, his lack of memory was a side effect of the trauma he had suffered before his execution.

Killed by the Palestinians or the Israelis?

"Does it really matter which? Or which side I originally fought on?" he asked in turn. "There is enough wrong on both sides to push the balance scales up and down, back and forth. If I was a man of war before, then I lived by the sword and died by it, as well."

Now he claimed to be fighting a different kind of war, a spiritual war. A war for the souls of those who had been told they had none.

Why?

He felt that there had to be some unseen but meaningful purpose that had brought him back in the flesh to walk the earth when he should have been long gone to rot and worms by now.

I had to ask the question though he clearly had addressed the issue long before: "You're sure that you actually died?"

"Not only am I sure that I actually died," he answered, as Brother Mike gently raised me to a sitting position, "but I question the use of the term 'resurrection' as it applies to me. When one speaks of a resurrection, it usually connotes a return to life—the condition of life. With all of the applicable attributes."

The hulking, hunched giant tucked pillows behind me as gently as my mother would.

"I," continued Father Pat, "am still dead. I do not breathe unless it is to draw air through my chest to speak. My heart does not beat. I do not sweat, sleep, or eat. And so, since awakening from what should have been my final sleep, my eternal sleep—I do not dream."

"You're a zombie?" I suggested.

"Have you ever met any?" he asked with that same oddly wry smile.

"Well, actually, yes." I think my smile must have matched his for the moment.

"They continue to decay," he pointed out. "Their reflexes, thought processes, response times, are slow. They are poster children for entropy. The organic breakdown may be slowed in some cases but it is never entirely held in check." He raised a gray hand and examined his own, dead-colored fingers. "I, on the other hand, seem to remain perfectly preserved. Well," he chuckled, "not 'perfectly.' But I can run and jump and dance and even swim and pass myself off as a living man if you don't look too closely."

I nodded groggily. "A little makeup—a good·foundation base— would solve that problem."

Massive Mike offered another bowl of blood to me but I dozed off before I could manage a single sip.

That night I had a dream that was most passing strange.

I dreamt that I was awake and watching an unearthly parade. Creatures that were half human and others far removed from that evolutionary tree passed by—shuffling, slithering, flapping, crawling—wending their way in a nightmare procession past a line of flickering torches and down into a great pit. Flames flickered down below, out of sight, but the treetops that ringed the pit danced in and out of the shadows, lit and darkened moment by moment by submerged firelight.

And when the nightmare horde had gathered, an assembly of death and damnation that congregated like the personified sum of humanity's darkest dreams, a voice rose from the pit as if from a dark general rallying his troops.

"The fourth chapter of Proverbs is particularly evocative for some of us," he called out in ringing tones. "The prophet writes these words: 'For they sleep not, except they have done mischief; and their sleep is taken away unless they cause some to fall. For they eat the bread of wickedness, and drink the wine of violence.'"

The congregation murmured at that and few voices bore resemblance to anything human.

"You, who crouch in darkness and shun the light, does your nocturnal nature make you evil?"

Faint growls formed a vague answer to the question.

"If so, then so must the bat be evil. And the owl . . . I'm certain that the owl appears quite evil to the field mouse."

Growls became throaty chuckles.

"And what of the firefly and the moth? Is the chorus of cricket and frog a dirge of death or a lullaby for sleep? We might as well follow mislaid logic to its extreme and declare the moon and the stars to be elements of immorality and wickedness.

"Man hates the darkness because he fears the unseen and the unknown. And, in like manner, he fears that which is not like him.

"But are we not like him? Do we not fear that which we do not understand? What we cannot see? Do we not fear living humans for their power to move about freely and fearlessly in the burning, blinding, killing light of day?

"We may say it is our nature to kill, our nature to do what men call evil because we are the spawn of darkness. But the eagle kills by day and the cavefish swims peacefully in eternal night. There is no line of moral demarcation between the darkness and the dawn.

"We may choose violence because we know no other way. We kill to eat. We kill to keep our enemies from us. Do we kill because it is our nature?"

I nodded, murmuring: "Nature, red in tooth and claw . . ."

Are God and Nature then at strife? quoted a soft voice off to my right. *That Nature lends such evil dreams?* Brother Michael stood stooped and hunched in the darkness beyond the torchlight.

"Tennyson, anyone?" I said with a small smile.

Brother Mike made no response other than to study me with gray, hawklike eyes.

" 'Who loved,' " I ventured, " 'who suffer'd countless ills, Who battled for the True, the Just . . .' "

The giant hunchback just stood there, considering me with an expression that grew less human by the minute.

" ' . . . Be blown about the desert dust,' " I offered, " 'Or seal'd within the iron hills?' Then . . . something about dragons . . . too bad, I bet you'd like that verse."

. . . *Dragons of the prime,* he said. Only his lips didn't move. *That tear each other in the slime . . .*

"He likes it!" I said, remembering that this must be a dream. "Hey, Mikey!"

O life as futile, then, as frail! came the words inside my head. *O for thy voice to soothe and bless!* The crippled giant began to fade back into the deeper darkness. *What hope of answer, or redress? Behind the veil . . .*

Then he was gone.

" . . . Behind the veil," I whispered.

Then I was gone: the dream was ended.

I rose on the third day.

Let me rephrase that: I got out of bed after three days of rest and recuperation.

I unwound the bandage about my middle and contemplated the fist-sized weal of pink new flesh where a gaping hole had been blasted just four nights before. I should still hurt like hell but I felt marvelous.

Physically, that is.

The blood made an undeniable difference. After months of supplementing my waning diet with embezzled packets of refrigerated blood products and aperitifs of plasma, getting it fresh and undiluted was akin to walking out of Dorothy's monochrome farmhouse and into the scintillating colors of the Land of Oz. I felt more than alive, I felt *vibrant.* I felt *younger.* I felt as if I were radiating health like a space heater pouring out waves of infrared heat and light.

Was this how Erzsébet Báthory felt after draining one of her virgin victims? If so, I could understand the hunger and need that

drove her down into her dark dungeons. I could still condemn—
but also fully appreciate how going down into that darkness
brought warmth and light of a different sort to the soul trapped
in ice.

Every time I had tasted crimson nectar, hot and lively from
pulsing veins and straining flesh, I could not imagine returning
to a repast of cold remains. Only a decaying sense of morality and
an unraveling guilt had succeeded in reining me in so far.

To keep from being totally swept away on this sensory flood
of health and vitality, I tried to capture a thread of that guilt. The
blood was given freely, Father Pat had said—no presumed guilt
there. So I focused on my other victims: my wife and daughter,
killed in the crash brought about by my first convulsive transformation; Dr. Marsh, murdered by New York's enforcers during their
first attempt to track me down; Damien's death and Deirdre's
suicide, the results of protecting me from Báthory's minions; Suki,
possibly still paralyzed from my leading her into a confrontation
with Liz Bachman last year; and, most recently, the deaths of Billy-
Bob Montrose and Teresa Kellerman during the assault on my
house.

My mere existence, alone, had resulted in so much pain and
death to others, how could I even contemplate performing a
conscious act that would bring further harm to an innocent life?
Better I should have climbed into that crematory oven behind Mr.
Delacroix and rid the world of two bloodsuckers for the price of
one.

Except I promised to protect his daughter and avenge his death.

And, so far, I hadn't done anything to be proud of in that
department. I might disagree with Father Pat's assessment of my
role in the grand scheme of things but, perhaps, we could find
one point of convergence: I owed Erzsébet Báthory a death. And
if that made an ending to my own encroaching madness and
monstrous transformation, then so much the better.

Someone had laid out clothing for me: jeans, boots, flannel
shirt—a bit warm for Louisiana, even in late fall. *Unless you exist
on the edge of unlife and need a little help in the body heat department.* I dressed and found that everything more or less fit though
the boots pinched a bit.

I pushed the tent flap aside and walked out into the late afternoon twilight.

We were deep in the swamps and a propinquity of trees provided a dense canopy of interlacing branches that blocked the waning sunlight like heavy cloud cover. Beneath the leafy ceiling the world seemed submerged in a dim green-tinted ocean and I moved into its depths like a deep-sea diver exploring a strange new world.

The camp was a haphazard arrangement of tents and makeshift tables and chairs set out and about. I couldn't be sure about the interiors of the other tents but the general area appeared to be deserted.

"Feeling better?"

I looked again and saw what I should have seen before: my three Fates sitting in the shade of a lean-to. Number One was knitting . . . something—it was too soon to be able to tell what. Number Two was working an ancient spinning wheel, producing a stream of yarn for Number One's project. Number Three was carding wool in preparation for the spindle of Number Two's wheel. In the distance, down by the bayou, I could see a knot of sheep. A giant, hunched form moved among them, distributing food.

"Um, yes," I said, remembering that I had been asked a question.

"Do you still want us to work on your chakras?" Number One—Marilyn—asked.

"Uh, sure."

"You do realize that your energy fields are pretty close to being balanced right now," Number Two—Lynne—added. "If we change the spin on those chakras that are currently running backwards, it will throw you out of balance until the proper rotation is restored."

"And that's bad?" I guessed.

"Depends on how long you're out of balance," Number Three—Angela—explained.

"You're balanced halfway between being alive and undead," Marilyn elaborated. "Even though we're attempting to move you away from the undead state, you might start to wobble from the balance point as we adjust your centers."

"Meaning I might tip over into the undead zone?" Not the direction I was hoping for.

"That's not too likely," Lynne said reassuringly.

"That's ni—"

"More likely you might tip over into a dead state," Angela amended.

"Angela!"

"Well, it's true. And you said we should tell him so he could make an informed decision."

"Well there's such a thing as tact."

I held up my hands. "What are the odds?"

Marilyn's knitting needles paused. "I can't give you odds. Your condition is unique so I can only tell you what is possible, maybe probable. I think it's probable that we can do this but I cannot tell you how long it may take or whether it will require many sessions. It will probably be very uncomfortable. And you may not like it."

"May not like it?"

"The end result," she said, looking me hard in the eye. "Right now you have the best of two worlds."

"The best—" I almost choked.

"You're stronger, faster, more . . . attenuated . . . than a human being. I doubt you will age like one. You don't have the full limitations that afflict the living dead nor have you succumbed to The Hunger or The Rage."

"Yet."

"You should have more faith in yourself."

"Why? Because everybody else does?"

"Everybody has to put their faith in something, Chris. And someone. Where and in whom do you put yours?"

I didn't have an answer, smartass or straight. I just nodded at the threads coming off the Fates' spinning wheel and finding a pattern between the clicking needles: "Anyone I know?"

"Jack," said Marilyn.

"Jack?"

Lynne shook her head. "You don't know Jack."

Angela giggled.

"Jack is my grandson," Marilyn said.

"That's your grandson?"

"It's going to be a sweater for my grandson."

"Ah. Okay . . ."

Angela giggled again as Lynne and Marilyn exchanged looks.

"Would you like to begin tonight?" Marilyn asked. "We could meet in your tent after the service."

"When shall we three meet again?" Lynne murmured.

"In thunder, lightning, or in rain?" Angela chimed in.

"Girls!" scolded Marilyn.

"Um, yeah. Sure." I started to back away.

"By then you may have had enough time to make up your mind," Lynne said.

"I'll bring my scissors, just in case," Angela called as I turned and ambled off a little briskly.

I think they all giggled that time.

Wandering about, I noticed a row of extinguished torches, set into the ground on tall poles like some sort of fifties-style Tiki-patio-party theme. Beyond them lay a small clearing where the ground dropped away into a bowl-like depression that was ringed with descending rows of split logs, laid on their sides to provide bench seating. At the nadir of the concavity was an open grave, a mound of dirt piled high beside it. All that was missing was the coffin.

"Welcome to our chapel."

I turned and looked for Father Pat but he was more elusive than my three faux Fates.

"Up here."

I looked up and, after a moment, was able to distinguish his form amid the latticework of leaves, branches, and garlands of Spanish moss.

"I'm checking the bayou for boats," he said, starting to climb down. "Ivonna said there were people a couple of miles to the south, yesterday. It's rare anyone ventures into the swamps this far, but you may still be worthy of a search party or two."

"Ivonna?" I said as he stopped about ten feet above the ground to disentangle a binocular strap that had snagged on a branch.

"You've met. She brought you to us the night you were shot."

I considered that. "Green hair?"

"That's the one. She's a russalka."

I nodded slowly. "She's a bit far from home."

He dropped to the ground and shrugged. "Home is where you hang your shroud."

"I thought home was where they had to take you in when nobody else wanted you."

He laughed and began plucking strands of gray-green moss from his clothing. "That's good! That's very good! Because that's what we're really all about."

"Your little congregation?"

"Yes, Chris, though I'd prefer to think of us as a family or a community. Congregations tend to be so iconoclast."

I gestured toward the pit. "You have a chapel. You preach sermons. I know you Roman Catholics are always trying to reinvent yourselves but—"

Father Pat held up his hand. "I'm not Catholic. At least, I don't remember being a Catholic while I was alive. But then I remember less and less about being alive with every passing day."

"You wear a Roman collar and everyone calls you 'Father' Pat."

He fingered the white square at his throat. "Symbols. Symbols are very important in matters of faith, in the realm of the unseen and the unknowable. As important as they are to the people of the daylight, they are even more potent to the children of darkness."

"So the collar and the title give you some measure of control over them."

"Control?" He gave me a long, penetrating look. "Oh. Oh, I see. You think I'm some kind of snake-oil salesman. That I'm using religion as a means to power." He smiled but there was little humor in it now. "I certainly wouldn't be the first to find advantage in using theology to amass a following. It certainly has been profitable to those with media outlets. But look about you." He swept his arm about in a broad gesture. "Where is my wealth? And even if I had access, who's going to permit a radio or television ministry to the undeniably damned?"

"According to the sermon I heard a couple of nights ago, you don't seem to subscribe to the concept of damnation."

"Oh," he said quietly, "I wholeheartedly believe in damnation. Don't you?"

"Oh yes," I said, trying to match him for quietness and not nearly succeeding. "That's why I question your motives. Hope is a cruel message. And people will seek power over others for no gain but power's own sake."

"Power to do what? Raise an undead army? With messages of peace?"

I shook my head. "There's nothing unusual about a religious war. Every generation sees millions murdered in the name of God. Offering forgiveness merely sooths the conscience and makes it easier to pull the trigger or break the commandments."

"And withholding it motivates us out of hopelessness?"

"There's a thin difference between motivation and manipulation."

"Manipulation?"

"I had an interesting conversation with a Chicago enforcer a while back. He told me about the fears of the soulless. Of the fear of endless darkness that awaits them beyond this pale existence. They don't go gentle into that good night—they rage, rage against the dying of the light because they have no promise of salvation! It's a cruel, *cruel* circumstance that gives you your opportunity. Bad enough that they're damned—that we're all damned! But you come along and tell them there's a heaven after all. That they can be heirs of light and salvation, as well. Well, God *damn* you, sir, for that! Except there is no God and you are worse than any serpent in the Garden of Eden. You offer a false hope where there is no hope!" I stopped, stunned at the depth of emotion that had come welling up from that dark place down deep inside.

"A lie is a terrible thing," he agreed, "especially when it shapes whole lives to hopelessness and despair. You, you speak the lies so smoothly, so effortlessly, because *you've* been told those lies all of your life. They've blinded you to the simple truths, the pure truths, and made you a judge to shallow appearance and prejudice. How dare *you*, sir! Who are *you* to come and say to anyone 'You have no soul, you have no salvation?'

"You accuse me of manipulating these beings with a message of hope when you would smugly perpetuate a falsehood of hopelessness without the intellectual honesty to question your own borrowed suppositions. The problem, Mr. Cséjthe, is that you *are* damned. Damned by the hardness of your own heart. Damned for wanting to close the doors of heaven against those that don't seem to measure up to your standards of redemption. Damned for wanting to hold them down in the darkness to share your miserable companionship."

"So," I whispered, "you do believe in damnation."

"Of course I believe in damnation, you fool! I already said so. Men like you and I, we know a great deal about damnation. But I live in a larger universe and I know there are greater things, more powerful things, than damnation. Things like love and forgiveness."

"And you get to dispense them, right?"

"Yes!" he thundered, his face catching a patch of sunlight that had slipped between the latticework of leaves. For a moment he seemed to glow like an illuminated saint on ancient parchment. "And so do you! We *can* forgive the wrongs done to us! And if we petty, vindictive, imperfect creatures can find some measure of love and forgiveness in our own shriveled hearts, what wondrous, immeasurable treasures might be poured out of that great heart at the center of the universe?"

"What about the rules?"

"Whose rules? What claptrap, pinch-hearted preachers have you been listening to? Did you hear my sermon and miss the whole point? There's only one sin in the whole Bible that is unforgivable. And as long as you don't commit that sin, there's hope, Chris! Hope! There's still a chance to redeem the life you thought was past redemption!"

"Who are you to offer hope?" I asked bitterly.

"Who are you to suggest anything but?" he shot back. "You think there is no hope? You believe Nietzsche's 'we are all apes of a cold god' shit?"

"Marx," I corrected, "not Nietzsche."

"Doesn't matter who said it, only who believes it. If you believe it then maybe it *is* too late for you. Maybe you've crossed that line of no return, achieved that unpardonable state, and lost your salvation forever."

"Yeah," I said, "*tell* me about my salvation."

"That's not my place, Chris; and it's not my message. I don't tell people that the grave is a closed door. You think the cross represents the message of the New Testament? The true symbol of the Christ is not an instrument of torture but the empty grave! That's our message: we are the Church of the Open Tomb! If His resurrection was a miracle and a blessing, why should ours be a horror and a curse? If God created us, He would not condemn us without reason. If there are shadows upon our souls, it is because there is a light within us, as well."

He paused and looked away. "There's just one catch."

"Sure," I said, "there's always a catch. What is it?"

"Free will."

I just looked at him.

He looked back.

"Of course," I said. "You have to have free will or there is no guilt. If we're the puppets of some higher power then there is no real responsibility. Ergo, no sin."

"Very good, Grasshopper," he said, inclining his head. "And since God allows us our own agency, forgiveness is very tricky."

"Ah," I said, "at last: the hook. You've been tossing that F-word around like it was totally free."

"God's love is free, my brother. It fills our every day like warm, life-giving sunlight." He frowned. "Hmmm. Perhaps that's not the best analogy for you. Certainly not for most of my congregants. Anyway, the point I'm trying to make is forgiveness is a gift. That's what makes it tricky."

"Beware of gods bearing gifts?"

"Poor Christopher—can't decide whether to wield his sarcasm like a sword or like a shield. Try again."

The thought finally crystallized: "You're saying the unforgivable sin is rejecting the gift of forgiveness."

He nodded. "It sounds like a catch-22 but it's really quite simple: forgiveness is a gift. And while a gift is bestowed freely, you have the power to accept or reject it. If you reject it, you choose your own damnation and God cannot interfere with that choice without making you His puppet.

"That's what's wrong with people always wanting God to destroy evil. To eliminate evil, He would have to prevent wrong choices."

I nodded slowly. "No wrong choices, no free will."

"Which would be worse?" Pat mused. "Apes of a cold god or puppets of a warm one?"

I stared off at the sunset reflected in the brackish waters of Bayou Gris. "It might not be so bad," I murmured after awhile: "if Shari Lewis was God."

Father Pat nodded. "And Buffalo Bob her prophet."

✧   ✧   ✧

I went to Father Pat's macabre matins that night. Not as a supplicant or believer but more along the lines of a skeptic on vacation. It was an intellectual cheat to judge something I hadn't fully examined.

But how do you examine God? Hold up theological hoops and see if He (or She or It) jumps through them on command?

I was still thinking this whole swamp front mission was nothing more than a theological circle-jerk when Father Pat began the midnight sermon.

"Those of you who were here a month back," he said, standing in a ring of fire that would have impressed Johnny Cash, "will remember a series of readings I offered from the Qur'an, holy to Islam. For the past month we have opened the Old Testament of the Hebrews and the New Testament of the Christians. Tonight I'd like to begin with The Four Noble Truths of Siddhartha Gautama, better known as Buddha, the 'Enlightened One.'"

I was sitting up in the nosebleed section—the ground-level edge of the great pit—and so the late arrivals jostled me. I moved down the log bench to make room for some vampires as Father Pat continued.

"All life is suffering. That is the first Noble Truth. Any questions?"

The vamp next to me gave me a nudge. "The question is," he whispered, leaning toward me, "are you a sufferer or a sufferee?" His laughter was more like a spasmed wheeze.

"Noble Truth number two: Suffering originates in desire. Ah, I see some brow-ridges going up on that one. "

The rest of the congregation had joined my bench mate in muttering. I wondered if they had fed just before coming to the service. I could smell the blood on my companion's breath even half turned away from him. "When the desire hits *me*," he murmured, "you can be sure somebody's gonna suffer." Phew! If his breath were any stronger I'd be able to type and cross match his last meal.

"Well, we'll come back to that point in a moment," Pat said as another pair of late arrivals crowded me on the other side of the bench. "The third Noble Truth of Buddhism is: Suffering can be escaped only by complete suppression of desire."

The undertone of muttering became an undertow of growls and I wondered how savvy our Preacher Pat really was. Whatever faith or denomination, tell 'em God loves you no matter what and that feel-good vibe makes true believers of us all. Start in on personal responsibility and the pews start to empty.

If we were lucky they'd start to empty before it got ugly.

"So," continued the voice to my right, "does this creepy creed practice baptism for the dead?" Another wheezy chuckle.

"I think the Mormons have the corner on that franchise," said a new voice to my left. "Hey," I got nudged, "have you noticed how this scooped-out depression makes a great amphitheatre?"

I nodded, trying not to breathe: The vamp on my left had a worse case of hemotosis than the one on my right.

"Well, it makes an even better trap."

"Mmm," I answered, wondering where this was going and whether now might not be a good time for me to be going, as well.

"Now bear with me," Pat was saying.

"One man with a flamethrower could destroy half of this gathering before they could turn around," my new seatmate explained. "Only a handful would have any chance of getting out, at all."

"So imagine what four men with flamethrowers, spaced equally around the perimeter could do," added the vamp on my right.

I started to stand but powerful hands grasped my arms and pulled me back down. Another pair of hands settled on my shoulders from behind and held me in a grip of lead and iron.

"Desire," Father Pat said, "can only be overcome by following the Noble Eight-Fold Path of right views, right intentions, right speech, right conduct, right livelihood, right effort, right mindfulness, and right concentration."

"I think you boys are missing the point of the sermon," I said quietly.

His response was just as quiet but it echoed in my head like a shout: "The countess wants to see you."

I told them what the countess could do instead and it wasn't something I would normally say or anyone would normally do in church. Guess I wasn't not a total convert, yet.

"If you won't do it for her," said a new voice behind my ear, a familiar voice, "then do it for me."

I turned and studied the play of distant firelight across the features of Terry-call-me-T's face. She leaned forward and kissed me on the cheek.

From Jesus to Judas, my Sunday school lesson was just about complete.

Chapter Twenty

I didn't do it for her or the countess.

I did it because it would be just like Erzsébet Báthory to kill a hundred over the obstinacy of one. As I walked toward the bayou, surrounded by a phalanx of fanged bodyguards, a large hulking shape rose up out of the shadows.

It was the hunchbacked giant, Brother Michael.

"Do you wish to leave?" he whispered. The whisper rumbled like distant thunder and I fancied I saw a dim flash of lightning as he twisted a great gnarled branch in his huge white hands.

This gentle giant suddenly seemed more dangerous and powerful than any unbent human I could imagine. But whatever his hidden strengths, I knew he was no match for a half-dozen vampires. And even if there had been any possibility of taking Báthory's minions there was still the implicit threat of four additional operatives with flamethrowers back at the pit. I had to defuse this confrontation before it escalated.

"Yeah, Mikey," I answered, "I've got some unfinished business."

The big guardian gazed down at me as if the others were of no consequence, staring as if I were a small child telling an obvious fib.

"Are you leaving of your own free will?"

Ah, that free will thing again. As if any of us truly have free will, choices without price tags . . .

The vamps around me were tensing, preparing to engage the hunchback if he offered any further resistance. I couldn't let that happen.

"Gotta go, big guy; I'm late," I said, moving toward him and forcing him to give ground. "Gotta see a man about a hearse, gotta make like a banana and split, make like a tree and leave, make like a mule train and haul ass . . ."

Brother Michael stepped aside and allowed us to pass but his face was stony with disapproval. My expression was more pleasant to look at but hurt a lot more. We walked down to the water's edge with his eyes burning into my back like twin laser-sights.

The next part was interesting.

Vampires do not like water.

Which makes hygiene problematical for some of them: Deirdre's excursion in my shower was one of those little triumphs of mind over nature. But the H_2O factor isn't generally too much of a problem unless there's a lot of it and it's headed in some direction: vampires, as a rule, don't cross running water.

One of the charms of a bayou, however, is that it isn't going anywhere. Oh, technically there is a current, but not so's you'd notice: toss a cork in the water on a windless day and that sucker will be floating close to the same spot twenty-four hours later.

So maybe it wasn't such a feat to get half-dozen vampires into a boat and send them to fetch me. But given Countess Báthory's methods and reputation, she'd probably have coerced them to shoot the rapids and go over a waterfall if necessary. We waded into the cold black water with a lot of hissing and feral grunting. We were almost up to our waists when we reached the boat that was anchored about twenty feet from the shore.

As we turned about and paddled away I wondered what would happen if I jumped back into the water.

"Before you make any attempt to escape," growled a familiar voice, "now or in the future, you should remember that we know where your friends are. Your cooperation is a guarantee of their safety."

"Sandor," I said with fake enthusiasm, "you old bowling ball, you! Still jealous that I have a neck and you don't?"

He growled but said nothing more. A moment later the outboard motor coughed to life and we trolled toward the deeper, central channel of Bayou Gris.

"What's that?" Terry-call-me-T asked, pointing off of our starboard side.

I caught a glimpse of a head with long emerald tresses before it submerged. "T . . ."

"Call me Theresa."

I looked at her. "Theresa?"

"It's my name."

"It's . . . Okay, what happened?"

She looked at me with those big, luminous eyes, eyes that weren't so innocent now. "Isn't it obvious? Nobody had to explain it to me."

"I've been distracted."

"The bullet that punched through your body and then mine caused me to bleed out. I died."

"That much I had pretty well figured out at the time," I said dryly.

"Our blood commingled through our wounds before I died," she continued. "It actually infected me faster than if you had opened a vein and allowed me to drink. I died and was reborn in a matter of minutes."

"So," I mused, "I am your Sire." All I lacked for now was the nomination for Deadbeat Undead Dad of the Year. I cleared my throat. "I'm a little surprised at your lack of loyalty, my dear. You know it's considered bad form to betray your Sire to his enemies."

She shook her head. "That's not how it works, my dear Professor Haim—or should I say Cséjthe? It is the countess who rules our clan: all allegiance is due her first, undivided by petty alliances over who made whom. You may be my Sire but she is our mother and my Dam."

"Damn," I said.

Sandor cuffed me. "You will show proper respect. The countess is the embodiment of a great and royal bloodline. Your blood, if related at all, is diluted by generations of common, mongrel stock."

I rubbed the back of my head. "Jeez, Sandy! If you've got such a jones for the aristocracy, how come you're not in Dracula's entourage?"

"My brothers and I are sworn to the Gutkeled Clan. Our fidelity is to the countess and her issue." He cuffed me again and constellations appeared even though the night skies remained overcast.

"Well, that might include me then, big guy. So stop popping me in the head."

"Even the children of royalty must be disciplined. Especially when their mother commands it."

"Too bad you're not a mother, Sandy," I said. "Oh wait, maybe you really are."

He reached out to pop me again and I caught his wrist. I yanked, overbalancing him, and the whole boat rocked. I braced myself, disallowing his recovery as the boat tilted the opposite direction and then yanked again. We both stumbled against the gunwales and I released his wrist to give him a little boost. The boat didn't capsize—a result too good to be hoped for—but Sandor made a most satisfactory splash as he tumbled into the bayou.

The other vamps weren't prepared for such a contingency. They scrambled to the side, coming a lot closer to rolling us over than I had. Thrusting their hands in the water they groped in vain: Sandor had sunk like a stone and wouldn't be coming up again on his own. A weighted rope would have a one-in-a-hundred chance of falling within his flailing grasp and we didn't have one of those on board. The only good their efforts accomplished was to enable me to kick two more over the side before the rest swarmed me.

They were sufficiently pissed and frightened that I only had to endure a dozen or so kicks and punches before the blessed curtain of unconsciousness postponed the pain until the next day.

My jailors brought me word this morning that Erzsi Majorova has been caught and beheaded. There will be no more trials, no more witch-hunts. I, alone, remain; walled up high in my tower, surrounded by crucifixes and selected pages from the Christian Bible that have been nailed to the walls between their binding symbols.

Katarina visits me some nights when the moon is new and the guards are more restful. Just last week she came to my window and told me that my time would not be long, now.

I wonder where she sleeps?

The townspeople all believe her to have quit Cachtice after the first trial. But she is watchful lest I break my promise.

She is restless for my death, I think. She wants to travel but dares not leave me lest I grow bold in her absence.

She wants to go to . . . him.

As if he would consort with a Beneczky when Báthory-Nádasdy was not good enough for his patrician ways.

Still, her power grows.

Though my dungeons have long stood empty and she must feed secretly and carefully now, her power continues to increase.

If she lives long enough—two, maybe three, lifetimes—she might equal him in strength, power, and cunning.

Should that day come not even the old dragon could withstand her. And then the world may well burn . . .

Maybe the concept of an afterlife was overrated.

At least the idea of waking up was proving to have less and less appeal. You can only wake up to pain so many times before the phrase "eternal rest" begins to take on a very literal attraction. Never mind Hell—Heaven in all of its various descriptions must involve some form of participatory involvement and, anymore, I just wanted to sleep the Sleep of Oblivion.

Alas, I had a bladder that wasn't suited for eternity. I rolled over and cracked an eyelid.

My prosthetic fangs sat in a glass on the nightstand just a foot-and-a-half away. They looked all sparkly-clean: maybe someone had dropped in an Efferdent tablet.

A couple of feet beyond, ensconced in a large, stuffed chair was my former student turned undead understudy, Theresa-call-me . . . uh, Theresa. The dark circles under her eyes appeared to be the real thing—no Goth makeup need apply here.

"You're awake," she said.

"You're anemic," I replied.

"Yeah. Well. That's your fault."

I sighed. "That's not surprising. Lately everything seems to be my fault."

"I don't have fangs," she pouted. "Your blood isn't pure."

"Perhaps," I said, pushing back the covers, "but everyone seems to want it." I was naked beneath the covers. "So, you're infected with only half of the combinant virus." I pulled the covers up to my chin. "Where are my clothes?"

She got out of the chair like a reluctant child. "I'm not a real vampire," she whined. "I don't know what I am."

"You're not dead and starting to rot in some cold grave," I said. "You're not a full-fledged monster."

She crossed the room and opened the closet. "I can't bite people. I can't suck their blood. Not without using a knife or something."

"I stand corrected. You probably are a monster." I disconnected from that line of thought and wondered what the dean had said when informed that I hadn't shown up for my night classes this past week.

"So," she asked, her voice partially muffled by the depths of the closet, "what clan are you?"

"Clan?"

"It's pretty obvious that you're not Nosferatu, and I've had enough conversations with you to know you're not Malkavian. You don't dress like a Ventrue."

"That's good to know."

"You don't act like a Toreador . . ."

"Olé."

"That leaves Tremere, Brujah, or Gangrel."

"What the hell are you talking about?"

"Clans. The Camarilla. The Masquerade."

"I don't go to parties," I said. I certainly shouldn't have gone to that one at BioWeb.

"Our Lady has promised to complete my transformation . . ." Hangers rattled. " . . . if I take care of you properly." She emerged with my clothing. Not what I had worn last but clothes from my closet back home. I looked around the room. It was furnished and appointed like a luxury suite at one of the finest hotels. I definitely was *not* home.

"Welcome to the Hotel California," I muttered.

"What?"

"We are all just prisoners here of our own device," I quoted.

She looked at me as if I were speaking an alien tongue. I suppose I was.

"And how am I to be taken care of?" I asked rhetorically.

She stopped by the chair. Draped my clothing over its back. Began to unbutton her black blouse.

"I'm not interested," I said flatly.

"How do you know until you've had a sample?" she asked, reaching the belt and undoing the buckle.

"I'm not promiscuous."

"Don't be silly," she said, easing the zipper down on her black slacks. "Everyone is promiscuous when the conditions are right." She shrugged the blouse from her shoulders. She wasn't wearing a bra. "Besides," she continued, shimmying out of her pants, "even if you can't get it up, you'll need to feed. It's easier when there's no clothing to get in the way."

I shook my head. "Poor Theresa-call-me-T-call-me-I-don't-know-what. You've read Goth fantasies penned by failed romance writers who would have you believe the undead nightlife is all fucking and sucking. Well, welcome to the dreary version of the nightfolk's nightmare. It's all about having power over others, trading lives like they were commodities—a means to mastery or mastication. Right now you're special because you're neither human nor vampire. Once you're truly turned, you'll be the lowest of the low on the undead food chain."

She stepped out of the last remnants of her clothing and crawled onto the bed. As twenty-something bodies go, hers was better than most but I had resisted Deirdre's charms and this little would-be vamp wasn't even in her zip code.

More importantly, she wasn't Lupé.

"Get out," I said. "This is the last time I'm going to ask nicely."

"Not until you've tasted my blood." She kept coming, crawling over my legs.

"I don't want your blood."

"Nobody wants my blood," she whined, deliberately slowing her progress as she reached my hips. "They say it tastes funny. It used to taste sweet."

"I'll bet Rod would still like it."

She grinned suddenly. "Once I get turned all the way, I'm going to pay ole Rod a visit." She chuckled in a most unpleasant way and I could see now that the sweet young coed in the coffee shop was forever dead and buried. "Yep. Ole Rod will unlock his door some night when he sees it's me and I'm alone. He'll invite me in and lock the door behind me. And I'll make sure he turns up the music before we start to party." A thoughtful expression flickered in her feral eyes. "I'll have to pick something appropriate.

Maybe something by Skinny Puppy or Switchblade Symphony. Something long and loud, though . . ."

"You're going to kill him?"

"Kill Rod?" She considered the question. "Everyone dies eventually. But I'll keep Rod around for as long as possible. It will be easy. He has a couple of pairs of handcuffs and an old, wrought iron bed. Now the master will become the pupil and the pupil, the master." She giggled. "I shall sip from his testicles."

That did it. I tossed the covers aside, bundling my unwanted bed guest, and got up. By the time she was able to unwrap herself I was stepping into my underwear.

"Don't leave!" she cried.

"Don't stay," I shot back.

"She'll punish me if I don't do as I'm told!"

"Dammit!" I threw my pants back down on the chair and grabbed her as she crawled to the edge of the bed. "It doesn't matter what you do!" I yelled, grasping her by the upper arms and shaking her like a rag doll. "She'll punish you anyway! That's what she does! That's what she *is*!" I threw her back on the bed. "Look, I'm sorry you took a bullet that was meant for me! I'm sorry that you died! I'm even more sorry that you've come back the way you are now! If I had any guts I'd do you the immense favor of twisting your head off right now!" I stumbled back and sat heavily on the chair arm. "But that's not my call. I *can't* be held responsible for anything anyone, here—you—or she—or her merry band of mutants—does! I can only take weight for what *I* do. Or what I don't do! If she puts a gun to your head, I *won't* be hostage to her finger on the trigger!"

I looked up at the ceiling and shook my fist at the room in general. "I don't know where the microphones and cameras are hidden but I know you're watching and listening. You can hold me! You can kill me! But I won't let you *twist* me! So let's stop playing these silly-ass games and get on with it!" Easy words to say. I wondered what I would actually do when push turned to shove.

I stood up and started dressing.

"What about me?" Theresa whimpered from the bed.

"Get dressed," I said. "I'll help you if I can. I just don't know that I can. Where's Deirdre?"

"Your blood slave? She's Our Lady's blood slave now."

"What! What do you mean?" All sorts of horrific images crowded to the forefront of my consciousness.

Before she could answer, the door opened and four very scary-looking people entered the room. I say "people" but that's not strictly true. They had been people once—a couple of hundred years ago. Now they were just people-shaped avatars for something far older and way less human.

And they were big. Had we all been human, any one of them could have beaten me to a pulp, five minutes max. Preternatural biology taken into account, I might last thirty seconds going *hemo y hemo,* tag-team style.

The nastiest-looking one stepped forward. "Put in your fangs," he commanded. "You are a ridiculous creature without them."

I slapped my biceps and pumped my arm. "Bite me, fangboy." Hey, if they were going to kill me, I might as well hurry the process.

"You killed Sandor," the spokesman answered with a severe look. "And Klaus and Gyorgy, alone and outnumbered."

I put my hands on my hips and just stared. "I didn't order you guys to get into a boat and go out on the water. It wasn't my fault you weren't wearing the mandated floatation devices. And it wasn't my idea to be piped aboard the Sloop John V. So don't be busting my chops over something that never would have happened if you cretins would just leave me the hell alone!"

"Before that, you dispatched Medea and Ivor with the assistance of your wamphyri servant."

I supposed he was talking about the little incident as Deirdre and I were leaving for the sucky BioWeb gala.

Then he did something unexpected. He smiled. "You are an unnatural creature. . . ."

"Oh, gee," I said. "Coming from someone who sleeps in graves and is a sniveling lapdog for that crazy Romanian slut, well that just stings. A little."

I didn't think a vampire could go all apoplectic but three of the fearsome foursome looked like they were about to stroke out. "Do you know," another one of the bloodsuckers sputtered, "of whom you speak? Do you know who our Dark Mistress is?"

"Yeah, yeah," I said, waving dismissively, "she's Ronald McDonald and we're all supposed to be her Happy Meals."

The one to the right snarled and lunged for me. Although starting from clear across the room, he was practically on me in a half of a second. He was certainly faster than me but I was anticipating this and *I* wasn't moving in a blind rage. I fell back on the bed, swinging my foot up. I caught my assailant right between the legs and launched him over me to go crashing, headfirst, into the wall on the other side of the bed. Pity; while he was unconscious he would miss out on all that invigorating throbbing where I had kicked him.

I sat up and looked at the remaining three. "Next?"

The leader had folded his arms across his chest but now flung one arm to the side to restrain the other two. "As I was saying, you are an unnatural creature—no fangs and lacking the full power of The Chosen. But you killed Sandor. And that earns you my respect. If you fully Become, you will be a most formidable warrior!"

"But . . . but . . . he dishonors Our Lady," one of the vamps protested.

"Perhaps," he agreed slowly, "or perhaps it is she who dishonors herself. But his blood may be hers and so our oath may bind us to him, as well. In any event, we have our orders and it is for her to choose his reward or punishment."

I stood up, knowing it was too late to bait them into making any further mistakes. But I could certainly keep trying. "You know, all that Master/Mistress/Slave/Sire/Blood-oath crap was all the rage three or four centuries ago—but this is America and the twenty-first century now. Wake up and smell the democracy. Feudalism is futile-ism now, and you people are way overdue for a paradigm-shift. If you don't like our all-men-are-created-equal policy then go back to the old world and hang with the guys who still dream of building empires with car bombs and ethnic cleansing."

"A pretty speech," said a new but familiar voice from the doorway, "but you lack an understanding of the importance of family." Erzsébet Báthory smiled from the doorway. "Prosperity aside, just to survive one must be able to trust in those about one. To have and give loyalty when the rest of the world would hunt you down and destroy you. And it is the natural order of things that the place of some is to obey while others are to be obeyed."

"Don't be lecturing me about the importance of family," I seethed. "My family is dead."

"Because of Dracula," she countered. "And we will speak of his whereabouts soon. But in the meantime I want to run a couple of tests." She reached behind the doorway and then entered the room dragging Deirdre by the arm.

Dragging was the operative word: Deirdre was practically unconscious, her legs splayed loose and unresponsive behind her as she was pulled across the carpeting and deposited at my feet.

"What did you do?" I knelt down and slid my arm beneath her shoulders. Deirdre's head lolled back and I could see her bruised face and the multiple bite marks on her neck and throat. The little black dress was shredded, and her normally pale skin was nearly translucent and marked with more wounds. Some were teeth marks.

Some were not.

"She would not help us find you," the countess said matter-of-factly. "I know you share a Blood-bond—much stronger and better appreciated than your link to this one." She pointed at Theresa, who cowered among the bedcovers.

"You've tortured her!" I slid my other arm behind her legs and lifted her up. Theresa barely got out of the way in time as I laid Deirdre on the bed.

"You make pretty speeches about equality, but the truth is she is so much your Thrall that I was unable to open her mind with mine. That left the old-fashioned methods. . . ."

"And you *love* the old-fashioned methods," I said bitterly as I realized how badly I had misjudged the redheaded vampire.

"Yes," Báthory said, seeming to savor the memory. "And her blood was sooo sweet. I didn't know whether to take her to my bed or my bath."

"My blood used to be sweet," Theresa whispered.

"Well, it's not now!" the countess said with sudden viciousness. "And since he has no interest in it or your body, your only value to me is what you can tell me about the power in *his* blood!"

"But I don't know anything," she whimpered.

"Maybe your mind is ignorant," the countess replied, "but your flesh knows some secrets. Perhaps they will yield them to the knife." She turned. "Graf, take this piece down to Dr. Krakovski in Special Research and tell him to prepare for a detailed vivisection."

"What? No!" I tried to body-block her fanged footman but he was on-balance and expecting resistance. He threw me into the same wall that had backstopped his fellow servitor just minutes before. He even had the time to be gentle so that I didn't completely pass out. That was thoughtful: I was able to appreciate Theresa's frenzied screaming as she was hauled out of the room. I wasn't able to regain my hands and knees until her wails had faded down the length of the outer hall.

"Kurt, help him up."

"Yes, my lady." Mr. Spokesman grabbed my collar and hoisted me into the air.

"Put him on the bed. Next to the other test subject."

I was deposited into a loose embrace with Deirdre. She moaned and leaned into me.

"She needs blood, Cséjthe. She's been drained to the point of Second Death."

"Why? For what purpose?"

"I want a demonstration of what your blood can do."

I raised myself up on an elbow. "You know what it can do. It makes Theresa taste funny."

Erzsébet Báthory shook her head. "It raised her from the dead. Vampire blood does not have that power."

I didn't like where this was going. "Sure it does," I argued. "That's how you make more vampires. You drain a human to the point of death and then give them your blood."

"*Almost* to the point of death," she corrected. "They must still be alive to drink. Your little resurrect took place after she died. And she's not strictly a vampire now. Laboratory analysis of the samples you gave Dr. Delacroix indicates anomalous elements that aren't consistent with living or undead hemoglobin. Your blood is different. Why? How did that happen? I need to know what it can do."

I thought about the tanis-leaf extract I had sampled last year and its effect on the resurrected flesh of Kadeth Bey. Then I remembered how the secret sharing of lycanthrope blood had elevated me to another level of undead existence—the rarified status of a Doman with the power to translocate.

Except I wasn't undead so there really was no precedent for what I had become. And no map or manual for what I would become. I looked into Erzsébet Báthory's eyes and vowed I would stop my own heart before I divulged Lupé's role in any of this.

"You want a taste?" I asked, thinking, if she would just get close enough . . .

"Drink from you without knowing what secrets are locked in your veins? Even without the Ogou Bhathalah warning me against its power, I would have waited to see its effect on another, first. I have not survived the centuries and become *voivode* of New York by being reckless."

"*Voivode?*" I hissed. "Of New York?" I shook my head. "Hey lady, I remember Rudy Guiliani. I watched him on TV. You're no Rudy Guiliani."

"So here's my first lab test," she continued, ignoring my response. "I've seen how your blood affects a human who was already dead. I want to see what happens when one of our kind receives the Dark Gift from your veins." She nodded toward Deirdre. "She will die the Second Death unless she feeds within the hour."

"Maybe it would be better if she did," I said slowly.

"That will be up to you."

I shook my head. "I didn't do this to her, you did. Her death is your responsibility."

She laughed. "You parse words like a lawyer, Cséjthe. Do you think her death will move me in any fashion? The question is, will her death move you? One way or another, I will have my test. How that test is assayed is in your hands." She gestured toward Deirdre's still form. "She needs sustenance and her time is running out."

I waited for her to "push" me.

Based on our previous encounter, the mere idea of defiance would be ludicrous: better than a marionette, she could work me like a hand puppet.

But she didn't push. No mental coercion followed the verbal command. She would not, however, wait forever: if she wanted to see a vampire sample my blood, she probably had a long line of loyal and willing volunteers waiting in the wings.

Screw them; I would resist as best I could. Under the circumstances it would be a totally futile attempt to exercise free will, but a man has his pride. With Deirdre, however, it was different. My culpability in Damien's death and her suicide put me under an obligation that Báthory had no need to invoke or press. I owed Deirdre a life—hers, if not mine.

And I could not bear to see her suffer.

I reached across her white, motionless body and retrieved my artificial fangs from the glass on the nightstand. Instead of fitting the prosthetics over my natural teeth, I used them to open a vein in my forearm—much as Deirdre had done when she had used them to savage her own wrists the year before.

Blood welled up, overflowing the cut as I pressed the wound to her slack lips.

For a minute, maybe two, there was no response. Then she shuddered, swallowed convulsively, and I felt the ghostly trace of her tongue as it explored the opening in my flesh.

"Come on," I whispered in her ear, "your turn to pull at it."

She moaned against my arm and her eyes fluttered open. Focused on my face. "Chris," she gasped, breaking the seal of her lips upon my skin. Her eyes roamed about and fixed on the countess. "No . . ."

"Hush now," I murmured, smoothing her tangled hair away from her battered face. "Let's get you strong again."

I moved the wound back to her mouth but she turned her head away.

"No," she protested weakly. "She's using me to get to you."

"She's already got me," I said calmly. "And if you don't take my blood, someone less deserving will." I turned her face back toward mine. "The blood-bond, remember? This is my favor returned." I used the teeth to deepen the wound and brought it to her mouth again.

She allowed it but just lay there passively, her eyes locked on mine, as the blood followed the path of gravity down her throat.

"How touching . . ." Báthory said sardonically. "Kurt, why is it that your Brethren have ceased to show such solicitousness toward me?"

"My Lady," I heard the alpha vamp answer, "we are as devoted and steadfast today as we were when we entered your service two centuries ago."

"That is not entirely true, Kurt. Sandor's devotion had only grown since he took his oath to serve the House of Cachtice, but I have sensed a growing disenchantment among some of the rest of you. Now that he's gone, I feel less secure." Maybe, but the tone of her voice suggested she wasn't exactly quaking in her stiletto heels.

"Madame, I assure you—" If Kurt meant to assure anyone, he would have to work on getting more sincerity into his vocal inflections. Deirdre was beginning to suck gently on my arm, the extra glands beneath her tongue secreting anticoagulants to counteract my own blood's accelerated clotting factor. While Báthory accused and Kurt remonstrated, the bruises on Deirdre's face began to fade and a pink blush began to infuse the unearthly pallor where her skin was unmarked. The discussion retreated into a background of white noise and my vision faded into a red haze that persisted even after I closed my eyes. I laid my head down beside hers as I felt something more than the blood pass between us. My head began to spin and I wondered if she would be able to stop before I was drained dry.

Maybe that wouldn't be such a bad thing.

She stopped.

She began to convulse.

"That's interesting," I heard Báthory say.

"Deirdre!" I gathered her into my arms. "Somebody help me here!"

"We'll need a diagnosis." Báthory snapped her fingers. "Jahn, Kurt, get her down to Krakovski. Tell him to prepare Red Clinic Two."

As the other two vamps moved toward the bed, Kurt cleared his throat. "Gold Clinic One is just down the hall."

"Red has a double setup. We may want to do a side-by-side."

My head snapped around and I stared at her. "A *what*?" Jahn and Kurt started to take her out of my arms. "Are you talking about a double vivisection?"

"It won't be a vivisection if she's dead, it will be an autopsy."

I shook my head and refused to relinquish my grip. "You can't autopsy a vampire! Not unless you're doing spectrographic chromatography of the ashes!"

Deirdre's seizures suddenly stopped. Between that and the superior strength of two vampires, I lost my grip and fell back on the bed.

"Be thankful, Mr. Cséjthe, that I'm not sending *you* down to Krakovski's lab for analysis." She didn't add the word "yet." She didn't have to.

I wasn't thinking about that, however. I was focused on Deirdre as Kurt and Jahn carried her toward the door. If I had let Deirdre die I would have saved her. Instead, my act of "mercy" was going to make her remaining existence one of utter horror.

I heard a moan rising up from the floor behind me: the vampire I had thrown into the wall was beginning to stir. There were three other fully conscious vampires in the room. If I'd had my silver-loaded Glock, the odds would have still been out of my favor. Unarmed and woozy from blood loss, I didn't have a chance in Hell.

Which was pretty much where I was now, I figured.

Chapter Twenty-one

"Oh my God!" I said, doubling over, "I'm going to be sick!" I jumped up off the bed and ran toward the bathroom, clutching my stomach. The bathroom was roomy—luxury-sized just like the bedroom. The tub was a doublewide Jacuzzi and the twin sinks were half-partitioned off from the rest of the facilities. There was no window, only a fine-meshed ventilation grill capping ductwork that would give a rat claustrophobia. The door had a lock and I pushed the button in for the illusion of privacy. If Báthory or her minions wanted in, neither the lock nor the flimsy door would give them a second's pause.

I sat on the toilet seat and bowed my head. I had but one chance and it was a slim one.

Since I first learned about vampiric translocation about a year before, I had managed to successfully pull it off fewer than a dozen times. My last attempt—following my little tussle with Je Rouge, Mr. Delacroix's brief resurrection, and hosting my post-mortem accident victim—was the first time I had managed to pull it off while under stress.

I usually failed, even when meditating under the most ideal of conditions. The question was, could I do it now? Hostile forces surrounded me. Deirdre and Theresa were on their way to pro-tracted, horrific deaths. The third most ancient and powerful vampire I had ever known was just on the other side of a door that was one step up from papier-mâché.

My only chance was that my luck had hit bottom hard enough for me to hitch a ride on the rebound.

"Christopher . . . are you all right?" The door was barely a barrier to Báthory's voice.

"Leave me alone!" I yelled. "I'm sick!" I flushed the toilet for corroborative sound effects.

"Poor Christopher," she crooned. "I'll come back when you're feeling better." The sound of retreating footsteps was encouraging—until my hypersensitive ears heard her say: "Awake now, are we? I'm locking him in but I want you right outside the bathroom door, just in case. Think you can handle it, Viktor?"

"Y-yes, my lady!"

"Because if you can't, we can roll an extra gurney into Red Two."

Two sets of footfalls moved toward the outer door.

I tried to relax. I couldn't unclench my teeth.

Don't think about how little time you have. This is the only way past Báthory and her goons. This is the only way to reach Deirdre and Theresa. The only way.

The only way.

Only way.

The tunnel.

Tunnel.

Breathe.

Breathe.

Stop breathing.

Death.

The tunnel.

Death is but the doorway . . .

To new life . . .

We live today . . .

We shall live again . . .

In many forms . . .

Shall we return . . .

Return . . .

Return . . .

I didn't know what forces still roiled through the charged atmosphere of BioWeb's labyrinthine facilities, but this time there was a sensation of movement, like tunneling through murky water. I felt my hackles rise and, with them, the fur along my spine. I ran in the darkness upon all four limbs, my snout straining for the scent that would lead me to Deirdre. A golden thread of pheromones looped off to one side and I followed, falling, tumbling.

I came out of the tunnel and into the brightness, rolling across the floor and into the backstop of a row of cabinets. I lurched to my feet to confront the vampire named Jahn. He was standing behind the autopsy table where Deirdre struggled against heavy straps buckled about her wrists and left ankle. Her right foot flailed about, Jahn having only made it that far when I popped in. Clearly, the sight of a naked man tumbling out of empty air was more of a major distraction than two naked women strapped down and apparently unable to move: Jahn's jaw dropped open, which made Deirdre's forceful, upwards kick all the more devastating as her foot smashed into his chin. His head snapped back and he went over backwards like a stunt double in a chop-socky kung-fu movie.

Jahn was down but not out. I had just enough time to unbuckle Deirdre's left wrist restraint before Jahn popped up like some giant, creepy Jack-in-the-Box from *Vamps-R-Us*.

"Look out!" Deirdre exclaimed unnecessarily.

"You're naked!" Theresa shrieked even more unnecessarily. "Omigod! Why are you naked?"

Jahn didn't attack me immediately. The whole "appear out of thin air" thing was not only a major showstopper, it was a provenance limited to the undead "ruling class." Manhandling the enlisted fangs and the occasional nosferatu noncom was one thing. Jahn might be Elizabeth Báthory's creature, but this was probably the first time he'd been confronted by someone with a Doman's credentials from the outside and off his home turf.

"They're *mine*!" I declared, following each word with an emphatic *push*. "You have *no* right! The law of the *wampyr* says you have *no power* over them! No *rights*!"

Jahn looked conflicted. Actually, he looked a little cross-eyed; he apparently hadn't come all the way back from that kick. This was probably why Deirdre was able to sucker him again.

This time her foot shot up, missing his face by a good three inches. He blinked as Deirdre's leg completed a ninety-degree arc, toes straining for the ceiling. "My lady commands—" he said, sounding for all the world like his tongue had developed a charley horse. He never got the chance to finish the sentence: Deirdre's leg came crashing down, catching Jahn behind his head at the base of his skull and propelling him face-first into the stainless-steel surface of the autopsy table. There was a soggy crunching sound as flesh, albeit undead, collided violently with reinforced steel alloy. Deirdre's subsequent attempt to pin him down with a scissor-lock about his neck was thwarted when Jahn dissolved into a loosely knit clump of dust and ashes.

"Wow," I said, as Deirdre rolled to her side and unbuckled her right wrist restraint, "now that's what I call a real ash kicking."

"Hey!" Theresa called. "Could use a little help over here!"

I was helping Theresa with her ankle straps when the door opened and Krakovski strode into the room. He stopped. Took in the sights of scattered ashes trailing across dissection table one and puddling to the floor, a naked redhead going through the cabinets in search of something to wear, a naked brunette nearly free of her restraints on dissection table two, and naked me who wasn't scheduled to be here. At least, not yet.

Krakovski was the only one dressed. And he was wearing (by God!) one of those white, button up the side, lab tunics that all the mad scientists used to wear in 1930s cinema. But he had enough "naked" fear in his eyes to make up for the unclothed state of the rest of us.

He opened his mouth and started to turn. To sound an alarm? To flee? Neither mattered: while his face was still turned toward us, his forehead sprouted a metal handle. A thread of blood traced a tiny tributary beneath the scalpel's grip and sought an estuary between Krakovski's bulging eyes. He collapsed as Deirdre raised two more surgical knives, throwing fashion, in her right hand and hefted a bone saw in her left.

"I'll keep the door covered," she said, "while you two get dressed."

There were extra surgical smocks in one of the lockers. I fastened the ties on Theresa's back then took the scalpels and covered the door while Theresa fastened mine and Deirdre dressed. The smocks gaped down the back but it was a vast improvement over "streaking" for the nearest exit.

Selecting handfuls of cutlery from the surgical tray, we crowded the door. Before I could ease it open, Deirdre grabbed me and pulled me around to face her. "You came for me," she said, her eyes shining. "Thanks . . ." She pulled my face down and pressed her lips against mine. Maybe it was because I hadn't caught my breath before the kiss started: I was definitely lightheaded when she finally broke the seal of her mouth against mine. It took another moment to forcibly uncurl my toes. "I won't forget what you did for me!" she vowed breathily.

I opened my mouth to say that she had done all the heavy lifting, I had just showed up; but she clutched the front of my smock with one hand and closed the other around my right hand, which was holding the bone saw. "Promise me!" she demanded fiercely, "that you won't let them take me alive!"

I looked over her head at the dissection tables where the heavy leather straps lolled like predators' tongues. "I promise," I said.

"Just get me out of here," Theresa moaned.

"I'm way ahead of you," I said.

Actually, I was only a little ahead of them both: they crowded my back as I eased the door open a crack. The outer chamber was deserted.

We moved through the anteroom and cracked the next door. It opened into a fourth-floor hallway. At least that's what I assumed from the number on the door across the hall. "Come on," I said. We moved out into the deserted corridor and headed for the stairs.

<Cséjthe . . .>

I staggered: the voice inside my head didn't hurt so much as it caught me off guard.

"Chris?" Deirdre reached out to steady me. "What's wrong?"

I made a shushing motion with my hand.

"What do you want?" I murmured.

<I want to know if you are all right. Viktor says you haven't come out of the bathroom, yet, and that it has grown very quiet in there.>

"So he's worried? How sweet."

<He's not so much worried as he is bored. I am the one who is worried. Viktor just wants to go to bed.>

"Didn't he just take a nap against the bedroom wall? Well, tell him to go ahead. I'm going to take a long, hot bath."

<You should think about going to bed soon. I have a very comfortable bed down in my quarters.>

We reached the bend in the hall: no stairwell. The stairs were another building's length away, at the end of the adjoining corridor.

"Not sleepy. Slept all night."

<*You don't have to sleep to enjoy a comfortable bed.*>

"Grandmother, what big teeth you have."

<*What does that mean?*>

"Vice is nice but incest is best?"

Theresa's eyes grew large while Deirdre's narrowed.

<*Assuming you are one of my descendants—something Kurt and the others will not accept until we test your DNA—there is ten times the distance between us as between what you call "kissing cousins." And if you believe in that collection of fairytales called the Bible, you must believe we are all guilty of incest since we all must come from the family of Noah.*>

I sighed. "What do you want? You're not attracted to me sexually. And definitely vice versa. So what would be the point?"

<*An alliance of power, my dear Cséjthe. I have it. You want it.*>

"Sez who?"

<*I have certain things that you want.*>

"Really? Like a pristine vinyl pressing of Blitzstein's Airborne Symphony—the Bernstein and Welles' performance?" We reached the end of the hall without being seen and opened the door to the stairwell.

<*I was referring to the lives of your friends.*>

"Yeah? It was my understanding that you were having my friends dissected."

<*Perhaps they will survive the process; the wamphyri are a very hardy species. But I was speaking of other friends. You have a fondness, have you not, for Dr. Delacroix? And then there is your secretary Olivia, and her nephew. You seem to have developed an affinity for dark meat, Cséjthe: compelling evidence that we are not so genetically similar.*>

"Hey, fuck you, witch, and the broom you rode in on."

<*You might guarantee their safety by swearing fealty to me in front of the others.*>

"You want me to swear at you in front of an audience, I got no problem with that."

<*You are my prisoner, Cséjthe. I don't require your cooperation; I can take what I want if necessary.*>

"Then why negotiate?" We were almost down to the third-floor landing.

<Come to bed with me and I will tell you.>

"Haven't I seen this movie on late-night cable? Oh yeah, 'An Affair To Dismember.'" But I knew what she really wanted. Sex magick, a powerful ritual of binding that would cement my allegiance in the eyes of her tribe and bind me into servitude with unseen cords of power. Her only true desire was her need to turn me into some emblematic trinket to be added to her charm bracelet of power.

<I could have Viktor break the door down and bring you to me.>

"Now that would be a fatal mistake."

She snorted, producing a really unpleasant sensation between my ears. *<You may be stronger and faster than an ordinary human but you are no match for a full-blooded vampire.>*

"Which is why I'd have to force him to kill me."

Now Deirdre's eyes grew wide while Theresa's narrowed.

<You are making this far more difficult than any reasonable person should. The sun will be up shortly and—>

"Oh *shit!*" I said. My voice boomed and echoed up and down the stairwell.

<What is it?>

"What is it?" Deirdre and Theresa echoed.

"Dawn is coming!" I said. "Run!"

We ran. Over the slapping thuds of bare feet pounding down the stairs I heard the whisper of Báthory's voice as she ordered Viktor to break down the bathroom door. In a few minutes she would probably have a full-scale security alert and the building in total lockdown. A few minutes beyond that and it probably wouldn't even matter: Once the sun came up we would be effectively trapped in the building for another twelve hours, anyway.

<Cséjthe? Where are you?>

"Looking for Red Two. Where did you take them, you bitch?"

<You're bluffing. You've been bluffing all along, haven't you? You've already rescued them and you're trying to get out of the building. What will you do then? Burn?>

"Sure. Better ash than hash."

<Such bravado. And such a clever, clever man. I have obviously misjudged you.>

"Well," I puffed, "that's one of us."

<Stay. Stay willingly and I promise to let the others go and pro-
vide them with safe transport.>

"You promise?"

<Yes!>

"Ooo, there's something I can take to the bank! A promise from
Bloody Báthory!"

Deirdre reached out and touched my arm as we hit the door
on the first floor and spilled out into the hallway. "She offering
you a better deal?"

"More like a bitter deal."

"Don't take it!" she said fiercely.

A security guard appeared around the corner of an intersect-
ing corridor. From the look on his face I guessed that no one had
sounded any alarms. Yet.

"Eeek!" Deirdre squealed, suddenly sounding very girly. She flung
her arms out and put on an extra burst of speed. "Help me! Save
me!"

The guard instinctively reached for his side arm, but the sight
of a squealing, jiggling redhead running toward him in an abbreviated smock set one group of reflexes against another. The
resulting hesitation cost him: instead of embracing her uniformed
savior, she ran him down and stomped on him for good measure.

While she dealt with one roadblock I dealt with another.

Reginald, I called, *Reggie!*

—What?— Not possessing a brain that had been rewired for
telepathy, the lobby guard's voice was very faint in my head. If I
hadn't opened his mind and poked around inside on my first visit,
I wouldn't even have the vaguest of connections now.

Unlock the front door.

—What? Who's there?—

Just do it, Reggie! Even at this distance I didn't have to push,
just nudge. My initial contact with Reginald was paying off in a
manner I hadn't originally envisioned. *Oh, and Regg . . . what kind
of a car do you drive?*

—Subaru station wagon. Yel—yellow.—

Doesn't anybody buy American anymore? *Parked out front?*

—Su—sure.—

I need to borrow your keys, my man. Have them ready. I sensed
a growing resistance and had to push now.

—*Ow.*—

Sorry.

We rounded the corner at the end of the hall and headed for the main lobby, just seconds away. An alarm began to blare in strident pulse patterns.

"We're not going to make it!" Theresa wailed.

It looked like she was right. As we burst into the glass-walled vestibule at the front of the BioWeb complex it was obvious that the darkest part of the night sky was merely gray. The horizon was already limned with threads of gold and a blush of pink. Maybe "Je Rouge" was going to get us after all.

As we ran up to a rather dazed-looking Reggie, holding a set of keys in his trembling hand, Elizabeth Báthory's voice rang out.

"Stop!" she cried from above us.

We looked up. The Witch of Cachtice stood at the railing of the second-floor balcony. She was not alone. Jamal, wearing a smock similar to the ones we all sported, dangled limply from the vampire's grip about his neck. I wondered how long she had been holding him in reserve as a potential hostage?

"Surrender or I kill him!"

Maybe.

Maybe she already had—her test release of the Blackout Virus could well have already signed his death warrant.

Deirdre looked at me with haunted eyes. "I—I can't!"

I nodded slowly. "No. No, you certainly cannot." I looked back up at my secretary's nephew, who coughed feebly in Báthory's grasp. "But I have to stay." I looked back at her. "Do you understand?"

She nodded. "If you survive the day, I'll find a way to come back for you!" she whispered.

"Now you're just being silly." I swiped the keys out of Reggie's hand and threw them at her. "Run!" I yelled.

The sun peeked over the horizon as Deirdre slammed through the front door. "It's too late!" Theresa screamed as golden beams of light began to poke holes in the distant line of trees to the east. She began backing up even as Deirdre ran down the front steps and into the smooth, blacktopped killing field of the parking lot.

"Some rescue," Báthory sneered, releasing her hold on Olive's nephew. He fell at her feet with a muted sigh. At that moment it came to me that I hadn't stayed to save Jamal . . .

...I had stayed to destroy the Witch of Cachtice.

Or die trying.

At that moment Deirdre reached the yellow Subaru at the far end of the lot.

She dropped the keys. In her haste and panic she ended up kicking them under the car.

"You should have left well enough alone, Cséjthe," Báthory crooned. "With me, she at least had a chance."

"I saved her," I said with more defiance than I felt. "This was her choice."

Báthory laughed. "Darkness spare me from your idea of salvation, Cséjthe! I thought burning was reserved for the damned!"

As she recovered the keys and stood, the rising sun caught her full in its pure and intensifying glare.

"Too bad we don't have popcorn," Báthory added.

Theresa made a gagging sound and a moment later I heard the sound of running footsteps retreating back down the corridor behind us.

I couldn't look away. I felt it was my duty to serve as witness to Deirdre's sacrifice. And I was counting on it to magnify my rage for the killing yet to come.

Now, I thought, now the solar radiation will be triggering the biochemical combustion that vampire flesh is heir to. Now her blood will start to boil.

Seeming to realize it was too late, Deirdre stopped trying to fit the key to the troublesome lock in the door. She turned to face the fiery orb of the rising sun, to acknowledge her own last moments of mortality.

Please, God, I prayed; if You exist, let it be quick.

But it wasn't quick.

The seconds dragged by.

Ten.

Twenty.

A half-minute.

The sun became too bright for us to bear, even through the heavily tinted glass. I moved back into the shadows and shielded my eyes. As I did, Deirdre finally reacted.

She convulsed. Spasmed. Leapt as if shocked or stung.

Then—the most shocking thing of all—she began to dance!

Standing in a lake of molten gold, showered and drenched by the bright, unbearable light of the growing day, Deirdre danced and whirled, arms flung out to gather more light and heat unto her pale, unmarked flesh.

Finally she stopped.

Blew a kiss toward the first floor of the lobby.

Then, very deliberately, extended her middle finger in an unmistakable salute to the second-floor balcony.

"Guard!" Báthory screamed, "bring that woman to me!"

Reginald began to shake off his dazed expression as Deirdre unlocked the door of his station wagon. I stepped up and tripped him on his way to the front door. As we watched Deirdre drive away I heard Báthory say: "Mr. Cséjthe, you are a very dangerous man."

She had no idea.

Chapter Twenty-two

Holding me against my will was problematic now that they knew I could translocate.

Even though it's widely believed that a vampire has the power to become as mist or fog and pass through cracks or keyholes to enter or escape any dwelling or chamber, most of the undead don't really have this particular trick up their rotted sleeves. That's how I took Báthory's minions by surprise the first time. Now that they knew I had the power of a Doman, they had to scramble for a new game plan.

Making it doubly difficult was the fact that I wasn't bound to a coffin or the need to sleep during the day. As long as I didn't have to snooze and they did, I had the advantage.

On the other hand, they had hostages. And human allies who were armed and trained to deal with undead advantages.

Not to mention a pharmaceutical solution to the insomnia problem, as well.

BioWeb, among its other potions, philters, and witches brews, had a broad assortment of tranquilizing agents. Lieutenant Lenny Birkmeister and his quasi-military goons sent me off to dreamland shortly after Báthory and her undead minions retired for the day.

In short order I find myself back in Cachtice Castle, my dream state propelling me four hundred years into the past.

Past the discoveries and arrests.

Past the trial and executions.

The nether regions of my stone-and-mortar namesake are empty, devoid of prisoners.

I wander through Erzsébet Báthory's chamber of horrors and wonder how we could be frightened by thumbscrews and racks in stone-walled cells yet completely relaxed in glass and chromed labs where vials of anthrax and Ebola hibernate in stainless-steel coolers.

Here is the iron cage with the razored bars, spikes and twisted blades turned inward to provide the countess with her showers of virgin's blood. There, the whipping post with troughs to collect the unguents for her beauty regimen. Nearby an oubliette with a platform reminiscent of the autopsy tables in Red Two, the trays for knives and needles toppled to the floor, the instruments of the crimson harvest disposed of—or collected as grisly trophies by the mob that stormed the slaughterhouse beneath the witch's dark tower.

A sound on the stairs and I step back into the shadows. Only there are no shadows: the torches and lamps have gone dark and cold and this is but a dream where I can see with no light and walk with no physical presence.

The witch enters the chamber, runs her hand along the side of the rack in an affectionate gesture. "It was good while it lasted," she says as if recalling a moment of bucolic nostalgia. "Their terror seemed more exquisite back then. Even using the same instruments, duplicating the same settings, doesn't seem to heat the blood quite so eloquently today." She raises her eyes and gazes steadfastly into mine. "The pain, the horror," she says, "enhances the blood. It is like a potent spice that triples—quadruples—the potency of its power. And the taste . . ." I repress a shiver at the smile that curves her lips like a smoothly drawn bow. "Do you have any idea? One sip from a tortured virgin and you'll never go back to the merciful strike, the unconscious prey, the—"

"Okay!" I interrupt, "I *get* it! You're a *cortisol* freak. Or is it the elevated histamine levels that floats your boat?"

"My mistake was in using human servitors," she continues. Her eyes drop and she seems to speak more to herself—as if I am a ghostly presence in her dream instead of the reverse. "I subsequently recruited my chief retainers from the undead aristocracy. Peasants may be more overt in their enthusiasm but the highborn understand duty better over the long haul. I was ill-served by this lot but I learned invaluable lessons . . ."

Her eyes rise and lock onto mine again. "What lessons might I learn from you, Dragonspawn? What might you have learned from your Dark Sire?"

I shrug. "You mean beyond 'no good deed goes unpunished'?" I shake my head. "You can forget tracking Dracula down through me. I don't know where he is. I don't even want to know where he is. We don't exchange Christmas cards or share instant messaging, and he's totally out of my Rolodex."

"You share a blood-bond. And he is near."

I think my eyebrows rise: it's hard to tell in a dream, and a drug-induced one, at that. "He is, huh? Well, that's more than I knew."

She extends her hand in languid gesture. "Well, you still have your uses. . . ."

"You sweet talker, you."

"Join me. I have much that I can teach you. Many pleasurable things . . ."

It suddenly occurs to me that Erzsébet Báthory is supposed to be locked up in her tower and not walking about down here on the Dungeon Nostalgia Tour 1712.

"You can't understand until you've tasted the wine of pain," she continues dreamily, reaching out to touch my lips, "the bouquet of sweat and fear, the Bordeaux of blood and bruises . . ."

I slap her hand away. "There's all kinds of tasty, body-amping, mind-blowing poisons in the world, lady, and each one comes with a price tag. There's no point in taste-testing the ones I can't afford."

"I can give you a free sample."

"There's no such thing as a free taste," I say, flexing my knees. "I've got enough regrets without you adding to my list!" I launch myself into the air, passing through the ceiling like an insubstantial thought. I continue to rise into the cold night above the courtyard. I had sampled the illusion of flight in childhood dreams, but the sensation this time is crisp and definite despite the haze of barbiturates in my system. I rise up and up, the black thrust of Erzsébet's tower just a dozen feet to starboard.

I hesitate as I reach the slitted window of the countess' chambers turned prison. My senses grow sharper in the cold, crystal night air. I consider the moonlight upon the dark stone walls around the narrow aperture, how it is contrasted by the lamplight flickering from within.

A face appears on the other side of the mortared slot. A face made familiar by a handful of blurry woodcuts and an ancient portrait in oils. Momentary confusion gives way to epiphany. I continue my ascent, rising up and up toward the brightness of the moon—toward a new understanding of history and the reverberation of conspiracy and deception across four centuries. I rise out of the darkness of dreams and troubled sleep, climbing on a collision course with truth and maybe . . . just maybe . . . four-hundred-year-old vengeance.

I awoke to find a gray-eyed, gray-haired, gray-suited man sitting beside my bed. Behind him and at the foot of the bed—I turned my head—and on the other side, were five no-nonsense humans. Their postures marked them as military even though their clothing was devoid of any markings of rank or insignia. The way they held their weapons suggested they were familiar with preternatural biology and knew exactly what to do if I twitched the wrong way.

I eased my hands up and slid them behind my neck, lacing my fingers together to cradle my head. I stretched a little to wake the rest of my body. "Good morning, General," I said, as if it were the most natural thing in the world to wake up to his nondescript face. "Or is it good evening, now?"

"It's good afternoon, Mr. Cséjthe," he answered. If his voice or his face implied any hint of a smile, I had totally missed it. "You've thrown off the tranquilizing agents faster than we anticipated."

"I've always had trouble sleeping in," I said. "By the way, if you're going to have a key to my bedroom, I think we should be on a first name basis. I mean, 'General' is so . . . general. General who? General Electric? General Quarters? General Mills?" I gave him my best "gee whiz" look. "Hey, if you're General Mills, would your headquarters be in Battle Creek?"

His lips thinned into a humorless parody of a smile. "You're a smartass, aren't you, boy? I know your type. Mock authority, scoff at discipline, spit on the flag . . ."

"Whoa there, Hoss!" Apparently I twitched too much: tasers, trank guns and automatic weapons shifted into firing position. "You can cuff me and smack me around and bore me to tears with sappy little speeches about the sanctity of your cause; you've got the men and the firepower and the hostages to keep me from walking out the door. But I won't have my patriotism questioned by the likes of Nazi Fascist traitors like you and your little pseudo-military circle-jerk here!"

He backhanded me but the position was awkward for him: it barely stung, didn't draw blood and I don't believe I even blinked. Hey, I had just given him permission, anyways.

"Mind if I sit up?" I asked. "It might help you get a little more leverage on the next one."

"You have no right to make accusations when you don't know what you're talking about," he said with a mildness that was the most unnerving thing I had experienced so far today.

"I know enough to make some educated guesses." I squirmed up slowly into a sitting position and eased my legs over the side of the bed. "You see, that's the thing about Evil: It always has tunnel vision. You people never seem to get the fact that the expedient course of action is rarely the moral one. For you, the end always justifies the means and collateral damage is always an abstract concept."

"You still don't know what you're talking about."

I rested my forearms on my knees and stared at the carpet between my feet, trying to rally my reserves of anger and energy. "Wrong. I'm talking about genetically tailored influenza viruses. Or something that walks and talks like the flu but packs a punch like an end-of-the-world plague. More importantly, it kills the right people."

"And who are the right people?" he asked, the picture of mildly interested innocence.

"Apparently they're whoever you say they are," I shot back. "Right now it looks like the elderly is one group of the right people—that's your Greyware Project, right? And African-Americans are the second group. Operation Blackout. Concise, descriptive, and clever: not like that baffling codespeak that the real military would use."

"There are higher purposes—"

"Yeah, tell me about your 'higher purposes.' I've got a pretty good handle on the 'what' and the 'how.' It's the 'why' that eludes my intellectual grasp."

He just stared at me and the look on his face suggested I wasn't worth the waste of breath that an explanation would require. Damn! It always worked in the movies: super-villain has hero within his power and gloatingly reveals all the details of his secret plans. Guess I didn't rank high enough on the Nemesis Chart. On the other hand I wasn't strapped to a sliding table with an industrial-strength laser pointed at my crotch.

Since clever and caustic witticism weren't producing the desired effect, I cheated. I gave him a mental nudge. I wasn't sure it would do any good: Faf and Mouse were seemingly immune, but it didn't cost anything to try.

I gave him a second nudge.

Then a gentle poke.

Extended psychic fingers and gave his cerebellum a squeeze.

Bingo; the grunts might be inoculated against vampiric mind melds but the general wasn't.

"Imagine a lifeboat," he said.

"Oh, this sounds familiar," I muttered.

"A lifeboat that has a forty-man capacity," he continued. "Maybe you can haul a few extra bodies aboard, let another dozen cling to the sides; but take on sixty or more passengers in any form and that boat's headed for the bottom. Now put that boat in the water with a hundred people trying not to drown. You can save forty, easy. Probably fifty if some of them stay in the water and hold on to the sides. But everyone's going to want in that boat and—as soon as the magic number is reached—everybody drowns. You can *let* that happen or you can try to guarantee the maximum possible number of survivors. The only way you can do that is by keeping the ones out of the boat who were going to drown anyway."

"Sort of a modern anti-Noah," I observed, "deciding who lives and who drowns."

"You may not like it, son, but do the math. If unpleasant decisions are not made then something even more unpleasant happens. You can be responsible for everyone dying just because you didn't want to get your hands a little dirty."

"So," I said, "seeing as how we're somewhat removed from the ocean, I'm assuming this lifeboat is metaphorical. An analogy. So, let me guess what we're really talking about. Entitlements? Social Security?"

"I may have misjudged you, son. You're not as stupid as you look."

"Keep calling me 'son' and I'm going to start entertaining thoughts of fratricide."

He smiled. Even getting all loose-lipped under my mental dominance, he was still trying to push my buttons. "Social Security is supposed to be in serious trouble by 2024 or 25," I continued, trying to hide the fact that he was moderately successful.

"It's been in trouble a lot longer than that and we're going to hit the wall a lot sooner than that. Deficit spending and the war on terrorism have drained the entitlements programs ahead of schedule, and Congress can't keep the lid on our pending bankruptcy much longer. When the government checks start bouncing there will be panic, economic collapse, anarchy. What would you do? Sit back and let it happen?"

I still didn't know if this guy was legitimate brass or bogus militia, but his numbers were the real deal. Once upon a time—back in the 1930s to be more precise, less than half of the general population was expected to live past the age of sixty-five. It took sixteen people paying into the Social Security trust fund to pay for one retiree and, given early twentieth-century life expectancy, the ratios worked. Fast-forward to the close of same century and changes in medicine and economics had changed the math radically. Eighty-six percent of the population was living past retirement age and only four people of working age were available to support each retiree.

Now, in the twenty-first century, the baby-boom generation had begun lining up for their retirement benefits and Gen X lacked the population base to fund the growing tidal wave of Social Security claims. On top of that, the cost of Medicare was doubling every ten years and claims to other entitlements were expanding exponentially. The mathematical fix was savagely simple: As long as a worker produces, he or she has value to the system. Once they retire, they not only lose their desirability as producers, they become economic liabilities. The Greyware Project was the simple, direct solution, a biotechnical assist to the Darwinian laws of economic entropy.

There was just one problem with his logic—that is, assuming you didn't find the willful murder of human beings for economic stability to be morally repugnant. The general's equation measured *only* economic contributions and those within the corporate *payroll* template. It assumed that "productivity" ended on a certain schedule. It didn't account for the necessities of parents and grandparents and great-grandparents: the guidance and stability they provided for the base unit structures of society—children, grandchildren, and great-grandchildren. Families. Neighborhoods. Communities. And this narrow economic definition failed to consider that some cultural contributions aren't possible until enough years and experiences are stacked up in a lifetime to begin great works rather than close out the books on them.

Would the Greyware Virus care that Voltaire was 64 when he penned *Candide*? What about other literary works, like *Zorba the Greek*, written when Nikos Kazantzakis was 66; *The Trumpet of the Swan* by E.B. White at the age of 70; or *The Fountain of Age* by Betty Friedan, 72? Would the Social Security Solution take into account the fact that actor Tony Randall was the same age when he founded the National Actors Theatre or that Jessica Tandy won Best Actress Oscar for *Driving Miss Daisy* at the age of 80? How about Tony Bennet's singing career enjoying a renaissance in his 70s or Grandma Moses starting a serious painting career at the age of 78? Jazz violinist Stephane Grappelli and classical guitarist Andres Segovia touring to worldwide acclaim when they were in their 80s?

Never mind the *moral* repugnance of the Greyware solution—for every Alzheimer-tranced oldster drooling in a private ward in some entitlement-funded facility, there were hundreds of vibrant elders making their greatest contributions yet to the quality of communal life for society as a whole.

But how do you get these points across to the "Bottom Line" Institution? They've already reduced people to commodities long before they reach a certain age. Use 'em up, throw 'em out. They've served their purpose; never mind that the money they're entitled to is the money they've paid into the system over their lifetimes. Once the cow stops giving milk, it's time to make hamburgers.

The general nodded as if my silence indicated consent. "We are talking about the survival of the greatest country on the face of the earth."

"If we're reduced to this then maybe we're not so great as we think we are."

"There are historical and societal precedents," the general argued. "The American Indians—"

"You're going to cite me the example of what some of the nomadic, Plains tribes did when their elderly were too frail and ill to be cared for anymore. This is not the same thing. We're not talking about abandoning the elderly and infirm to live or die on their own: We already *do* that. We're talking about wholesale generational murder! So don't bring up the Hemlock Society or obsolete cultural groups like the Spartans. The only comparable cultural analogy is Hitler's Final Solution."

"This is nothing like that!" he roared.

"Yeah? The only noticeable differences I've picked up on so far is that you now have the technology to bring the Zyklon-B to the victims rather than the other way around. And no one's mentioned making soap or lampshades out of the elderly." I eyeballed him. "Have they?"

His face was red, now. "We are talking about survival, here!"

Or as a certain contestant on the Vietnamese game show *What's My Lai* once said: "We had to destroy the village to save it."

"Okay, I get the new Medikill program for the elderly," I replied, "but what's the deal with Operation Blackout? Isn't killing off a significant portion of the population sufficient? Or is it that bureaucratic attitude of a few million deaths here, a few million there—pretty soon we're talking genuine fatality rates?"

I don't know what I expected to come out of his mouth. That Blacks were a "mongrel" race as so many White supremacists were overly fond of saying? Well, that's sort of what it was, only dandified and dressed up as the second round of Useless People Economics 101. The general had more numbers ready and started off with the dramatic racial shifts in prison populations, statistics on crime and recidivism, poverty levels, school drop-out rates, joblessness, drug use, and—before I knew it—we were back to the Greyware issues of welfare and entitlements.

I tuned him out.

There was no point in even attempting a debate, internally or externally. The man was locked into his worldview and a cozy little conversation with *moi* wasn't going to change his accounting system or the way he crunched his numbers. I was better off nodding and agreeing and acting like a True Believer until I could get everybody to look the other way.

But then what?

Even without a roomful of Marine-wannabes there didn't seem be much that I could do about what I had learned. I felt like Mary Philbin unmasking Lon Chaney, pulling back the spooky veneer and finally getting a glimpse of the true horror underneath that was BioWeb.

The issue here was even larger than the issue of wiping out millions—potentially billions—for the shortcomings of a few thousand. I had used the term "African American" when the truth was this virus wouldn't stop to check your citizenship papers at the borders. If this thing got loose and did what it was designed to do, it would dwarf all of history's past attempts at genocide. It truly would be the end of the world for an entire race, a monumental crime against humanity that would put the death camps of Nazi Germany and Soviet Russia, China and North Korea—all of history's horrors from the Black Hole of Calcutta to the Trail of Tears to the Bataan Death March—in the category of "felonies and misdemeanors."

And that was just for starters. The follow-up question was: *for what degree of ethnicity are you adjusting this virus?*

Had the general and his band of brown-shirt patriots considered the fact that issues of racial "purity" and separation of the races were fairytale concepts at odds with the human genome? Perhaps his great-great-grandparents had introduced a little mulatto blood into the family tree. Would he find himself coughing out his last lungful of life alongside his distant cousins in some hospital ward a few months from now? Would we all?

Or was Operation Blackout geared to the genetic subsets for melanin—a different genetic issue than that of "race" or ethnicity?

I was impatient. I didn't want to waste any more time doing a verbal dance with Generalissimo Muscle-ini, here, so I took the direct approach. Probing his mind with mental fingers, I tried to roll his brain—much like I used to turn over stones by the river to hunt for night crawlers.

And, as in my childhood fishing expeditions, I found them: the general was quite mad.

It was a quiet and elegant psychosis, not loud and vociferous like George C. Scott's General Buck Turgidson in *Dr. Strangelove*. More of an understated and unconscious, Anthony Hopkins-esque type of lunacy—not in the rabidly self-aware mode of Dr. Hannibal Lector but more along the subtle manners of Corky the ventriloquist in *Magic*.

I picked up a couple of interesting impressions as I considered the scramble of mentalpedes wriggling about the base of his skull.

First, he wasn't standard Government Issue, after all. Private militia, then—though he retained a strong conviction that he really was working covertly for Uncle Samuel.

Was it possible? Presidents, senators, and congressmen came and went with every election, but generations have whispered of a shadow government—unanswerable to the populace or its chosen but transitory representation. Might other gray men infest the corridors of power in D.C.? Shadowy gray power mongers who knew no masters beyond their own star chambers and secret societies? Might colorless, darkling hearts and minds birth such evil schemes and then entrust them to self-styled patriots-in-exile?

Perhaps. But I could not know the truth from this man's mind. It had been sane, once. Sane in the sense that bigotry and narcissism could rule a man and not impede his rise to power. But he had been twisted beyond his own feeble abilities for evil. The monster who ruled the East Coast undead had used her powers of psychic persuasion to reshape the general to her own dark purposes. A man who fancied himself a commander of men was nothing more than a spear-carrier for a campaign that was beyond his damaged understanding.

I opened my psychic fingers so that everything disappeared beneath the surface again with a little, telepathic "plop."

So it was a waste of breath to argue right and wrong: all I

could expect to get out of a debate was an extra layer of security around Yours Truly. If I was to have any chance at throwing a monkey wrench into the works, I would have to act the part of team player.

And figure out how to smile without gagging.

By the time I had considered my real options and brought my attention back to General Genocide, he had finished his statistical analysis and had moved on to cultural comparisons to other disadvantaged groups—essentially how the "chinks" and "gooks" scored higher on the school LEAP tests despite the "niggers" home advantages of language and American culture . . .

I forced a grin. "Really, sir; I was just yanking your chain. You'll get no argument from me about the Black problem."

At least not right now when all the guns were on his side of the room.

"But," I added, "I'm afraid I get a little testy when I think about my dear old grandmother getting a dose of BioWeb super flu."

The general gave me a look that suggested he knew horseshit when he heard it, saw it, or smelled it and he wasn't, by God, about to swallow any of it.

"So, here's one of my negotiating points," I continued. "I sign on with you guys and she gets the vaccine."

"You don't seem to understand, son," he said, missing the whitening of my knuckles on that last word, "your ass is ours and it don't matter whether you decide to cooperate or not."

On that issue he was terribly misinformed: there was a vast difference between them *having* me and my being "cooperative." I intended to demonstrate the difference in no uncertain terms.

I just hadn't settled on a lesson plan, yet.

"Do you need to use the bathroom, son?"

"Huh? No. Why?"

"Because the countess wants you presentable this evening. She's planning on some formal ceremony shortly after sundown and it wouldn't do for you to soil yourself before I have to deliver you. Then we have a midnight flight to catch: her highness wants you bundled back to her base of operations in New York where her security situation is a lot tighter." A thoughtful look passed across his face—a rather misleading expression from what I had seen so far. "We'll have to trank you a third time, I guess."

"A third time?" I asked.

"The third time will be for the traveling."

"What about the second, then?"

The general's answer consisted of one word and a nod: "Sergeant."

A tranquilizer gun coughed and a hypo-dart smacked into my leg, injecting its dose on impact.

"Looks like you'll be a little late for the ceremony, son," he said, getting up from the chair and brushing himself off, "but I can't have you pulling any shenanigans on my watch. After sundown you're their responsibility."

To use or to lose, I heard his mind echo as he headed for the door.

My eyes started to flutter. This was just great! Unarmed and alone, I had just hours to arrange the fall of this high-tech House of Usher. Never mind that I had no practical plan and now I was going to spend most of that time drugged and unconscious.

Was I ever going to catch a break?

Ah, Lupé, I cried, *I'm sorry I never got the chance to tell you how much you meant to me. That I'll never see your face again. That the world may well go down in flames and I won't be there to hold you—*

=*Hold on there, big guy, the cavalry's coming for you!*=

Deirdre?

=*Now admit it: Are you really so sorry to have the advantage of a blood-bond under the present circumstances?*=

Are you all right?

=*All right?*= She laughed and my toes curled in a most unnerving manner. =*Yeah, I'm all right! I'm not a physical or mental prisoner of Bloody Báthory, I'm not strapped to an autopsy table for Krakovski's amusement, I'm alive!*=

You are alive?

=*I just ate a cheeseburger—my first solid food in over a year. It was delicious! And now I'm standing outside in the sun. I think I'm starting to tan!*=

Pretty amazing.

=*You don't understand; I could never tan before I became a vampire!*=

Where are you?

=Hiding out at your friend, Mr. Montrose's, place. Did you know he practically has his own Civil War museum? I've never seen so many muskets in my life. It's like an ancient armory.=

How did you wind up there?

=Your other friend, that fortune-teller, she was waiting for me at your place. We ditched the Subaru and she drove me to the Montrose estate. Told me to wait here. She's out, rounding up some of your other friends—=

Other friends?

=I never knew you had so many friends.=

Neither did I.

=She wanted me to give you a message.=

Yeah?

=She said to tell you to remember Ephesians six-twelve.=

That's it? That's the message?

=Yes. What does it mean?=

I have no idea.

Actually that wasn't true.

I hadn't darkened a church door since the deaths of my wife and daughter except to steal holy water from the Catholics. And it had been more than a couple of decades since I'd had to memorize Bible verses for Sunday school. But a few passages had stayed with me down the long years of a secular life lived and Paul's warning to the saints at Ephesus was one of them.

"For we wrestle not against flesh and blood," the Apostle had written, "but against principalities, against powers, against the rulers of the darkness of this world, against spiritual wickedness in high places."

=What are you thinking?=

That I ought to give up wrestling and take up bowling.

And that, for a juju woman, Mama Samm seemed awfully conversant with the New Testament. Of course, if you're gonna get down and get jiggy with the end-of-the-world references, the Bible was, by and large, the text of choice for most of North America. . . .

=Well, I'm supposed to wait for her here. And I'm supposed to hide if the police come by.=

Montrose is dead, I told her. *My old adversaries-in-arms put an*

*antitank rocket into his truck and blew him up with it. The cops
will probably send someone by in the next day or so for a cursory
investigation. Since he didn't die at home it isn't really a crime scene
but they'll want phone numbers for next of kin, anything that might
shed light on relationships . . . business dealings . . . connected to his
death . . .*

I shook my head, trying to clear it.

Is anyone else there? I sent what I hoped was a clear image of
Chalice Delacroix and the Be-bop, re-bop, zoot-suit guy.

=*I think I'm alone, but the lock on the back door is broken and
it looks like there's been some kind of a struggle.*=

I shook my head again. It only served to make the room spin.

=*But what is happening? You're starting to fade!*=

*I've been drugged . . . probably be out until dark. Then they're
moving out around midnight. After we're gone you need to get
Pagelovitch . . . his people . . . to get their hands on explosives . . .
plastique, dynamite, hell . . . make Molotov cocktails if you have
to . . . but this place has to be destroyed!*

And I told her as much as I could until my brain completely
fuzzed out. The next to the last words I heard inside my head
repeated her promise to come back and rescue me.

No, I told her. *It's too danger . . .*

=*I'm hooking up with some of your friends. In fact, Mama Samm
said Billy-Bob——*=

Hello Darkness, my old friend.

>*Cséjthe.*<
The voice was ancient.
>*Cséjthe . . .*<
Sonorous.
>*Cséjthe!*<
And chilling.
>*Cséjthe?*<

Did I mention familiar? Prince in exile Vladimir Drakul Bassarab
was providing narration for my next dream sequence.

It's about time, I answered groggily. *Where have you been, Old
Dragon?*

>*Hither and yon, child. My business takes me many places.*<

I smiled in my sleep. *You lie like a rug! You've been on the run ever since that little mutiny on the East Coast that dethroned you and set up Liz Báthory in your place.*

>*Ah, Erzsébet! I hear you've finally made her acquaintance.*<

Well now, maybe I have and maybe I haven't. Did you actually do the face-to-face before she sent you packing?

>*'Ware, Cséjthe; I've impaled entire villages for showing such disrespect.*<

Blah, blah, blah. If Báthory's in town, you're probably no farther away than the Eastern Hemisphere.

>*You might be surprised.*<

Whatever. Look, why don't you make yourself useful for a change. I need a memory.

>*A what?*<

A memory. Of your last time together.

>*Speculation and gossip! Prince Vlad Dracul Bassarab and the Blood Countess never met.*<

I saw you together.

>*What?*<

In her tower. You called her Betya.

>*!*<

I just want to see her as she was back then.

I had to wait but, eventually, images flitted through my head. Four-hundred-year-old memories. A fall of black raven's-wing hair. Amber, catlike eyes. Skin like fresh milk, white and startling in its contrast to the darkness around her. An exotic, twenty-something, Slavic woman approaching the peak of youthful beauty. She outshone all of the young maidens who had been gathered into her castle, her holding pens. For now, at least. Even her lovely and mysterious young domestic, Katarina Beneczky, whose beauty was said to approach that of her royal mistress. Some would later claim it was Katarina's striking good looks that contributed to the favor she found with the tribunals even as they walled the countess into her chambers and put the rest of Erzsébet's staff to torture and grisly death.

It was hard to tell from Vlad Drakul's remembrances: he had taken no notice of a serving maid. His attention had been focused on the mistress of Castle Cséjthe; Beneczky's image was only a shadow in his memory. And even now those projected memories were peeling away as I awoke to the lurching momentum of a wheelchair.

My wheelchair.
Entering one of the BioWeb elevators.
Five minutes to curtain, Mr. Cséjthe.
Break a leg.
Knock 'em dead.
It's show time!

Chapter Twenty-three

Even though the floor was no longer flashing beneath the foot-rests of my wheelchair, I had trouble focusing on the carpeting as we rode the elevator down. So far my ears were sharper than my eyes: I recognized Kurt's voice immediately.

"We are allied with fools and incompetents," he complained behind me. "The countess wanted him awake by sunset and yet they drugged him a second time. She is furious!"

"She would certainly be more furious if he had escaped after awakening this afternoon," said a second voice—Graf, maybe—it certainly wasn't Jahn. "I understand their caution."

"Bah! If he was going to escape, he would have left with the bloodhair at daybreak."

"Maybe he feared the sun . . ." Since I had never heard Graf speak, I would only be guessing so, for now, I dubbed him "Skippy."

"If so, then he would hardly attempt an escape in the middle of the afternoon. He stays out of obligation to the hostages. He is honorable, this one." Kurt sighed. "Perhaps he is older than they say he is. Honor is such a rare commodity in this generation."

"Perhaps," Skippy allowed, "but I still understand their caution. He killed at least five of us now and he is only half as strong and half as fast as the rest of us. He is dangerous, this one!"

"Yes," Kurt agreed, "yes he is. He has the powers of a Doman, and some say that he is more Sire to Dracula than the Prince of Wallachia was Sire to him. Last year he destroyed the Egyptian necromancer, Kadeth Bey—something entire armies had failed to do for over four thousand years. His blood gives his chosen immunity from the sun and he has secrets that Our Lady both fears and desires."

"I would have second thoughts about facing him in single combat."

"You fear for your physical existence," Kurt said. "I fear more for his power to break my oath."

"You call him Warlock?" The awe and fear in his voice almost made me grin. Of course Skippy's use of the term was the ancient alias for "Oath-breaker," not the pop-cultural designation for a male witch, popularized by femophobic sexists and instructional television like *Bewitched*.

"*She* calls him Cséjthe," Kurt countered. "We swore an oath to the bloodline."

"We swore an oath to serve the House of Cachtice!"

"Cachtice, Cséjthe, linguistic hair-splitting. They are one and the same."

Skippy wasn't mollified. "But Erzsébet Báthory is eldest survivor and head of the bloodline. She is royalty. If he is of the blood, he still must swear fealty to her or be destroyed. If he does swear and she embraces him, he has no authority but that which she grants him. There can be no conflict. Our oath binds us to the eldest head of the line."

"Perhaps."

A frantic note crept into his voice. "There is no perhaps! Unless you choose to break your own oath and turn rogue."

"Not rogue," Kurt mused, "not if I am allied with another Doman."

"No," Skippy admitted. "Not rogue. But just as dead. You would ally yourself with a Halfling who has no demesnes. His werewolf lover has abandoned him, his two Thralls are less wamphyri than he, one of whom would betray him for the Embrace of any vampire lover, and you would have the combined might of the East Coast demesnes arrayed against you. To what purpose?"

"I would have my honor," Kurt replied quietly.

"Honor? *Ptah*," spat the other. "Your discontent is well-known, my friend. The countess has her eye on you. See what your honor gets you when push comes to shove!"

The elevator stopped and the doors slid open. I kept my head down but rolled my eyes up as we moved into the corridor and around the corner: Gen/GEN was just down the hall. Feeling was starting to flow back into my fingers and toes but it was too little and too late. I couldn't run and I wouldn't hide.

I could only play the meager hand that was dealt me.

Any variant of poker and I was screwed; my only chance was a hand of Fifty-two Pick-up . . .

They wheeled me into an office just two doors down from the Gen/GEN lab.

The woman who had once introduced herself as Elizabeth Cachtice was waiting for us. "Mr. Cséjthe, can you stand on your own?" she asked curtly.

A very dazed-looking Chalice Delacroix was by her side, still wearing the little black cocktail dress she'd had on the night of the BioWeb fundraiser. One strap was broken, possibly during the scuffle at Montrose's place, and a dark breast nudged the loose fabric aside like a Hershey's kiss attempting a curtain call. She swayed like a young tree in a high wind.

"Countess," I replied, trying to match her tone and mask my concern, "can you sit on it?"

Báthory's response was immediate and swift. She swung her arm, sweeping the top of the desk clean; the lamp and the phone went flying to crash against the far wall. "I don't have time for this," she hissed. "I have a video-conference set up in the genetics lab and two dozen envoys from the various enclaves waiting for us! I need you up! I need you healthy-looking! And I need your unquestionable obedience! All in the next ten minutes!"

"Well then," I drawled, still having a little trouble with making my mouth work properly, "it seems you've got a little problem."

"Have I?" Her eyes glittered in the backwash of the crumpled lamp on the floor. "Let's see if I can kill a bird and a bat with one stone!" She threw Chalice down on the desk and pinned her wrists above her head with one hand. More stunned than dazed now, Chalice gave no evidence of resistance but Báthory tightened her grip so that the muscles in her forearms bunched. "Bring him here," the countess ordered.

I was rolled up to the edge of the desk. Báthory handed me my teeth. I just stared at them in my hand. Was I ever going to spend a day in this place without someone handing me my fangs? Kurt took them from my hand, opened my mouth, and slid them into place. I didn't know which was more surprising: that he did that or that I let him.

The command was given to hold Chalice's legs, and Skippy moved to grasp her ankles. She groaned as the two vampires pulled, stretching her on her back across the desk. Báthory reached down with her free hand and ripped the front of the little black dress from neckline to hem.

"I caught this little bitch down in the containment labs last night! She was destroying the viral loads for Operation Blackout! I have already executed the security personnel who should have prevented such a thing from happening. The only reason that *she* is still alive is that *she* contributes to my hold over you. If you do as I say, she may *live* a little longer. If you disobey me, I will flay her alive and render her body fat into bath soap!"

"What do you want?" I asked carefully.

"First of all, I want you to drink."

"Drink?"

"Her blood. I need you to be able to walk and function with the appearance of health and the assumption that you are acting of your own volition."

"And then what?"

"We will go into the Gen lab and you will swear fealty to me before a roomful of witnesses with a camera recording the event for the other enclaves as well as my people back home. There will be an exchange of blood: mine for yours. Normally we both would drink, but I'm not sure that it is wise for me, given the unusual effects your blood seems to have on both the living and the undead. So, I will hold your blood in trust. You will drink mine as part of your blood oath to me. Then the oath will be administered and sealed. I expect you to speak and act as though you do these things of your own volition and that you do it willingly, if not eagerly.

"Make no mistake, however: I will maintain a psychic hold on your mind. You may not do anything without my permission. At the first hint of rebellion I will shut down your higher brain functions and you will become my puppet. And after this evening is over and we are back in my stronghold, back east, I will kill her as slowly and painfully as I can devise while you watch and listen. And when I am done, you will be forced to eat her remains. Some of which will be pre-chewed. Do I make myself clear?"

I swallowed bile and nodded.

"Do we have an understanding?"

"S-sure," I said. "N-no problem. I was just afraid you were still going to force me to sleep with you."

I knew it was mistake even before I said it but the words just came tumbling out of my mouth like eager puppies looking for mischief. Báthory's hand curled, her fingers becoming curved talons, and she raked Chalice's belly, trenching red furrows in her dark skin with inhumanly sharp fingernails.

"There, Mr. Cséjthe," Báthory crooned with stomach-churning sweetness, while Chalice moaned and twisted in the vampires' grasp, "I've prepared your trough. Drink up."

I opened my mouth to—to—what? Defy her? Threaten her? I had no leverage. Anything but unquestioning obedience on my part was only going to make things worse. After a moment's hard thought I spoke anyway: "I'll drink if you leave the room."

"And why should I do that?" Báthory wanted to know.

"I'm shy."

Báthory's verbal evaluation was somewhat different and a lot more vulgar.

"I'll drink," I tried again, "but I don't want an audience. This is a difficult thing for me. Feeding is . . . is . . . very private for me."

"Private?" Báthory's lips curled in an unpleasant smile. "I don't care where you bite her, Cséjthe. I am not leaving you alone until our business is done in the next room. Now we're running out of time." She reached across the desk, grabbed a handful of my hair, and pulled my face against Chalice's wounded stomach. "Feed!"

I rolled my face away from Báthory, smearing Chalice's blood across my nose and cheeks. As I did, I bit down hard on my lower lip, making twin punctures in my flesh with my artificial fangs. My own blood began to dribble down my chin and I turned my face back, backwashing my own blood into the torn flesh of Chalice's abdomen. As I turned, she sucked in her stomach, forming a shallow basin for the blood to pool in. I caught a little reverse tide, as well—more than I had counted on and it flooded my eyes, my nose, and my mouth. I swallowed convulsively and nearly choked.

It was like tasting whiskey-laced honey and crank.

During my gradual transformation over the past year or so I had supplemented my diet with blood that had been clinically donated, packaged, frozen, stored, thawed, reheated, and eventually served in cradles of plastic or porcelain. Those rare occasions that I had tasted of a living host was when the blood was freely offered—a gift given, not forcibly or painfully taken.

This was utterly different.

As strong as the burning brightness of Chalice's blood had seemed when I sipped from her arm a few nights before, it paled in the supernova of now. It was as if her body had transformed into some kind of bipolar brewery and crystal meth lab, distilling the neural cracklings of her synapses and pain receptors into arterial white lightning. It was a heady blend, containing neurotransmitter lattice-works of codified adrenaline and compressed dopamine poppers that exploded at the back of your eyeballs, sizzled across the channels of your cerebral cortex, crawled through your chest like a prickling army of electrified lemmings, and detonated like depth charges in the murky depths of the hindbrain. It was like tasting colors and sounds, a symphony of dark energies that surged and thrust and hummed and spun, sucking me down and down into warm, pulsating wetness.

Dimly, I realized I was pushing my face against her tortured abs, trying to burrow like a mole into darkness. I pushed away but it took great effort.

I wiped at my bleary eyes: Báthory's amused face swam into view. "You've never really slaked your thirst with the wine of violence, have you Cséjthe?" she mocked. "Pain is the greatest aphrodisiac."

I wanted to say something rude and vulgar. I wanted to deny the dark power that had suddenly enveloped my senses and stripped away the veneer of humanity, but I was suddenly bereft of reason, of rational thought.

Of humanity.

I looked down but my eyes wouldn't focus. I wondered if Chalice had escaped and then wondered who or what I was even thinking about. The desk was a smorgasbord of chocolate sweetmeats, a buffet of fudge brownies and devil's-food delicacies, a cacophony of caviar and cocoa. And the stripes of cherry topping were like an irresistible dessert, a homing beacon to the tongue, the gravity well of a dark and mysterious star. I felt my face drawn downward, pulled by irresistible forces, and then, for a moment, could see flesh and blood in human form once more.

Chalice . . .

I had to save her.

I had to *have* her!

The difference of one little letter: "s" or "h." Save her, *have* her, save her . . . *have her* . . .

So thirsty . . .

No.

Hungry!

I bit down on my lower lip again and the pain was like a sleepy sensation buried under an avalanche of thrumming desire and appetite. Blood dripped from my mouth as I lowered it toward her chocolate sweetness. Crimson drops pattered across the scarlet slashes and her belly fluttered like the dance undulations of an Egyptian houri. She whimpered and I felt the tattered remnants of self-control snap taut like a threadbare flag in a sudden gale, a furnace wind from the soul.

I lowered my head (God help me, I couldn't stop myself) and I pressed my lips to her wounds. But I held that line against her velvet skin. More viral-loaded blood drooled from my mouth and I used my tongue to lave it into the open furrows, fighting the gripping, tightening, squeezing impulse to delicately slip its tip down and in, to gently probe, to slide—

I snapped my head back and Chalice moaned again. There was a different quality to the sound escaping her throat, this time. An undercurrent of a sigh. A sub-harmonic of surrender. I blinked and it seemed as if the cuts across her stomach were smaller, now. More shallow. I turned my face toward hers and saw that she had raised her head; her eyes were clear and locked on mine.

"The Blackout virus," she whispered. "It's a genetic tar baby—"

Báthory released her wrists and slammed Chalice's head back against the desk. Her eyes rolled up in her head and she was gone.

My eyes searched her face, her throat, her upper body for any indication of breath. I reached to feel for a pulse and Báthory was around the desk before I could touch the side of her neck.

"No time for that," she said harshly, taking my arm and hauling me up and out of the wheelchair. "You can play with your new toy as soon as we're finished with the night's festivities."

I was able to walk now but Kurt took my left arm and Skippy my right and they proceeded to support me between them like a vampire sandwich. Báthory stepped into a small washroom to the side of the entrance and produced a couple of wet towels. "Here," she said, tossing them so that one actually settled over my head. "Clean him up and then bring him in as soon as he's presentable."

She exited the office without a backward glance.

It took more than a couple of damp towels. I ended up with my head in the sink before it was over and about three-dozen paper towels and a whole roll of toilet paper before I was ghoulishly presentable.

During the process, I looked up at the face in the mirror.

It wasn't mine.

It was Chalice's.

And she looked even less substantial than I usually did.

Chalice?

/Chris . . . I have to tell you . . ./

My God, you look like a ghost!

/I'm not sure but I think I am . . ./

Oh my God! I've killed you!

/Don't be an ass . . . that bitch killed me after you did everything you could to save me. . . ./

Oh dear Lord, I am so, so sorry!

/We don't have time for this . . . listen . . . I have to tell you something . . . something important . . ./

Uh, okay.

/They came looking for us at your friend's house . . . there were too many of them . . . I think they staked the boy. . . ./

I felt a pang in spite of the fact that he was an annoying little twerp: I hadn't really disliked him all that much.

/After they brought me back to BioWeb, they put me to work under the supervision of one of the security guards . . . with Krakovski gone

and the big move scheduled for tonight . . . oh, this is taking too long to explain . . ./

Just cut to the chase.

/The genetics of race is both more complicated and more simple than you might believe . . . skin color and hair texture and facial features are only superficial variations in the human race that are based on climatological influence rather than true genetic divisions . . ./

I know. The externals of human appearance are actually determined by less than 0.01 percent of our genes while patterns of thousands to tens of thousands of gene markers determine other distinguishing characteristics like intelligence or susceptibility to certain diseases—things that really matter. *I don't think the general has a clue as to what kind of a genetic smart bomb he's sponsoring. I figured it must have a melanin trigger—*

/It does . . . and it's very indiscriminate as a result . . . some Hispanics may be more susceptible than some Negroids . . . and more than a few Caucasians may trip the viral trigger, as well./

That doesn't sound like it's very well designed.

/Oh, it is . . . for its actual purpose, that is. You're right when you say that the general doesn't know what he's turning loose on the world. But the Blackout virus is actually a ruse, a classic example of misdirection./

So it doesn't really work?

/Oh, it does after a fashion. My people are seeing twice the mortality rate from this strain of the flu than from any previous year. There will probably be some kind of increase for other population vectors, as well. But it isn't a doomsday virus. Except to the people who die from it./

So what is the point of developing this—what did you call it? Genetic tar baby? If it's only marginally more effective than Mother Nature and bound to set off alarms at the CDC, USAMRIID, and every genetics research facility around the globe?

/That, it turns out, is precisely the point. As soon as the word gets out that there's a flu bug that singles out people of color the shit is going to hit the fan. There will be demonstrations, riots . . ./

To say the least.

/I am saying the least. Because once it comes out that the virus has been artificially tailored, the white establishment becomes public enemy number one./

"Anarchy," I whispered.

Her ghostly reflection nodded in the mirror. */To say the least./*

So, the end result is a social meltdown that is potentially more destructive than, say a virus with a fifty-percent mortality rate!

/See how easily you're distracted by the social implications of the secondary virus? That's the real point of Operation Blackout. Any damages accrued are just bonus points. The real, end-of-the-world haymaker is the Greyware Project!/

I shook my head, trying to clear it as much as deny this new premise. *They're both bad news but I think the Blackout virus— God, doesn't that sound like something straight out of the Klueless Klutz Klan—is the greater and more immediate threat in end-of-the-world terms.*

/That's what everyone will think. Resources may be divided in attempting a cure for both but the greater attention and pressure will be directed toward the melanin marker. That's part of her plan. To give the Greyware virus a chance to spread unchecked./

And?

/The influenza is virulent: Everyone will get it!/

But it only kills old people, right? I shook my head again. *I don't mean that like it sounds.*

/It kills both the elderly and the unborn./

So the very old and the very young?

/I'm not talking about human fetuses. This flu is a super-combinant virus—much like the virus that turns the living into the undead. Except it's designed to operate backwards./

And a big "huh?" here.

/You told me the vampire virus was composed of two separate viruses, one which lives in the bloodstream, the other taking up residence in the saliva. Your condition is unique because you were only infected with one of the two virae./

Okay . . .

/Well, that's how you get a white-supremacist paramilitary organization to work with a bunch of vampires: Greyware was originally conceived as two-stage, piggybacked virus. Virus A: the flu, a general, low-grade, all-purpose infection that would infect everyone but be no more virulent than a mild cold. In fact, its base design is more along the lines of the cold virae than the influenza models. Virus B: piggybacked onto A as the all-purpose

transporting agent, it was designed to trigger upon encountering telomeres of reduced lengths in the host's cells. It didn't have to be powerful to kill hosts of advanced age. Younger victims either would not trigger the secondary agent or would be healthy and strong enough to throw it off with little difficulty. That was the initial design./

But Báthory tampered with the design?

/Yes. The blueprints I saw last night show a tertiary virus, piggy-backed behind B. Virus C is actually wired directly to A and uses the mild, flulike symptoms to mask its own purposes./

Which are? The connection suddenly flared in my mind. *Oh dear God! The unborn! It's designed to sterilize the host!*

The ghost of Chalice Delacroix inclined her head. */As one generation passeth away . . ./*

So passeth the end of the world. And no one will notice until it's too late. I stared into her translucent eyes. *Are you sure?*

/I would need a month or more of research and testing to be sure. But she certainly believes it. And the documentation lays it out in no uncertain terms. The only thing that doesn't make sense is why would a vampire want to bring about the end of the world? Or, at the least, eliminate her food supply?/

That's easy.

/It is . . . ?/

Yeah. The short answer is, she isn't.

/She isn't . . . ?/

A vampire. I think she's something else. Not only some thing, but also some—

Skippy yanked me away from the mirror. "Come on, man. Time to join the family."

I got in two backward glances as they walked me out the door. The mirror was as empty as the eyes of the corpse sprawled across the desk.

"Gentlemen," I said as we trundled down the hall to the door marked Gen/GEN, "the countess may be the Big Boo around here and I know that if she says 'bat,' everybody flaps . . ."

Skippy grinned but Kurt was listening very carefully.

" . . . but if anyone other than myself so much as touches that poor girl back there, I will dedicate the rest of my unlife—however short and difficult—to fucking them up beyond all recognition."

I hadn't raised my voice but Skippy stopped grinning. "Do I make myself clear?"

Kurt nodded. "Crystal."

Gen/GEN looked different packed with people. There were about a dozen vampires, another dozen human soldier-types, and yet another dozen or so humanoids that were neither alive nor undead but as different from one another as the inhabitants of a Hieronymus Bosch painting. Shakespeare said that there were more things in heaven and earth than we could dream of—perhaps he was referring to the denizens of that twilight realm in-between. Báthory, it appeared, had drawn most of her recruits, allies, and servitors from an otherworldly zip code.

The military attendees dressed uniformly (if you'll pardon the implied pun) in gray shirts with black ties and pants. Again, no insignia but that unmistakable carriage and attitude that set them apart and suggested martial discipline and training. The BioWeb vampires were dressed semiformally. No ties or joint color coordination but they dressed so as not to raise eyebrows as they passed among humans on the outside. The rest were a sartorial mixed bag: they dressed more like extras from *The Rocky Horror Picture Show* than envoys and ambassadors from unworldly realms. Perhaps this was the contingent from the Peewee Herman Dimension.

Since no one was wearing paper hats and booties I figured the need for "clean room" standards was at an end. That or perhaps paper-wear just wasn't festive enough for the fête that was about to commence.

I stood off to the side, flanked by my escorts who were doing their best to look more like an honor guard and less like my handlers.

I tried taking my mind off my broken promise to Robert Delacroix by contemplating the logistics of tonight's departure. If we were supposed to fly, I wondered whether the juxtaposition of a plane's wings and fuselage presented any impediment to vampires with hypersensitivity to a cruciform design.

Obviously the drugs still retained some finger-holds on my cortical folds.

Meanwhile, Liz was working the room.

There was the usual blather about being united in an important cause and how great things would come to pass due to the efforts of those gathered here tonight. I wasn't following too closely as I was trying to fight my way through the residual buzzing in my head and reach out to Deirdre.

Either the lines were down or she wasn't answering.

Now Báthory was putting an interesting spin on the events of this morning. About how her research had uncovered some unique properties in the family bloodline—proving, by the way, her incipient superiority over lesser vampires and humans and, thus, her divine right to rule as she saw fit.

Yadda, yadda, yadda . . .

Then there was the matter of The Dragonspawn—how he had been sired by Dracula, achieved the powers of a Doman and more, had slain a dozen vampires, himself, including Drac and the ancient sorcerer Kadeth Bey—it took me another moment to realize that she was talking about me. The big buildup was designed to lend significance to our pending alliance by magnifying my own importance.

Blah, blah, blah.

Finally, she announced that a little demonstration was in order.

Theresa was brought forward (sorry Toots, you can run but you can't hide) and she looked terrible. Not as bad as she would if Krakovski hadn't been scalpel-tated this morning, but bad nonetheless.

What are you doing? I asked, shooting the thought straight at Erzsébet's forehead.

It furrowed as if in pain. <*I think another demonstration is in order,*> she shot back.

If she intended to mindsmack me, the last vestiges of the tranquilizer must have still cushioned my brain from the brunt. That or the ingestion of Chalice's amped hemoglobin was reinforcing my own shields and defenses.

Hey, I'm still a couple of pints low from this morning, I reminded her.

<*You just fed.*>

That was a snack, not a meal. The idea of referring to Chalice Delacroix as a snack was repugnant but I made the emotion work for me. I sent that ambiguity back at her in the guise of uncertainty, along with: *Not to mention the residual dope in my system, thanks to your toy soldiers. Might throw off your demo in ways you haven't considered.*

She scowled and glanced over at a video camera on a tripod and wired to one of the lab computers. Hello: we're live for the folks back home in the Big Apple. Don't want any screw-ups that can't be re-spun later.

<Well, later then. For now I'll keep her nearby for insurance.>

Yeah, you're in good hands with All-Stake. Looking at her face I was forcibly reminded why I never went out on a second date with a woman who didn't have a sense of humor.

"Join me, Mr. Cséjthe," she commanded aloud. She backed it up with a mental booster shot that pulled me away from my fanged bookends before I even had time to consider the directive. The Báthory Dog and Pony Show was under way in Supermarionation.

She motioned to me to approach and I staggered, stiff-legged, across the room to join her before the crowd. *If you want to see me do my thing, pull my string.*

A lab tech joined us. It wasn't Spyder. I wondered how ole Spyder was and whether any of his brains had actually leaked out of his ears. It sort of felt like mine was having a little slippage in that direction.

The tech slipped a needle into my forearm and withdrew two vials of blood in short order. Another tech swiveled the camera as one of the vials was carried over to a testing tray and prepared for analysis.

Here, and before the world—or at least the East Coast underworld—my lineage to the Báthory-Nádasdy line was to be revealed and validated. Too bad I was properly dressed instead of hanging out of one of those backless gowns we had appropriated this morning: it was the perfect moment to moon the audience.

It took just a few minutes for the results to be analyzed and verified: I was descended from the House of Cséjthe. But apparently not the House of Nádasdy. I thought of the Countess Báthory's storied premarital dalliance with a gypsy lad and the baby girl who was spirited away into the unknown mists of history.

So, it was true: on some level of generational reckoning, I was a bastard after all.

She handed the blade to me and mindwhispered: <*I'll make the cut at the base of the neck and away from the artery.*>

The knife was in my hand but it might as well have been hers: she was still pulling the "strings."

"*Now* would be a good time," I murmured.

<*A good time for what?*>

>*To give Mr. Cséjthe the gift and curse of free will, Betya.*< I felt Báthory's hold on me evaporate.

<*Who is that?*>

"The Blue Fairy, Geppetto," I said, taking advantage of her surprise and confusion to pull her into my embrace. "Guess who just became a real, live boy."

I might be slower than a full-fledged vampire but I had the element of surprise: within the space of a single heartbeat I was standing behind her, my left arm clamped about her throat and my right hand pressing the scalpel-sharp blade against the back of her neck. "Nobody move!" I yelled. "Or I'll slice through her spinal column before anyone can say 'heads up'!"

The crowd looked more amused than upset. Was that because they knew I didn't have a prayer of getting out alive or because this passed for entertainment in the soap opera of succession?

"What do you want?" she croaked, being very careful not to add any pressure to the golden edge nestled between her third and fourth vertebrae.

"From you? Nothing. I've already got what I want from you." I nodded toward Kurt, who was still holding the crystal goblets, one of which held the dark, rich red essence of the countess' four-hundred-year-old veins. "I want Kurt, however, to give your blood to the lab tech. I want to see what happens when they run your genome through the database."

She tensed in my grasp. "My genetic profile is already in the database!"

I shook my head. "I don't think so. If it were, you wouldn't be able to connect me to the Báthory line. Erzsébet Báthory's grave is in northeastern Hungary, in the village of Ecsed. I believe her genetic samples were collected years ago so that the database wouldn't be corrupted with incorrect data. The wrong genome in the wrong field and flags would start popping up all over the place as you added hereditary listings."

It was time for another speech and Báthory used the ⸢
tunity to diagram my place in the coming New Order. Wh⸢
yakked, another voice began to whisper in the back of my⸢

>Cséjthe . . .<

Huh?

>Cséjthe, are you anywhere near an exit?<

Vlad? That you? I thought you were a drug-induced dream⸢
ment.

>We're outside the building. If you can get close to an exit, ⸢
how do you say—bust you out.<

You're here? In Louisiana?

>In Monroe. Right outside BioWeb's rear emergency exit.⸢

You came to rescue me? Talk about morte ex machina! ⸢
someday my prince did come!

>How can you jest at a time like this? You do not know Er⸢
Báthory!<

I think you're probably right.

>Can you slip away?<

No can do, Uncle Morte. I'm surrounded by hostiles, still t⸢
ing off some kind of tranquilizing agent in my bloodstream, an⸢
being mindstrung like a puppet: my body is not my own.

>We share a blood-bond, Cséjthe. I may be able to break her⸢
on you and reinforce your will over your own flesh and bloo⸢

May? I don't suppose you'd be willing to improve the odc⸢
coming inside?

>That woman has kept me on the run for decades and you⸢
me to walk into her lair now? You ask too much, Soulgiver.<

What did you call me?

"Cséjthe," interrupted our Mistress of Ceremonies, "it is ⸢
for you to take The Oath."

Kurt approached with a pair of crystal goblets and a small go⸢
knife. I guess they needed something ceremonial and, in ma⸢
involving undead flesh, silver was a big no-no.

Our dominatrix of ceremonies took the knife first and ran⸢
blade across the side of her neck. A living woman would h⸢
produced an arterial spray that would have spattered the far v⸢
Báthory's carotid artery produced a dribble that was quickly cau⸢
in one of the crystal goblets before her preternatural flesh rese⸢
itself with no hint of a scar or blemish.

"This is absurd!" she protested.

"What do you expect to prove?" Kurt asked.

"He's stalling!" Báthory exclaimed.

"Am I?" I asked. "It's a matter of history that the Countess Báthory dictated her last will and testament to two cathedral priests from Esztergom on July thirty-first, 1614. Three weeks later she was found dead, face down in her sealed chambers, by one of her guards."

"I was faking," she snapped, starting to squirm again. "How do you think I arranged my escape?"

"Good fake," I said, cutting into the back of her neck so that the edge of the blade touched the top of a vertebrae knob. She immediately stopped moving. "Erzsébet Báthory was fifty-four when she died and showed it. Did you fake that, too?"

"Kurt!" she cried, "he is cutting me!"

The head of her undead household stood next to the lab tech, clutching the crystal goblet of his mistress' blood in agonized indecision. "My lady, what would you have me do?"

I jerked her into a tighter embrace. "Run the blood, lapdog; or the countess dies the Second Death!"

He hesitated another two beats, then thrust the goblet into the technician's hands. "Run the countess' DNA," he ordered. "Hurry!"

"What are you doing?" Báthory screeched.

"Saving your life," her servitor replied.

I was hoping for the opposite result.

Chapter Twenty-four

"Let me tell you a little story while we wait," I said as the sequencer began the process of scanning and sorting the genome of New York's vampire Doman.

"Once upon a time—a little over four hundred years ago, in fact—there was a baby girl born into the house of Báthory. It wasn't enough that she was produced by centuries of savage Darwinism laced with significant episodes of inbreeding, she had the additional advantage of growing up among relatives who practiced witchcraft, bestiality, torture, and twisted cruelties beyond the scope of most human imaginations."

Around the room the expressions ranged from "been there, done that" to "so?"

"As a child of the nobility," I continued, trying to keep them quiet and in their seats for just a couple more minutes, "she had wealth and privilege and essentially *carte blanche* permission to do as she pleased without fear of consequence or retribution. It was, in other words, the perfect greenhouse for cultivating a monster."

"You state the obvious!" my captive protested.

"Yes," I agreed, "yes, I do. Just as I would if I spent the next hour recounting the Blood Countess' many cruelties, the torturous deaths visited upon the young women of her province. I could state the obvious in telling the old story of how Erzsébet Báthory, a vain and selfish woman, struck a servant girl one day and discovered that the girl's blood made her skin appear more youthful where it had been splashed. Obvious, well-known—and, patently, untrue."

"What do you mean, untrue? It is true!" she cried. "That is how it started!"

I shrugged but didn't relax my hold on her. "Perhaps you're right. I wasn't there and you were so maybe *that* part of the story is true. Perhaps you planned it that way and staged it so the other servants would witness the event. The story certainly helped you when it all began to crumble and the tribunals were called."

"This serves no purpose!" she exclaimed.

"Maybe not," I concurred. "Maybe it's just a little conversation to pass the time until the results come in."

>Cséjthe, she is trying to mind-bend the man operating the computing machine.<

Well, block her, Old Dragon! If she interferes with the results, I'm dead and ninety-nine percent of the world will follow in short order.

>You ask much!<

For myself? Maybe. For the rest of the planet? Suck it up and try being useful for a change.

>I will not forget your impertinence when this is over . . .<

Oh, bite me! "Liz, baby, leave the poor lab tech alone and let him finish running the scans without interference."

"Someone's blocking me!" she said through clenched teeth.

"How about I cut just part way through your spinal cord now? It will certainly change the distraction level for you." She shut up and seemed to strain a little less. "So, where was I? Oh, yeah. Over six hundred virgins drained of blood during a single decade. What a time that must have been! Imagine trying to find six virgins now, never mind six hundred. Makes you long for the good old days."

Kurt had moved to flank the lab tech by the computer monitors. "You," he asked me, "have a point to make in all of this?"

"Gee, I sure hope so," I said. "Now help me out here because I'm still somewhat of an outsider on all the undead etiquette. I mean, if there's a Miss Manners for monsters or Emily Post for the posthumous, I've missed the advice column. So, isn't it customary when you become a vampire that you're automatically a vassal to the one who made you?" I snorted. "I can't believe I just used the word 'vassal' in a public discourse."

Throughout the gathered assemblage heads nodded and turned to see what might be the inclinations of their neighbors. No one had given any indication of wanting to rush me yet and I figured I had a decent chance of surviving a few more minutes as long as I kept them entertained. And, of course, the golden knife less than a centimeter away from my hostage's spinal cord.

Kurt cleared his throat. "Yes. You are obligated to your Sire or Dam and, by extension, to theirs, all the way up to the surviving head of that particular line."

"So," I asked, "what's with the oath? Isn't it sort of *ipso de facto* that we're all family, with the requisite pecking order? Why administer a formal oath?"

"There are some crossovers upon occasion," he answered. "Yourself, for example. Dracula was your Sire yet you are—or were— taking the oath to swear fealty to the House of Báthory."

I gave my captive a little shake. "Do I look like someone who was *willing* to take an oath of fealty? How about you and your buddies, Kurt? You and the rest of the old guard here have mentioned your oath. Was it taken willingly? How about the rest of the European aristobats? And why an oath? If she made you, why did she have to bind your loyalty in a blood-oath?"

His face was like stone. "The countess did not grant us the Dark Gift. Each of us was the head of our own line before we took the oath and swore fealty to the Bátor clan."

"So . . . your only allegiance to this woman is through the oath you've sworn to the Báthory line. Which might sort of include me by genetic disposition."

He nodded, well, curtly. "Except she is eldest and head. And she is noble born, a countess."

I nodded. "You Old World guys really do have a major hard-on when it comes to the aristocracy. I always thought the undead pecking order was based along the lines of oldest and strongest or something like that."

Kurt's smile was humorless. "You are young. And, like the young, you want to believe that the universe is fair, that justice will always prevail. It takes age and wisdom to see things as they really are. Even your country is young, its history no more than a child's compared to the rest of the world. America likes to pretend that 'all men are created equal' when it clearly knows better and operates otherwise."

I sighed. "Okay. So, I guess you're pretty firm in your dedication to the nobility."

"Nobility and its bloodlines," Kurt affirmed. "Even if she did not grant the Dark Gift directly, she is still noblest and eldest among us."

I nodded in agreement. "Blood will out."

The computer beeped.

"Sounds like the results are in," I said.

My prisoner made one last desperate attempt to squirm out of my grasp. *I could use a little help here!* She suddenly slumped in my grasp and I almost dropped her. *Jeez, Drac, I thought you were on the run all of these years because you were overmatched.*

>*I had some help this time. Can you get out now?*<

I didn't have time to answer as Kurt was moving toward me. "What did you do?" he demanded.

"Easy, Captain Kurt, she's just unconscious," I said. "See, she's still—well, not breathing, of course—but she's still, um, corporate."

He slowed his advance. "The countess is all right then?"

I shook my head slowly from side to side. "No, Kurt," I said carefully, "the countess is dead."

"What? But you said—"

"Erzsébet Báthory," I elaborated, "died some four centuries ago in her tower in Cséjthe Castle. The woman who's been giving you orders for the last three hundred years is an imposter." I looked over at the lab tech who was staring at the monitors and probably programming an additional run of tests into the sequencer. "Isn't she, man?"

He hesitated, then nodded. "She's not even a close match to either of the Báthory of Nádasdy lines."

"Then who—?"

"I can't prove it," I said, measuring the distance between the door and yours truly, "but I believe the real Witch of Cachtice was a woman named Katarina Beneczky, one of Countess Báthory's maids."

"What? How? I thought they were all put to death."

"Not Beneczky. She was the only one on the countess' personal staff that was found innocent. She was set free by the same tribunal that sealed Erzsébet in her tower and executed the others."

I looked around at my audience. Gee, this was like those old-fashioned, locked-room mysteries where all the suspects sit in the parlor while the inspector explains the case to everyone. I continued, hoping I wouldn't pull a "Clouseau."

"While Erzsébet developed her sadistic proclivities early, I believe it was Katarina who turned that private obsession into crimes of monstrous proportions. She used the dark arts to bind the countess and the others to her will. Using an aristocrat was the perfect tool and the perfect cover for carrying out her nefarious schemes." I shook my head. "I can't believe I just used the word 'nefarious' in a public forum."

The entire room appeared to be shocked by this turn of events but Kurt seemed utterly thunderstruck. "Then that means . . . that we . . . that I . . ."

"Yep," I said, "you swore a blood-oath of fealty to a commoner, a peasant."

The other vamps in the room turned to Báthory-turned-Beneczky's majordomo, their expressions asking the same questions: what have we done; what do we do?

"Except," I continued, "you really didn't." They all looked back at me. "If I understand the situation correctly, you all swore in word and in your hearts, to serve the Countess Erzsébet Báthory and her House. Not . . ." I paused for effect, " . . . some servant girl passing herself off as the countess. So, you're free."

Now came the part where I explained to everyone about what terrible things the counterfeit countess had plotted and how important it was for us to join forces to keep these terrible plots from going forward.

Before I could launch into that part of my vague plan, some guy in the fourth row of chairs stood up. "Do you know what this means?" he asked, smoothing back his hair. He had three horns, curved close to his skull and peeking through his pompadour like the stripes of a skunk.

Maybe this was my opening.

"It means," he continued, "that you no longer have a viable hostage!"

And then again, maybe not. "Hey," I said, "I've got an idea. Let's do 'The Time Warp,' again . . ."

Several audience members, rising from their seats, hesitated. "What?" a couple of them asked.

"It's just a jump to the left!" I said, hurling Beneczky toward them and running for the door.

It would have been a clean break except for the two vamps guarding the exit.

Each one possessed speed, strength, and reflexes that were inhumanly superior to mine: between the two of them, I didn't stand a chance. Anticipating my charge, they went into side-by-side crouches, each dropping one knee to the floor to brace themselves and then—

Inclined their heads?

Instead of attacking they were kneeling and assuming a position of obeisance!

I looked back over my shoulder and saw that most of the other vamps were facing me and doing the same. Everybody else just looked confused. Myself included, I suppose.

Kurt raised his head and addressed me: "Sire."

"Sire?" I felt a little stupid as most of my brain was still working out the problem of my escape. "How can I be your 'Sire' when you're older than me?"

"Master, then," he conceded. "We have sworn our oaths to the House of Báthory and, as of now, you are our Blood-liege by default."

I looked around at all of the kneeling vampires. "Just like that?"

He nodded.

"Don't you want to run a few more tests? Make sure she isn't the real Countess Báthory?"

"No, Master. We have had our doubts for over two hundred years. It is like a fulfillment of prophecy: the true Báthory heir has come to free us from centuries of false servitude."

"Yeah, well—"

"Under your reign, the Eastern Demesnes will become a great empire, ruling the night for a thousand years!"

"Um," I said.

>*Cséjthe? Can you get away, yet? What is happening?*<

Well, I'm not sure. But I think I've just been offered your old job.

>What?<

=You need to get out here!=

Deirdre?

=A bunch of trucks and vans just came through the front gate and have pulled around to the loading docks at the rear of the buildings. There must be a hundred guys running around in fatigues and Ninja-casual, waving automatic weapons and preparing some sort of loading operation.=

They're loading their weapons?

>No, Cséjthe, they are loading the trucks. I certainly hope that I did not absorb your genetic proclivity for obtuseness from the trans-fusion of your blood.<

Tough toothies, Vlad; beggars can't be choosers. I turned back to Kurt. "Beneczky has set a plan in motion that will destroy most of the world's population. We've got to stop it!"

"Will it affect vampires?" Skippy wanted to know.

"Does it matter?" Kurt growled. "If our supply of food becomes extinct then we are harmed, as well. Besides, our Master commands—that, alone, should be enough!"

The presumed Katarina Beneczky began to stir and was promptly hoisted to her feet by two large vamps. Correction: her feet now hung a few inches above the floor. They carried her over to where we could speak to each other without yelling but maybe she was oblivious to that fact: the ersatz Erzsébet began yelling anyway. And her choice of words was anything but aristocratic.

I reached out and pinched her mouth shut. "I don't have time for niceties," I said, forcing as much menace into my subvocals as my human throat could manage. "I want this whole operation called off right now! Do it and I might let you live. Refuse and I'll kill you right here and now!"

She glared at me but she stopped struggling and, when I removed my hand, she spoke more civilly. "I can't. It's out of my hands now. In fact, it has always been out of my hands."

I was afraid of this. I was about to suggest locking her up in something airtight when Kurt walked up behind her and twisted her head off. There was a soggy "pop" and our dusting was not unlike that of an ancient vacuum cleaner exploding.

So much for one of my theories: Katarina Beneczky was a vampire, after all.

"So ends the treachery and falsehood of four centuries," my new majordomo announced. "What would you have us do, now, my lord?"

"Um," I said again. "Follow me." I was going to have to have a talk with him later about taking me literally.

As I exited Gen/GEN and started down the hallway, my eyes were drawn to a trail of blood that stippled the carpet and led toward the stairs. Looking back I could see that the trail emerged from the office where I had left Chalice Delacroix's body less than a half hour before. "No!" I ran and slammed the door open.

The back trail of blood led to a now-empty desk.

I whirled.

>*Cséjthe? Are you coming?*<

Not now, Pops, I'm busy!

>*What could be more important than saving the world?*<

I'm following the path of the Grail. I was back out in the corridor and running toward the stairs. "Kurt, take all the vamps you can down to the loading docks and stop those trucks from leaving!"

I winced as he said: "Yes, Master."

"Call me Chris."

"Yes, Master."

"You're doing that on purpose, aren't you?"

"*Yes, Master.*"

A phalanx of undead glided by, speeding toward the elevators. "Aren't you going with them?"

"No. My place is with you, now. They know what to do."

We started down the stairs. "Kurt, do I really strike you as a likely candidate for aristocracy?"

"Let me put it this way," he said as we flew down two flights of stairs in the space of a double heartbeat. "You are as likely a candidate for nobility as we are likely to find among this sorry generation."

"Gee, Kurt, that's almost kind of sweet."

"Everyone is entitled to their opinion, my lord, but I would hate to have to kill you for expressing it publicly."

Another frenzied half-circle at the next landing and down another flight. "When you put it that way," I said, "it gives me hope that this relationship might actually work out."

Exiting out of the stairwell and into the first-floor corridor, I reversed direction and continued to follow the scarlet spoor toward the back of the building.

"You're headed for the voodoo altar, aren't you?" my undead shadow asked.

"I think someone is." I rounded the corner and found the remains of Chalice's black party dress, shredded and abandoned next to the trail of bloody droplets. It was no longer salvageable in any sense of the word so I tossed it aside. Blood from the dress clung to the palms of my hands and I had to resist the compulsion to lick them clean.

"You know what bothers me?" I asked as I wiped my hands off on the wall.

"It would be hard to guess," he answered. "Compared to my former Doman, so much seems to bother you."

"It's the vast amounts of blood involved in the Báthory legend." I started down the corridor again. "I mean, even if the countess and her inner circle were all vampires—which history has pretty well disproved—they couldn't consume more than a fraction of the blood produced in any given month. So what was the deal?"

"According to legend, the countess bathed—"

"But if she was being manipulated by the real Witch of Cachtice," I interrupted, "the motivation for spilling such vast quantities of blood might have been Beneczky's alone. What purpose was served through so much pain, death, and exsanguination?" The subbasement stairs were coming up and the bloody trail left little doubt that someone or some*thing* had taken Chalice Delacroix's body to the *djevo* underneath the building.

"Blood magic," suggested Kurt, "though I do not know what sort of necromancy would require such a volume of life essence." We plunged down the stairs. "Perhaps it was all meant as a sacrifice of some kind?"

"But to who? Or what?" The secret door at the bottom of the stairs was open but I slowed down as I needed time to adjust my eyes to the darkness beyond. "Too bad I can't ask Katarina Beneczky."

"I doubt that she would have answered the question—at least not truthfully."

"Well, I guess I'll never get the chance to find out now, will I?"

"You said you would kill her if she didn't—"

"Is the word 'bluff' in your lexicon? Remind me to teach you how to play poker."

Kurt sounded wounded: "I prefer chess. One does not bluff in chess."

"No? We really must play a match some time. Perhaps *after* the end of the world."

The candles were still guttering in their alcoves along the inner corridor. I gave them a glance. And then a second look as I moved into the dimly lit passageway.

"What is it?"

"Those candles. They were red the last time I was down here. Now they're black."

"What does that signify?"

"Something, I'm sure. If this place is still being used as a Vodoun temple, then color would be significant in identifying the Loa who are invoked here. My guess is the Ogou clan has been cleared out and something else has checked in."

"What?"

"Something that likes the color black. Now hush."

He hushed but the quiet was broken by another voice. "Koki Oko," a voice sang in the distance.

"O wa djab-la!" It was a woman's voice, high-pitched and eerie.

"Koki Oko ki anba . . . nèg mare nou!
Koki Oko, ki anba, nèg mare nou
Koki Oko, ki anba, n'a lage!
Koki Oko, o wa djab-la . . .
Koki Oko, ki anba, nèg mare!
Koki Oko, o wa djab-la . . .
Koki Oko ki anba, nèg mare nou!"

"Jesus," I whispered.

"What is it? What do the words mean?"

"I'm not sure," I said quietly, hoping my voice wouldn't carry in the sudden silence following the song's end. "I recognize two or three of the words. Djab-la is a Vodoun name for a wild spirit. It's a distortion of the French word *diable* for devil—only its connotation here is more in the magical realm than the spiritual."

"Could have fooled me. What's Koki Oko?"

"Um, the translation wouldn't do it justice. Let's just say the song was oriented somewhere between naughty and nasty."

The voice started again, this time chanting instead of singing: "Amen. *Seculi venturi vitam et. Mortuorum resurrectionem in baptisma unum Confiteor. Ecclesiam apostolicam et catholicicam, sanctum, unam et . . .*"

"That sounds like Latin," I said.

"It is," Kurt agreed, "but it is gibberish. The words make no sense."

" *. . . prophetas per est locutus qui . . .*"

"Maybe," I said, moving ahead, "and my Latin's a little rusty but there's something familiar about some of that gibberish."

It made sense: Vodoun was such a distorted blend of African Mystère and Catholicism that Latin might well be invoked along with variants of French, Spanish, and the Fon language of West Africa.

" *. . . mortuos et vivos judicare Gloria cum est venturus iterum et. Patris dexteram adsedet . . .*"

"Wait a minute," I said as we came to the *hounfort* and entered the temple area. "I may not know my masses beyond a Te Deum and an Agnus Dei, but isn't that the Nicene Creed?"

Kurt considered the chanting more attentively.

" *. . . Scripturas secundum, die tertia resurrexit et . . .*"

"Yes. It's being recited backwards."

"Thought so."

"What does it mean?"

"It means something very bad. Voodoo is always getting a bad rap from the Hollywood treatment—"

"Yes," he said, "they do the same disservice to vampires."

I let that one slide. "Rada—or 'right hand' voodoo—is a positive religion. Even Petro—the left hand or sinister perversion of the African mysteries—wouldn't hold their services underground like this. So whatever we have here is something off the map."

" *. . . coelis de descendit salutem nostram propter et . . .*"

As we started across the *peristil*, I could see the altar room beyond the sinister maypole of the *poteau mitan*. Someone had come in since the conflagration accompanying my last visit and cleaned up. Black drapes now hung on the sides of the alcove but the back wall was left uncovered. There, on a series of small shelves, were racks of tiny glass bottles—DNA sample vials like the ones in the Gen/GEN lab upstairs. The flames from thirteen ebony candles did little to illume the dark décor but here the glass containers seemed to glow with pale red and blue phosphors— much like the alternating glow from the BioWeb sign outside. A swatch of scarlet was draped across the altar table, appearing in the pulses of blue light, disappearing in the counterpoint bursts of red illumination.

" . . . *saecula omnia ante natum Patre ex et . . .*"

The rest of the Ogou paraphernalia had been removed from the area but the crimson dress had been salvaged. Symbols, Father Pat had said, are very powerful agents in systems of belief.

I was beginning to form a theory concerning the nature of Cachtice's blood sacrifices.

"Isn't that Chalice Delacroix?" Kurt whispered.

She had been nearly invisible against the backdrop of darkness but now that my attention was drawn and my eyes adjusted, I could see the woman standing by the altar. She wore nothing but her own skin and a faint, golden limning of light from the votive candles on the altar. An arm-shaped thread of gold extended toward the swirl of red and a moment later a crimson flash of fabric unfurled, setting a dozen and one points of light a-shiver. She wasn't dead! Chalice had survived!

"What is she doing? Kurt whispered.

Chanting was the first answer that came to mind as I moved toward her. But as I circled around the great wooden post and got a better angle and a closer look I wasn't sure that it was Chalice after all. Four lines of clotted blood still striped her stomach, but her umber flesh seemed vaguely out of place, as if subtly redistributed. It was like clothing that you are used to seeing on one person being worn by another: the colors and patterns are identical but the shape and drape differ, even on similar forms and figures.

" . . . *invisibilium et omnium visibilium . . .*"

She turned her head and my heart seized up in my chest. Chalice's moss-green eyes might appear to be black in the near darkness of our surroundings but these eyes glittered red and orange with a light that was not all reflected candle-flame. Her mouth moved in an unnatural way and the teeth within appeared to be filed to triangular points as if they were retro-engineered for tearing flesh and separating gristle from bone.

" . . . *Deum unum in credo,*" she finished and smiled. Her mouth grew inhumanly wide. "Cséjthe! How good of you to come!" It definitely wasn't Chalice Delacroix's voice!

"Wh—who are you?" I asked.

"Don't you recognize me?" she purred. No, that wasn't the right word: "purred" suggests something feline. But cats are warm-blooded creatures and there was nothing warm-blooded here. She turned and posed provocatively, the red silk flung over one shoulder. "Didn't you get a good look?"

I stopped moving toward her. I was already closer than I suddenly wanted to be.

"How about another taste?" She sauntered toward me, one hand caressing her bloody belly. "You took so little before. A few sips, really."

"You're not Chalice," I said, taking a step back.

"What is a chalice?" She came toward me, step by step. "A glass? A cup? A drinking container? I contain blood; would you like another drink?"

I took another step back. "No."

"No?" Her eyebrows went up in a parody of surprise. "I thought you *liked* me. I thought you *loved* the taste. Wasn't I yummy? Yummy in the tummy?"

"Don't," I said.

"Yummy in your tummy?" she asked, closing the distance between us with a dreamlike inexorability. "Didn't you find my tummy yummy?"

I got a better look at the fabric draped over her shoulder and stopped backing away.

"You look very thirsty, Cséjthe. Maybe even a little hungry. Would you like a little nibble before the fun begins? A little taste? There's room on the altar for two. Or I could stand here while you kneel . . ."

"I know who you are," I said.

"Yes, I think I'd like that—you on your knees . . ." Flickers of light from ancient sacrificial fires danced in her eyes and she began to hum.

"You're Marinette Bois-Chèche," I said.

She shook her head. "I am your chalice . . . your goblet . . ."

"Yeah, more like my hob-goblet." Somewhere in the back of my brain a beeping sound commenced, signaling that I seriously needed to be backing up now! Instead I stood my ground, wrestling with the problem of Katarina Beneczky and Marinette Bois-Chèche. Were they one and the same?

In Vodoun, the spirit Loa manifest by possessing a human body. It's called "mounting the host" who is referred to as a "horse" as the spirit "rides" the human. Chalice—whether truly dead or still alive—was gone and the most dangerous, bitter, and vengeful of the Petro Loa was sitting in the saddle and applying supernatural spurs.

"Kneel, Cséjthe . . . kneel and drink . . ."

I hesitated and felt invisible bands of pressure close about my head. While there was no doubt about my ability to physically overpower Chalice Delacroix, this was an entirely different matter. Given the manifest changes in her physicality while the Loa had her boots in the stirrups, I had serious doubts about the efficacy of any direct resistance. I could remain defiant and see just how high Marinette could ratchet up the grief-o-meter. Or I could apply the principles of Ju-jitsu and use her centers of balance against her.

I sank to one knee and felt the pressure lessen.

"Kneel . . . and feed . . ." She stepped up to me and, reaching behind my head, pressed my face to her belly.

I embraced her legs with my left arm and ran my right hand up the smooth curve of her flank in a leisurely caress.

"Taste the blood of the Loa," she crooned. "Taste the power . . ."

That wasn't my goal. The touch of her cold, blood-slicked flesh was actually the last thing I craved at this particular moment but I had to endure it to keep a promise. I had turned out to be no damn good at keeping my word to Chalice's daddy but the world's fate might well be sealed tonight if I failed in my charge from Mama Samm.

A funny thing happened in the midst of my deception: The Hunger began to return. In spite of the revulsion I felt for the atrocities rendered upon Chalice Delacroix's flesh this night, I felt the ancient lusts begin to stir as the scents of blood and sweat and musk bathed my nasal epithelial receptors. My hindbrain began to wake from its ten-thousand-year slumber, stretching limbic limbs and flooding my veins with a hormonal soup of predatory impulses and drives. *A few moments more,* I told myself as my right hand roamed higher, palm surfing the wavelets of muscle-sheathed ribs. *It was unavoidable, it was necessary,* I told myself, sipping at the dark wine that trickled by the well of her navel; *she must believe me compliant, complicit . . .*

Compromised . . .

The power that transmogrified Chalice Delacroix's flesh and shaped it to the will of Marinette Bois-Chèche burned in her blood like bitter whiskey and sweet rum. Lightning from the Ogou forge crackled there and something latched onto my tongue, drawing it into a whirlpool of sensation, a whorl of power, a vortex of violence.

The plan had been to catch the demon Loa off-balance but it was I who had suddenly lost my own footing. Even as I took her dark essence into me I felt my will, my resistance, my very conscience being drained. Metaphysical fangs were biting into my own heart, a vampiric feeding frenzy had begun: even as my body took on unaccustomed physical strength and power, I felt my inner strength ebb and fade.

God help me, I thought frantically. *I can't disengage!* I tried to think of a prayer, a scripture that would help me pull out of this Tantric tailspin. Psalm 121 began with: "I will lift up mine eyes unto the hills, from whence cometh my help." When I looked up, the only hills I could see undermined my resolve that much more.

Then I saw a flash of scarlet and my attention was drawn to the red dress still draped from her shoulder, now inches from my questing right hand.

She sighed and caressed the back of my head. "Deeper . . ."

I strained my hand upward . . . an inch . . . then another.

"Ooo," she cooed, "devour me!"

The monster inside was breaking loose, ripping the chains of conscience away with brutish strength and subhuman rage. In moments it would be free.

"No," I murmured, crimson threads gumming my lips.

Her hand fell away from the back of my head and I looked up.

Her head was tilted back, her own gaze turned upward, as well. "What?" she asked, slowly, dreamily.

"I've had about all I can stomach," I said more clearly as the fingers of my right hand closed on the hem of the dress. As I yanked it from her shoulder, I pulled her legs out from under her with the sweep of my left arm. I bounced to my feet even as I heard the back of her head thud against the earthen floor.

"Kurt!" I yelled.

"Here, Master," he answered from a few feet away. "I couldn't move!"

"Can you move now?"

"I think so, yes."

"Then the last one out is a rotten corpse!"

We ran for the exit. Kurt should have been twice as fast as I but he followed closely while keeping me in front; guarding my back, no doubt.

"What are we doing?" he asked as we scrambled into the outer corridor and headed for the stairs.

"Saving the world!"

"By running away?"

I held up my scarlet trophy. "By preventing the Whore of Babylon from putting her red dress on!"

"I don't understand!"

My reply was drowned out by the thunder of our feet pounding up the stairs.

"What?" he yelled as we reached the first floor.

"I said: Neither do I!"

We turned and ran for the rear exit and the loading docks.

"It can't be that simple!" he protested.

Of course, it wasn't. . . .

Chapter Twenty-five

As a full-fledged battle raged outside on the BioWeb grounds, Kurt and I exited through the loading docks and found a half-dozen vampires hiding behind a large, canopied truck.

"What are you doing?" my new majordomo demanded. "They're only humans!"

"Hey," I muttered, "watch the profiling."

"Some of them are armed with lasers," Viktor answered.

Kurt and I exchanged looks. Bullets were one thing. An extremely well-placed shot or a heavy barrage of poorly placed shots might prove fatal—but most of the time guns were nothing more than a painful inconvenience to the undead.

Weapons utilizing amplified or coherently focused light were another matter, entirely—think sunrise in a continuous deadly stream. Marinette Bois-Chèche might have duped the general in the lab but he was no dummy in military matters. He had arranged for most of his troops to be rendered hypno-immune to vampiric mind control and armed them with weapons deadly to living and undead flesh alike. Already they had made ash out of a dozen of New York's best fanged enforcers.

"What do we do now?" Kurt asked.

"Do I look like a man with a plan to you?"

He shook his head. "Actually, you look more like a frat boy who ran through a plate glass window fleeing a panty raid. Wipe your face."

I opened my mouth. Felt more threads of blood decorate my oral cavity. Closed it and wiped my face with the dress. "We've got to keep them from driving out the main gate with their cargo," I reasoned. "Okay, everybody fall back to the inside of the building!"

We turned and ran like hell. All but two of us made it back inside the loading docks.

Mirrors, I thought as we pounded toward the front of the building, *we could rip mirrors off the restroom walls*—and have our legs cut out from under us a moment after we held them up as shields.

Along the way some of the vamps acquired BioWeb security firearms. It didn't look to be much of an advantage—few of them seemed to have any real expertise with twenty-first-century weaponry.

Oh man, we are really screwed.

=*Is that what you've been doing in there while I was busy organizing a rescue operation?*=

Deirdre?

=*We're still waiting for you, Chris, but the action has shifted around front. In a few moments we're going to need all the help we can get or the militia is going to drive off with three truckloads of viral cultures.*=

We're on our way but I don't know what we can do.

=*Got any guns?*=

I looked around. *Maybe a half dozen side arms, a couple of rifles.* We charged through the lobby and out the front doors. I would have preferred to reconnoiter but you don't play it safe when the end of the world is getting ready to drive out the front gate. We split up immediately to prevent a clustering of targets for the opposition. We were in luck: A few gunshots rang out but there was no concentrated response.

=*That will have to do until the rest get here. Though I'm not sure our troops will know how to use them.*=

My follow-up "Huh? What troops?" to that was derailed by the arrival of a black van.

Okay, I get the need for tinted windows and eschewing the waiting-for-an-accident-to-happen ragtops and sunroofs.

But would it be such a violation of the undead code to drive a vehicle that explored other colors of the spectrum? Maybe a green sedan or a red pickup or a blue sports car? But, no; it's always a black paint job when a citizen of the night is at the wheel.

Okay, guilty as charged, I thought as the black van smashed through the lowered security bar and was followed by a familiar-looking black 1950 Mercury Club Coupé with a chopped silhouette and a raggedy hole in the roof. Both vehicles swerved across the parking lot dodging shots fired from the side of the main building. They rolled to a stop on the grass just beyond the edge of the asphalt.

As I ran toward my car, the driver's door opened and my zoot-suit buddy clambered out. He turned, seeming oblivious to the chaos unfolding from the far side of the lot and heading in his direction. As he retrieved his wide-brimmed hat, the door to the van opened and the driver that emerged was a creature unlike any I could recall seeing despite this past year's subscription to the Necronomicon Yearbook.

His head looked like the burned tip of a safety match and the rest of him was hardly any better—a charred, gray-and-black caricature of an elongated tar baby with skin like soft asphalt. He limped around to the back of the van and opened the rear doors.

"Hey," said The Kid, "nice flivver, man. Needs some detailing but if you're ever in the market to sell—"

I swung my attention back to Mr. Hep-as-hell. "I thought you were dead."

He grinned, displaying fangs that were long and strong. "I am, Big Daddy! I'm dead as hell and I'm not taking it anymore! I've got it made in the grave." He moved toward the rear of the van.

"No," I said, "I mean, I thought they had staked you or something."

"You jiving me, Daddy-O? We're too tough for these GI-Joseph wannabes. Ask ole Bubba, here."

Matchstick man turned his crispy head and wheezed something unintelligible.

I stared at him, at them. "You're telling me this is Mr. Montrose?" I turned to the crispy cadaver. "Billy Bob?"

He bobbed his charcoaled cranium.

"You'll have to pardon my associate's lack of lingo, Gringo," J.D. explained. "His throat hasn't yet recovered from imitating a blowtorch. He needs a month in the ground with a hemoglobin IV drip going full bore. Too bad war ain't more convenient."

As he spoke, the ground opened up a few feet away and a corpse rose up from the earth like a passenger on a sidewalk freight elevator. He wore a tattered wool greatcoat with a shredded six-button cape. Piping that might have been white over a century ago lined the outer legs of his trousers, formed "V"s above his cuffs, and striped his collar. A tarnished officer's sword and scabbard hung below a faded red sash that circled his waist. On the opposite side a pair of yellowed gauntlets were folded over the sash near his hip. A nearly fleshless hand came up to a ghastly brow and I heard a muffled "chik," the sound of bone striking bone as the dead man snapped off a smart salute.

"Muh men are at the ready," the cadaver said, holding his salute. "With yuh permission, suh, we will engage the enemy."

It took a moment but I finally remembered to raise my own arm in a return salute. "Uh, certainly, Captain. Whenever you are ready, of course."

"Of course, suh." The official exchange completed, he turned to the crispy vampire who was emerging from the back of the van and tugging on a long, wooden case. "Sergeant, have you brought us our ordnance?"

Montrose bobbed his head and lowered one end to the ground as the earth behind the captain opened with three more popping sighs. As the case was opened, three more dead soldiers approached in varying stages of recomposition. The hideously burned vampire handed a tarnished, tan-handled revolver to the officer and gurgled something.

"You're giving them antique weapons?" I asked incredulously, thinking of the modern armament carried by the general's paramilitary troops coming around the corner of the building.

"Nothing but the best," The Kid answered. "He says that's a Cooper double-action percussion revolver—he got it on eBay a couple of years ago for twenty-two hundred dollars."

Two corpses, one wearing a gray sack coat with four brass buttons, the other a faded blue frock coat with a two-inch collar—stepped forward and hefted the box. Inside were ancient long-barreled weapons. "1842 Springfield muskets," The Kid said. "Twelve hundred and fifty dollars apiece if you buy from a collector who's legit."

Another dead guy stepped up, wearing a twelve-button shell jacket of indeterminate hue. Only the red wool twill taping had retained sufficient color from its previous excursion above the ground. He was given an armful of handguns—flintlock single-shot pistols and a couple of later model percussion single-shot versions.

A squad of corpses approached and one of them opened the van's sliding side door. More boxes were hastily unloaded, and their museum-exhibit armaments hurriedly distributed. Carbines manufactured by Starr, by Sharps, by Smith. Muskets bearing the imprints of Enfield and Greene. P.S. Justice and Mississippi rifles. Even a couple of short-barreled minié rifles. It was a treasure trove of firepower, The Kid explained. Here was a Colt Model 1852 Police Revolver with a thirty-six-hundred-dollar price tag, there a Springfield Model 1863 Type 2 Rifle musket worth twenty-five hundred dollars on the collectors' circuit. Powder and shot were flung to waiting, anxious, and fleshless hands. Some of the ammo boxes tumbled to the ground and I picked up the lid of one that had burst open.

Poultney's Patent Metallic Cartridges
Patented December 15, 1863   12 Caps
For Smith's Breech-Loading Carbine
No. 1   50-100 Caliber
Address, Poultney & Trimble, Baltimore, Md.

"Here they come!" someone yelled.

A musket was flung into my hands, a .69 caliber smooth-bore from all appearances. On the lockplate the date 1849 was clearly visible as was the cartouche. There was some pitting at the breech from the mercury fulminate and there were a few "dings" here and there in the wood and metal, but it was remarkably well preserved and, with a start, I realized it could do more serious damage at close range than the modern, hard-jacketed, high-velocity ammo that was about to come flying in our direction.

Too bad I didn't know how to load and fire the damn thing!

I suddenly remembered the silver-loaded Glock in my glove compartment. I ran back to my car and flung open the passenger door. It was easier to slide onto the bench seat while I groped for the zippered carry case. As I opened the glove compartment the door beside me closed. A moment later the lock stem sank down with an emphatic clack.

"Mister Chris . . ." said a familiar voice.

I turned and looked behind me with equal portions of fear and annoyance: I really *had* to start checking the backseat before getting into my car at night.

Mama Samm's white robe and turban seemed to shed a soft light, more than equal to the full moon on a cloudless night. Sitting beside her was a tall, thin man dressed in a black frock coat and top hat. His blue-black skin was daubed with white paint in a pattern that approximated a crude skeletal motif on his face and shirtless torso. He sat in a rigid pose and, after a moment, I saw that his arms were bound to his sides by dozens of loops of scarlet thread.

"So, dis is de one," he said, considering me as one might regard a social introduction to a professional telemarketer. "He don' look de type."

"Nevertheless," she admonished him. She turned to me. "Christopher, may I introduce his royal highness, Baron Samedi of the Gédé clan."

I started to extend my hand out of polite habit and then stopped as I noticed the threads precluded any kind of practical handshaking. High-fives were definitely out of the picture.

"Nice to meetcha," I said, nodding my head. I turned back to my friendly neighborhood fortune-teller. "Does this mean we can get this whole mistaken identity thing settled and close out the cemetery tours to my doorstep?"

"Do not think I am ungrateful for your assistance while I was indisposed," the Loa of the Dead said, "but as soon as I am free I will reclaim my rightful place as adjudicator for de dead!"

"Great," I said. "I think I have a pocketknife—"

"He cannot be freed by physical means," Mama Samm explained. "He is bound by foul sorceries. Only powerful, sympathetic magic can free him. You must free the others, the Gédé and Ogou that the witch has taken hostage. She has turned their power against him and against each other."

I looked out at the confusion that was unfolding beyond the Merc's tinted windows.

Captain Worthington's cadaverous corps had engaged the gray guard and, while the general's men had the advantage in numbers and weaponry, the Civil War dead had the benefit of already being dead.

And then there was the home turf advantage. "The South shall rise again," I murmured as, here and there, the turf split open and rotted hands and arms came thrusting out of the ground to grab mercenaries' legs. Trousers would begin to smoke in the grasp of those chemical-laced fingers and it wasn't long before the screams of the living drowned out the Rebel yells of the dead. Lasers and tracers lit up portions of the churning grounds, igniting an emerging corpse here and there. Some fell and were quickly consumed where they lay, their desiccated remains serving as wicks for the combustible witches brew that had permeated the earth. Others ran into the midst of the troops trying to load the trucks and took them down in fiery embraces. One vehicle caught fire and its subsequent explosion set up a chain reaction queue of blazes down the length of the idling caravan. Drivers ran to separate one of the trucks as yet untouched from the rest of the burning transports.

I reached for the door handle. "We've got to outflank those remaining trucks," I said. "Nothing else will matter if even a portion of the virus leaves these grounds!"

"Others must fight that battle," she announced more than said. "You must resist the Whore of Babylon."

"Yeah, well I've already knocked the wind out of her sails."

"*Listen to me!*" The fortune-teller was large and in charge, and her voice was suddenly sharp: "You cannot physically gainsay her, you can only do damage to the vessel she inhabits! If you kill the horse that she rides, she will only abandon it and seek to straddle another. You must *resist* her! Do not engage her in a physical contest, for you cannot win and you will not accomplish your objective!"

"You know, your on-again, off-again accent isn't just slipping—it's gone on an extended vacation."

"You need to focus on your objective," she snapped.

"And my objective is to free the hostages?"

"Speak of de she-devil," the baron said. A bloody and unsteady Marinette Bois-Chèche in the avatar of Chalice Delacroix staggered out the front door of the BioWeb building. She stopped and looked out over the series of skirmishes that sprawled across the grounds and parking lot.

"Go!" Mama Samm urged, "Go now! Do not turn to the left or the right! You must go down into the pit and free them before she can stop you! Do not stop to help the others, their support will come from other quarters! Do not allow yourself to be turned aside by The Beast!"

The passenger door lock popped up.

"The Beast?" I asked. "What—"

The ground trembled and a network of cracks and fissures spread across the parking lot like an Etch-a-sketch gone berserk. Asphalt buckled and heaved as Marinette/Chalice capered and danced upon the staired entryway. A reptilian skull the size of a Volkswagen popped up in the midst of Row F, scattering a dozen advancing mercenaries.

"What the hell is that?" I yelled, popping the door open and sticking my head out for a better look.

"The dragon," PFC Blankenship informed me, running past with a rust-eaten bayonet affixed to his musket.

"The Beast," repeated Mama Samm from behind me. "Or one of Its Shadows, at least."

It shouldered its way up through chunks of blacktop and bars of concrete retainers, scapulae like giant kite-shields flinging artificial stone in deadly arcs onto hapless men and vampires, alike. I tried to unzip my pistol case but the zipper was jammed.

"Run!" Mama Samm yelled, "Your gun is of no use for the task that you must do! Go and do it quickly! Before it is too late!"

I started to move toward the building but stopped and turned back. "Where are these hostages?" I called.

"In de pit!" Samedi answered.

I started to open my mouth when he added, "Dey are not human, Cséjthe; dey are Zombi!"

Okay. Sure. It was all coming together for me, now.

Not!

I started for the building anyway. What else was there for me to do? I had a handgun with silver Glaser loads that I couldn't get to, an elite paramilitary force that wouldn't be threatened if I could, a fossilized Tyrannosaurus Rex doing *Jurassic Park* meets *Night of the Living Dead* in the parking lot, and a bunch of dead hostages I needed to rescue before they—well—got any deader.

So help me, if I got through this in one piece I was going to find a safe line of work—maybe testing bulletproof vests or repo-ing motorcycles from the Hell's Angels.

Bloody Bones rampaged to the western end of the parking lot and lowered its gargantuan, toothy skull to the steps where its Dark Mistress waited. Marinette/Chalice climbed up its inclined snout and turned to seat herself upon its grooved cranium as it reared back up and turned in search of fresh prey.

"Chris!"

I looked across the blacktop battlefield and saw Deirdre in dark pants and shirt, motioning for me to come and join her. A cluster of unhuman companions surrounded her: Pagelovitch and his lieutenants, Father Pat in ecclesiastical garb with the requisite collar, and Brother Michael wearing his rough, brown homespun robe and leaning upon his great staff. My three Fates stood together, clasping hands, looking like nothing so much as the Powerpuff Girls, all growed up. I even fancied I saw Marilyn floating a few inches off the ground!

Back behind them was an indistinct mass, like a gathering thunderhead that had settled to the earth. I couldn't be sure at this distance, but I had the distinct impression that every grave in the parish had opened and an army of the deceased was marching on the BioWeb complex.

But would they get here in time?

I wasn't the only thing that turned to look at the sound of Deirdre's voice: Bloody Bones and his dark rider were taking note of my comrades, as well.

It took a giant step in their direction.

Then, another.

"Hey!" I yelled without thinking. What the hell, thinking was overrated anyway.

I dropped the zippered-up Glock and flapped the red dress like a matador's cape. "Over here! Hey Tyro, Tyro!" Mama Samm had said don't do battle with Marinette—but she never specifically told me I couldn't fight The Beast.

And even in that I wouldn't be disobeying her: as the mountain of fossilized bones turned and regarded me with empty eyesockets there was no question that I would be giving it any kind of a real fight either. Just a momentary distraction if I was lucky enough to last another thirty seconds. Maybe that would be enough time for the others to scatter and take cover.

"Cséjthe!" Mama Samm called from behind me, "This is not your battle! Keep going!"

Yeah, right. Then whose battle was it?

As if to answer my question, Father Pat stepped forward and opened a book in his hands. I couldn't hear his voice from where I stood but I could imagine the text was probably from the Bible. Even money on the seventeenth chapter of the Book of Revelation.

Then Brother Michael caught my attention by doing a most unusual thing.

He straightened his bent and hunched form.

He stretched and the hump across his shoulders bulged and strained the fabric of his robe.

The back of his garment tore open and a bundle of white tumbled out even as his large, powerful hands wrenched his staff apart.

There was a flash of silver as a long, double-edged blade emerged from its gnarled, twisted sheath. I barely had time to register that the hunchbacked giant's walking staff was actually a great sword in disguise when my eyes were drawn away to the enormous white sails unfurling from his massive shoulders. They opened and spread, fanlike, behind him: two more kite-shaped forms like giant scapulae covered in swan's down and white eagle's feathers.

Like wings.

With a harsh cry, Michael launched himself into the air, brandishing a silvery sword that was now bursting into flame like a deadly Olympic torch.

"*Holy . . . !*" I yelled, at a loss for a second word. There are not many words you can use when you've seen your first angel.

"Cséjthe," Mama Samm hurried up beside me and took my arm, "hurry! There isn't much time!"

"But..." I said, starting to point.

"Have you lived so long among the creatures of darkness that you cannot imagine the existence of creatures of light? Come! Even an angel may not turn back the Darkness if he fights alone. You must free the zombi!" She gave me a shove as six-inch teeth of stone clacked shut just inches from the snowy pinions on one of Michael's wingtips.

I began to run again, fighting every impulse to turn back to watch.

"Cséjthe!" The voice belonged to Marinette Bois-Chèche: now I dared not hesitate nor turn back. I hurtled up the front steps and slam-danced through the front doors of the lobby.

The pit, the pit, free the zombies in the pit, they had said. But where was this pit? Downstairs was the obvious direction but the only space approximating a pit that I had seen was the *hounfort* and *djevo* that had served the Mambo's terrible dark powers.

Well, I had to start somewhere. I turned and ran down the north corridor toward the back of the building.

>*Cséjthe...*< The voice of Dracula echoed through my head.

"Nag, nag, nag," I groused. *What is it, now?*

>*I did not want to leave without saying goodbye.*<

What? You're leaving? Now!?

>*I think it in my best interests, whatever the outcome, to return to the shadows while some still remain.*<

Now the temptation to turn around, run back out of the building, find him and throttle him became the greater temptation to resist. *You run away now voivode, and it's pretty well over between us!*

>*Ah, Cséjthe; no more Christmas cards?*<

You candy-assed mothersucker! Let the word go out that Cséjthe stayed at the battle's heart while Vlad the Pretender slunk off in the darkness like a frightened cur.

My head was suddenly full, then suddenly empty as I pounded around the corner at the back of the building, homed in on the extra staircase leading to the subbasement.

I stumbled to a stop three steps down. It was like stepping down into an icy swimming pool. A palpable force was flowing up from below, impeding my descent while assuring me that I was on the right track after all. Somewhere below was some kind of *angajan gris,* providing power for Bois-Chèche and her monstrous steed. And, presumably, the Zombie hostages that I was supposed to liberate.

I forced my foot down to the next step and shivered as the cold crept another six inches up my leg. Faster—I had to move faster; time was running out.

Speaking of time, I was supposed to be in Stubbs Hall right now giving an exam on my last three lectures—the final two of which I had failed to show up for. Mark a teaching career as just one more thing in my life that was pretty much over. I stared down into the churning darkness: whatever I had to face down there, it couldn't be much worse than facing the dean and trying to explain my absences and dereliction of class duties. "Oh y-yeah," I said, teeth chattering as I stepped down again, "s-sorry D-dr. F. I g-got mixed up in s-some underworld act-t-tivies. N-not m-mafia or organ-n-ized c-crime . . ." I stepped again and the cold pulled at my waist. " . . . j-just dead g-guys. Y-you know, l-like vampires, z-zombies, c-corporate t-tax attorneys. . . ." I kept forcing myself down, one step at a time until the frigid darkness lapped at my chin. "Oh, f-fu—"

I submerged.

Even though I was forcing my way down through preternaturally charged air, the sensation of moving underwater was inescapable. I tried holding my breath but was forced to take in another lungful as I reached the bottom of the stairs. It burned all the way down into my chest, like a shocking first gasp of wintry, arctic air, but seemed to have no further ill effect other than to lower my internal body temperature to match my extremities. In some ways it helped. Like a swimmer who adjusts after that first minute's shock to the body, I found it easier to move as I acclimated to the temperature around me.

My vision seemed to improve, as well: the single bulb that lit the stairway's end glowed feebly in the murk but I could still make out the details in the iron *vèvè*. The false wall was still open—a testament to another hasty exit. My entrance was a little less hasty.

The candles that lined the passageway to the *hounfort* had gone out but tiny red flecks of residual heat still glittered here and there amid the smoking wicks. They guided my way down the corridor like glimmering runway lights in a dense fog. By the time I reached the temple area my chest was laboring like that of a diver who had exhausted himself in swimming against the current.

The candles upon the altar in the *djevo* were still burning, but they were not the source of the red and purple lights that bathed the *peristil* in an eerie glow. A shadow emerged from the silhouette of the *poteau mitan*: Theresa.

"So," she said, "it comes to this."

"It comes to what?" I asked carefully. A long machete that had recently adorned the altar was now held loosely in her right hand.

"A test," she said.

"Test?"

"To see who is worthy to be a Dark Master." She stepped away from the great pole and tightened her grip on the carved wooden handle.

"I don't recall seeing any tests in the Dark Master syllabus," I said, taking a counter-step to the side.

"The countess has promised to complete my transformation if I stop you here." She took another step toward me.

"Again with the promises," I said, edging another sideways step and working a gradual curve about the great post. "Remember what I told you about the Countess Báthory's promises? Well, she's no longer around to keep or break her word."

"You're lying. I can still hear her voice inside my head."

"That's not—" What? Stop and explain that the countess wasn't really the countess but the chambermaid?

Who wasn't actually the peasant girl Katarina Beneczky but the avatar for something ancient and demonic whose name might be Marinette Bois-Chèche?

Or, even more likely: Lilith, the Whore of Babylon and the Mother of Demons?

Aw, the hell with this! I had enough trouble wrapping my own brain around this grotesque game of guess-who. Time was running out and the last thing I needed was Transylvania Barbie here acting out all her dysfunctional relationships with a bigger knife than Rod's: Bois-Lilith could still have enough time to open the

Fifth Seal, red dress or no. "Dammit, Theresa, she's bad!" I yelled. "She's bad! You know it . . . you *know* it!" I hesitated. "Dear God, tell me I didn't just do a Michael Jackson cover."

In response, the machete flicked around and just barely missed my arm.

I danced back a couple of steps and circled forward again, trying to keep the broad post in the area between us. It wasn't real shelter but I couldn't retreat without abandoning my mission. And, under the present circumstances, she might well be able to outrun me.

"Do you know what your problem is?" she grunted, recovering all too quickly from the wild swing.

"That I vote for individual candidates and not along party lines?" I couldn't orbit the pole forever, eventually I was going to get dizzy.

"You were given an immensely powerful gift and you've squandered it."

"Why? Because I don't conform to your idea of a Dark Master? What am I supposed to do? Grind my enemies to dust? Create undead dynasties? Dress like Duran Duran?"

"Power should never be wasted on those too timid to use it!" she said, swinging for my shins on the word "use."

I jumped the blade. "You know the problem with people who crave power is they always want it to rule over others." I dodged to the other side of the pole. "When the real root of their discontent is their inability to rule over themselves."

"If you leave now, she might let you live. She will need a new aristocracy to help her rule and you could be exalted with those of us who are to be her Chosen."

"Oooh, *chosen*! It sounds so special—especially in that 'help rule the world' context. Well, I got news for you, Terry-call-me-D-for-Damned: even if your Dark Lady makes Queen For A Day, she's only offering temp jobs."

"Not as temporary as your situation right now!" she grunted, trying a figure-eight pattern of slashes. "And you'd say *anything* to keep me from *killing* you now!"

"I don't think there's anything I could say that would keep you from trying." I dropped to the ground and tried a one-leg sweep. She danced back from the arc of my foot but it threw her off balance.

"You think I *want* to kill you?" she panted. "I don't have a *choice*!"

I scrambled back up on my feet as she regained her balance. She swung again, rage and frustration powering the machete with unnatural force and speed. I ducked and leaned back but the tip scored my brow, leaving a burning line of pain across my forehead. The blade met a more solid target at the end of its trajectory, *thunking* into the wooden pole and burying its tip deep in the reluctant hardwood.

"You don't *have* to kill me," I remonstrated as she tried to pull the machete free. "You have a choice. You have a lot of choices."

"I'm dead!" she shrieked.

"Everybody dies," I said. "You've still got more options than most."

"I am an unnatural creature! I will be hunted! I cannot go out by day! I must ally myself with those who have the power to protect me!" The blade, for all her frenzied tugging, remained resolutely buried in the wood.

I stepped to the left and extended my hand. "I will protect you."

"You?" The offer seemed to enrage her. "How can you protect me when you cannot even use your Dark Gifts to protect yourself?"

"Ccsssééééjjjttthhe!" The voice boomed down the corridor and arrived in the temple area like one of the seven trumps of doom.

As the sound of her new mistress' voice, Theresa's eyes grew wide with terror and desperation. Her hands came up, fingers curled like predatory claws. I took a step back to the right, maneuvering the post back between us. Unarmed, she might not be able to kill me but if she could keep me busy until the demoness rode in on Chalice Delacroix, the delay would be just as fatal.

She shrieked her rage and fear and desperation, launching herself around the great pole. I turned and fled, keeping a tight trajectory around the pole so that I could peel off and head toward the altar. Before I could, however, I had to duck: the machete remained embedded in the post and cut across my orbital path like a deadly crossing gate. I almost didn't see it in time and felt a few hairs lag behind as the blade skimmed the back of my head. Behind me, Theresa's shriek was interrupted by an abrupt "urk!"

"*Ccsssééééjjjttthhe!!*"

In spite of the approaching sound of the Doomsday Loa, I had to stop and look back. Theresa's fury had blinded her to the edge-on blade in her path. Her body staggered a few more steps past the machete still embedded in the wood at shoulder height. Black fountains of blood spurted from her neck. Her head rolled on the dark ground beneath the fixed blade. Then her body stumbled and fell. Began to twitch and jerk.

I turned away. I hadn't the stomach or the time to watch any more. I ran toward the red-and-purple glow that emanated from the altar.

Chapter Twenty-six

The glow came from the walls of the *djevo*.

The curtains had been pulled aside to reveal shelves built into the three walls surrounding the altar. The shelves were crowded with row upon row of tiny glass bottles: it looked like a liquor cabinet for a 747.

Except those little liquor bottles the flight attendants dole out don't glow in the dark while these little containers looked like tiny jars of captured fireflies. Little living pulses of bioluminescence flickered, trapped inside ranks and files of glass prisons.

Only . . .

Only they weren't fireflies . . .

"Zombis," I whispered to myself, "*zombi astrals!*"

I had come down here looking for shuffling corpses, wondering where Bois-Chèche could hide that many bodies. Now it suddenly made sense.

The *zombi astrals* were an efficient way of keeping the Loa as hostages: trap their spirits in a specially prepared bottle and harness their *ti-bon-ange* as a power source. From the look of things, she had not only trapped the astral forms of the Ogou and Gédé clans, she had hooked these zombie batteries up in a paranormal parallel circuit to augment her own magicks!

Which meant I was not only on a mission of mercy to rescue

the imprisoned Loa, I was sent down here to throw the circuit breaker on Bois-Chèche's power source. I reached for the nearest bottle and twisted the cap off—or at least I tried to. The cap didn't twist. It didn't pull, either. In fact, it didn't move at all.

"Ccsssééééjjjttthhe!"

"Bitch, bitch, bitch . . ." I could hear her approach—she was emerging from the hallway and entering the peristil, now.

I pulled and twisted harder.

Nothing.

I dropped the bottle and grabbed another. It was stuck just as tight. I bounced it off the altar table but it rebounded like shatter-proof plastic.

The machete! I turned and ran toward the pole but Chalice Delacroix's body was already there, waiting for me.

"Cséjthe," she crooned, "you keep running away."

"Yeah," I said, trying to figure my maneuvering room, "take a hint."

"But I don't want you to run away. I want to be with you. We have so much to offer one another."

"Like what?"

"Like the world," she purred.

"You mean, what's left of it after you're done?"

"And, of course, there's this . . ." She ran her left hand over the ripe brown curves of Chalice's body. The other she kept behind her back. She seemed to get a bigger thrill out of the caress than I might ever hope to.

"Who the hell are you?"

"Who would you like me to be?"

"I wish you were still Chalice Delacroix."

"And so I am."

I sighed. "We both know that you're using her as a meat pup-pet. The real Chalice Delacroix is not anywhere in the vicinity. Four hundred years ago you pulled the strings in Cachtice castle and laid the blame for your unnatural appetites on Elizabeth Báthory. For a while I thought you might be Katarina Beneczky, but that was probably no more your real name then than Chalice Delacroix is your real name now."

"Such a clever boy."

I shook my head—and used that gesture to break eye contact for another scan of the room. "Not so clever, really. First I peg you for the true Witch of Cachtice. Then I discover that you are not only *not* the real Countess Báthory, you're probably not her undead maidservant, either. Or maybe you're both—seeing as how you can leapfrog from one person's body to the next. Did you start out in the countess' body and then escape to Beneczky's when the party wound down? Or did you arrive on the scene wearing Katarina's face and form and pull the strings from the shadows?" Another thought occurred. "Or did you move around, dressing in the bodies of the various servitors in Castle Cachtice?"

"Castle Cséjthe," she corrected. "That was so long ago, why does it matter now?"

"Because I want to know who you really are. Or what? Now I'm supposed to believe that you're Marinette Bois-Chèche, the Queen Bitch of the Voodoo pantheon."

"As I said, such a clever boy!"

"If I am it's because I've finally figured out that Bois-Chèche is just another mask, too."

"Really?"

I shook my head. "I've dropped that particular word from my vocabulary this past year. No, I don't think you're Loa, at all. I don't believe any single Loa has the power—or even the motivation—to imprison all the other Loa and their multiple aspects. Certainly not a lesser aspect like one of the Marinettes. The only thing you have in common with them is your ability to mount a human host and use their body as your own."

A thought struck me. "Or maybe you don't . . ."

"Maybe I don't?"

I tried shuffling a little to the left: I really wanted to know what she was holding behind her back. "The Loa mount living humans to use as their 'horses.' Maybe you can't do that unless they're dead. More reason to peek behind the mask."

"Is my real name so important?" She turned slightly, keeping her right hand obscured.

"It is if you're a demon."

She laughed. "And knowing my name would give you power over me?" She shook her head. "I have many names!"

"Trot out the list. I got all night."

"Ah, but I do not. *Tempus fugit.*" She shrugged, her right hand still hidden behind her back. I glanced at the machete still buried in the pole. There was no way to grab it without stepping within her reach.

Unless . . .

My right hand twitched and I tried willing the weapon to my hand. Hey, I figured if I could translocate my own body and the ghost of my dead wife was really just the psychokinetic feedback of my own virus-enhanced gray-matter, I should be able to pull the old Luke Skywalker/light-saber/Jedi mind-trick.

"We have much in common, Christopher." She took a half-step toward me. "More than you have with any of those others."

I shook my head. "You're not human. I don't think you ever were," I elaborated. "As I said, you've got the mojo to imprison entire clans of Vodoun spirits and channel their energies to augment your powers. You've been around for at least four hundred years and I'm betting even longer than that." *Come to me,* I thought at the machete, *come to my hand.* "Not a problematical lifespan for a vampire and your last vessel seemed to meet all the prerequisites . . . but you change bodies like Bruce Willis changes hairpieces." *Come to me.* "And you don't use blood for physical sustenance. You use it ritualistically and there's some kind of power connection involved."

"There is power in the blood."

"Yeah, that's what everyone says: you, Mama Samm, Dracula, Jimmy Swaggert . . ."

"Vlad Dracul?" She smiled. "I had heard the stories, of course, but I had not noticed until now."

"Noticed what?"

"How much alike the two of you are."

I forgot about the machete for a moment. "Take that back!"

"Your pride, your arrogance . . ." she sighed, " . . . that fatal romantic streak . . ."

"Fatal . . ." I mused, returning to the subject at hand. I twisted my own hand a little more and fancied I could see the machete quiver a bit. "You waltz into a castle where the mistress is a closet sadist and suddenly there's a shortage of virgins and a surfeit of blood. If the countess had been half the sorceress she was accused of being, she never would have been caught and imprisoned, much less held until her death. She was your instrument before, during, and even after the trial."

She smiled. "Some instruments beg to be played."

"Flash forward to now. I don't know who you were and what you did during the centuries in-between but I bet a little research—" I stopped and cocked my head, the possibilities spinning in my mind like a dark pinwheel. "So what *was* it like inside Hitler's bunker?"

Her mouth made a little moue of a smile. "Not nearly as entertaining as the gas chambers at Birkenau and Majdanek."

I was speechless. It's no secret that the good die young, but I had never really appreciated how evil could live on and on until just this minute.

"So much death," she cooed, "so much destruction. I thought that my reign was about to begin." Her eyes and her mouth softened in fond remembrance. "Hiroshima . . . Nagasaki . . .

"For ten thousand years I have waited for a lever large enough to unhinge the world. A taste here, a sip there, always waiting for the final feast of souls. I thought the splitting of the atom would open the Fifth Seal. But like every other dark technology, the means always required more pawns than I could co-opt."

"Until now," I said, finally finding my voice. "You *are* Lilith, Mother of Demons!"

She laughed. "A fanciful theory for a man who didn't believe in vampires a year ago and still doesn't believe in ghosts, even now."

It almost felt like a physical blow. Suddenly the machete was forgotten as my hands clenched impotently. Jenny's absence was now like a hole in my heart, personal delusion or no.

After a moment I said quietly: "I believe in evil. Always have. And while I can't explain or believe everything I've seen or been told this past year, I've learned that I can generally trust my instincts."

"Instincts," she snorted, "you men of the twenty-first century aren't so different from your Cro-Magnon ancestors."

"Who knew you," I retorted. "Called you by many names: Lilith, Erishkaigal, Hecate, Medea, Medusa, Pandora, Tiamat—from ancient times, the Whore of Babylon."

"Sounds like you've got it all figured out." She reached out and pulled the machete from the great wooden post with her left hand as if plucking a petal from a flower.

"The important stuff," I agreed. "I know about the tri-part

combinant virus, about what it's really engineered to do. And I know that you can't win: even the dead are rising up to stop you. Even now your mercenaries are being routed, your plague trucks burned, your labs destroyed. Maybe I can't stop you from getting away but I think you will be a long time plotting to get another foothold in this world."

"I was wrong, Cséjthe." She smiled, the triangular points of her teeth seeming to elongate in the eerie violet light. "You are really not so clever, after all." Her right hand came out from behind her back. It held a syringe.

I took a step back.

"Now I am become Death, the Destroyer of Worlds," she said.

"Yeah?" I couldn't take my eyes off the syringe. *I dared not.* "You don't strike me as very Shiva-like. There's a greater resemblance to Kali. Is that who you really are? Are the gray men your New World cult of thugees?"

"As you said, I have many names. You would need to speak them all to banish me back into my cave."

"Cave," I said. "That would match up with the legends of Lilith." So now what? Should I say "Lilith be gone"? I said it.

She laughed. "As I said, I have many names. You, however, have only one. Cséjthe stand still." The hand holding the syringe came up.

I took a second small step back: so much for her own powers of invocation. "Let me guess. All that research, all that work. The virus samples intercepted. Destroyed. Your troops in disarray. The plan is finished." I cocked an eyebrow. "Unless . . ."

She nodded. "Unless . . ."

"You infect at least one person before you leave this night," I concluded. "Better to have multiple infection sites, varying ways of introducing the virus to dense population centers. But one person could still be enough to start the viral chain reaction."

She nodded again. "I would prefer the surety of my former plan but I will work with what you've left me."

I took another step back. "Which is me. You want me to be your Typhoid Harry."

"I would infect myself but this body is already dead. It cannot host the virus and sustain it." The syringe came up, the machete stayed down. "The infection is relatively mild. It doesn't hurt, really."

She nudged the plunger and a drop swelled at the tip of the needle. "Just a little prick."

"Isn't it always," I retorted. "Even when it comes to bringing the world to an end."

"If it isn't you, Cséjthe, then it will be one of your friends who discovers your bloody remains." The machete came back up.

"Oh, now that's not so bad. I was afraid you were going to talk me to death."

Anger and madness flashed in her eyes and the machete flashed up over her head, where she held it aloft for a long moment. Then, she smiled. "Company's coming. What does a girl have to do to be alone with you?" She gestured. Spoke a word that sounded ancient, felt substantial. The air behind her began to shimmer.

"Did you ever stop to think that if I am the woman foretold in the Bible, it would be your Christian duty to help me fulfill the prophecy and hasten God's Day of Judgment?" She took a step toward me.

"Did you ever stop to think," I countered, taking another step back, "that the Council of Trent elected to retain the Book of Revelation by just one vote back in the sixteenth century?" I watched the striated patterns of the biceps and triceps quivering under her chocolate skin.

Coming . . . I set myself.

She looked a little confused. "Your point?"

Coming . . .

"It wasn't *my* vote!" I said, jumping back as the machete flashed down into the space I had just occupied.

"Abeko!" cried a familiar voice as I stumbled back further, driven before the figure-eight patterns of the whirring blade. I couldn't look away lest I be pureed but Bois-Chèche, or whatever the hell her real name was, seemed to stagger a bit.

"Abito!" the voice called harshly, and: "Abro, Abyzu, Ailo!"

"Don't look now," I gasped, barely avoiding the machete for the seventeenth time, "but I think your pager is going off."

"Alu! Amiz! Amizo! Amizu!"

"I have power enough," she grunted back, "to destroy you all!"

"Ardad Lili! Avitu! Batna!"

I ducked the blade once more. "Yeah? Well apparently only enough to do us one at a time. And only while you're wired up to your ever-Gédé power source. So, tell me the truth before I pull your plug: are you AC or DC?"

"Bituah!" cried the voice that I finally recognized as belonging to the angel I had once called Mikey. "Eilo! Gallu!"

I sneaked a glance past her shoulder and caught a glimpse of the granite-faced creature on the far side of the peristil. He was leaning forward, his hands spread wide and pressing against the shimmering air. His great white wings fanned out behind him, straining with effort while the great sword quivered, point-first in the ground like a martyr's cross. "Geloul!" he shouted, "Gilou!"

My distraction from the closer blade had immediate and painful consequences: the tip of the machete sliced across my forearm in a fiery line.

" 'Ik, 'Ils, Ita!" cried the angel.

"You can say that again," I muttered.

"Die, damn you!" the Whore of Babylon shrieked.

It suddenly came to me, what had been missing from my life for so long, now. "Pleasant conversation," I murmured, barely avoiding the blade again.

"Izorpo . . . Kalee . . . Kali . . ."

I stumbled back against the altar table and flung out my injured arm to keep my balance. There was a sizzling sound behind me. I didn't fall because I had run out of room to fall back in. Or to. Or something. I dodged left.

"Kakash . . . Kea . . ."

She swung to her right. This put me in line with the blade.

My whole left side went numb as the great knife cracked a couple of ribs and then bit down into the flesh between. I tried to grab the blade and got the point through my left palm for my clumsy efforts.

"What?" she taunted, as I spun in the opposite direction, trying to roll away and staunch the twin gushes of blood. "No witty repartee?"

"Damn you!" I gasped, half distracted by sizzling sounds that were increasing all around me. "Now I'm gonna need a tetanus shot!"

"Kema . . . Kokos . . . Lamassu . . ."

There was a muted popping sound. And then another. And I staggered as a wave of dizziness washed over me.

"Odom! Partasah! Partashah!"

My vision began to haze—first red and then purple and I knew I had just run out of time. I threw my arm about in a last-ditch effort to delay a fatal thrust.

"Patrota!"

More popping sounds.

"Petrota!"

Sounds of breaking glass.

"Nooo!" the creature called by all of these names, and more, moaned.

"Podo!"

My blurred eyesight suddenly resolved into sharp focus and I grabbed the blade with my right hand.

"Pods!"

It felt like holding a flattened, red-hot poker but I did not let go.

"Raphi!"

Strength returned to my arm, my body. My head began to clear.

"Satrinah!"

I stole a glance over my shoulder and saw shattered glass vials scattered across the table, crisscrossed by spattered patterns of blood.

"Talto!"

I tossed my left hand back and watched as a thin spray of crimson spackled two shelves of zombi astrals on the left wall. The glass trembled, popped, and shattered. A haze of red lights misted toward us.

"Thiltho!"

"No! No! No!" Babylon's Bint shrilled.

"Zahriel!"

I jerked the machete from her grasp, slicing my hand to the bone as I did. Hurling it aside, I spun to my right, smearing my bloody palms across the remaining bottles on the right and rear racks. I barely had time to duck as three-dozen vials exploded, freeing purple pinpoints of light.

"Zefonith!" Michael shouted triumphantly. I looked back in time to watch as the angel pushed through the invisible barrier that had held him at bay. He pulled the sword from the dark ground and brought its fiery blade up to an attack position as he rushed toward us.

Chalice Delacroix's body rose into the air as she flailed her arms and kicked her legs. Judging from her body language and the red and purple firefly lights that swarmed and swirled about her form, the levitation act wasn't her doing. She opened her mouth and started to scream. Twin streamers of crimson and violet flashed down her throat and muffled her cries. Her staring, bulging eyes began to glow an unearthly green and great tears, yellow and thick like oily piss, ran down her cheeks and dribbled from her chin. The eerie emerald light spread to the whites of her eyeballs and grew in intensity. There was a final POP! as if a large zombi astral bottle had shattered and the lights in her eyes flashed and went dark. Her head lolled to the side, her body went limp. Chalice Delacroix fell to the ground as Michael ran up, his sword raised for a killing stroke. The mist of red and purple fireflies spun in a galactic farandole and dispersed, scattering across the hounfort and peristil, and zipping out through the corridor in the direction of the stairs.

"Wait!" I yelled, throwing my arm across her body to shield her from the angel's sword. Michael's reflexes spared me the irony of surviving a demon's machete attack only to lose my arm to an angel's sword.

"She's dead," he intoned. Picture Lurch doing voice-overs for Dr. McCoy in *Star Trek—The Original Series,* of course.

"Then what's your hurry?"

"The demon Lilith will have left a shadow of corruption upon her soul. Better she should perish here and her soul be remanded to heaven than have it slowly succumb to the spiritual cancer that will surely follow."

"Are we talking Predestination? Or just rolling the dice based on House odds?" I knelt and slid one arm beneath her back, the other under her legs. "Because I'm heavily invested in the Free Will portfolio and that means it's not my place to make that sort of decision for another person." I glanced up at the sword that remained poised above the two of us. "Somehow I don't think it's your place, either." I shouldn't have had the strength to lift her but the Loa had imparted some preternatural strength and energy reserves as they passed through me to attack Lilith Bois-Chèche. The sword came down slowly as I staggered to my feet. I had no sooner regained my balance than I nearly lost it again as the ground erupted nearby and Baron Samedi ascended from the bowels of the earth.

The dark man in top hat and tails (sans red threads) eyed the angel and the flickering play of flames along the great silvery blade that he held at his side. "Damn, Hefe!" he said, "you're a bit out of your element, aren't you? This here is my home turf."

"Our ground," corrected the corpse of Captain Worthington as he climbed out of the hole that the baron had created upon his entrance. "Muh men and Ah have stood post here for more than one hundred and fifty years. Tonight we have met the enemy in combat and retaken this ground."

"Very good, Captain." Mama Samm came huffing and puffing across the dirt floor from the far end of the peristil. He saluted her and she returned the salute without the slightest hesitation. "I bring word from Sally Crow."

The Confederate corpse stiffened—there was a joke there somewhere but I was too tired to figure it out just now—and the dark ground all around the *hounfort* and peristil erupted as dozens of Civil War soldiers ascended from the earth. "Attention!" barked the remains of their commanding officer.

"At ease," the old fortune-teller said gently. "The juju woman who cursed you has lifted her judgment. She says, your wrongs are forgiven you and that your faithfulness and valor have secured your rewards. You may go home, now. Go home to your homes and families."

Soldiers unknown and unknowable removed their tattered caps. Death grins softened to smiles. Some trembled, others bowed their scabrous heads as she continued. "Go home. Linger there awhile to remember the people and places that you fought and shed blood for. And when you are ready for the true honors and glories that you have won," she raised her massive arms, "kiss your great-great-grandbabies in their sleep, leave a scattering of ashes to bless the ground, and report to the One who commands all those who fight for causes just and right."

A wind sprang up as the dead men turned and began their leave-taking. It blew through the corridor as arms were clasped, moaned across the dancing ground as comrades embraced for the last time, and swirled about each soldier, causing ragged garments to flap, bones to click and clack, desiccated flesh to crumble. In moments each mummified myrmidon was rendered into columns of ash and grit and powder, spun into dust devils of decay and dissolution, and lifted on a chariot of air that carried the last earthly remnants of their physical existence up and back out through the corridor—from whence, I assumed, they would be blown to those places where their progeny lived and loved today.

I wondered briefly which ones would come home to empty fields or parking lots or shopping malls and which would find their descendants in apartment complexes and strange-looking houses far from the lands they'd known. I had only a moment for the question to form before the ground began to shake again.

Now what? No one appeared and the ground continued to tremble. "All right, already," I said, "come on in."

"No one is coming," Baron Samedi said. "This place is beginning to descend."

"Descend?"

He nodded. "It is a place of death and now is its time to die. You must leave now or perish with it." He reached out and took one of Chalice's limp hands in his own. "Come, child. Awaken and walk with me."

She stirred in my arms. Opened her eyes as a sleeper newly awakened might. "What . . . ?"

"No time for questions, now," the baron said. "Come with me and we will find your place among the dead."

"The . . . dead?" She looked from him up to me. "I don't understand."

"Can you walk?" I asked. "We've got to get out of here." A table-sized chunk of ceiling crashed down just twenty feet away from us. "Right now," I added.

"She no longer belongs to the land of the living," the baron argued.

"Doesn't mean she belongs in the realm of the dead," I countered. "And I can speak somewhat knowledgably to that subject." I turned and found my path blocked by the big angel. Beyond him I could see Deirdre, Father Pat, and The Kid coming out of the corridor. "Am I gonna have to go around you or through you, Mikey?"

He reached out and plucked Chalice from my arms, handing me his sword in her place. "I can carry her to safety this day," he said softly. "I cannot speak to her future."

"Can we help?" Deirdre called as we turned and began to move in their direction.

"Yeah," I said loosening up into an ungainly run, "don't block the exits!"

"Hey," I heard J.D. say off to the side, "lookit what I found!"

There was no time to pay him any mind, we were all running back for the corridor and the stairs beyond as the poteau mitan snapped with a loud bang and the ceiling fractured like thin ice. Concrete began to fall in earnest and I quickly found myself dropping back into last place. Everyone else was ahead of me and the baron had apparently exited the same way he had entered.

Just as the angel ducked through the doorway to the corridor about five tons of cement came crashing down to cut off my escape route. I had two choices left. Find the baron's tunnel—if that was how he actually traveled beneath the earth—or translocate on the run.

Aside from my fundamental doubts about Loa locomotion, I tend to be a bit claustrophobic. "Death is but the doorway," I murmured, dodging hundred-pound cement hailstones, "to new life . . ." The aftertaste of Loa power hummed in my veins and I could feel the transdimensional shift begin with a clarity that I had never felt in previous attempts. "We live today," I shouted, "we shall live again!" There was a growing thunder rumbling toward me from behind: the subbasement was turning into a concrete waffle iron and the lid was about to close! "In many forms," I cried, putting on a burst of speed, "shall we return!" I leapt into the void between the atoms of the cement rubble that was avalanching my way.

It felt like running into a stone wall.

The ceiling caved in.

Chapter Twenty-seven

The next thing I knew I was standing in the parking lot with a bashed and bloody nose. I turned and watched as the main building trembled and tottered, cracks slashing through its sandstone façade as though some great, invisible beast was mauling it with fearsome claws. All around, like foundering lifeboats, the outbuildings collapsed and sank into the churning ground.

Cracks became fissures as the roof caved in and the windows blew out. The north side sank first, tilting the broken building like the H.M.S. *Titanic,* poised for its watery descent. All about the ground heaved and bucked, throwing up muddy clods like a boiling beef stew. Grassy turf rolled like breakers against the asphalt beach of the shattered parking lot.

Don't wait on me! I thought furiously, *Get out! GET OUT!*

"I don't think they are going to make it."

I looked over at Baron Samedi, who seemed to have popped up out of nowhere.

"Can you help them?" I asked.

He pulled a cigar out of his jacket pocket and bit off the end. "Why should I?"

Why should he? After I had freed the Ogou and his Gédé clans from their imprisonment by the demon Lilith? I opened and closed my mouth a couple of times. Then I snatched the top hat off of

391

his head and settled it down at a rakish angle atop my own cranium. "Go on back to Haiti, Hefe; there's a new baron in town."

He stared at me suspiciously. "I thought you wanted out."

I shrugged. "Gonna need some new friends if my old ones get killed tonight."

He stomped his foot angrily and descended back down into a gap in the buckled asphalt.

The main building had sunk to where the second floor on the south side and the third on the north were now disappearing into the churning soil. As to what had undermined the foundations of the complex, I could only guess. Was it the biotoxic witch's brew of chemicals that had leaked or been dumped during the past several years, the movement of the restless dead beneath the earth this past century and a half, the emergence of the "dragon," or maybe even the juxtaposition of powerful magicks and opposing elemental forces?

Perhaps all of it and more. I would have wished it Godspeed on its trajectory to Hell but my friends were still inside. And destined to remain, it seemed: the second level of the foyer was now buried beneath the churning mud. I began to weigh my chances of translocating back in when a bubble appeared.

It swelled into a dark brown membrane above the roiling grass and quickly expanded into a large, opaque dome. It grew until it could garage a school bus and then quivered as a hand stretched through its dirt-flecked skin. The hand was daubed with white paint, the skeletal markings of the Baron Samedi. The fingers closed to a fist, then suddenly opened again.

The bubble burst and the Loa of the Dead emerged from its soft crater, leading a chain of beslimed escapees, holding hands like an overly affectionate chain gang.

Behind them the rest of the main building sank into the morass and murk with a gaseous, bubbly sound.

The flush of the House of Usher.

As I stood at the edge of the pit and watched my friends struggle out of the muck and mud, I folded my arms across my chest and said, "Gee, guys, what kept you?"

Grins opened in the masks of mud and caked dust but I quickly learned that it was more than simple relief at seeing me alive. "I'm thinkin' the more pertinent question, Big Daddy," J.D. shot back, "is how come you're not wearin' any threads?"

✧   ✧   ✧

"Terrorists?" Detective Ruiz repeated for the fifteenth time.

Pagelovitch nodded, his eyes holding hers in a tight, hypnotic gaze. "That's right, Lieutenant. BioWeb was working on a super-secret government weapon and Mr. Haim here was deputized to help us ferret out some suspected saboteurs. . . ."

I sighed, closed my eyes, and leaned back against the rear doors of the ambulance while a paramedic finished bandaging my ribs.

"Nice stigmata."

I opened my eyes and considered the spots of blood on my bandaged hands and the red stripe blotting through the pad taped to my side. "We all," I said carefully to Detective Murray, "have our cross to bear." His Mona Lisa smile was playing peek-a-boo through his goatish beard. "Shouldn't you be paying attention to the debriefing?" I asked. Pagelovitch was apparently going to have to sell his story a second time.

"Naw," he said, tilting up the brim of his porkpie hat just enough to reveal a pair of small horns at the edge of his hairline. "There are eight million stories in the Naked City; yours is just one of them." He chuckled and turned away.

"*Naked* city, indeed," Deirdre remarked, pulling at the thin sheet I had tied about my waist. The paramedic picked up his case and went in search of other injured parties. "Looks like I get to drive you home," she added with a mischievous waggle of her eyebrows.

"Have you seen my car?" I asked sourly.

She looked over at the colander bodywork on my Merc and said "oh" in a little voice.

"Besides, even though I've talked my way out of going to the hospital," I added, "I'm not so sure Pagelovitch has talked Ruiz out of packing me off to the pokey yet."

"You see, Professor Haim was supposed to be the bait to draw them out into the open," Pagelovitch was explaining as he stood next to my bullet-riddled Mercury. "That's why they attacked his house."

Ruiz didn't stop staring into the Seattle Doman's hypnotic eyes but said: "I don't get the bit about Kandi Fenoli's corpse."

"Er, it's classified," he answered, fighting a smile. "I'd tell you but then I'd have to kill you. . . ."

Deirdre shook her head. "Then maybe I shouldn't hand you this, quite yet." She hefted the zippered handgun pouch holding my silver-loaded Glock.

"You may as well keep it for all the good it's done me." I stared at the remains of my car. "What a mess. My house is riddled with bullets, the napalm in my front yard has probably made it impossible to grow anything but kudzu and crabgrass for the next decade, the dean will probably schedule my termination meeting on the seventh floor of the library just so he can throw me off the balcony, and now there's some kind of paramilitary militia group out there that I can officially add to my enemies list. T.G.I.F."

Deirdre had unzipped the gun pouch and was checking the Glock's magazine. "T.G.I.F.?"

"Thank God it's Friday."

"Um, not to be a nitpicker but, actually, it's Saturday." She rammed the clip back in the grip. "Just a little better than an hour before dawn."

"I guess we'd better head back to the house."

"We've got extra beds at the hotel," Pagelovitch said, turning away from Ruiz and walking toward us. "It will be more convenient—especially since we will be starting back to Seattle at sundown. We *all* will."

I gritted my teeth and struggled to my feet. "The answer is still no."

"Well, you can't stay here. You would be rogue and everybody now knows where you live."

Deirdre had started to tuck the Glock into her handbag but she hesitated now, waiting to see how this was going to work out.

Kurt came around the far side of the ambulance, saying: "He isn't rogue, he is Doman."

Pagelovitch pounded his fist against the side of the ambulance. He couldn't be that exasperated; it only dented a little. "The other Domans won't permit a new enclave! We've already discussed this!"

"Not a new enclave," Kurt clarified, "Christopher Cséjthe is now the Doman of the New York demesne."

"What?" The Seattle Doman was taken aback. "Him? You must be joking!"

>Believe it, Stefan.<

"Vladimir Drakul?"

We all looked around but Dracula was nowhere to be seen.

>*Yes, I am still here.*<

"If you think to return now that the countess is dead—" my majordomo began.

>*Nay, Kurt; I am an observer, now. I have no taste for intrigues these days.*<

"Coulda fooled me," I muttered.

"This—this pup—will not last a month in New York," Pagelovitch protested.

Ruiz was taking in the audible portion of the debate with open-mouthed curiosity. "Come on, Dorcas," Murray took her by the hand and tugged her back in the direction of their unmarked car. "Let the Feds sort out who's got jurisdiction over Mr. Haim."

"I keep forgetting," she said, stumbling along in a daze, "which one is FBI and which is CIA."

The Prince of Wallachia chuckled inside our heads. >*This one is much more dangerous than you suppose, my friend. Twice now he has destroyed timeless foes that not even I could withstand in my prime. I think New York might well fear his coming. Fare well, Cséjthe, the Dragon's blood burns brightly in your veins.*<

And then, just like that, his presence evaporated from our collective consciousness.

"Did you hear that?" Pagelovitch finally asked with a disconcerting grin. "Dracula called me his friend!"

The sky was noticeably—well, not lighter but definitely less dark. Leave-takings were a hurried affair. Father Pat and "Brother" Michael would take Chalice Delacroix back to their encampment, now hidden even deeper in the swamps. There she could rest and heal and questions as to her future might be asked and eventually answered in a safe and nurturing environment. I tried to shake hands with the dead cleric but he slipped between my bandaged hands and embraced me. Breaking the hug with a hearty backslap he whispered that he would be in touch.

Neither option was feasible with the angel as his hands were filled supporting Chalice Delacroix's limp form. She was conscious, however, and asked me to lean in close.

"Thank you for my life," she whispered, kissing my cheek. "Your blood has saved me."

I shook my head. "Jesus saves, I only invest." I smiled. "I just bought you some time. Just as you did for me."

And, in the end, isn't that all we can really do for each other?

The Kid came roaring up in a 1932 Ford Cabriolet that made my '50 Merc look state of the art. Its Gibson body was high-gloss midnight purple with red-and-orange flames ghost painted as emerging from the hood's vented side-panels. It had straight pipes, a dropped front axle, Just Hobby rails, and the chopped roof had been stowed. The license plate read: NOS4 AH2. He reached back and popped open the rumble seat and then turned and leaned over the driver's sill. "If you need a ride, better jump inside! This crate rates, but it's gettin' late!"

I glanced back at my Swiss-cheesed junker and sighed. "Guess it's not too likely we'll get a cab out here at this hour." As Deirdre and I started for the car, Kurt gave instructions to his brethren and hurried to join us.

"We will make our traveling arrangements after sunset," he told me as The Kid opened the passenger-side door for me.

"Whoops," he said as I started to climb in beside him, "gotta make some room."

"Uh, Kurt," I said as The Kid picked up a bowling ball-sized object from the front seat, "about the New York gig . . . this bears a little more discussion . . ."

The vampire's face fell. "If you will not rule over us, then who will?"

I postponed that question as I sat beside The Kid and he plopped Theresa's severed head in my lap.

"See what I found down there in the dungeon," he announced, proud of his discovery. "Turn it from side to side: it looks like her eyes follow you no matter which way you move it!"

With a sinking feeling, I realized that it was true. Theresa's eyes moved in her head, her eyelids blinked. Her mouth opened and closed.

"I seen stuff like that: autonomic reflexes and stuff," J.D. elaborated as Kurt and Deirdre climbed into the rumble seat behind us. "Kinda like those chickens that run around after their heads get chopped off."

"I don't think so," I said slowly as he popped the clutch and started maneuvering the Ford around the buckled stalagmites of asphalt. "I think she's still alive."

"What!" We screeched to a halt and Kurt's and Deirdre's heads bracketed mine as they leaned over my shoulders. J.D. took the head out of my grasp and held it up for a better look. "If she's alive, how come she don't say nothin'?"

A numbed and disembodied portion of myself took up the intellectual analysis. "She has no lungs to move air through her vocal cords."

"But, if she don't got lungs—and I mean the breathin' kind, you understand—then how can she still be alive?" He looked up and found a vampire, a semi-vampire, and a former vampire all staring back at him. "Oh."

Kurt cleared his throat. "Perhaps a better question is how much alive is she?"

I looked back at him. "What do you mean?"

"How much awareness remains? Does she retain actual consciousness? Does she still enjoy higher brain functions?"

"Somehow," Deirdre murmured, "I don't think 'enjoy' is an applicable term, here."

"And you would do well to remember that," I told her, "considering your own circumstances."

"What do you mean?"

The Kid raised the head in one hand and touched his own brow with the other. "Alas, poor Yorrick! I knew her well!"

I plucked Theresa's head from his grasp. "This isn't funny."

"What do you mean 'my own circumstances'?" Deirdre insisted.

"We'll talk about it later," I told her. "Our main concern right now is what do we do with her."

"I want to talk about it now," the redhead persisted. "You gave both of us some of your blood. I'm no longer a vampire. She's no longer . . . well . . . connected."

"Well connected," J.D. chortled, "I like that."

"I'm alive and so is she," Deirdre continued, "though neither of us should be."

"See, now 'alive' is one of those subjective terms—" I began.

"Are you telling me that if I get all chopped up that I won't die either?"

"Well," I shrugged, "that thought had just crossed my mind."

"Cooool," opined Mr. Jump 'n Jive Jittersauce.

"Not so cool," answered Kurt. "Imagine being trapped in a fire, falling under the wheels of a subway, being crushed in a building collapse, blown up by a terrorist bombing—"

"I've got the picture," Deirdre said sourly. "Is it true? Could the same thing happen to me? *Can* I die? And, if I can't, is any damage to my body permanent?"

J.D. sobered as he appeared to consider existence without the regenerative powers that a vampire enjoys.

"The problem is," I said, "I don't know how we'd go about finding out without . . . without . . ."

Deirdre nodded.

"The sky is turning gray," Kurt observed. "This matter should be debated elsewhere."

The Kid nodded and started the car back toward the road.

"I think I may turn this matter over to Pagelovitch before he leaves," I said as we drove past the abandoned guard station. "There are labs and medical facilities back at the Seattle demesne and I trust Dr. Mooncloud."

"There are labs and medical facilities in New York," Kurt offered.

I sighed. "I guess there's no putting this off." I turned to J.D. who was whistling "I Ain't Got Nobody" and said: "Cut that out." Then I turned back to my majordomo and said: "Here's what I want to do . . ."

We made it back to what was left of my house in good time. The Kid hadn't replaced the Lincoln V-8 or the Lincoln Zephyr transmission but he had kept the original parts in pristine condition and replaced other elements with an eye toward integration and performance. The interior was tricked out with VDO classic gauges, including clock and tach, and we rolled through the predawn gray on Hildebrand Sprint wheels—Michelins, big and little with the narrow whites out.

"I was thinkin' about chopping the hood," he was telling me as we wove up the tree-canopied drive, "and adding a B and M blower—"

I touched his shoulder and pointed at a lighted window on the second floor. "Someone's up there." A shadow ghosted along the section of ceiling that was visible from the car.

The Kid killed the lights and engine and set the brake as we coasted to a stop. "Give me my gun," I said as Deirdre and Kurt scrambled out of the folding backseat.

She just looked at my bandaged hands and snorted.

"Doggone it!" I muttered, easing the passenger door shut behind me. "I don't know why I ever bought the damn thing in the first place!"

There was a quiet argument going on when I reached the front porch.

"I am his adjutant," Kurt was whispering, "I should go in first!"

"But you haven't been invited, so you can't cross the threshold," Deirdre argued.

"But I am more powerful and less vulnerable than you! Invite me in and let me handle this!"

"Guys, guys," I said, pushing between them, "it's my house, I'll go in first. You're both invited in to follow behind and provide backup."

"But—" the redhead began.

"Funny thing," I said to her, easing the scorched and broken door aside, "I don't remember inviting *you* in to begin with."

I expected to find the downstairs littered with the remains of desiccated body parts but the primary evidences of the Birkmeister's assault on my digs had been cleaned up. The bullet holes remained in the walls and the windows were still broken but all signs of my dead visitors had been cleared away along with the shattered furniture and busted lamps. The carpeting had been rolled up against the far wall and the floor beneath appeared to have been recently mopped. A serious attempt had been made to remove any evidence of the previous conflict.

Deirdre rechecked the Glock and headed for the stairs.

"Get back here!" I stage whispered.

"Who's there!" called a harsh, guttural voice from the top of the stairway. We looked at each other but no one answered. Now the sound of growling drifted down the stairs to our ears.

I suddenly knew and was afraid. I was in no way ready for this— had no conceivable defense and now all of us were in danger: it would have been far better for me to come here alone.

An inhuman shadow appeared on the wall of the stairway as she began to descend the steps.

"Run!" I whispered to the others. "Hide!"

A long muzzle came into view, filled with sharp teeth. Canine lips were drawn back in a snarl. A hairy, clawed hand gripped the banister.

"Get out," I urged, "before she sees you!"

Too late: she had reached the landing and had as clear a view of us as we did of her.

J.D. came scurrying through the doorway and into the living room just then. He skidded to a stop and took in the wolfish head, the clawed hands and feet, and the thick pelt of fur that covered her from head to taloned toes, including the single, human pair of mammary glands.

"Whoa," he said. "Dog looks like a lady!"

The creature turned and growled directly at me.

"Hi, Honey," I said, trying to conceal my dismay, "sorry about the mess."

The kitchen was relatively undamaged and I busied myself preparing a repast for my company while Lupé went back upstairs to change—out of werewolf mode and into fresh clothing, that is. Lycanthropy is hell on your wardrobe when you transform without undressing first. Tomorrow would likely bring another shopping spree.

Drinks were easy: Lupé had been back for a couple of days and the fridge and cupboards had been restocked. I poured vintage blood bank for Kurt and J.D., V-8 juice for Deirdre, then put the kettle on to brew green tea for Lupé and myself. Surprisingly, I didn't need any hemoglobin: the extra properties in Chalice Delacroix's charged bloodstream—whatever they were—seemed to have more than made up for what the machete had cost me.

Lupé was back downstairs before the water started to boil.

Introductions commenced. Explanations ensued. Lupé seemed especially interested in Deirdre's appearance and part in all of this. They had known each other back in Seattle but my S.O. was particularly interested in why the redhead was here instead of back at the hotel with Pagelovitch. No parts of the past week's narrative were fabricated but, for brevity—among other things—a lot of details were edited out.

"So, let me get this straight," Lupé said when we had finished detailing our various portions of the story. "Certain elements—possibly within our own government—have been developing a bioweapon that they hope to use against their own population to reduce the federal deficit . . ."

"Could be inside, could be outside paramilitary self-styled patriots," I interjected.

" . . . and the leader of the New York demesne, who everyone thinks is the Countess Elizabeth Báthory . . ."

"But isn't," I added unnecessarily.

" . . . gets involved by offering the unique, transmutagenic elements of vampire DNA to assist in reverse engineering the architecture of a combinant, mutative, super-virus . . ."

"All the while building in a doomsday trigger and creating a decoy virus to cover her tracks," I elaborated.

" . . . because she's really an ancient demoness with a yen for The End, foretold in the Book of Revelation . . ."

"And not Marinette Bois-Chèche, who she pretended to be while enslaving the other Loa to use as supernatural power sources for her sorceries," I added.

" . . . and in the process of unraveling her secrets, defeating her evil schemes, and freeing the Loa from her sorcerous imprisonment, you've put our address into the database of every vampire enclave in the world, the government, the so-called gray men, and made us a stopping point on the grateful dead's map of the homes of the stars . . ."

"Well—" I said.

" . . . you've tasted vampire blood . . ."

"Vampire blood?" J.D. wanted to know.

"Deirdre's. I can smell her coming out of his pores," she explained. "And she's tasted his: He's leaking out of her quite strongly."

"Um—" I had forgotten about the acute sensitivity of a werewolf's nose.

"He was dying," Deirdre tried to explain. "And some of that blood was second-generation vampire blood—"

"Not to mention the scent of human blood—fresh from the vein and not refrigerated in plastic—as well as something more. Chris?"

"Demon infected," I answered. "I thought it was Loa-laced at the time."

J.D. looked at me with renewed respect. "Cséjthe, you dog!" His eyes shifted to Lupé's less than admiring expression. "Sorry, ma'am."

"I come home to find the house in a shambles. It was probably a lot worse than what I found, but I arrived to find a cleanup crew of corpses washing down walls, mopping floors, and hauling away trash bags filled with what, I don't even want to guess!"

"We might as well move anyway," I said dejectedly. "I think I lost my job."

"Move? How are we going to sell the house in this condition?" She got up and walked over to the answering machine by the telephone. "At least I have a little good news to give you in exchange for the devastation and chaos you provided for my homecoming."

She pressed the playback button and the dean's voice crackled from the tiny speaker. "Sam . . ." I didn't hear the next few words, I was trying to figure out whom he was talking about. Then I remembered: To the university and most of the rest of the world I retained the carefully forged identity of Samuel Haim. " . . . must confess I was not amused when I was told what you were doing. Using theatrical makeup and costuming to transform yourself into a corpse while lecturing on Themes on Death in American Lit— well, at best it seemed like pandering and, at worst—well, as I said, I was not amused. But the registrar has reported a three hundred percent preenrollment increase for your class next semester and I dropped by the other night to see for myself. And I must admit that I was impressed. Even from the hallway I could tell that the students were alert and paying close attention. The discussion was spirited and insightful. I'm not keen on gimmicks but the content was scholarly and comprehensive while engaging the entire class. I think I can soothe any ruffled feathers from the rest of the faculty if you'll commit to two or three compromises. First, think about toning down the makeup. You weren't just unrecognizable, you were positively ghastly. And lose the rotted-meat smell. I think the visual stimulus is quite sufficient without layering on any olfactory realism. And, finally, no more references to the preponderance of 'dead white males' in our curriculum." The recording beeped and started on a message from a telemarketer selling aluminum siding. Lupé hit the delete button. "No point in keeping this one: aluminum isn't bulletproof."

I stood up as the teakettle began to whistle from the kitchen. "Baby, I'm . . . sorry."

"Sorry? *Sorry?*" Even in her human skin I could see the little hairs standing up on her arms and the nape of her neck. "I come home and have the hell scared out of me, thinking you're dead, and all you can do is say you're sorry!" She grabbed the front of my shirt and jerked me off my feet pulling me against her. "I didn't want to go on living! I couldn't—" Her eyes were brimming with tears as she crushed her lips against mine and kissed me passionately.

Kurt and J.D. wound up sharing what was left of the foldout couch in the den.

Deirdre refused the guestroom, insisting on keeping watch downstairs while we slept.

The sheets and pillowcases had been changed on our bed and if Lupé's nose had detected anything of a suspicious nature, she had yet to mention it.

It was nearly eight A.M. when I closed the bedroom door and thumbed the lock for the illusion of privacy. I turned and looked at my werewolf lover who had just emerged from the bathroom, brushing her long brown-black hair. The powder blue nightgown that she wore softened the athletic lines of her slender torso while the baby oil she had rubbed on her arms and chest made her skin glow like polished cherry wood. She was what I affectionately call a big-nosed girl, the features of her face carved more for piquant sensuality than delicate beauty.

As she saw me she smiled and her features were transformed from comely to dazzling. "Christopher," she whispered, "how I've missed you!"

"How?" I echoed. "How *have* you missed me?"

Her lips curled into something truly extraordinary. "Let me show you." The nightgown was up and over her head in the blink of an eye. She was on the bed before it hit the floor. Although she probably crooked her finger almost immediately, it was all of another minute before I noticed that particular detail.

A couple of minutes more and the very best detail was revealed: all was forgiven.

✧   ✧   ✧

"Chris?"

"Mmm?" While my preternatural biology did not require me to sleep during the day, the last few days and nights (not to mention the previous forty-five minutes) had taken their toll: I could hardly keep my eyes open.

"Explain the part about how you are now the Doman of the East Coast undead."

"Mmm. You want the how? Or the why?"

"The why, I guess. Assassination is the political advancement method of choice in most enclaves and New York makes Machiavelli look like Mary Tyler Moore."

"That's why I'm not relocating to the Big Apple." Her expression made it clear that that was not going to cut it. "Look," I said, "if I don't take the position, whoever does is going to come after me anyway. And the ensuing battle over that vacancy will guarantee the rule of the biggest, baddest neck-biter around. While I'm in charge, I can try to institute some changes that might save human lives and protect my own backside, as well."

"Why don't you just declare the East Coast demesne disbanded?"

I gave up on my slow slide into dreamland and sat up against the headboard. "Are you kidding? Even if there was a chance that the majority would accept such an edict, can you imagine the resulting loss of life if hundreds of vampires went suddenly rogue? No, better a benign Doman, working to change the system from within. Assuming Kurt can act as my minister-by-proxy."

"He doesn't seem very happy about it."

"Would you in his shoes?" I fluffed my pillow and tucked it behind my back. "Still, without me being physically present, an ambitious assassin has a more difficult road to advancement."

"Assuming we move."

"I think that's a given." I turned to her. "You're taking this awfully well."

"The house isn't important to me; you are."

"I figured your nose would be all out of joint over Deirdre."

Her eyes searched mine, sifting for . . . something. "Should it be?" She propped herself up on one elbow and gazed up at me with an expression of careful tenderness. "You are a hero. A Doman, now. In fact, you are something beyond anyone's knowing at this point. Your . . . relationship . . . with Deirdre was never simple to begin with and now you owe each other your lives. Am I jealous? Of course I am. Do I understand? I think I do. Am I insecure? She is very beautiful. And I can see that she is devoted to you. And if I were not around—"

I touched my finger to her lips. "But you are around. You haven't said yet whether you're back to stay."

She smiled—a little sadly, I thought. "It's a fair question, I suppose. I left because I was jealous of a woman who was either a ghost or a figment of your imagination."

I opened my mouth but she shushed me. "It didn't matter which at the time. I was jealous and I couldn't abide what seemed a crucial lack of privacy. I came back when I realized that sharing you was better than giving you up completely. And then I find out that the dark sorceries that were unleashed seem to have banished your ex-wife from our lives and so this whole separation was moot."

I closed my eyes. Ghost, spirit, or mental hallucination, I hadn't had the time to properly mourn Jenny's final departure.

"Anyway," Lupé continued, "I feel that a living, breathing woman is much easier for me to deal with than a memory given a ghostly presence. Deirdre has no place else to go right now, you need an enforcer to watch your back, and I, at least, don't have to worry about a certain blithe spirit haunting our bedroom."

"So you're back to stay." It was less of a question, now. Father Pat had preached forgiveness but Lupé's silent sermon this past hour had been far more eloquent.

"Well . . ." she tugged the sheet down and treated me to a rousing vista, " . . . I might need a little convincing . . ."

I reached for her. "Did you say 'little'?"

Her response was interrupted by the sound of the shower turning on in the bathroom.

She looked at me. "Deirdre's downstairs."

I looked at her. "I locked the bedroom door."

Steam began to drift from beneath the door to the adjoining bathroom. "Chris?" Jenny's voice echoed from the tub's shower enclosure, "where's the shampoo?"